OTTERLY IRRESISTIBLE

BOYS OF THE BAYOU GONE WILD

ERIN NICHOLAS

ISBN: 978-1-952280-12-2

Editor: Lindsey Faber

Cover photo: Wander Aguiar

Cover design: Najla Qamber, Qamber Designs

THE SERIES

Boys of the Bayou-Gone Wild
Things are going to get wild when the next batch of bayou boys falls in love!

Otterly Irresistible
Heavy Petting
Flipping Love You

Connected series...

Boys of the Bayou
Small town, big family, hot-country-boys-with-Louisiana-drawls, crazy-falling-in-love fun!

My Best Friend's Mardi Gras Wedding
Sweet Home Louisiana
Beauty and the Bayou
Crazy Rich Cajuns
Must Love Alligators
Four Weddings and a Swamp Boat Tour

Boys of the Big Easy
Hot single dads in the sexy city of New Orleans

Easy Going (prequel)
Going Down Easy
Taking It Easy
Eggnog Makes Her Easy
Nice and Easy
Getting Off Easy

ABOUT THE BOOK

Broody wildlife veterinarian Griffin Foster is done. Done trying to save the world. Done getting attached. He's been fired twice for standing his ground and now he's going to be content--by God--in small-town Louisiana, in a small veterinary practice, where there will only be small problems.

Quiet and boring, though? Um, no. He's been adopted by a loud, crazy Cajun family with a tiny petting zoo for him to care for. Hey, it's not endangered tigers at a nationally renowned zoo, but a family of otters--and all the gumbo he can eat--isn't a bad deal.

Until she shows up. Again.

The sunny, gorgeous optimist who stole his heart--and his favorite shirt--two months ago. Who clearly hasn't heard the word "no" enough in her life. And who is the first woman to put even a tiny crack in his don't-get-attached wall.

Charlotte "Charlie" Landry is the new marketing consultant for the family swamp-boat tour company and petting zoo. It might not have been her plan, but she is all in, ready to grow the business. Whether the hot, grumpy vet likes it or not.

He doesn't.

Worse, sparring with his unforgettable one-night stand is more fun than he's had in a long time.

But watching wears-designer-dresses Charlie find her dream job amongst a bunch of goats, alpacas, and otters is a surprise.

And her helping him find his passion again is...well, irresistible.

Dammit.

1

"Sugar, I adore you too. But you can't follow me everywhere. It's inappropriate for you to be here right now."

Charlotte Landry paused and tipped her head at the sound of the deep male voice coming from the west side of her grandmother's bar.

The guy didn't have a Louisiana accent. If he had, it would have been obvious on the *Sugar*. That was one of the best-drawled words down here—especially when combined with a playful smile.

There was no reply from "Sugar," but this sounded juicy. Why was it inappropriate for her—or Charlie supposed Sugar could be a guy—to be here? Was she—or he—an ex? Was Sugar a secret fling, and no one could see them together?

Charlie knew she shouldn't eavesdrop, but it wasn't as if she'd snuck up on this conversation. She'd been across the street at her grandmother's house, using the bathroom since the bar bathroom had a line seven deep, and was on her way back to the party.

She reached up and felt the fake eyelash she'd needed to reattach to her right eyelid. She really hated the things. She had yet to master their application. However, they did make her eyes look incredible. A girl had to do what a girl had to do sometimes.

She pressed her lips together. She'd also reapplied the lipstick, even though she knew the tube she was using cost more than the dress her grandmother had bought for the weddings. Charlie wasn't trying to show off. She was a walking, talking billboard for the makeup and lashes she was wearing tonight. Working in marketing for a makeup company required her to wear the products—even to a casual wedding reception at her grandmother's bar in a tiny bayou town in Louisiana.

Okay, she wouldn't have *had* to wear them here. She just sometimes forgot how laid back and casual things really were in Autre, Lousiana. Even weddings.

"We simply can't be together every minute of every day. We've talked about this." The man's deep voice was low and calming even as he delivered the news that Sugar wasn't welcome here.

Charlie felt her eyebrows lift. Ooh, Sugar was a little needy it seemed. She—or he—felt they needed to be together constantly? Charlie took a few steps closer to the corner of the building. She probably shouldn't listen in, but as much fun as the wedding reception was inside, the moonshine, wedding cake, music, and Cajun tall-tales weren't going anywhere. There was always more food, booze, and bullshit with that group inside. She could spare a few minutes.

"You also can't bring your friends with you when you're stalking me," the man said.

Charlie looked around. Had his stalker brought an entourage? Was it for a flash mob? Or for a kidnapping? Really, neither would've surprised her here in Autre. Which was one of the things she loved about this town. The definition of crazy was different here than anywhere else she'd ever been. And not exactly frowned upon.

She also wasn't afraid to admit she was willing to stick around for a flash mob. Or a kidnapping. She would, of course, call for other people to come out if it turned out to be a kidnapping. Okay, or a flash mob. So it wasn't as if the guy was actually going to end up stuffed in a trunk of a car. She was just waiting to see which of those scenarios she was dealing with.

"Don't you think it's time to go home?" the guy said to his stalker. "Come on. I'll take you."

Oh, good, he was a nice guy. Even if Sugar was harassing him, he was still willing to be sure she—or he—got home safely.

Dammit, did this mean Charlie needed to follow them? In case the kidnapping happened away from the bar? Or what if Sugar had a hatchet and duct tape waiting for the guy back at her place?

Or, maybe worse, what if Sugar waited to sing and dance for him in her living room? Charlie would miss the whole performance.

Now she was invested. She was going to have to follow them. Crap. She really wasn't dressed for traipsing around in the dark. Or the light. Her Valentino Garavani Rockstud ankle-strap pumps were *perfection*. And not at all comfortable for any kind of distance walking.

But she really didn't want to miss the flash mob.

Surely it was going to be a flash mob, right?

Or a striptease. At least.

Charlie decided if she were going to do a flash mob for a guy she stalked to a wedding, she'd choose Taylor Swift's "Love Story". Obviously.

She was in town for her cousins' weddings. Yes, plural. Three of her cousins had gotten married today, and she was now attending the reception held at her grandmother's bar. Considering the guy was confronting Sugar just outside the back door of the bar, Charlie assumed he was a wedding guest as well.

The Landry family never did anything small, and that, apparently, included weddings. Of course, growing up in Shreveport, Charlie sometimes forgot the easy-going, laid-back ways of the bayou, and now that she had been working in Atlanta, that was even truer. Hence why she'd worn a pale pink strapless cocktail dress that hugged her breasts and waist and had an uneven hemline that nearly touched the ground in back to a wedding where the grooms wore blue jeans, and some of the guests were alligators. Literally. For one of the couples' vows, they'd taken a pontoon out into the bayou to a little cove, and there had been alligators floating in the water listening in.

She also had on Valentino heels, fake eyelashes, fake nails, and hair extensions.

Yeah, she might have overdone it.

And yes, some of her cousins had already given her shit about the fake fingernails.

But she did love this dress, these heels were her favorite thing in her closet right now, and her highlights had turned out amazing.

Still, as much fun as the food, dancing, laughing, and one-upmanship was inside, she wasn't above enjoying a little romantic drama outside on her way back from the bathroom.

"Come on, Sugar," the man said. "Let's get you home."

Charlie literally had her fingers crossed for the first strains of Taylor Swift when she heard the stalker reply for the first time.

"*Behhhh!*"

Charlie jumped, then frowned. Okay, she hadn't been expecting that.

She peered around the corner of the building. There was a man sitting on the back step of her grandmother's bar.

And he was surrounded by goats.

4

He was holding one goat's face in his hands and was talking to it directly. The other goats seemed content to munch on the grass and weeds that grew along the edge of the gravel drive that led to the back of the bar. But this goat was, as far as Charlie could tell from six feet away in the dimming light of the evening, gazing at the man adoringly. There were also two ducks and a potbellied pig. Most of them seemed unconcerned with what was going on, except for the one duck who was standing like a bodyguard next to the goat having the intense conversation with the man.

Surprisingly, none of that was the most startling thing about the scene in front of her.

No, *that* was the fact that the man on the step was the extremely good-looking man who Charlie had previously asked to dance at the wedding reception. And who had turned her down.

It wasn't just that he'd turned her down, though without getting too full of herself, Charlie could admit she wasn't all that used to men telling her no. It was also that she knew they had chemistry. She'd caught him watching her across the bar earlier in the evening, and when she had slid in next to him to order another drink, he hadn't given her much space. Nor had he seemed annoyed with her taking up any of *his* space.

Still, he'd turned her down when she asked him to dance. Without an explanation. He hadn't claimed a sprained ankle or being a terrible dancer or having a girlfriend. He didn't have a ring on his left hand.

So yes, even before she saw him sitting on the back step with a goat—correction, nine goats, two ducks, and a potbellied pig—she had been wondering what the hell his deal was.

It was probably the not-being-used-to-being-told-no thing, but something made her walk around the corner of the building and say, "So, does she think that's a carrot in your pocket? Because it sounds like you're not that happy to see her."

The man's head came up quickly and, if she wasn't mistaken, he gave a little sigh when he saw who she was.

But surely, she *was* mistaken. People didn't often tell her no, and they very rarely sighed when they saw her. Or if they did, it was certainly in relief. Charlie was a very well-liked person. She was an optimist, she was a hard worker, and she always tried to make the best of every situation. She was a damned delight. And if this guy had taken ten minutes to dance with her, he would have known that.

"I can't believe I lost out to a goat," she said.

The man continued to pet the goat's head as Charlie approached.

"I mean, I assume that's why you turned down my offer for a dance." Charlie stopped in front of him. "Because for the life of me, I can't think of any other reason."

"Not wanting to dance with you couldn't possibly have been the reason?" His voice was a low rumble, and his tone was dry.

Charlie lifted a shoulder. "Nope." Charlie scanned the menagerie around him. "This is your fan club, huh? I might actually be hoping for Taylor Swift even more now."

The guy was looking at her as if *she* was the weird one. But he was the one with the goat standing between his knees looking at him as if he was a salt lick, and it was majorly sodium deficient. And despite his Old McDonald role-playing, Charlie had to admit she and the goat might have something in common.

She looked at him for a long moment, then asked, "You're not going to ask me about the Taylor Swift comment?"

"I've found that when you ask people questions, it keeps conversations going."

Ah, he wasn't much of a conversationalist. Got it.

Charlie smiled what she knew had to look like a sly grin. There was nothing more fun than drawing someone into a reluctant conversation and charming them with her wit and charisma.

This guy was pushing a lot of her buttons. He was good-looking, he was clearly a friend of her family's since he was at these weddings, and, most of all, he was trying to resist her.

She didn't flirt her way through life, exactly, but she'd rarely met another human she couldn't win over if she wanted to.

"Well, I overheard you telling your friend that it was inappropriate for her to be here and that she couldn't stalk you with her friends, and I have to admit I was hoping for a flash mob to break out."

"And you thought Taylor Swift would be a part of that?"

Charlie grinned. Score one for her. He'd just responded to her despite clearly not wanting to. Even better, he was talking to her about Taylor Swift. She had no idea how she knew, but she was certain that this man did not say the name "Taylor Swift" on any kind of a regular basis.

"I was just going through the songs that I would use if I were arranging a flash mob for the guy I was stalking."

"You're stalking a guy?"

He was still talking to her. Charlie's smile grew wider. "I was thinking about stalking the guy who turned me down for a dance at a recent wedding reception, but it seems like I'll have to get in line."

The man stretched to his feet. The goat backed up, but only a couple of steps. The duck did as well to avoid being stepped on. The potbellied pig lifted her head to see what was happening. Everyone else continued grazing.

Well, not everyone else. Charlie took the opportunity to sweep her gaze over the man from head to toe. Twice.

He was tall, at least six foot three inches. He had dark hair, but she hadn't been close enough in good lighting to decide if it was dark brown or black. It was a little shaggy, curling sexily against the collar of his shirt. He had at least a day or two's worth of stubble on his jaw, his skin an I-work-outside-in-the-sun-a-lot tan. All she could tell from earlier in the bar was that his eyes were dark. She would very much like to be close enough to tell what exact color they were. He'd smelled really good in the bar.

He was dressed, as all the men at the wedding reception were, in dark jeans and a button-down dress shirt. His shirt was now untucked, the top two buttons unbuttoned, and the sleeves rolled up to his elbows.

He started walking away from the bar toward the dirt road that ran in front of her grandmother's establishment, without another word.

Charlie watched him go for a few steps, the adoring goat trotting beside him and one of the ducks waddling along behind them. The rest of the animals seemed oblivious to being left behind.

He turned and looked back at the animals. "Come on, everybody."

A couple of the goats lifted their heads, and the potbellied pig glanced over, but no one seemed inclined to move. Charlie crossed her arms, fighting a grin.

He sighed and started back.

"Seriously, it's time to go home." He got behind a couple of the goats and nudged one of them with his knee. The goat bleated at him and gave him what Charlie could only describe as a glare.

"Let's go, Dopey." The man nudged the goat with his knee again.

"Is insulting them the best way to get them to do what you want?"

He gave Charlie an irritated look. "Dopey is his name."

"You named him Dopey?"

"I didn't name him anything. I didn't name any of them anything."

"So they're not your goats?"

"They are most definitely not my goats."

Charlie was definitely fighting laughter now. "So she fell in love with you, and she's not even yours? You don't feed her or anything?"

He shrugged. "What can I say? When you've got it, you've got it."

Charlie snorted. "I'm feeling a little better about us not dancing together."

"Worried about my animal magnetism?"

Actually, she was starting to worry about his charm. It was there, even if it took a little bit of digging to get to it, and it was surprisingly potent. "I'm not sure that I want to be in the same fan club as Lulubelle here." She gave the goat a mock appraising look. "I would never wear that collar with her hair color." The goat had a pretty green collar on that looked completely fine with her mostly brown coat.

Now the guy stopped and turned to face Charlie fully. His gaze tracked over her from her hair to the toes of her Valentinos and back again. "Yeah, you seem pretty... put together."

He bent and put both hands on Dopey's rump and pushed, leaving Charlie to wonder if being "put together" was a compliment from this guy or not.

She was going to go with *not*.

"By the way, her name is Sugar," he said.

Charlie laughed. "So that was not just a term of endearment?"

"It most definitely wasn't."

"But how can you resist someone who obviously loves you so much that she would follow you all the way down here to this wedding?" Charlie looked around. "Come to think of it, where did she come from, Mac?"

He frowned. "Mac?"

"As in Old McDonald had a farm?"

"Cute." His tone made it clear he didn't find it cute at all.

"Right, they're not your goats," Charlie said.

He was still talking to her. Kind of. She couldn't explain why, but she really liked that. She often wanted to keep people talking. Talking was one of her favorite things to do. She was very good at it even when the people she talked to didn't think they wanted to talk or listen to her. In fact, that was when she did some of her best work. Marketing and PR had been an obvious choice when it had come to deciding her college major. Her father had laughed, shaken his head, and said simply, "The world isn't going to know what hit it."

Dopey finally took a few steps, but none of the other goats seemed inclined to follow. The guy turned to nudge another goat, which caused Dopey to stop moving. The remaining duck that wasn't following Sugar got offended by the other goats being pushed around, and she squawked, flapped her wings angrily, and went waddling off—in the opposite direction.

"Dammit, Alice," the man exclaimed.

That seemed to annoy the pig, who decided to go find a quieter place to eat and went wandering toward the front of the bar.

"Hermione," the man said, raising his voice slightly, calling after the pig. "I *really* like bacon. And pulled pork."

Charlie snorted again. He looked over.

"Did you say her name is Hermione?"

He sighed.

Charlie grinned at him. It was. The pig's name was Hermione. "I know you didn't name her—though it would have made it even better if you had—but I have to tell you, something about hearing you say *Hermione* really delights me."

He rolled his eyes. She couldn't see it in the dark, but she was sure of it.

"I get the impression that you're pretty used to people

wanting to delight you," he said, turning to nudge another goat. Who didn't want to be nudged.

Hmmm, also not exactly a compliment. But not really an insult either. It could have probably sounded like an innuendo, actually. But this guy didn't seem like the innuendo type.

"It's true," she admitted. "People like to make me happy."

"Why is that?"

That was an interesting question. But *she* liked to make other people happy, so it seemed that they should feel the same way in return. "Probably because *I'm* delightful."

"You don't say."

Yeah, he didn't seem convinced. "If you'd danced with me, you would have known that."

"I'm not too easy to... delight."

She felt her lips curl into a smile.

His brows rose. "What's that?"

"What's what?"

"That smile."

She shrugged. "Just a smile."

"No." He shook his head. "That's an oh-that's-really-interesting smile."

"Is it?" She pretended not to know what he was talking about. But it *was* really interesting that he wasn't easy to delight.

People who were hard to delight were her catnip.

"It is," he confirmed.

"I don't know what you mean."

"I'm not really the dancing type."

"Uh-huh."

"And delightful isn't a word I use any more often than *Taylor Swift*."

"Okay."

"You're still smiling."

"Huh."

And apparently, good-looking, six-foot-three-inch guys with scruffy jaws, who had a soft spot for goats and who weren't easy to delight, were more like chocolate-covered catnip with colored candy sprinkles.

Because he was *not* getting rid of her now.

Not until he admitted that she was delightful. And that he should have said yes to that dance.

He sighed. "So are you going to help?"

"Help with what?" She had a list already started in her mind of things she'd like to help him with. Like getting him out of his pants.

"The goats."

Yeah, those weren't even in the top ten.

Charlie looked around. Then back at him. "Do I seem like the type of girl who would be helpful with goats?"

She'd spent every summer of her life in Autre until she'd turned nineteen and landed her first marketing internship as a part of her college program. She wasn't *not* the type to help with goats. She'd spent plenty of time dirty and muddy and not smelling so good when down here on the bayou. Some of the best times of her life.

But right now?

She was wearing Valentino. And her nails were totally inappropriate for this event, but they were spectacular.

"You really don't," he said simply.

Well, at least they were on the same page with that.

"But you're human and have two arms, two legs, and two hands. That's really all I need right now."

Charlie bit back her first retort in response to that being all he really needed from her. She was a lady. Kind of.

She was a Landry lady, which meant that she sometimes let the inappropriate comments slip out. But she'd been raised away from the bayou, unlike most of her cousins, which meant that she was typically able to swallow her inappropriate responses before they made it past her lips.

"How about I just go back inside and get you some help from in there?"

The man groaned, and he straightened fully. "Jesus, don't do that."

Charlie immediately realized what he was talking about. The people she would go retrieve to help him with this little situation included her cousins Mitch, Fletcher, Zeke, and Zander. And they would absolutely give him shit about this. She would have considered getting her nicer set of cousins—Josh, Owen, and Sawyer—but they happened to be the grooms at this triple wedding, and she couldn't imagine pulling them away from their new brides for goat herding.

Clearly, this guy realized which men she would most likely bring out to help wrangle the animals. That he didn't want to deal with them made her think he knew her family rather well.

She looked from him to the goats, then back to him, then to the pig, then back to him again. She blew out a breath and said, "Fine. But you're going to owe me."

He hesitated for just a moment, then said, "I may regret this, but I think owing you might be better in the long run than dealing with the Landry boys."

Charlie decided not to tell him that he was *incorrect* in that assumption.

Not that him owing her wouldn't be fun, but where he might end up getting mocked, possibly even bruised, and definitely muddy hanging out with her cousins, it would be an event that he would soon forget about. It would simply be another night hanging out in Autre with the Landrys.

But hanging out with *her* was not something that he was likely to forget for a long time. At least if she had her way.

2

"Okay, just tell me what you need me to do," she said brightly, suddenly more enthusiastic about this task.

If this guy and his tiny hints of charm also had a little bossiness and a whole lot of competence underneath—and he continued with this general air of reluctance about spending a lot of time with her—this was going to be way more fun than even her grandpa's moonshine at a triple family wedding.

And her grandpa's moonshine had been known to lead to things like fireworks and skinny dipping. In other words, *lots* of fun.

"I need to get these animals back across the street," the man said.

"Across the street?"

He nodded and tipped his head in the general direction of the Boys of the Bayou office. The company offered swamp boat and pontoon tours of the bayou and fishing expeditions. It was owned and run by, as it so happened, the three men and one of the women who had tied the knot tonight. It had been her grandfather's business before he'd sold it to her cousins, so it had been in the family for years. It was a staple in Charlie's life, and she had spent many wonderful summer days on those boat docks and out on the bayou on those boats.

The office was situated across the dirt road from Ellie's bar.

The Landry family, other than Charlie's father, all lived and worked within a twenty-mile radius of one another, and the little town of Autre was home to a multitude of Landry family businesses. In addition to the bar and swamp boat tour company, there was also a construction company, an accounting business, a mechanics garage, and many others. Her cousin Zander was even the town cop, and her cousin Kennedy had recently been elected mayor. The Landry family more or less ruled Autre, Louisiana. It was a unique and very special place, and Charlie loved it with her whole heart.

"You're going to put the goats in the office?" Charlie asked.

"No, I think I'll put them in their barn."

Charlie glanced toward the swamp boat company again. "Their barn?"

"The barn that's next to the swamp boat docks," the man said.

"Why is there a barn next to the docks?"

"Because that's where they put the petting zoo."

"There's a *petting zoo*?" She really should start reading her grandmother's emails more carefully.

Ellie would have definitely filled Charlie in on a new petting zoo. But Ellie's emails tended to be as long as the stories she told out loud. And she didn't hit ENTER very often. The emails were solid blocks of running text, and they made Charlie's head hurt a little, even as they made her smile.

Plus, Charlie's schedule had been crazy lately. She was leaving for a new position with her company in two days. In Paris. Yes, France. She was going to be working in Paris, freaking France.

So yeah, she'd been a little busy. Still, it seemed that her mom or dad or one of her sisters would've mentioned that their cousins were starting a petting zoo as a part of their tourist business.

"There is a petting zoo. Boys of the Bayou Gone Wild." The man seemed put out by the mere suggestion of a petting zoo, not to mention the reality of one.

Charlie felt a little smile curling her lips. The man seemed a little put out in general as it had to do with goats, ducks, and pigs. It seemed that perhaps he had more to do with this dinky zoo than he wanted to have, especially if he knew one of the goats well enough to consider her a stalker. But adding the Gone Wild to the Boys of the Bayou business name was pretty clever.

So this man worked for her family's new business. And while the goats seemed to be a bit of an irritant in his life, he was gruff but sweet with them. There was just something about him that made her think that he was a good guy. If her family had hired him and worked with him every day, she had absolutely no reason to worry about crossing a dark dirt road and going into a barn with him at night when no one knew where she was.

"Well, the petting zoo is news to me," she said. "But that's fun."

"Oh yeah, it's a ton of fun." His tone was dry.

Charlie grinned. "Well, I don't know what a petting zoo has to do with swamp tours, but has it increased business or revenue?"

"I have no idea. The business's accounting is not in my job description."

Got it. "So you just take care of the animals?"

She loved to dress up in Valentino heels and loved to do her makeup, and though she hated fake eyelashes, she definitely enjoyed cocktail dresses and a great blowout. However, she'd always been attracted to blue-collar guys who worked with their hands and weren't afraid to get dirty.

She attributed that to growing up spending summers on the bayou. She was a Louisiana girl, raised in Shreveport, but there was something about the small-town bayou boys that, especially as a teenager, she'd noticed were just a little bit *more* than the city boys she was used to.

She was blessed to have a large number of male cousins who happened to have a lot of friends who loved to spend time swimming and fishing off the Boys of the Bayou docks just outside her grandma's house and bar.

Charlie definitely had an affinity for rugged, outdoorsy, hard-working men. And even if he didn't have a Louisiana drawl, she liked the gruff edge to this guy and his inadvertent charm. Southern boys could turn the charm on and off like a faucet. This guy seemed to be unaware he was being charming.

And then he scooped Sugar up in his arms and started across the road, shepherding three other goats along in front of him. "You comin'?" he called back.

To her, Charlie assumed.

It took her just a moment to gather her wits. It was probably the biceps bunching that got her a little flustered, but the way he cuddled Sugar against his chest as if he had done it before made Charlie feel a little warmer than she had a moment ago.

She looked around, still not entirely sure what he expected of her, exactly. But clearly, she was supposed to somehow get a group of animals away from Ellie's, across the street, and to the *barn* that she had, so far, not even noticed in the hours she had been in town.

"Okay, let's go, guys," she said to the goats, who were still munching grass and not paying a bit of attention to her. One of them lifted its head and blinked at her. "Yeah, you, let's go." She jabbed her thumb in the general direction the man had headed. The goat blinked again, and then went back to eating grass. Charlie sighed and called after the man, "Hey, what are the rest of their names?"

He turned back. "Are you just trying to get me to say goofy goat names?"

"They have goofy names?"

"They're named after the Seven Dwarves. The goats are, anyway."

Charlie grinned. "What about the ducks?"

"The Brady Bunch."

Her eyes widened. "Jan? Bobby? Marcia? All of them?"

He sighed, obviously not as delighted by this fact as she was. "Yeah."

Charlie laughed. "And is there a Harry and Ron to go with Hermione?" she asked of the pig.

"Yep."

Charlie loved everything about this. "Tori and Maddie and Kennedy named them, right?"

"Of course."

Oh yes, he knew her family well. Kennedy was her cousin. Tori and Maddie were two of the brides tonight and Charlie's new cousins-in-law. And yes, the Landry *girls*—even those who were Landrys by marriage rather than blood—were as much trouble as the boys. Especially when they got together and ganged up on someone. Like a poor, unsuspecting, put-upon farmer from...

"Where are you from?" she asked. Yeah, it seemed out of the blue, but his lack of accent stood out down here.

He clearly agreed it seemed out of the blue. "Here. Now."

"But before here."

"D.C."

"That's where you grew up?"

"Nope."

Mr. Congeniality was going to have to try harder than one-word answers to turn her off. Especially now that he was holding a goat like someone would a puppy. Or a child. No matter how annoyed he seemed, he liked the animals, and that was sexy.

"You sound like you're from the Midwest." She did *lots* of calls and meetings with people from around the country.

"Good guess."

"If I didn't know better, I'd think you wanted to *keep* talking to me."

"Why would you think that?"

"Because it would be a lot faster and end the conversation sooner if you just answered the question. The way you're going, you're just making me more curious and more determined to keep talking."

He sighed. "Kansas."

She grinned. She'd figured out how to push at least a couple of his buttons. "Kansas. Yep, that sounds right."

"Maybe if you start talking to the goats, they'll decide to come to the barn to end the conversation too."

She nodded, not even a little insulted. He acted annoyed with the goats but was actually kind of sweet to them. It seemed he was treating her similarly. She was okay being on the same level as the goats with this guy. "Maybe. Good idea." She turned. "So, guys..." Then she looked over her shoulder. "Wait. They're not *all* named after the Seven Dwarves. There's Sugar. And there are more than seven remaining."

He sighed. "You're going to keep asking me about their names, aren't you?"

"Absolutely."

He looked resigned. "There's Sugar and Spice. They're sisters."

"Does Spice adore you too?" Charlie teased.

"Nope. They all love Josh. The pigs too."

Charlie could see that. Josh was a sweetheart. And he was married to Tori, the soft-hearted, animal-crazy veterinarian from Iowa that he'd met at Mardi Gras a couple of years ago. He probably got big brownie points with her for being sweet and spending time with the animals.

The man pointed to the goat furthest away from the group. "That one's Stan. His real name is Satan. Owen named him. But the girls think that's mean so they call him Stan instead."

Charlie laughed. "Does he live up to the Satan name?"

"He's the one who opens the gate for Sugar," the man said as if that was all the proof she should need.

Charlie looked at the goat in his arms. "He likes Sugar?"

"Nah. He just likes to be a pain in the ass and knows that opening the gate is the best way to piss off the humans."

The guy was *talking*. Like, multiple words in a sentence and multiple sentences in a row. It was about goats, but honestly, Charlie was pretty charmed by all of this.

"So, Sugar, Spice, Stan..."

He sighed but pointed again. "Vinny."

"Vinny?"

"Short for Vincent Van Goat."

There was just a beat, and then Charlie snorted. "No way. Is he missing an ear?"

"He is. Are we done now?"

"What? No! I need to know what happened to his ear!"

"I shouldn't have made that a question," he said. "We are done now."

Charlie shook her head, still smiling. "But that leaves only five goats with dwarf names."

He started to turn away.

"And there are seven dwarves," she said.

"Huh."

He was definitely not into this. Or he was pretending anyway.

"I've met Dopey." She glanced at the goat, a little surprised to realize that she remembered which one he was. "That leaves Sleepy, Bashful, Sneezy—weird name for a goat."

He just shrugged.

"Happy, Doc, and Grumpy," she finished. "Which one's which?"

"No Doc. Or Grumpy."

"Why not?"

"Tori is Doc."

Charlie smiled. "That's cute. And..." A thought hit her, and she narrowed her eyes even as her grin grew. "Who's Grumpy?"

"Ran out of goats."

"Uh-huh. But they didn't name one of these Grumpy because..."

"No idea."

"Are you sure it's not because they already had a Grumpy... in you?"

He lifted a brow. "Are you going to actually be helpful now or not?"

That wasn't a denial that *he* filled the role of Grumpy.

She loved every damn thing about this petting zoo so far.

"Oh, I'm not going anywhere," she told him. "I'm definitely going to help."

He sighed.

Feeling suddenly lighter and happier than she had in a long time—and that was saying something as she was generally light and happy, not to mention on her way to Paris soon—Charlie turned back to the animals.

"Okay, now that we know each other better, how about you all be sweet and head back to the barn? We can keep this party going over there?"

Not one animal even looked at her.

"Hey, Stan?" she called. "You're clearly a leader. How about you show me that you can do some good with all that staunch determination and lead everyone back to the barn?"

"You can't be serious," the guy said. "*Talking* to them isn't actually going to work. You know I don't really think that."

"Talking is what I do."

"No kidding."

She just lifted a brow. "So what should I do instead?"

Maybe he could give her an opening for charming him into putting that very nice, smirky, sarcastic mouth against hers and...

"Nudge 'em," he said simply.

Now she blinked at him. "What?"

"Nudge them," he said again.

"Just... nudge them? As in, push them?" She narrowed her eyes. Were they talking about goats? Or were they maybe talking about grumpy farmers who needed more than a subtle flirtation to make a move?

"Sometimes that's all they need."

Okay then. She was going to keep that in mind.

"So..." He nodded toward the goats.

She blew out a breath. Okay, so for *right now,* they were talking about goats.

Charlie approached the smallest of the animals. He—or she—looked up at her. "Hello, I'm Charlotte. Would you please accompany me across the street back to your barn?" She heard the man's snort even from a distance. That made her smile even though she was still stuck with the problem of herding goats.

The goat, of course, didn't move a step.

"I would very much enjoy it if you would grant me the pleasure of your company across the street at your barn," she told the goat.

This time the goat didn't even lift his head.

Charlie propped a hand on her hip. "I don't feel that we know each other well enough for me to actually put my hands on your body, so it really would be easier if you would just head in the general direction of your barn."

"For fuck's sake." Suddenly the man was back beside her.

He bent and lifted the goat, and Charlie couldn't help but think this had worked out very well. She hadn't had to touch the goats, but she hadn't been entirely unhelpful to him.

Okay, that wasn't true. She had been *completely* unhelpful to him. But she hadn't left him out here with the goats alone, and she hadn't gone back inside the bar and told her rowdy cousins on him.

The man pivoted and pressed the goat to her chest. Instinctively her arms went up and around it. He let go.

And just like that, she had her arms full of goat.

Charlie gasped, partially in surprise and partially because it only took her a millisecond to think about the fact that she now had a barnyard animal up against her Alex Perry cocktail dress.

"Oh my God, you have to be kidding," she said to the man.

"When nudging doesn't work, sometimes you have to get hands-on."

Charlie blew out a breath. She was tucking that away with her other ideas about how to handle *him* too. But she was preoccupied at the moment.

And not so sure she wanted to kiss him after all.

No, that wasn't true. She still wanted to kiss him. Especially now that he was standing closer.

Even if she had to kiss him over the back of a goat.

Which probably meant she *really* wanted to kiss him.

She'd *definitely* rather do it without a goat between them though.

She could throw a fit, of course. He was probably expecting that.

She could put the goat back down. She could stomp off in a huff. She could still sic her rowdy cousins on the guy.

But in spite of the fact that she was holding a goat and she didn't even know the guy's name, she wanted to stay out here with him.

"If I am going to literally carry goats back to a barn," she said, noting that the man seemed to be waiting for her to throw exactly the kind of fit that she had just entertained in her mind, "you're going to have to keep talking to me."

"What is it that you think we need to be talking about?"

"Whatever I want."

"Why do you get to pick?"

"My eight-hundred-dollar cocktail dress is now going to smell like goat," Charlie told him. "I think that's only fair."

"Eight hundred dollars? Jesus. Maybe that's what's making it look so good."

Okay, now she was shocked. "Did you just say I look 'so good?' As in, you just gave me a compliment?"

"Well—" His gaze roamed over her, and, despite the goat in her arms, he seemed to like what he saw.

Charlie felt her body heat.

"I think I gave the dress a compliment," he finally said. "I mean, if you're willing to pay that much, you must have something pretty awful to cover up. And it's doing a fine job of it."

She felt her brows climb. But she also felt the urge to laugh. That comment was a lot more in character for him than an outright compliment. And it was weird that she already thought she knew his character, wasn't it?

"Is this where I'm supposed to offer to prove that there's nothing horrible under this dress?"

His gaze flew back to hers. He straightened slightly and took a breath. "No. *Hell no*." He shook his head.

Her eyes widened as he took a step back.

"I mean, no, sorry," he went on. "That's not what I meant."

Oh, now he was flustered. She kind of liked that, too.

Gruff, accidentally charming, sweet with animals, funny

even if he didn't mean to be, and chagrined about possibly being ungentlemanly.

Who was this guy?

Charlie tipped her head to the side. "This goat is getting heavy. Make me the deal for more conversation in exchange for being a shepherdess, or I'm heading inside with this goat in my arms to get you some different help."

The man seemed to believe she was serious and once again realized that he did *not* want any of the Landrys inside the bar to come out at this moment. But he also relaxed, grasping that she wasn't offended by his comment about her dress.

"Why do you want to keep talking to me so badly?" he asked, seeming genuinely curious.

That was a really good question. One she was still trying to answer. "You turned me down for a dance. And don't want to keep talking to me."

"And that makes me a challenge or something?"

If she wasn't mistaken, there was a flicker of humor, and even interest, in his eyes.

"Yep," she said simply.

"So, if I'd danced with you, I could have avoided all of this?"

"Yep." Then she added, "Though if we'd danced, you probably wouldn't have been outside to find Sugar had come over looking for you."

He *almost* smiled again. Instead, he shook his head as if he couldn't quite believe her audacity. She wanted to laugh. Audacity was a highly prized characteristic in her family.

Finally, he gave a short nod. "Fine. We can talk. But you can't be a shepherdess. They're goats. So you're a goatherder."

She wrinkled her nose. "Oh, that's not nearly as cute."

"It's gotta be cute?"

It did because that seemed to bug him. She nodded. "Cute is always the way to go."

He made a noncommittal grunting noise at that.

She laughed. "How about just between us we call me a shepherdess. No one else needs to know that we weren't absolutely, technically correct."

Instead of saying "no, that's ridiculous," or just going along with it because that really would be a lot easier—something a lot of people realized pretty quickly when dealing with Charlie —he said, "Do people ever say no to you?"

That was a really good question. It showed that he was catching on.

She pretended to think for a second. Then shook her head. "Not that I can remember."

He sighed. "No going slowly with the animals just to drag out the conversation."

Charlie laughed. And noted that he hadn't said yes or no to the shepherdess terminology. "You think I'm going to find you so fascinating that I'm going to want to drag out the conversation? It's occurring to me right now that taking animals to a barn is going to involve a lot of animal smells. I haven't met a man in a long time that could keep me interested enough that I would tolerate the smell of a barn."

"Is that right? Now that *is* interesting."

Charlie opened her mouth to respond, though she wasn't sure with what, but before she could, the man turned and scooped up another goat and started off across the street again.

He found that interesting? Which part exactly? The part where she wasn't really a barn type of girl? Surely that wasn't a huge surprise to him. It must be the part about her not finding a guy lately that she had had such an engaging conversation with. Or perhaps it was the part where she thought that he might provide such a conversation.

Whatever it was, he found something about her interesting, and that made her happy. Which was stupid. She liked people to like her, of course. But making people like her wasn't usually that difficult. Why did she care if *this* guy found her interesting?

Why did she find it so satisfying that she'd made him smile? Or almost smile anyway. And seriously, why was she in a cocktail dress and heels and carrying a goat?

But she was.

Charlie started after him, quickly finding that balancing in heels while carrying a goat was a little bit more complicated than walking in heels *without* carrying a goat. She also was fascinated to find that the other goats started to follow her as she headed in the general direction of the barn. Or at least what she assumed was the general direction of the barn since she had yet to see the structure.

Sure enough, as she rounded the corner of the bar, crossed the street, and followed the sidewalk leading away from the boat docks, she found herself approaching a wooden structure that could only be described as a small barn. It was tucked back under a cluster of trees and was inside a very typical wooden fence with a dirt yard in front. The space had two large boulders, two plastic barrels, and three feeding troughs. There was also a large basin of water.

The man set the goat he was carrying down and then turned to take her goat from her. His attention went to something behind her—she assumed the rest of the goats following her—and he smiled.

Charlie just stared.

She knew she was staring. She knew that was a crazy reaction. She knew that he was going to notice that she was staring and that it was a crazy reaction. But she couldn't stop.

Without the smile, he was sexy, hot, and rugged. She'd found him incredibly attractive inside the wedding reception and had actually been very disappointed that he'd turned down her invitation to dance.

However, him *smiling* did things to her stomach that no man had done in a very long time. Possibly ever. And it was that thought that gave her the greatest hesitation. It was one thing to flirt. It was one thing to charm. It was one thing to poke at a guy who was a little gruff and didn't think he wanted to have conversations with her. It was one thing to tease the guy who turned her down for a dance.

It was quite another to have a man smile and make crazy, warm, curly, tingly, twisty things happen to her insides that she'd never experienced before.

Whew.

It was a really good thing that she was only in town for this wedding. She was getting on an airplane in two days to go to Paris. She wasn't hanging out on the bayou for any period of time. She wasn't spending the summer here as she had for so many years. She was out of here tomorrow night.

And suddenly that seemed not only practical but like a really good idea.

It wasn't that she was scared of the guy. Quite the contrary—she found herself wanting to spend a lot more time with him. She had no desire to return to the wedding reception. She was even considering what it would take to scatter the goats so that they would have to stay out here and round them up again.

This guy rattled her. And all he had done was smile.

"You okay?"

Just as she'd expected, he was watching her with a puzzled look, as if he couldn't figure out why she was standing there, not moving or saying anything.

Charlie pulled herself together. Kind of. "Now what?"

And she wasn't talking about the goats.

He took the goat from her, their hands brushing, and dammit, she felt some tingles. That was crazy. She loved tingles. Tingles were awesome. In fact, if a guy didn't give her tingles after three dates or so, she usually ended it. Tingles were required.

For dating. For guys she wanted to have hot, fun sex with.

For guys she would consider potentially getting serious with. For that last group, tingles were *absolutely* essential.

Tingles, however, had no place in a petting zoo barn with a guy whose name she still didn't know and who had turned her down for even a simple dance. Especially a guy who lived in a tiny town in Louisiana when she was on her way to Paris in forty-eight hours.

3

G riffin had never seen a woman in a cocktail dress holding a goat.

He supposed it was likely that most men could say that. But it turned out that he'd been missing out on one of his major fantasies.

This woman was stunning. She would have been stunning in a potato sack. He knew better than to actually believe that the eight-hundred-dollar—*holy shit*—cocktail dress had anything to do with how beautiful she looked.

He'd been incredibly attracted to her from the minute he'd seen her across Ellie's bar. Which was why he had turned down her offer to dance. He knew better than to get attached in this little town.

Frankly, he was already struggling with that.

Autre, Louisiana, had a way of getting under a person's skin. Even his. He'd learned the hard way not to settle down anywhere, not to get attached to a place or to the people there. But Autre had proven, in the six months that he'd been here, to be dangerous to even the best-laid plans of a guy who had a pretty high, firm wall around his heart.

It did, however, seem typical of the way his luck worked that when he'd successfully resisted temptation at the wedding dance and escaped outside for some air, that the same gorgeous blond who had been tempting him with nothing more than, "Do you want to dance?" and then a genuinely surprised look on her face when he declined, would be the person to find him talking to goats.

It was no surprise that this woman didn't hear no from men very often. In fact, even Griffin, who had no trouble saying no to just about anyone, had almost immediately regretted his answer. Not enough to change his mind and go after her, of course. Until she'd walked up and asked him about the metaphoric carrot in his pocket.

Of course, she had to be funny, clever, bright, friendly, and charming on top of looking like sex on a stick in the cocktail dress and heels she was wearing.

Even when he'd lived in D.C., he hadn't gone for the hours-in-the-salon-chair type. This woman screamed high maintenance. She wore heels that were not only completely impractical for walking around the bayou town but were the type of shoes that fought for attention with the form-fitted cocktail dress that hugged her breasts and hips. It was clear that she also spent a lot of time on her nails, and no one's lips were the color of hers naturally.

Still, he had been inordinately pleased to see her once he'd gotten over his surprise, and nothing about their conversation had done anything to dim his interest.

Which in and of itself was a shock. She was a talker.

Griffin was not.

But then she'd held a goat. In a cocktail dress and high heels.

And he suddenly had a new fetish.

She hadn't fought it. She'd barely glared at him. In fact, she'd used the goat, and the potential goat smell on her dress,

31

as a bargaining chip. For some reason, this woman wanted to keep talking to him and spending time with him. That, again, made her unusual.

There'd been a time when plenty of women had wanted to spend time with him. But that had been before he'd become a surly, unpleasant pessimist. Even women less friendly than this one found him to be a bit of a downer. Or an asshole.

But he hadn't really been much of an asshole with this one so far. He'd tried. Half-heartedly. He'd been a little gruff, and he definitely made it clear that conversation was his least favorite pastime, but he'd told her the animals' names. The ridiculous animal names. He'd also teased her about the talking. And he'd commented on how she looked in her dress.

He shouldn't have done that. Not only because it definitely could've come off as creepy, but because he shouldn't have been noticing how she looked in the dress in the first place.

He also got the impression he shouldn't give this woman any hints to his inner thoughts. And not just the lusty ones. She would use them—all of them—against him. Somehow he knew it.

Griffin set Sleepy down on the floor of the barn. The goat scampered off to explore the barn as if he'd never seen it before.

The other goats darted about the enclosure, two of them climbing up on one of the boulders, another headbutting one of the plastic barrels. Alice and Mike, the ducks, waddled off to find the rest of the Brady Bunch. And Hermione had already reunited with Harry, Ron, and Dumbledore.

Sugar, of course, hadn't gone far when he'd put her down. Sugar loved him. He didn't understand it any more than he understood why this human woman wanted to keep talking to him, but in his weaker moments, he could admit that Sugar was cute. And it never hurt a guy's ego to have someone, or something, adoring him.

Other than Sugar and Hermione—who was scared of thunderstorms—the rest of the animals in the barn could give a rat's ass about him. In fact, most of them didn't like him. They associated him with being poked and prodded and stuck with needles. But such was the life of a veterinarian. If he needed an ego boost and Sugar wasn't enough, he could always go over to the otter enclosure. The otters were smitten with him. They chittered to him like he was a long-lost friend every time they saw him. They could actually give this woman a run for her money when it came to chatter. And they were *a lot* louder about it.

Okay, yes, sometimes he snuck them treats, and yes, when no one else was around, he sat down and let them climb on him, and he'd pet them and talked to them, but he also poked, prodded, and stuck them with needles.

He watched the woman turn a full circle, taking in all the details of the barnyard. He knew the exact moment when she noticed Al, one of the alpacas.

Al had come to the fence that separated his pen from the goat yard and was now peering over, checking out the commotion.

Their emu, Elmo, then wandered over to see what Al was looking at.

The woman spun to face Griffin. "Is that a llama?"

He almost smiled but caught himself just in the nick of time. "Actually, it's an alpaca. That's Al."

His full name was Al Pacacino. And Griffin *really* hoped she wouldn't ask. He also did *not* want to tell her about Alpacalypse, Alpacasso, Alpacaman, or Alpacapella.

They couldn't call them all Al, of course. Al Pacacino was the oldest, so he got the nickname. The rest, Griffin mostly referred to as number two, number three, and so on. He most definitely didn't want to tell her about Chewpaca. Who he did, in his weaker moments, call Chewie.

Elmo was the only emu. For now. But Griffin definitely feared they would add more, and they'd all be named after Sesame Street characters.

"Oh my God, I really need to read my grandmother's emails more carefully," Charlie muttered, shaking her head.

"What do you mean?"

"I'm sure that she would have emailed me about alpacas in Autre."

"Your grandmother lives here?" Yep, he shouldn't get involved with her.

Her eyes narrowed. She seemed to be thinking something over before she answered. "She does. And I think that's all I'm going to tell you."

Yeah, now he liked her even more. "We're not going to share a lot of details?"

"You don't seem like the detail-sharing type of guy."

"But you seem very much like the detail-sharing type of girl." He knew he could walk out of here knowing her favorite flavor of milkshake, her birthday, and her shoe size if he wanted to. Which made his attention drop to her feet again, and the shoes that screamed, *Look at us! Aren't we sexy as fuck?*

Yes, yes, they were.

She nodded. "Typically yes. However, I think that it might be in my best interest right now to be a little less *my* usual type of girl and a little more *your* usual type of girl."

That pulled his attention right back to her face. He took a step toward her without really meaning to. "What do you think my usual type of girl is?"

"Casual. No strings attached. Willing to share only first names and no other details."

Griffin wasn't sure what exactly his heart rate was reacting to, but his pulse had definitely picked up. "And why might that be in your best interest right now?"

"Well, you turned me down for a dance earlier, but that was before we had a chance to really talk."

"And you think now that we've talked, I'm going to be more open to the idea of dancing?"

She laughed. "Actually, I think now that we've talked, you might be even *less* inclined to say yes to a dance." She paused. "Or anything else."

Again, he took a step forward without consciously deciding to make his feet move.

He liked her. She was talkative. God, was she talkative. She was clearly high-maintenance. She was also bright and bubbly, though she hadn't quite crossed over to perky yet. But this was the most interesting evening he'd had in a very long time. And he worked around a bunch of crazy, loud Cajuns, and his days were filled with otters, alpacas, and potbellied pigs. His days were not boring. And yet, this woman was definitely the most fun he'd had in a while.

She was also absolutely gorgeous.

Had he mentioned that? Yes, he had. Even without a goat in her arms.

And then there was the goat thing. She hadn't picked the animal up by herself, and she'd commented on the smell, but she'd carried it to the barn, and she was still here. In the barn, in the middle of the smell.

"So you're thinking of asking me to dance again?"

She tipped her head. "Actually, I've moved on to the anything else part."

His pulse kicked up another notch, and he took a step forward again. He was now close enough that he could reach out and touch her. And God, he wanted to reach out and touch her. That was a huge red flag. He shouldn't be touching anybody. He shouldn't like anyone this much. Certainly not someone that he had just met and knew next to nothing about. But she certainly had a point about his type of girl.

He was definitely a casual, no-strings-attached type of guy. Now. He hadn't always been that guy, but definitely, over the past few years, he'd become that guy. It was just safer.

"Define 'anything else,'" he said, his voice gruffer.

Now *she* took a step forward. This was way more than being within touching distance. The air around him heated slightly, and he caught the scent of expensive perfume over the scent of goat. He supposed it took an expensive perfume to be smelled over the scent of goat. That was certainly a point in the *pro* column for pricey perfume.

"The good news is that 'anything else' does not include dancing..." She paused. "Or talking."

Well, damn. He was on board.

For better or worse, despite the fact, he had flashing warning signs in the back of his mind. In spite of the fact that he had successfully kept from doing anything stupid since he had been in Autre—and there was a tiny niggling voice in the back of his head telling him *this* was going to be stupid—he said, "There are a lot of things I like better than dancing and talking."

She smiled, and he felt a punch to the gut. It wasn't the first smile he'd seen. She'd been smiling and laughing since she'd walked up on him and Sugar and the rest of the gang outside the bar. In addition to being talkative, she was a very smiley person, which should have put her in the not-my-type category. Smiley people were happy people. And happy people didn't put up with growly people, like him, for long. It was a sure set-up for disappointment for someone.

But he really liked her smile. And this smile in particular. This one said *we are totally on the same page, and this page is going to be a hell of a lot of fun.*

She took one more little step forward, putting her directly in front of him, her breasts centimeters away from brushing against his chest. Her forehead was right in front of his mouth, at the perfect height for kissing. Which meant that without her shoes on, her head would tuck right under his chin. The perfect height for hugging.

Griffin rolled his eyes at himself. He was thinking about this woman being the perfect height for hugging? Really? It was one thing to be immediately attracted to her and to have her charm him past his general dislike of conversation and socialization, but it was quite another for him to be measuring her hugging height at this point.

"There's just one thing I need to know," she said.

"Okay."

"Brace yourself. I'm going to ask you something personal," she warned. "But I do think that it is important."

Personal. That was definitely one of his least favorite words. He hesitated but could not ignore the fact that his palms were literally itching to run over the smooth expanse of her shoulder and upper arm bared by her strapless dress. If he didn't touch this woman and kiss her at least once, he was going to regret it forever.

That was the strangest thought he had maybe ever had, but it was enough to make him say, "What do you want to know?"

"What's your first name?" She paused. "Just your first name. I don't need your last name."

"Griffin."

She smiled. "Hi, Griffin. I'm Charlotte."

Charlotte. It fit her. Beautiful, slightly sophisticated but warm.

Warm? He thought of her name as *warm*? That was maybe the second strangest thought he'd ever had.

"There is one other thing I need to know about *you*," he said.

Her eyes widened. "Wow, *you're* going to ask me something personal?"

He lifted a brow, letting her know he noted her sass. "Are you from here?"

He really needed the answer to that. He was going to be incredibly disappointed if the answer was yes, but if she was from Autre, and they just hadn't crossed paths until now, this was the time to know. He could still shut this down. Which he absolutely would if she was local. This woman gave him all kinds of I-could-get-attached vibes, and he needed to nip that in the bud.

"I'm not."

Air rushed from his lungs before Griffin realized he'd even been holding his breath.

"In fact, I'm *really* not from here."

"What's that mean?" She'd already given him the best answer she could have.

"I'm actually moving to Paris in two days. I got a new job."

He blinked at her. "Paris?"

"Yes, Paris. France."

Okay, *that* was the best answer she could have given him. Another country? Another continent? That was fantastic. He gave her a big smile. Her eyes widened, then she blinked at him as if stunned.

He reached out and ran his hand from her elbow to her bare shoulder. Her pale skin was soft and silky, and he felt relief at finally making skin-to-skin contact with her. But even better than the actual feel of her skin under his hand was the tiny shiver of awareness that went through her body.

"I happen to be a huge fan of Paris," he said. With his hand on her elbow, he drew her closer.

She came forward willingly. "You've been to Paris?"

"No."

She gave him a small knowing smile. "You're a fan of me going to Paris in two days."

He nodded.

"You know most girls would probably be insulted by that."

"I'm getting the impression you're not most girls."

"Thank you very much, Griffin."

They leaned in at the same time. Her hands came to rest on his waist while his gently gripped her upper arms. Their mouths met. The kiss was soft. But only for about three seconds. That was all the time it took for his body to say, *Oh, yeah, we want all of this right fucking now.* Then she pressed closer, slid her hands higher, and opened her mouth too.

He ran his hands from her upper arms over her shoulders to the back of her hair, where he cradled her head in his palms, his fingers tangled deep in the silky blond tresses.

Her hands slid up over his ribs to his biceps, where she gripped him, pulling herself up onto tiptoe.

She gave a tiny moan, he growled in the back of his throat, and their tongues met, stroking hungrily.

She tasted even better than she looked. And considering that he wasn't sure he had ever met a woman who had gotten under his skin so quickly, that should've been the biggest red flag of all. Instead, he relished the hunger crashing through him.

It had been so long since he'd felt raw emotion. He didn't let himself anymore. He'd learned to lock it down and had, for the most part, been pleased with the results of that. Ignoring those emotions. Keeping them pushed out of his consciousness, kept him on an even keel, and if not happy, at least not angry and resentful.

But raw emotions didn't just include anger and rage at injustice and a desire to fight and argue and protest. Desire and the need to possess were also true raw emotions. Emotions he hadn't felt in an exceptionally long time. And this woman was bringing them all rushing to the forefront. He was incapable of stopping it.

He tore his mouth from hers and looked down. Her blue

eyes were darker now, swirling with emotion as well. She was breathing a little faster, her likely expensive-as-hell lipstick completely smudged. He lifted one hand to his bottom lip and ran the pad of his thumb over it. He drew it away and looked down to see the dark pink stain on his skin. He liked that. Her mark on him. It was a strange thought, and one he didn't want to delve into at all, but he did acknowledge it.

"You okay?" he asked.

Her eyes widened slightly. "What in the world would make you think I wasn't okay?"

"Just making sure."

"Well, Griffin, I'm *very* okay, and I promise that if at any point I become not okay, you will be the first to know."

Yeah, he really liked her.

"Deal."

He captured her lips again, kissing her deeply, stroking his tongue against hers, wondering how she could taste so amazing. Had it really just been so long since he'd been with a woman?

But it hadn't really been all that long. He hadn't been celibate since coming to Louisiana. He just hadn't been emotionally involved. Of course, he hadn't been emotionally involved in a lot longer than that. Still, there was something about this woman that made his hunger feel more urgent, and everything about being with her, sweeter at the same time.

It was really good she was going to Paris in two days.

She moved her hands to his chest and gripped his shirt in her fists. She tipped her head, slanting her mouth under his, and gave a needy little moan.

Something about her being needy made his gut clench, and a very primal instinct surge forward, demanding he take care of every need she had.

With his mouth still on hers, he started walking her backward. It was about six steps to the nearest wall. Of course, it was a barn wall, but a part of his brain—a part that was quickly becoming the most insistent and impossible to ignore—cared only that it was a firm surface.

Once she'd bumped into the wall, he pressed close, running his hands down her back to settle on her hips. She arched closer to him, the sweet sound she made now sounding less *oh-please* and more *oh-yes*.

Stupidly, he was urged on, knowing that he had done something to satisfy her. He ran one hand lower, cupping her ass and bringing her up against him more fully. Now her moan was purely *more-of-that*.

He kissed along her jaw to the sweet spot behind her ear. Damn, he didn't know what they put in this perfume, but he wanted to smell it all over his pillows and sheets. Hell, he wanted to smell it all over his skin. But only if it was transferred from her skin to his.

Her fingers dug into his shoulder blades as she tipped her head back. She arched closer to his mouth and the hard length of his erection behind his fly. He slid his hand from her ass to her upper thigh and lifted her leg. Her skirt was loose enough that the material fell away from her thighs, hanging behind her. The back of the skirt was longer than the front, and the hem now brushed the barn floor. And there was now a lot of enticing bare skin. The position also allowed him to settle between her thighs against the soft spot where he instinctively needed to be.

"Griffin," she gasped.

His name, said like that, from this woman, was exactly what he needed without even knowing he'd needed anything.

All of this was crazy. The way he was feeling, the way he was thinking about this woman, his stupid, irrational, emotional reactions to her.

But she wasn't from here, she was leaving, and she was going to be far away and untouchable. And she knew the score.

That was key. She didn't want his last name any more than he wanted hers. All of that made this safe, and the emotions he'd been holding back for all these months now seemed to have an outlet. A sweet-smelling, soft, silky, sassy-flirty-funny-charming blond outlet.

Now that the lid was off, it seemed he had feelings and desires spilling out all over the place.

But he wasn't going to have to clean this mess up. It wasn't even going to be a mess.

"More. More, please," she pleaded in a breathless voice.

This woman was the best thing to happen to him in months.

And he wanted to say thanks.

He pressed his hard cock against the V of her thighs. She gave a happy sigh. He smiled. God, there was something about being with someone who let you know exactly how they felt and that *you* were the one making them feel it. Especially when the feelings were good.

He had people and situations where he hadn't minded making people feel pretty damn bad too. Sorry. Full of shame. Regretful. Even angry. He didn't care. Sometimes people deserved to feel those things too.

But this woman, tonight? She deserved to feel very, very good. Because yeah, she was making *him* feel better than he had in a long time. Now that he'd let the thought in, let the emotions flow, there was no denying it.

He stroked his open palm along the back of her thigh as he kissed his way down her neck to her collarbone. Her hands moved up to the back of his head, her fingers spreading through his hair.

"Thank you for wearing a strapless dress," he said against her skin.

Her fingers curled into his scalp. "I would've gladly unzipped anything for you."

He gave a huff of laughter but continued kissing across her collarbone to the base of her throat. He gave her skin a little lick and suck and then kissed down to the top edge of the bodice of the dress.

"In fact…" She reached behind her, and he heard the faint rasp of a zipper. The material at his chin loosened, and he realized she'd unzipped the top of her dress.

He lifted his head to look into her eyes. She met his gaze directly.

"You sure about this?"

"What did I tell you about me being okay? I will let you know if my status changes."

"I just want you to know that with the taste I've already gotten, I'm about this close to already being addicted to you."

Heat flared in her eyes, even as a smile teased her lips. "Then let's keep going. I'd really like to get you all the way to addicted."

Griffin felt the corner of his mouth twitch. He wanted her more than he'd wanted anyone he could remember in a very long time, but he also felt the constant urge to smile in the time he'd spent with her, and dammit, if he didn't still have the urge to hug her.

Just then, he felt a familiar, hard bump against his leg.

He looked down. Sugar looked up at him and gave a short, loud bleat.

She was feeling neglected.

Dammit.

"Go away," he told the goat.

She head-butted his leg again.

He nudged her with his knee. "Go find Spice and Stan." He glanced at Mike, the duck, who was never far from Sugar. "Do something."

Mike was very unhelpful most of the time. But he loved Sugar and followed her around like a puppy. While she followed Griffin around like a puppy. It was ridiculous. And annoying a lot of the time.

"Hey, Sugar," Charlotte said. "You can have him back in about an hour, okay?"

Griffin looked at her. "An hour, huh?"

"Approximately," she told him with a sexy smile.

He suddenly wanted a lot more than an hour.

Dammit.

"Hey!" Charlotte suddenly exclaimed, looking down.

Sugar had now head-butted her. But harder than she did Griffin. With Griffin, it was for attention. It now seemed she was actually getting aggressive with Charlotte.

The goat bleated at her and then grabbed a mouthful of Charlotte's dress.

"Hey!" Charlotte said again, grabbing the skirt of her dress and trying to tug it away.

"*Enough,*" Griffin said. The dress was going to get torn, or Sugar was going to take another bite and get some skin this time.

He leaned over and grabbed the goat. He turned and set her away from them and gave her a little push. "Get lost."

Then he turned back to Charlotte, took her by the waist, and picked her up as well, carrying her to the nearest empty stall. The floor was covered with hay, and there was less light in here, but there were no animals in it at the moment, and the door would shut, keeping any more curious—or jealous—creatures out.

He set her down, pulled the door shut, and latched it.

Sugar trotted over and stuck her head between the slats. She gave them a pissed-off, "*Maaaaa!*"

"Ignore her. She'll go away," he told Charlotte, who was holding the top of her dress against her breasts to keep it from falling down.

He really wanted it to fall down.

"A lady should never tolerate being ignored," Charlotte said. "She should dump you."

"I agree."

She nodded and glanced at the goat. "Also, she should *not* watch her crush get it on with someone else. Have some self-respect, Sugar."

Griffin felt himself snort softly. "Get it on?"

"I didn't know if I should use bad words in front of her. How old is she?"

"Six."

"Yeah, I definitely shouldn't say 'fuck' in front of her."

But she should *absolutely* say it in front of him. To him. As in begging him for it.

He reached for the blanket that was draped over the short wall that separated the stall from the next one. He draped it over the door, letting it hang to the floor on the inside—where Sugar couldn't grab it with her teeth and yank it down.

With her view blocked, Sugar gave another long, pitiful "*Maaaaa.*"

"Wow, she's got it bad," Charlotte said.

"And you're still here in spite of the smell, the hay, and the cock-blocking goat."

Which was damn amazing.

He didn't know another woman he'd want to kiss and "get it on" with who would tolerate any of that.

"Technically, she's not cock-blocking," Charlotte said, reaching for him and pulling him close. "She's *trying*. But it's definitely not working."

"You know," he said, running his hand up her arm again, "you're pretty damn delightful after all."

She gave him a full smile at that. "Told you so."

"That makes you feel pretty cocky, huh?"

"Oh, *that* doesn't make me cocky. I've been cocky for a long time. But it does make me happy."

He knew he shouldn't say it, even as the words occurred to him. This was exactly the kind of thing that he shouldn't even be thinking, not to mention admitting out loud. Still, it was his voice that said the words, "I think making you happy could be a really fun hobby."

She nodded. "If that's the case, you definitely need to put your mouth back where it was."

He lifted a brow, dropped his gaze to the top of her dress where it was now gaping away from her skin, and said, "I figured you'd like me being a little more talkative."

She lifted her hand to his head and pulled him forward, putting her lips against his before she said, "Hey, Griffin?"

"Yes, Charlotte?"

"This is me nudging you."

It took him just a second, but he remembered telling her earlier that sometimes to get the goats to do what he wanted, he had to nudge them. So Charlotte was going to nudge him here? That was absolutely unnecessary.

He kissed her deeply then ran his mouth down her throat, loving her shiver as his scruffy chin lightly abraded her skin. He stopped at the top of the dress and licked along the edge of the fabric. Then he took the silky material between his teeth and pulled it down.

Charlotte wasn't wearing a bra with the strapless, summery dress.

Absolutely fucking delightful.

The woman really was perfection. And he knew looking at her tantalizing naked breasts with the hard, pink tips that his addiction was going to be complete and possibly devastating.

Still, he gave a little growl and reached for her hands at the back of his head. With his fingers around her wrists, he pressed her hands against the wall of the barn on either side of her shoulders. The position caused her back to arch, lifting her breasts, and he bent to take a nipple in his mouth. He licked and sucked, drawing a gasp and a moan from her. Heat shot through him at the sound, making blood pound into his cock.

To this point, he'd found her funny, not quite sweet, but certainly friendly. But she was also full of sass. She had been completely unintimidated by his attempts to avoid conversation and send her on her way. He definitely liked her, which was more than he could say for some of the other women whose breasts he'd been this close to, but he was under no illusion that he needed to treat her gently or be romantic with her. And he definitely liked that about her too.

He wasn't a guy to mince words, he wasn't much of a poker player because his emotions always showed, and he'd gotten himself fired twice for speaking his mind. So he certainly wasn't a guy to hold back on how he was feeling when he was with a beautiful woman who seemed to want him as much as he wanted her.

"Don't move your hands." His command was short and gruff. He let go of one of her wrists so that he could cup the breast he was not currently worshiping with his mouth. Satisfaction coursed through him as Charlotte kept her hands pressed against the wall of the barn. He rewarded her by first rubbing a thumb over her nipple then rolling it between his thumb and forefinger before tugging on it gently. Her head fell back against the wall, and her eyes shut as she moaned his name. That got her more than a tug. He pinched her nipple and moved to take that one with a hard suck as well.

"Tuck both your hands behind your back," he ordered.

Charlotte did it without question. She didn't even open her eyes. She slid both hands down the wall and then behind her lower back. The position was amazingly submissive and incredibly hot. Griffin tugged the front of her dress down further, bunching the expensive material at her waist and leaving her torso bare. There was also something incredibly hot about knowing the fabric that had cost her eight hundred dollars and was now going to be wrinkled and dirty from a barn wall because she wanted him as much as he wanted her.

He ran his hands from her waist up to her sides, relishing the goosebumps that broke out over her skin. He kept both breasts in his big hands, thumbing the nipples, then tugging again as she whimpered. He alternated between pinching and sucking until she was writhing against the wall and begging breathlessly with hot little *please*s and *oh my God*s and *Griffin*s.

"I want more of you, Charlotte."

Her eyes flew open to meet his. Then she simply nodded.

"I want all of you."

She nodded again.

"Say it."

"Yes."

"Say yes, you can have all of me, Griffin."

Her blue eyes were nearly the color of the darkening night sky when they met his. She wet her lips. "Yes, you can have all of me, Griffin."

Heat and desire more intense than any he could remember gripped him. His cock ached for her, but he felt an even deeper need. It was more than just a physical completion that he was craving. He needed to know that she would think about this for a very long time to come.

Considering that he often forgot a woman's name within a week or so of spending the night with her, that was a particularly strange urge. He intentionally didn't remember names. It was subconscious now. A habit. But at one point, it had been very purposeful.

It was an asshole move to not know a woman's name when you took her to bed, but if you had no intention of an ongoing relationship of any kind, there was no reason to remember her name in the long-term. He often remembered the names of people he disliked more easily than he did the ones he liked, and he was sure a psychologist could have a heyday with that, but the fact remained that he didn't let people's names, or any details about them, sink in too deep. It was easier to not feel attached to someone whose name he didn't remember.

But in this case, with this woman, he wanted to sink deep and not just in the as-deep-inside-her-as-he-could-get-for-as-long-as-he-could way.

With his gaze locked on hers, Griffin reached behind her and grasped the tiny tab of her zipper. He pulled it the rest of the way down. She shifted away from the wall but kept her hands behind her back. A streak of satisfaction went through him. This woman was absolutely not the submissive type, but he loved that she was willing to let him call the shots here. Whether she just needed a chance to let loose and have someone else make some of the decisions, or whether she read in him the natural instinct to be in charge didn't matter. He was going to make this very good for both of them.

He tugged on the skirt of the dress, and it fell to a silky pink puddle around her heels. She wore a matching pink thong. And nothing else.

"Wow, I guess I was wrong," he said, his gaze raking over her.

"About which thing exactly?"

Her tone indicated that he'd been wrong about several things.

"Turns out there's actually nothing terrible underneath that eight-hundred-dollar dress."

4

Griffin gave her a smirk as he met her eyes again. "You are definitely overpaying for clothes, Charlotte. This body could make anything look good."

"Oh, don't get all complimentary now," she said. "I might start thinking that I've gotten past your grumpy façade."

The fact that the woman could stand with her hands behind her back, half-naked—hell, a lot more than *half*-naked—in a barn and still tease him and think she had the upper hand was admirable. Because frankly, she did have the upper hand. At that moment, Griffin realized that this woman could get him to do almost anything. It was really going to be in his best interest to keep that information from her.

"Façade?" he asked, taking a step forward. He put his hands on her waist and lifted her up out of the pool of pink silk on the floor. He set her next to it and backed her against the wall again. "You think I'm faking it?"

She tipped her head, studying him as if truly considering his question. "No, actually," she said after a moment, "I think the grumpiness is real. But I gotta say, it just makes me want to dig in and find out what that's about."

"Too bad you're leaving soon," he said, not at all sorry she would be leaving before she could poke around in his psyche. Because he had no doubt, she meant that. "And you are going to be very busy in the time we're spending together until then."

She opened her mouth, clearly to reply, but Griffin ran his hand down her back to her ass and then slipped his middle finger under the strap of the thong where it crossed her hip. He ran the digit back and forth between her skin and the garment.

Charlotte caught her breath. And stopped talking.

With what he was sure was a smug grin, he leaned in and said against her ear, "Do you know what some people think is an appropriate synonym for grumpy?"

She shook her head. Probably because Griffin's finger had moved to the front of her thong and was now brushing over her mound.

"Grumpy and bossy are often similar characteristics. And while you might spend more time with bubbly optimists than grumps, you don't seem to mind being bossed a little."

He moved his finger lower, brushing over her clit.

She pulled her bottom lip between her teeth but said nothing.

"For instance, if I told you to spread your legs a little, you would."

She swallowed hard. And nodded.

"I really like the way you just dropped your dress on this barn floor for me, Charlotte," Griffin said roughly against her ear. "And I might be grumpy and bossy, but I'm happy to reward people who do things I like."

His finger brushed back and forth over her clit, and he could feel the wet heat that had already dampened her thong. He dragged his mouth up and down the side of her neck. Her head tilted away, giving him better access to the sweet skin, and, much to his pleasure, her hands stayed behind her back.

"I think it would be hot as hell if this thong was down

around your ankles while I made you come with my fingers right here in this dirty barn that you are way too good to even walk into."

She shivered, and suddenly, he wanted nothing more than to make this woman come hard, right here and now, without a thought to the animal sounds, smells, or even their presence. Not to mention the fact that she had family, and likely friends, in a building only about a block away. He loved the idea of making her mindless with pleasure. And he loved the realization that he'd gotten her even this far already.

"Are you going to let me press your bare ass against this barn wall and make you come, Charlotte?"

She took a shaky breath, then said, "If you don't, I might have to cut off your balls and feed them to Hermione."

Griffin laughed, caught by surprise. He had no doubt that she was hot and wanted everything he was teasing her with, and yet she was still able to make quips and remind him that she was *letting* him boss her around because she enjoyed it rather than because she was mindless.

She was very aware of their location and the proximity to the barnyard animals as well as the human beings nearby, and she was choosing to be here with him like this with her dress on the floor and her sweet body exposed to him.

It was a good reminder. He did like to be dominant in the bedroom, but this was even better than being with a woman who was simply overcome by his prowess. Charlotte Last-Name-Unknown was here with him right now because she absolutely wanted to be.

"So are you going to take my thong off, or do I need to?" she asked. "Because to do that, I'll have to move my hands. And honestly, this position with my hands behind my back is really hot."

In spite of her sassy words, her voice was breathless. Griffin definitely took note of that, and he, no doubt, let his smugness show on his face.

"Oh, I can help you with that," he said. "But now I'm going to need you to ask me nicely."

Charlotte's eyebrows shot up. "I have to *ask* you to take my thong off?"

He shrugged, then lifted a hand to one of her breasts, teasing the nipple. "Yes."

"Don't you *want* to take my thong off?"

"Oh, I definitely want to take your thong off. But I'd very much like to hear you ask me to."

He was, in fact, tight and hard from head to toe in anticipation of seeing this woman completely naked and feeling all the sweet, tight, wet heat between her thighs. But playing with her was so much fun. He couldn't remember the last time he'd enjoyed sex this much, and he needed to enjoy it as long as he could since he was going to lose her.

Whoa. Griffin was immediately shocked by the thoughts of "losing" her. She wasn't his to start with, and he certainly didn't want to keep her.

Not since he'd set a box of photos and letters on fire before leaving D.C. had he kept mementos of any kind. He didn't have pets. He didn't keep animals other than the ones he cared for as a veterinarian. He didn't even keep takeout menus. He definitely didn't keep *people*.

There was nothing to be lost here. What his subconscious had surely meant was that he wasn't going to have another chance to enjoy this body or this woman's wit and sass. And yes, as surprising as it was, he was enjoying those things as much as he was the sight of her naked.

"Well," she said. "We could turn this into a game of chicken and see who gives in first on this whole thong-stripping thing." She looked around. "A game of chicken would be appropriate for our current situation."

He leaned in, pinching her nipple and sliding his hand further into the thong he wanted to rip from her body. Right now. His middle finger teased her hot, slick opening, and she gasped.

"Take your thong off for me, Charlotte." He slipped his finger into the second knuckle and paused. "Now."

She swallowed hard. "May I move my hands?"

Desire hit him in the gut, and his appreciation for her grew. She was far beyond delightful. She was damn near perfect. "You asking me that is going to get you well rewarded," he promised.

"It better."

He was smiling, but she wouldn't be able to see it with his face against her neck. He nipped her lightly, then said, "Yes, you may move your hands."

Her thumbs hooked into the straps of the thong, and she pulled it down to mid-thigh, where she let it go. The thong dropped around her ankles and those cock-teasing heels.

Griffin unapologetically leaned back to take a look. Charlotte propped a hand on one hip and let him.

She was amazing.

"Damn," he said, meeting her eyes again. "Thank you for moving your hands."

"How about you start moving *your* hands again now?" She gripped the front of his shirt and pulled him in for a kiss.

His hands gladly glided over her body, from her breasts to her ass, and then one hand settled between her thighs, circling her clit.

"Spread your legs." His voice was low and gruff.

She did. His finger slid into her, and they both moaned. She was tight and so hot, and his body was screaming at him for more.

He pumped his finger deep twice, then added a second, loving her breathy moan. He covered her lips with his as he thrust faster, adding pressure to her clit with the pad of his thumb. He rubbed in a gentle circle as he stroked deep with two fingers, kissing her hungrily. He wanted to feel and hear her come apart.

But a moment later, she pushed him back.

"I do have one more question for you." She was practically panting.

He hadn't stopped moving his fingers. "Okay."

"Do you have a condom?"

Now, he froze.

Of course, he didn't have a condom. He was definitely not the guy who walked around with a condom in his wallet on the sheer chance that he might have a random hookup in the barn. He carefully planned everything as much as possible, especially interactions with other humans. And he never took intimate interactions, like sex, for granted.

"I'm going to take your obvious shock as a no," Charlotte said.

"No, I don't have a condom." He started to lean back, withdrawing his fingers, but she quickly grasped his forearm.

"Oh, where do you think you're going?"

He looked down at her. He was very aware of the fact that his fingers were in the most intimate place they could be. "I thought maybe we had just discovered a reason to stop."

"You don't need a condom for your fingers."

Well, she had a point. A very good point, considering how much he did not want to remove his fingers from where they were.

"Are you going to make me ask you nicely for this too?" she asked.

He should. He really should. Not only would that be hot, it would make him feel back in control again after realizing he'd gotten to this point without remembering that he didn't have protection.

True, he was usually prepared for the *worst*, and nothing about the situation with Charlotte was qualifying as "the worst" anything, but he was very rarely caught off guard.

It was just another example of how this woman had been a surprise from the minute they'd started talking.

He leaned in and kissed her. That was way better than talking anyway. He was past the teasing. This woman had been mixing him up from the moment she'd asked about his metaphorical carrot. It was time to finish their very enjoyable time together and say good night.

If he were a stronger man, he would take his hands off her body, wish her a good evening, and walk his ass out of this barn right now. But he wasn't a stronger man. At least not with this woman.

Actually, he could imagine himself doing exactly that with any other woman he'd met. But the idea of walking away from Charlotte right now was unfathomable.

And he was suddenly not sure that Paris was far enough away.

Griffin moved his fingers, stroking her deep, his thumb rubbing over her clit, kissing her deeply. She moaned into his mouth, gripped his forearm tighter, and arched closer to his hand.

He was, indeed, pressing her against the barn wall. One of her hands was already holding his arm as if afraid he was going to leave her. The other came out and circled the back of his neck, holding him into their kiss, her tongue stroking his as enthusiastically as he was her.

She lifted one foot, still clad in one of her crazy shoes, wrapped her leg around his, and tucked her heel at the back of his knee. It opened her even wider, and Griffin read her plea clearly. He curled his fingers, stroking over her G-spot, feeling the resultant ripple of her pussy.

Now she tore her mouth away from his as she gasped his name.

"Griffin!"

Both hands dug into his muscles where she held him and her head thumped back against the wall behind her.

"Yes! Oh, Griffin! Yes!"

"You know I am really going to think about adding delightful to my regular vocabulary," Griffin told her. "Because everything about this sweet pussy, from how tight it is, to how hot it is, to how wet it is"—he thrust again, curling his fingers against her G-spot—"is absolutely..." He rubbed over her clit with his thumb, and she gasped. "Fucking." He circled her clit more firmly and fingered her faster as she moaned. "Delightful."

"Griffin." She gripped his arm even tighter.

"Yes, *yes*, Charlotte, just let go."

"You're so good at this."

"You are the best thing to happen to me in this town in the six months I've been here."

She cried out his name. He felt her clamp down around his fingers as she came apart.

He didn't know why that was what had sent her over the edge, but he was damn grateful to have felt and heard it. That was going to fuel some pretty hot nights to come.

Charlotte took a deep, shuddering breath and pulled him in for a kiss.

Griffin slipped his fingers from her pussy and gripped her ass against his hard cock. He swept her mouth with his tongue and relished the feel of her pressing against him as if he hadn't just gotten her off.

This woman could have any man she wanted. He was certain of that. And it was more than just her delicious curves and her long silky hair and big blue eyes. It was the way she carried herself, her attitude, her wit, and her humor. This was not the type of woman who got so much as felt up in a barn, not to mention stripped bare and made to orgasm. There was no doubt in his mind that she was treated to ritzy restaurants and had seen more than her share of flower bouquets and expensive bottles of wine. She didn't have to be here with him, but she was, and she seemed as into it as he was.

Finally, he let her up for air. Without condoms, their options were somewhat limited. But he didn't want to let her go yet.

Which was, of course, exactly why he should let her go.

"Well, I have to say, Griffin, you have some pretty delightful moments yourself. "

Then much to his surprise, she reached for his fly. "What are you doing?"

"How charming would I really be if I got mine but didn't give you anything in return?"

Her meaning was clear, as was the way she was unbuckling his belt and undoing his button and zipper of his jeans, but the smile said it all. It was a combination of playful and sexy that Griffin was sure could bring any man to his knees. But it also seemed clear that Charlotte did not think *he* was the one who was going to be going on his knees in the next few minutes.

She slid her hand into his jeans, stroking him through his boxers. Even with a layer of cotton between them, he had to lock his knees and brace his hand on the wall beside her head as pleasure streaked through him.

"Jesus, Charlotte."

"And just so I don't forget to tell you," she said, slipping her hand inside of his boxers and stroking with a flat palm, up and down his length, skin to skin. "You're the most fun I've had in this town in six months too."

He gave a short bark of laughter. "You haven't been here the past six months. Trust me, I would've noticed."

She grinned. "Then let's say the past couple of years."

"You're here regularly?"

"Definitely. Not as much in the past three or four years, but regularly, yes. I'd say I've had some of the best times of my life here. And tonight is definitely in the top three."

He was going to ask her about the other two. He really was. She simply made him curious. Which was a very good reason to be grateful that she wrapped her hand around his cock and stroked with a firm grip, and all thoughts left his head except: More. Of. That.

"Charlotte," he managed to get out between clenched teeth.

"Yeah, see, you're definitely thinking I'm charming right now."

"Charming's not the word that first comes to mind."

Hot. Amazing. Perfect. Special. Addictive. Dangerous. Those were all a lot more accurate.

"Is the first word 'ew,' 'gross,' or 'stop'?" she asked, still stroking him.

He swallowed hard, trying very hard not to just thrust into her fist and let himself explode. "No," he said roughly. "Not even close."

"Then I'll take it. Whatever it is."

Yeah, he had a feeling she'd like all of those words. Especially dangerous.

She started to dip her knees, her intent very clear, but Griffin caught her under one elbow. "Hang on."

"Oh, please don't try to be a gentleman and tell me I don't have to do this," she said. "I really want to. Besides," she looked around, "No need to be a gentleman now. I smell like goats, and I think my favorite pair of heels has some not-exactly-mud on them, and I'm going to have to throw them away after tonight."

Yet she was still here. He knew that meant something. He didn't know what exactly. He didn't know her well enough to know what that meant. He also didn't want to know. That was the way to get involved and for things to get complicated.

"Just give me a second," he said.

His hands went to the buttons on the front of his shirt, and her smile grew as she watched him unfasten them.

"I like where this is going so far."

He shrugged out of the shirt, then with a half smile laid it out over the hay on the floor at his feet.

She laughed, then nodded. "Thank you very much, Griffin."

"I wouldn't go so far as to say I'm a gentleman," he said. "But I don't want you getting any not-exactly-mud on those pretty knees."

She dropped to those knees without another word, and her hands opened his pants and pulled the denim and boxers out of her way. She took his cock in hand again, stroking firmly and confidently, before leaning in and licking his head.

She went from playful teasing to holy-shit-yes in just a few seconds. Griffin had to grit his teeth, and he slapped his hand against the barn wall as he braced himself again. If he fell over and cracked his head open and died right here on the floor, Sugar was going to be heartbroken. But it would be worth it. Charlotte had already proven that her mouth was one of his favorite things—the comebacks, the wit, the smiles. But when this woman applied her lips and tongue to his cock, Griffin definitely found heaven.

She sucked on his head, taking him about halfway into her mouth. She licked and stroked and sucked and licked again. He felt the pressure building. He'd already been on edge, and if he was being honest, it had started when she'd first approached him to dance. It had only gotten stronger since then. Now with her on her knees, happily giving him a blowjob, he felt his climax building quickly.

"Charlotte, baby." His hand went to her head, stroking over her silky hair and tangling in the thick mass.

She sucked harder and stroked him faster, taking him

further into her mouth. He let her work him over. He had no problem letting her take control here.

"I'm not gonna last long like this," he warned her.

"Good. I would feel bad if this took too long."

She flattened her tongue against the front of his cock and dragged it up to the tip slowly. Her eyes were on him as she took his head into her mouth, sucked hard, then took him deep. His fingers curled into her hair, and he groaned, feeling the pleasure coming from deep in his bones.

He wasn't above giving praise where praise was due. "Charlotte, I love your mouth."

She couldn't respond verbally, considering her mouth was full, but she squeezed the base of his cock and sucked harder as if thanking him for the compliment.

As she licked, sucked, and stroked, the hot knot coiling in his gut intensified, the pleasure pressing and building until it was an incessant, pounding, uncontrollable *need,* and he cupped the back of her head.

"Pull back or take me fully. I'm there, honey," he gritted out.

She squeezed his cock tighter and flattened her other palm on his ass, pressing him into her. She took him deeper, urging him on, and Griffin couldn't hold back any longer.

He came, her name a guttural groan filling the barn, his fingers gripping her hair.

She didn't pull back. She didn't even flinch. She stroked him with her hand and mouth as he worked on staying upright, the waves of pleasure shuddering through him.

When he finally shifted back, she let him go, looking up at him with a small smile. He sucked in a deep breath and held out a hand to help her to her feet. Gallant for sure. She took it and let him pull her up. He cupped her face, kissing her deeply. Her fingers dug into his back, kissing him with the same force.

They pulled back at the same time and just looked at each other for several long seconds.

"Thank you for the use of your shirt," she finally said.

Griffin laughed. A full, out-loud-from-his-gut laugh.

"It's my favorite, so it's *especially* nice that I let you... borrow it."

She grinned, clearly pleased with making him laugh, then swept her dress up from the floor.

"I'm a little new to the chivalrous thing," Griffin said as he pulled his boxers and jeans back into place. "But is now the time to offer to dry clean your dress?"

She stepped into the dress, shimmying it up her body and reaching behind her for the zipper. Now it was Charlotte's turn to laugh. "I actually don't know the etiquette following oral sex in a barn. But I suppose the offer is polite no matter what."

"Charlotte, I would very much like to pay for the dry cleaning of your dress."

Said dress back in place, though severely wrinkled and definitely smudged with dirt and what he hoped was only dirt, she propped a hand on her hip. "Well, thank you very much, Griffin, but it might be difficult with the dress in Paris in a couple of days."

"You don't think they have dry cleaners in France?"

"You'll have to transfer me the money. Is this your way of trying to find out more about me?"

He realized that was exactly how that sounded. He also realized it was a really good way to find out more about her. He also realized that he wanted to know more about her, that he knew less about her than he did about any other woman who had her mouth on his cock—ever—and that he really didn't know what to do at this moment.

"I suppose just handing you a few twenties would be crass?"

She laughed again. "Oh no, it wouldn't make me feel like a prostitute at all to have just gotten up from the ground after giving you a blowjob and having you hand me cash."

He couldn't help smiling, but he nodded. "Right. I suppose

that would probably erase the gentlemanly act of putting my shirt down on the floor for you to give me that blowjob in the first place."

She laughed, bent, and grabbed his shirt from the floor. She shook it out, then shrugged into it. She stepped forward, lifted onto her tiptoes, pressed her lips against his, then said, "I think I can take care of the dress. But I'm keeping the shirt. Maybe I'll even press these pieces of straw in my scrapbook as a memento of our evening together." She plucked a piece from her skirt and held it up.

He shook his head as she stepped to the stall door and pulled it open. Her sass had no limits. And now he was going home shirtless. "Think of me fondly whenever you smell goats."

She grinned. "Of course." Then she blew him a kiss, stepped out of the stall, and headed for the barn door. A moment later, she was gone.

Griffin blew out a breath. He shoved a hand through his hair and looked around. He wondered if he'd ever be able to come in here again without thinking of her.

He knew instantly the answer to that was no way.

He looked toward the door again and realized he'd gotten very lucky not having a condom.

Being condom-less had prevented barn-shaking sex with the most intriguing, gorgeous woman he'd ever met. It had kept him from having, even more, to miss about the first woman to make him actually think words like "delightful." He'd even said it out loud.

Yep, being condom-less had helped him avoid getting attached.

But just barely.

5

Two months later...

Griffin approached the side door of the veterinary clinic with a sense of resignation.

Maddie Landry's truck was already parked out front. She was supposed to bring his new assistant over to meet him this morning. The kid was going to be in Autre for the summer and was apparently a friend of the Landrys, or the son of a friend of the Landrys. Or something.

All Griffin knew was that he needed two more hands and someone who could answer the phone now that Tori, his boss and friend, was further along in her pregnancy and spending less time in the clinic. This kid was willing, and the Landrys wanted him to hire the kid. That was really all it took for him to say yes.

As much as he'd tried to stay unattached while in Autre, the Landry family made it impossible. If he were completely honest, he would admit that he had been welcomed into the family from minute one and had been fond of them all by minute five. The Landrys were a loud, rowdy, fun-loving family that had never met anyone who stayed a stranger longer than about ten minutes. Even if that stranger really wanted to stay a stranger.

So all it had taken was Ellie, the matriarch of the family and Tori's grandmother-in-law, to ask him—okay, she'd told him—to hire this Charlie kid. If the Landrys wanted this guy working at the clinic over the summer, then Griffin wasn't going to say no. It was his partner's family for one thing, and for another, Ellie had long ago won him over with her homemade pralines, her very generous pours of beer, and her blunt but affectionate advice.

Ellie thought Griffin needed to start living life. When he asked her why she thought he wasn't living life, she'd given him a look that said she was completely insulted by the stupid question and had moved down the bar to wait on someone else. When he'd asked her how she knew that he wasn't living life, she responded, "I've lived in this town for seventy-five years, have seen everyone in this town and hundreds of tourists in and out of this bar's doors, raised five children and have eleven grandchildren—seven of whom are boys—so I've seen a lot of stupid in my life."

When he'd asked if she was essentially calling him stupid, she grinned, winked, and said, "Anyone not living every day to the fullest is stupid. You take that however you want."

Griffin hadn't exactly put that advice into practice yet, but he heard the message, and he thought about it often. And now Ellie had asked him to hire some kid as his assistant for the summer, and he was absolutely unable to say anything but "sure."

He didn't need help with the veterinary work specifically. However, he did need someone who could look after the animals being kept at the clinic after surgical procedures, answer phones, do basic filing and scheduling, and be a second pair of hands. Like when he needed someone to hold down a cat, grab him another syringe, or help him chase baby rabbits that got loose in the lobby. And no, that was not just a theoretical scenario. He really could have used a second pair of hands on Tuesday when there were baby rabbits scattering in all directions.

He let himself in through the side door that led into the storage room. He heard Maddie's voice coming from the front of the clinic but was surprised to hear another female voice answer her. He stopped in the room to hang his cap on the hook by the door and toss his duffel bag onto a chair.

"So, what did you carve into the side of his Porsche?" Maddie asked. "Because I know you didn't just scratch a line in it with your key."

Griffin felt his eyebrows rise. This woman had vandalized a *Porsche*?

There was a husky feminine laugh. "Of course not," the other woman answered. "I wrote *I have a tiny dick.*"

Maddie laughed out loud, and Griffin stepped into the front of the clinic. Did he know the woman Maddie was talking to? Because if so, he was going to stay far away from her. A woman who carved insults into the side of a man's Porsche? That was someone he didn't want to tangle with. Of course, he'd like to think he wouldn't do anything that would warrant that kind of response, but he wasn't the most gallant at times.

He smiled to himself as he thought about the last time he'd even attempted to be a gentleman. It had been to spread his shirt out on a dirty barn floor for a stunning blonde to give him a blowjob. In spite of the fact that he was sure that wouldn't get him very many points with the chivalry police, he still liked the memory. A lot. And not just the blowjob. Though, that had been one of the best of his life. It was absolutely the woman involved.

The women were leaning against the front desk. Maddie was facing his direction, and her friend was facing away. They were both trim blondes, wearing t-shirts and denim shorts. Maddie was a couple of inches shorter, and her skin was sun-kissed from working on the swamp boats with her husband, Owen, and their other partners.

The other woman's skin was paler, and she had her long hair gathered up into a ponytail and pulled through the back of the white cap she wore. And as always happened, he thought of Charlotte. For the past two months, anytime he saw long blond hair and creamy skin and gorgeous curves, he immediately thought of the woman in the eight-hundred-dollar cocktail dress outside Ellie's bar.

This woman's baby blue t-shirt, cutoff denim jeans, and white canvas tennis shoes were absolutely nothing like Charlotte's outfit. The only thing they had in common was the hair color. Still, Griffin found himself thinking about the woman who had made him laugh, flirt, and actually use the word "delightful" more than once.

It wasn't that he never laughed or hadn't laughed in the past two months, but he definitely hadn't flirted, and the word delightful had *definitely* not crossed his lips.

Of course, he hung out with Landrys most of the time, and there were lots of words to describe them, individually and collectively, but *delightful* was probably not even in the top ten.

"Well, did he deserve it?" Maddie said of the way the woman had defaced the Porsche.

"Absolutely. And he had to drive that around for two days before he could get it repainted," the woman told her.

"Was it worth getting fired over?" Maddie asked.

"Oh, I'm super pissed that I got fired for that. But I'm more pissed that *he* didn't get fired."

Maddie shrugged. "He is the boss's son."

Holy hell, she'd done that to her boss's son's car?

The woman blew out a breath. "Yeah. And now *I* have to pay to get the stupid thing repainted."

"How much is that going to run you?"

"He gave me a quote for ten grand."

Maddie's eyebrows shot up, but Griffin wasn't surprised. A guy who owned a Porsche would want a very well-done paint job. And to repair something like a deeply gouged I HAVE A TINY DICK message in the door, they'd have to strip the paint, buff the whole thing smooth, and then paint over it.

If the guy truly was an asshole, as they were implying, he might even have a custom color that would be hard to match and that he might insist they get from the same place he had the car painted originally. He might even insist on them repainting the entire thing, so the paint job looked good.

"Well, ten grand isn't so bad. You had your big fancy job in Paris for a couple of months at least, right?" Maddie asked.

Griffin felt his spine stiffen, and he froze in the middle of the space behind the front desk.

Paris? He knew another blonde with amazing curves who'd had a great job in Paris. And now that he thought about it, that woman would've definitely keyed a man's Porsche if he pissed her off. He wasn't sure how he knew that, but for some reason, it fit.

"Yeah, but... Paris isn't cheap. And I had *a lot* of cappuccino. And I might have gone a little crazy on the credit cards with shopping."

Both women laughed.

Griffin felt his gut tighten.

This was Charlotte. It had to be. Charlotte was here. Back. In Autre.

Maddie nodded. "I can understand that. When I first moved to California, I needed a whole new wardrobe and everything. Or at least I thought I did."

"Needless to say, I don't have ten grand to pay the jackass off, so..." the blonde shrugged. "Here I am."

Yep. Here she was. Not just back in the states, but in Louisiana. In Autre. In *his clinic*. Why was she here in the clinic? Griffin couldn't have described how he was feeling exactly, but it felt a little like excitement and a lot like panic. He wasn't sure why, but Charlotte being back here, sounding as if she was here to stay, at least for a period of time, made him... worry.

Yes. He was worried.

And he wanted to throw her over his shoulder and head into the nearest room with a lock on the door.

He cleared his throat. "Hey, Maddie."

Both women straightened away from the counter and turned toward him.

His eyes were firmly on Charlotte.

Her blue eyes widened. Her mouth dropped open. Then her lips spread into a huge grin.

Not that he would've expected her not to recognize him. It'd only been two months. And they'd spent quite enough time in very close proximity.

"Griffin!"

She looked thrilled to see him. He wasn't sure why he was surprised by that.

Actually, he *wasn't* surprised by that. He was just still reeling from the fact that she was here.

Charlotte, the woman he had been unable to get out of his head for the past two months, the woman who he'd become obsessed within the space of about an hour, the woman who was supposed to be across an ocean from him at the moment, was now standing in front of him.

She looked amazing.

That cocktail dress from two months ago had absolutely not at all been a part of her beauty.

"Charlotte," he greeted. "What are you doing here?"

"I'm... back."

"You know each other?" Maddie asked.

Charlotte glanced at her. "Yeah, we met at the weddings in April."

Griffin nodded. "Yeah. We... talked at the weddings."

Charlotte's eyes met his, clearly surprised. Had he paused in front of *talked* on purpose? Yes, he had.

He needed to be careful here. Maddie was smart. It wasn't as if she wasn't going to notice him making weird pauses in front of normal words or that he was acting tense around Charlotte, who was clearly a friend of hers.

"Can I talk to you for a second?" Charlotte asked, stepping around the front desk and coming for him.

She grabbed his arm and started tugging him into the hallway behind the desk before he even answered.

Of course, she did.

He followed, aware that her touch on his arm was completely distracting and stupidly pleasant. No, it was much more than pleasant. He felt like he had been waiting for that touch for two months, and the feel of her skin on his again was like taking a huge lungful of fresh air after holding his breath for too long.

Stupid. Sending this woman off to Paris with nothing more than what they'd done in the barn had been the right move. In fact, they had done too much in the barn. In fact, they'd *talked* too much. They'd spent too much time together. He'd had too much of a taste of her, knew too many of her sounds, knew her smell too well. He was addicted to her, and he'd only spent an hour with her two months ago.

She paused for a moment, looked up and down the hall, clearly trying to figure out where they should go. Then she pulled him into the storage room. She pushed the door shut and turned to face him, still holding his arm.

"I'm so happy to see you," she said. "I'd hoped we'd run into each other, though I didn't expect it to be quite so soon."

So, she clearly hadn't come here looking for him. She didn't know he was the vet. How would she know that? She wouldn't unless she'd asked someone about him after they'd met at the wedding. And apparently, she hadn't asked anyone about him.

That annoyed him.

Which was as stupid as liking her hand on his arm. He hadn't asked anyone about her either.

"I'm shocked to see you," he told her, honestly. No one had mentioned Charlotte was going to be back in town. Though, why would they have mentioned that to him? No one had any idea they'd even met, not to mention that he was stupidly infatuated with her.

"Yeah, this whole... situation... kind of happened fast." She pulled her bottom lip between her teeth.

"Situation?" he asked. He'd overheard that she'd been fired. But was there more? "Are you okay?"

She let go of her lip to smile up at him with a sweet look. That almost made it seem as if she was a little infatuated too.

"I am. I mean, I'm going to be poor for a while, and I don't get to look at the Eiffel Tower every morning while I have coffee, but I'll be okay."

"Good." He meant that. Fuck. How? What did he mean that he really wanted her to be okay? That the idea that she wasn't had given him a moment of *I'll make it okay*. He was not that guy.

He wasn't that guy *anymore*. He wasn't a hero. He didn't swoop in and save things anymore.

She stepped closer. "I got in last night. Kind of late. I thought about going to look for you in the barn but then figured maybe it was a little past your typical goat herding hours."

That damn goat barn. He'd been right when he thought he

wouldn't be able to step inside that building without thinking about her.

"So what are you doing here? What happened to Paris?" There was a boss's son and a Porsche, but he'd love to know the whole story.

Dammit.

He didn't want people's stories. He didn't want to be involved. He wanted to keep things simple in his life, and the best way to do that, he knew from experience, was to just keep to himself.

"Oh, that... yeah, that didn't work out."

"You got fired. For keying the door of the boss's son's Porsche."

She sighed. "You heard all that?"

He nodded. "I did. What happened? He wouldn't dance with you?"

She looked surprised for a second, then she gave him a playful grin. "Oh, you know what happens when guys say no to dancing with me."

He wasn't sure if it was still the surprise of seeing her or that he'd built their time together up in his mind or what, but possessiveness slammed into him.

Which was stupid.

She'd danced with other men.

She'd done more than that with other men, he was sure.

He was the one who didn't have random hookups. He was the one who didn't carry condoms around just in case. He was the one who carefully weighed all of his human interactions and basically assumed the worst out of most of them.

He hadn't expected the worst out of the interaction with her, but he should have. Not only was he clearly a bit obsessed, but it turned out he was the only one feeling that way.

"Yes, I do." He started to step back from her.

But she grabbed the front of his shirt, keeping him close.

She peered up at him, her expression serious now. "Griffin, I was teasing you. Everything about that night was a very unique... situation."

He wrapped his fingers around her wrist and reached for the clinic's side door with his other hand. He tugged her out of the building, letting the door slam behind them. He wouldn't put it past Maddie to have her ear pressed to the storage room door. And for her to have already texted the rest of the Landrys with, *Charlotte and Griffin are shut in the storeroom together. On purpose.*

Once they were several steps away from the building, Griffin dropped his hold on her. The vet clinic was set on the edge of town, away from any other houses or businesses. It was actually behind Tori and Josh's house and was just another building on their farm, though it had its own drive and small parking area. There were stables and pens and pastures behind it because, well, Tori had never met an animal she didn't like, and if any four-legged creatures needed a home, they found one with her.

Griffin tucked his hands in his back pockets. "When you say it was a unique situation, you're referring to the barn?"

Charlotte frowned slightly, and he realized that he much preferred her smiling. It was a stupid, irrelevant realization, perhaps. But Charlotte was absolutely the type of woman who needed to be smiling.

"No, not the barn. Well, not just the barn. I've definitely never done any of that in a barn before. But everything about that night was unusual. I actually don't usually care if a guy doesn't want to spend time with me. I figure it's his loss if not."

"I'm guessing you very rarely run across men who don't want to spend time with you."

She lifted a shoulder, not denying it. "There was something about you that made it particularly... bothersome. I couldn't leave you alone. That never happens." She stepped closer. "I don't regret anything from that night. I was very excited to see you again when I got back. I've been thinking about you ever since."

"And you're back for how long?"

Griffin was a very smart man. He knew his feelings for this woman were unusual and possibly dangerous. But he'd been feeling them for two months. They weren't going anywhere.

Now she was here. She was telling him that she felt something between them too. He was not going to be able to ignore that. So, as he had in other circumstances in his life, he recognized that if he was going to fuck up, he was going to fuck up in a big way.

"Well," she said. "I'm not exactly sure how long I'll be here, but for a little bit."

"For a few days?" he asked.

"For sure."

"That's really excellent news. Especially considering I just rented a house and moved in and no longer have a roommate."

She smiled and stepped closer, running her hand up the front of his shirt. She smelled amazing. It wasn't quite the same expensive perfume scent from two months ago—and the fact that he remembered that so well should have been concerning to him—but she smelled like he wanted to bury his nose in her neck and breathe deep for at least an hour.

"So what are you saying?" she asked softly.

"Maybe we should pick up where we left off."

"Charlie!"

They were interrupted by the shout from Tori.

"Dr. Foster!" a man's voice called right after Tori's.

Charlotte and Griffin both pivoted to face the people approaching the clinic. Then Griffin frowned as he realized Tori was headed straight for them.

As was the man carrying a puppy with a little boy right behind him.

That was Michael LeClaire and his son, Andre. The puppy was Brownie, and he was new to the family. But he had a growth on his back leg that Griffin needed to operate on.

He and Charlotte turned back to one another.

"Dr. Foster?" she asked.

Griffin nodded. "Griffin Foster. Veterinarian."

"Oh... Shit."

He frowned. Then the realization hit him as well. "Charlie? Is she talking to you?"

"Yeah. This side of the family calls me Charlie."

Charlie. That was the name of the kid who was going to be his assistant for the summer.

Except... clearly it wasn't.

Then more of what she said sunk in.

"Did you say this side of the *family*?"

She nodded. "My dad's side. My mom's side in Shreveport calls me Charlotte."

Griffin stepped back, and Charlie's hand dropped away from his shirt. She was watching him with a confused look.

He took a breath. "Charlotte, I have a question for you."

Her expression said she already knew what he was about to ask. She nodded. "Okay."

"What is your last name?"

"Landry."

Griffin felt his whole body go cold. This was not at all how he had planned his day to go.

Not only was he obsessed with a woman for the first time in forever, but she was a *Landry*, the family who had gotten under his skin and made him feel attached in spite of every effort *not* to.

Charlie sighed, reading his expression. "I'm guessing that picking up where we left off is off the table."

"Yes, considering I'm your new boss."

6

D ammit.
      He was her new boss.

She had *really* not seen that coming.

Charlie's thoughts were interrupted as Tori joined them.

"Hi! I see you guys have met. Sorry, I'm running a little late," Tori said.

She was smiling at them brightly. Her long brown hair fell softly around her shoulders, and her cheeks were pink from rushing in the heat. Or maybe it was just a natural glow. She was also clearly pregnant. She was over halfway to her September due date. She looked amazing.

"Hi!" Charlie said, enfolding Tori in a hug.

Charlie loved her cousin Josh. He'd always teased her, just like the others, but he was a good guy, and she was so happy that *he* was so happy. She'd visited Autre a few times since Tori had moved to Louisiana from Iowa, and she really liked the other woman. She and Josh were absolutely adorable together, and everyone in the family was already head-over-heels for their baby.

"Has Griffin given you the tour?" Tori asked after they embraced.

Charlie glanced at the man she'd been surprisingly excited to see. She'd been thinking about him for two months. She'd been wearing his shirt around her apartment for two months. She'd had to wash it because of the goat smell, which had been too bad because it had washed a lot of his smell off too. Still, she liked wearing it and thinking of him.

Seeing him again had been one of the bright spots in her decision to come to Autre after her Paris plans fell apart. As was *not* living in Shreveport with her parents. Who had been telling her that she needed to learn to take a deep breath and not always react on pure emotion ever since she was six and threw orange Jell-O at Molly Hartman because Molly was being mean to the new kid in their class.

Curtis and Renee Landry were very disappointed in the Porsche incident and didn't really care to know *why* she'd done it. She'd said she wasn't sorry and refused to even attempt to apologize to her boss—or the woman's asshole son—and the, "Well, Charlotte, this is the real world, and you can't always just do whatever you want," from her dad had been the catalyst for her calling her grandmother and asking if she could crash in Autre until she got a new job.

She hated disappointing her dad. She admired him, and his entrepreneurship was the reason she wanted to help businesses grow. But while she'd inherited his drive and outgoing personality, she did not possess his calm, just roll-with-it attitude.

Of course, Ellie had said yes and had texted Charlie's dad to tell him to pull the stick out of his ass. See, Ellie hadn't even needed to know why Charlie had done what she'd done to Alan's Porsche. She'd just trusted that Charlie had a good reason.

It was funny to Charlie that her father had always been

considered a bit of the black sheep of the family *because* he was level-headed and sophisticated and polished.

That was why Autre had always felt like such a different world. She'd loved her summers here where, as long as you weren't hurting anyone else, anything went. You could stay out until sunrise, go barefoot all day, skinny-dip in the bayou—or jump in with all your clothes on—eat sweets for breakfast, and any and all other decadent things. She'd gotten drunk for the first time, had her first kiss, had sex for the first time, said the words "Fuck you" for the first time, and had gotten her first and only tattoo during her summers in Autre. The bayou had always been wild in her experience, and she loved it. She could say and do and be whatever she wanted when she was here.

She needed some of that right now.

Her job in marketing was fun and fulfilling. Mostly. But she'd been spending a lot of time over the past couple of years with people who wore suits every day and drank Super Food smoothies for breakfast, and hadn't gone barefoot probably since they were kids, and had very likely never skinny-dipped.

And it showed.

She needed a break. And the bayou was the perfect place for it.

"Griffin has... shown me some things," she finally answered Tori.

His gaze snapped to hers, and she couldn't help but smile at how startled he looked.

"But he didn't know I was going to be here today, so he hasn't had a chance to go over many details," she said, looking back to Tori.

"He knew you were going to be here." Tori looked at Griffin. "We told you about hiring Charlie as the new assistant."

He nodded. "No one mentioned who she was, exactly. I didn't expect Charlie to be the woman I didn't want to dance with at your wedding."

Charlie snorted, his comment catching her off guard. She wasn't sure if he'd meant to be funny just then, but he was. She grinned at him. "Hard to get rid of me."

He just lifted a brow. "Startlingly."

She laughed. She couldn't help it. She looked back to Tori. Her cousin-in-law seemed concerned.

"Is there a problem?" Tori asked.

Yeah, there might be a problem. Charlie *really* wanted to pick up where they'd left off, and Griffin now seemed set against that. Except that he *did* want to. Which made Charlie want to convince him it was a *very* good idea.

"No. Of course not," Griffin told Tori, even giving her a little smile. "If you want to hire Charlotte, then that's fine."

Tori frowned. "But we're partners now. I can't hire someone you don't want to work with. Especially because I'll be here less, and it will just be the two of you a lot of the time."

Charlie just crossed her arms and tipped her head, waiting for Griffin to respond to that. She was fine with it just being the two of them.

He, on the other hand, straightened his spine and cleared his throat. "It's not that I don't want to work with her. It will be fine."

"But you said no to dancing with her at the wedding?" Tori asked. "Why?"

Griffin was stoically *not* looking at Charlie now. She also found that amusing.

"I don't dance," Griffin finally said. "It wasn't anything to do with her personally."

"Oh." Tori didn't seem totally convinced.

"It's fine." Charlie reached out to pat Tori's arm. "Give me a couple of days, and he'll be *so* glad I'm here that he won't even believe he was once able to tell me no." She cast him a sly glance.

He still did not meet her eyes. Because he knew very well that he hadn't said no to her for long.

This was going to be fun.

"Dr. Foster! Brownie needs you!"

The little boy's voice cut into their conversation, and they all turned to look at him.

"Andre," his dad admonished. "You don't interrupt adults talking."

"You do when your dog needs help," Griffin said, stepping past Tori and crouching in front of the little boy. "You do whatever you have to do to take care of the animals that need you."

Charlie felt a little flip in her stomach as Griffin reached out and touched the boy's upper arm.

"We do need to get Brownie inside," Griffin agreed. "I'm sorry we were talking about silly things when you needed me."

Charlie figured that he'd intended the term "silly things" for her as an attempt to seem nonchalant about their conversation, but she knew better. Griffin Foster had been happy to see her. She'd seen it on his face. She might describe the situation between her and Griffin in a number of ways, but silly wasn't one of them.

But she also felt warmer watching Griffin with the little boy. He was fully focused on Andre now and seemed genuine when he said that the dog was more important than their conversation.

He was probably right.

Andre's eyes flickered to her.

"Hi, Andre."

"Hi, Charlie."

Griffin looked at her with an eyebrow up.

She shrugged. Yes, she knew his patient's family.

Charlie glanced at the boy's father. "Hey, Michael."

"Hey, Charlie." The big man gave her a grin. "How are ya?"

He was as good-looking now as he'd been in high school.

He had medium brown skin and dark brown eyes, a quick smile, and a deep laugh. She'd definitely had great taste in crushes back then.

"Good." She glanced at Griffin. Speaking of crushes, she had been *really* good a minute ago. Now she was feeling definite regret about not picking back up where she and Griffin had left off. "How's Naomi?" she asked Michael.

Charlie had hung out with his younger sister during her teenage summers here. She'd also flirted with Michael a lot. And had danced with *him*. At least three or four times.

"Naomi's good. Does she know you're back?"

"Well, my grandma probably told yours," Charlie said with a smile. "But I need to give Naomi a call. Can't wait to catch up."

"She'll love that."

Naomi had been an actress as a kid and spent most of her time in California, but she'd retired by the time she was fourteen and was just another Autre girl when Charlie had gotten to know her. Not that Charlie hadn't been a little star-struck at first. Or very star-struck. She'd watched every episode of Naomi's show. But the actress was very down-to-earth and had put her stardom behind her when she'd moved back to Louisiana.

Charlie had quickly gotten to know her just as Naomi, the girl with the amazing sense of humor and a family that reminded Charlie a lot of the Landrys. In good ways.

The LeClaires were loving and fun. And even better than getting to dance with a very hot and very sweet older boy, was being introduced to food like griot, the national dish of Haiti, by their mother. Monique was an amazing cook, and Charlie had never tasted better sos pwa nwa anywhere else better than when she'd tried it in Monique's kitchen.

"How has Brownie been feeling?" Charlie heard Griffin ask Andre.

She turned to watch the man and the boy.

"He seems okay," Andre told him seriously. "But he doesn't want to run around as much as he used to."

"Well, let's get inside and fix that," Griffin said.

There was something about his reassuring tone of voice and the way he met the little boy's eyes as if acknowledging that, while Andre was only eight years old, he was clearly the primary caregiver to this puppy and had the most reason to be concerned.

"Okay. I really want him to feel good and be able to play with me again," Andre said.

Charlie felt a prickling behind her eyes. Andre was clearly worried about his puppy, and Griffin was treating him with respect and giving the situation the attention it deserved.

"It's going to be okay. I'll do everything I can, and I promise that Brownie will be back to playing with you really soon."

In that moment, Charlie realized that if Griffin Foster told her something was going to be okay and that he was going to do everything he could to make it right, she would believe that one hundred percent.

Griffin stretched to his feet and addressed Michael. "Do you want to come in with me, or should I take him in?"

Charlie straightened, her eyes widening. Griffin had just told Andre everything was going to be okay. But why couldn't the boy go inside with his dog? Was something bad going to happen?

She stepped forward. "Dr. Foster, what are we going to be doing with Brownie today?"

He looked at her, clearly surprised at her interruption. She also knew, however, that he had noted the word *we*. Well, she was his assistant, wasn't she?

"*We're* going to be doing a minor procedure on Brownie's leg," Griffin said, glancing at Andre. "But it's not a big deal. Brownie is going to be fine. He's going to stay overnight with us tonight just to be sure though."

Okay, a minor procedure. That seemed good. And Griffin wouldn't lie to Andre. They weren't going to do a puppy switch or something. She didn't think.

"He has a bump on his leg," Andre told her. "I'm the one who found it, and Dr. Foster said that it was really good I said something so that we can take care of it before it was a problem."

Charlie made her eyes go round, and she crouched down in front of Andre the way Griffin had. "Wow, you are a really good puppy owner. Brownie is really lucky to have you."

Andre nodded. "I know. Dr. Foster told me that too."

Charlie could see in Andre's face that he was proud of himself, but he couldn't stop glancing at the puppy in his dad's arms. Clearly, he was worried.

"I'll tell you what, if your dad will give me his phone number, I can text you little notes about how Brownie is doing today, and I can send you a picture of him later."

Andre's eyes widened. "You could do that?"

Charlie nodded. "The only thing that I need you to do in return is to draw and color me a picture of Brownie when you're at home today. That way, after he goes home with you again, I'll be able to remember him. Because I think that I'm going to really want to be friends with Brownie."

Andre nodded. "I can do that. I draw pictures of him all the time!"

Charlie smiled. "I bet you're a really good artist too."

"I am."

Charlie looked up at Michael. "If you give me your number, I promise not to drunk dial you or anything."

Michael grinned, clearly remembering the time she *had* drunk dialed him when she'd been eighteen, and she and Kennedy had wanted Michael and his brother Anthony to go fishing with them. At midnight.

"What's drunk dial?" Andre asked.

Charlie grimaced and looked at Griffin, who just cocked an eyebrow. She got to her feet but said to Andre, "It's when you accidentally call somebody really late at night and wake them up."

Andre giggled. "You should *not* do that to my dad. He's grumpy when he gets waked up."

"All right," Michael said, putting a hand on Andre's head. He smiled at Charlie. "I'll be happy to give you my number for texts."

"Great."

"Okay, let's get Brownie inside." Griffin held his arms out, and Michael shifted the puppy to Griffin.

Griffin ran a big hand over the dog's head as he cradled the dog against his stomach. He handled it with confidence and gentleness, and Charlie couldn't help but think of how he'd been reluctantly sweet with the goats and the rest of the menagerie that had been clustered around him on Tori's wedding night.

Turned on by a guy who was good with animals? Check.

Turned on by a guy who was reassuring to a scared little boy? Double-check.

She watched Griffin as he carried the puppy to the side door of the clinic. Andre and Michael followed, and it wasn't until Tori said her name that Charlie realized she'd done a full pivot to watch Griffin disappear back into the clinic.

She swung back to face Tori. "Yeah?"

"Are you okay?" Tori was eyeing her closely.

Was she okay? That was a good question.

She was feeling a little discombobulated, as a matter of fact.

Just five days ago, she'd been in Paris, feeling pretty full of herself and good about life in general, eating croissants at a sidewalk café where she could gaze adoringly at the Eiffel Tower.

Now she was standing beside the veterinary clinic in Autre,

Louisiana, about to become the assistant to the man that she had more or less had sex with in a barn two months ago and whose shirt she still wore with only panties when she was lounging around her house. Who was now her boss.

Griffin was absolutely as gorgeous and delicious as he'd been back then. And that meant the moonshine she'd shot with her cousins and the general celebratory air of the event had not been part of her attraction to Griffin.

"So Griffin takes care of the petting zoo and everything with Boys of the Bayou Gone Wild?" Charlie asked. After seeing him with the goats, it was clear he spent a lot of time with them.

Tori nodded. "Yep. I'm sticking with most of my small animal clients, but he's taking on any new clients and the petting zoo and otters. He also handles a lot of the larger animal calls now that I'm further along." She put a hand on her stomach. "I fully intend to practice after the baby comes, but it would be great to be more flexible and maybe more part-time."

"Does he like working with the petting zoo?" Charlie was too interested in the guy. But it didn't hurt to know something about her new boss, did it?

Tori smiled. "Griffin likes anything having to do with animals. It's people he's not as crazy about."

That fit. Charlie didn't know him well, but Griffin Foster wasn't that hard to read, really. He probably shouldn't play poker. Even the night they'd met, it had been clear that, while the goats weren't supposed to be following him around, he was far more tolerant of them than he had been of Charlie insinuating herself into his quiet time outside the bar.

That hadn't lasted. He'd been fine with her being in his space after a few minutes. Sure, kissing and thongs and dirty talk had a way of getting to most guys, but she truly thought he'd liked more than that about her.

Griffin didn't strike her as "most guys." And that was going to make her stay in Autre this time a lot more fun, she had a feeling.

"So I'll be more Griffin's assistant than yours?" Charlie asked.

Tori nodded. "He's the one here most of the time. I do a lot of house calls."

"I'd guess most small town vets don't get a chance to work with a whole bunch of otters or even alpacas regularly," Charlie said. "He must enjoy that."

Was she digging for information about Griffin Foster? Absolutely.

But Tori laughed. "Oh, I'm sure our goats and alpacas and even the otters seem like a demotion to him."

"He doesn't like goats and alpacas and otters?" How did someone not like otters?

"He likes them. They're just not tigers and polar bears and penguins."

"Oh, well..." That was true. "But he didn't really think Autre would have penguins, did he?"

"No. But he worked for zoos before coming here. I think going from tigers to goats is still a little disheartening."

"Zoos? No way." Okay, that was cool. A zoo veterinarian? She didn't run into one of those every day.

"Yes, he spent time in Omaha at the Henry Doorly Zoo. He worked with all of the animals there at one time or another. Then he moved to Washington, D.C,. and was actually head of the propagation program for the tigers at the National Zoo."

Yes, very interesting. How often did a girl meet a hot guy who was great with animals and had been a veterinarian at the zoo? Accountants, lawyers, general businessmen, even mechanics and construction workers were a dime a dozen but zoo veterinarians?

"So how did he end up here? If he thinks all of this is a demotion, why did he leave D.C.?"

That wasn't nosy. Surely anyone who heard that Griffin had worked at zoos before and was now taking care of the goats in Autre, Louisiana, would wonder how that transition had happened.

Tori would not meet Charlie's eyes as she answered, "He just... needed a change of pace."

A change of pace, huh?

"And he just happened to answer your Help Wanted ad?"

"Griffin and I know each other from vet school," Tori said with a smile. "When I found out that he..." She seemed to consider her next words, "...needed a new job—" She winced a little as if that wasn't exactly how she meant to phrase that. "I offered him a position here as my partner. Even before I was pregnant, I was getting busier, and as we added the otters, I had more work than I can really keep up with. Griffin is a great guy and an extraordinary veterinarian, and I'm always happy to help out friends and colleagues."

Charlie put a hand on her hip. Tori Landry was a very sweet woman. Charlie liked her a lot. Tori was also not telling Charlie the whole story about Griffin. And she was *very* interested.

"Why did he need a new job?" Charlie asked.

Tori actually took a step backward, shaking her head. "Um... not my story to tell."

So there *was* a story.

"But what are the chances Griffin's going to tell me the story?"

"Probably not very good," Tori admitted. "He keeps to himself."

Dammit, now Charlie felt like this was a challenge. She wanted his story. And she wanted *him* to tell her.

There was very little Charlie liked more than a challenge. Chocolate croissants. A great cappuccino. A new pair of heels. And interestingly, just over the past two months, possibly baby goats.

No, she didn't like goats *more* than a challenge, but she did like baby goats more than she would have expected.

"But—" Now Tori was studying Charlie closely. "Why do you need the story?"

Because I haven't been this interested in a guy in a really long time. Or ever.

Charlie thought quickly. Did she need to be careful here? Would Tori not let her work here if she knew what had happened between her and Griffin two months ago? If so, why would Tori care about that?

Charlie realized at that moment that she wanted this job. Here. At the vet clinic with Griffin. But Maddie had mentioned her helping Boys of the Bayou out with some marketing ideas. Charlie was certain it had been Ellie's suggestion initially, but she appreciated that her family would give her a job. Even if it was out of pity. And temporary. She needed to come up with ten grand to pay off Alan's stupid paint job, so she couldn't be picky at the moment.

She could probably find a marketing job in New Orleans if she looked. But she didn't want a job in New Orleans. This was like every other trip she'd taken to the bayou—it was a break, a vacation, a short-term getaway. A chance to have some fun, kick back, not worry about anything for a little while.

But she had plans. Goals. Dreams, even. Watching her father build his business as she'd grown up had made her want to be a part of something like that. Where a company could be more than a business. Where it could become influential and make a real difference.

Autre was just a pit stop along that road, and no matter how creative she got about activities with swamp boats and goats and otters, it wasn't the big, meaningful work she wanted to do.

Still, in the short term, putting together a marketing plan for her family would keep her busy, and it would help them out. That would definitely make her feel good. Plus, some of her ideas could be mutually beneficial if things went her way.

And things very often went her way.

"He's my new boss. A friend of the family. I'm nosy." Charlie lifted a shoulder after giving three very good excuses.

Tori looked suspicious, but she nodded. "Okay."

"But you don't have to tell me."

"Good," Tori said as if that hadn't even been a possibility. "How about we head in, and I'll show you around?" Tori stepped to the clinic door and pulled it open. "Then Griffin really might need you in on the surgery on Brownie."

"Great."

Charlie followed Tori back into the clinic and took mental notes as Tori showed her around the building.

They had the storage room, four examination rooms, two surgical rooms, and the large room where they kept the dogs, cats, and other critters kenneled for their hospital stays. There were also two offices—one for Tori and one for Griffin.

Charlie lingered in the doorway to Griffin's office, taking in as many details as she could without seeming overly interested. The room was cluttered, with stacks of folders and papers all over his desk and in piles on the floor between the desk and window. There were also magazines and books, along with a couple of t-shirts draped over one chair and a jacket on the back of another. But that was as personal as it got. There were no photos or any other personal touches. She didn't even see a coffee cup.

The clutter with the lack of personal touches surprised her for some reason. She had no idea why. She didn't know the guy very well.

She knew that he was an amazing kisser. She knew that she really liked having his hands in her panties—well, technically, she hadn't had panties on when his hands had been where she really liked having them—and she loved the way he responded to blowjobs.

And that was it.

Except that he had a soft spot for animals, was good with little kids, and was funny and charming.

A funny, charming animal lover should at least have a mug that said *This Probably Has Dog Hair In It*.

She'd seen that mug online when she'd been scrolling for something else. She'd thought it was funny at the time, but it was weird that it came to mind now.

But yeah, she was going to get him that mug.

She liked the guy. What could she say?

"We'll go over several of the supplies, but I just wanted to show you around for now," Tori said. "A lot of the job is just answering the phone and assisting patients as they come in. We're not crazy busy all the time, so Griffin will obviously handle most of the actual work, but it's nice to have an extra pair of hands sometimes."

"I'm game for whatever," Charlie said. "I'm happy to help if I can."

"Well, it's great for me to know someone's here with Griffin," Tori said. "He is such a hard worker, and he's an amazing vet, but sometimes..."

Charlie gave Tori a little grin. There were few different ways Tori could probably fill in that blank, and Charlie was curious about all of them. "But sometimes?" she prompted.

"Customer service isn't Griffin's strong suit." Tori gave her a little smile that said she was trying to be diplomatic.

Charlie nodded. "Got it. So I will be handling the customer service?"

"Please."

Charlie laughed and followed Tori through the rest of the clinic.

"Feel free to poke around, so you know where things are,

but you won't be doing anything with the animals without Griffin. The surgical suites will need to be cleaned up after procedures though. I'll show you all of that."

Tori turned to the left and led Charlie toward the front of the clinic. "And this is our lobby and waiting area."

Charlie was listening. She really was. She heard something about cleaning up and that she should go in and look around. But she was definitely distracted.

She could hear Griffin's voice coming from one of the examination rooms. The door wasn't shut, and Griffin was inside with Andre and Michael, and Brownie.

She couldn't hear everything they were saying, but she could hear Griffin's low voice and soothing tone. It did funny things to her insides. He'd been charming, sexy, dirty, and funny with her. She very much liked all of those characteristics. But something about him being soothing and reassuring made her want to get closer to that room and listen in. She took a step in that direction.

"So you promise he'll be okay in time for my birthday?" she heard Andre ask.

"I promise that if he's not okay to come home for your birthday," Griffin said, "you can come here and visit him, and we'll have a little party right here. I would hate to think that your best friend in the world wouldn't be at your birthday party."

Charlie wanted to take her clothes off.

It was that simple. Listening to Griffin talk to the little boy about his birthday party and his best friend, the puppy, made her want him in a way that shocked her.

She was not exactly *excited* to be in Autre. She loved the town and being with her family, of course, but Autre was just a place for her to rest and re-set. She also wasn't excited to be jobless. She definitely wasn't excited to have her mother think that she had been majorly demoted and was now begging her family for charity. But if part of her time in Autre was going to be spent around Dr. Griffin Foster, things were going to be just fine.

"Charlie?" Tori asked, turning back

Charlie shook herself and looked at Tori.

"You okay?" Tori asked.

"Yeah. Sure." Stupidly horny, but actually, suddenly *delighted* to be here.

Charlie grinned to herself as she followed Tori into the front of the clinic.

"Welcome home," her cousin Sawyer said, straightening away from the counter where he'd been leaning. He was a big guy. Six-four and broad. He was wearing a black t-shirt with a Boys of the Bayou logo and faded blue jeans that she was sure had seen many a swamp boat tour. He had a jagged scar that ran down the one side of his face from an accident on the bayou, but he was still very handsome, especially with the big grin he gave Charlie as she stepped into the lobby.

"Hey, Sawyer!" Charlie rounded the corner of the tall front counter.

Her oldest cousin pulled her into a big hug. "I hear you've been causing trouble."

Charlie nodded. "As always."

"Glad some things never change." Sawyer patted her on the head. "You didn't have to use the right hook I taught you?"

"I would have if I'd thought it would hurt him as much as keying his Porsche did."

Sawyer laughed, a deep rumbling sound. "That's my girl."

"But, lucky for you, now that I'm here for a while, I'm going to make Boys of the Bayou bigger and better than ever."

"You don't have to sell us," Sawyer said. "Anything you do will be more than we're doing now."

"Hey," Maddie protested. "I've been doing stuff since I got back. We didn't even have much of a website when I showed up. And we've got alligator cookies and much better t-shirts now."

Maddie and her husband, Owen, another of Charlie's cousins, owned Boys of the Bayou with Sawyer, Josh, and Bennett Baxter, Kennedy Landry-Baxter's husband.

"Great. We can build on all of those ideas," Charlie told Maddie. "But I have a few other things that we can try while I'm here. And if you hate them, or they don't work by the time I leave, I'll take my ideas with me. But if you love them and it's going great, then I can easily help you guys keep the plan going even when I'm not here."

Maddie nodded. "Sounds good. I don't have a lot of time to devote to the stuff anymore because I'm helping with tours since we're getting busier. Which is a good problem to have."

Sawyer chuckled. "You love doing the tours," he said. "We would've hired somebody else to do the tours a long time ago or talked Mitch into taking some of them over. You're the one who wants to keep doing them."

Maddie grinned. "I really do."

Charlie nodded. "Then there's no reason for you to not keep doing them. I love marketing, and I'm great at it, so I am very happy to take this on right now, and we'll see where we're at in a couple of months."

"That's how long you're planning to stay?" Sawyer asked. "Just a couple of months?"

Charlie lifted a shoulder. She was officially in take-this-one-day-at-a-time mode. She'd been shopping on Avenue Montaigne just a few days ago and could still taste the socca. After her boss had fired her, she'd simply gotten on a plane, landed in New Orleans, and driven to Autre.

She'd known she could figure things out once she was back on the bayou.

Her short-term plan was to pay off the ten-thousand-dollar paint job.

And to make a better plan.

She was looking for jobs, but until something came along,

she was going to work as a veterinary assistant and help build the Boys of the Bayou.

At least she wouldn't have a gap on her marketing resume.

"So what do you think? New website design? Maybe we add some tote bags to those t-shirts?" Sawyer asked.

Charlie laughed. "Oh, Sawyer, you have no idea what I have in store."

Sawyer looked at Maddie again, then back to Charlie. "What's that mean?"

"It's much easier to show you than just tell you." Charlie moved behind the front desk and pulled out a large leather portfolio.

She unzipped it and laid it open on the top of the front counter. She had to move a small lamp, a potted plant, and a pencil holder out of the way. She pointed to the first page with a big smile.

Sawyer's eyes were wide as he took in the bright green, yellow, white, and black graphics that read *Boys of the Bayou Marketing Plan*.

"When did you have time to do all of *that*?" he asked, looking at the portfolio like it might bite him. "We *just* decided to talk about this." He glanced at Maddie. "Didn't we?"

She simply shrugged.

"Ellie told me we should talk," Charlie said. "And it's a long trip from Paris to New Orleans." And she'd been in first class with plenty of room and resources to work. She'd simply needed a printer when she'd landed, and those were easy enough to find.

Sawyer and Maddie both still looked a little stunned.

Well, they'd learn to go with it. Charlie was an idea factory. She didn't need a lot of time to pull concepts together. In fact, they often came in avalanches, flooding her imagination faster than she could write them down.

"Let's start on page one." Charlie flipped the first page of the portfolio, showing Maddie and Sawyer the initial new design of their logo. Now that the swamp boat tour company was also taking on the animal park and the otter enclosure, they needed a second logo for the animal portion of the business.

Maddie looked to Tori as if for help.

Tori just grinned and shook her head. "I'm thinking of hiring her for our marketing too."

Maddie took a deep breath and focused on the portfolio again. "We're getting a new logo for the Gone Wild stuff?" she asked.

"Yes, to start." Charlie watched their faces.

Along with being very good at judging how customers responded to marketing ideas, she was also great at reading body language. A lot of times, when she came into the picture, she was the first one to introduce clients to big, exciting marketing plans, and they could get overwhelmed easily. Her cousins were definitely going to fall into that category.

The Boys of the Bayou swamp boat tour company had been started years ago by her grandfather and his best friend, Maddie's grandfather, Kenny. It had started off as a couple of guys who would take occasional visitors out on the bayou to look around and fish and hunt. They quickly realized that people would pay them for the experience, and it had evolved over the years into a tour company they had passed down to their grandsons.

Sawyer, Josh, Owen, and Maddie's brother, Tommy, had kept doing what they'd been doing and just slowly built the company off of their reputation as charming, fun guys with a great knowledge and love for the bayou. After Tommy had been killed on the bayou and Maddie had come back to take over her portion of the tour company, things started to evolve.

They had been having some money trouble at that point, and Maddie had brought in another partner, Bennett Baxter, the first non-Landry to ever be involved with the swamp boat tour company. Of course, now he was a pseudo-Landry because he was married to Kennedy, Josh and Sawyer's sister. So the tour company had definitely stayed in the family.

However, thanks to Bennett's influx of cash, Maddie's initial marketing ideas, and just the general enthusiasm the family brought to the company, the business had continued to grow slowly over the past year.

But there was so much potential here. While this wasn't the big, exciting opportunity that Charlie was looking for in her long-term career, she was excited to help them out.

"While I think some tote bags would be a great addition to the gift shop," Charlie said, "I think that we can do more. We need to find a way to combine the swamp boat tour company and the animal experiences more intimately."

"What do you mean by that?" Sawyer asked.

"Well, the otters are probably a little more obvious," Charlie said. "But we might need to figure out a way to help people understand what llamas have to do with the swamp."

"Actually, they're alpacas."

Charlie turned as Griffin's voice sounded behind her. For just a second, Charlie lost her train of thought. That never happened when she was talking about marketing plans and doing presentations.

"Right, alpacas." She gave Griffin a big smile. He'd told her they were alpacas the night they'd been in the barn together.

He frowned.

"I'm not really sure that alpacas do have anything to do with the swamp," Sawyer said. He glanced at Tori with an affectionate smile. "We have alpacas because we have Tori, not because we live on the swamp."

Charlie pulled her eyes away from Griffin and focused on Sawyer. She nodded. "Right, which is why we have to try to make some kind of connection."

"But that's why it's funny," Maddie said. "Boys of the Bayou

Gone Wild. It's tongue-in-cheek. Alpacas and otters and goats aren't really that wild."

Charlie nodded. Maddie had filled her in on everything while they'd been chatting before Griffin showed up this morning.

The petting zoo was a very only-half-thought-out project. The animals were more of a side attraction. Something to occupy tourists while they waited for their boat tours. But Charlie thought they could change that.

River otters made sense. They had a connection to the bayou. In fact, the first otter, Gus, had lived under one of the Boys of the Bayou docks and had adopted the guys before they adopted him. Then he'd gotten a girlfriend, and they'd had babies, and the Landrys had decided to make him a more official space to raise his little family.

But alpacas and goats were a little more of a stretch when connecting the two portions of the business together.

"I get that. I think we need to get some turtles and frogs and other bayou animals in here. Or we can maybe even expand to some other Louisiana animals."

"Such as?" Griffin asked. He had his arms crossed and looked annoyed.

"Skunks. Foxes." She shrugged. "You'd probably know better than me." Though she'd looked up some native Louisiana animals.

"We're going to bring in skunks and foxes?" Griffin asked. "Why not a black bear? Or an alligator?"

"If you think we could—"

"No." He said it flatly and firmly.

And just like the way his soothing, reassuring voice had made her stomach swoop, so did his firm, don't-mess-with-me voice.

"But it could—"

"*No*, Charlotte."

Oh boy, and using her full name? Why did *that* make her hot?

"You're a zoo veterinarian. Surely you know the importance of people learning about animals and having a chance to interact with them."

"Wild animals need to be—deserve to be—wild unless there is a reason they are safer in captivity."

There was an intensity in his expression and tone that said he would not budge on this.

She could, of course, remind him that he was a partner here in the veterinary clinic but not in the Boys of the Bayou.

But she didn't want to.

She was *always* up for pushing her ideas and making her case. Sometimes she had to convince people to see things her way by laying out details and proof.

There was something about Griffin's adamant refusal here that made her nod instead. "Fine." She looked back to Sawyer and Maddie. "Then if we're going with the funny, tongue-in-cheek thing, we need to lean into it. We can get some other animals that kids can interact with, but that aren't wild."

Her mind was spinning with ideas. How could they play up the "wild" joke? Make it funny and interesting rather than "what the hell is this all about?"

"We can make a visit to the petting zoo a 'jungle tour,'" she said, as the idea formed. "We give the kids plastic jungle hats to wear while they're here." She gasped. "Oh, and a field guide. They can do a tour of our animals, learning facts, earning stickers, taking little notes. We can share the wildest thing each animal does. I mean, even if it's something not-wild-at-all, that will be interesting and fun. In fact, the *less* wild, the funnier."

She paced to the end of the counter, thinking. "Then once they're done with the petting zoo, they stop over at a little 'training center' where they learn about more dangerous animals around here—alligators, snakes, bears, and so on. The ones that are *actually* wild."

She turned and paced to the other end. "And we emphasize why it's important to respect wild animals and be careful when you come across one outside of a zoo." She nodded. "Yes, we can turn this into something more educational that way. Oh!" She spun around again. "We can have a little station with a laptop or tablet set up where the kids from other places can learn about the wildest animals where *they're* from!"

She grabbed for her notebook and a pen, knocking the pencil holder off the front of the counter. Pens scattered, but Charlie bent her head over her paper. And kept talking.

"Then they get on the swamp boats and can continue their tour by looking for and learning about alligators and herons and snakes and turtles and other things they might see out there, and what their *wild* environment is like."

She scribbled her notes, then stood back. Finally, she focused on the other people with her again.

She grinned at them all. "The alpacas and goats will be gateway-wild-animals."

"Gateway?" Maddie asked.

"We get kids excited about the animals that are cute and approachable, and it will pique their interest in learning about others. We'll just get progressively more 'wild' with what we expose them to. Then when they get home, they'll be more into learning about animals where they are."

Another idea hit her. "Oh! We can also set up an online forum. Kids can share experiences with us when they get back home too. Maybe they write us a little essay about wild animals where they live. Or draw us pictures." She bent over her notebook again, writing furiously. "We can have monthly prizes for sharing with us! Stuffed alpacas and alligators and pigs! We can have a whole section on our website with animal facts!"

She looked up. Her heart was actually pounding a little

harder than it was before. She loved brainstorming. It was her favorite part next to that moment when a client said, "Wow, this is working! We're so happy."

Sawyer was watching her with amusement, and Maddie was smiling. Tori looked excited. And Griffin...

Charlie turned to look at him.

He was staring at her as if amazed. Or horrified.

7

"For an added fee, they can then have a true otter encounter where they can feed and swim with the otters," Charlie said.

"No."

She sighed at Griffin's reaction. After all of that, all she got was a no? "Why not?"

"Swim with them? We don't need people tromping around inside the otter enclosure. That's not safe or secure for the animals."

It was about the animals again. She had to admit, that was attractive. Even if he was objecting to her idea.

"Is there a way to bring a couple of otters to a bigger pool to—"

"No," Griffin said before she even finished. "Transporting them back and forth would be stressful for them."

Charlie propped a hand on her hip. "What about feeding them?"

"You want people tossing fish into them?"

"I was thinking hand feeding."

"No."

"Why not?"

"Because humans don't listen to instructions and could do something that's dangerous to the animals. They could pass germs and disease. Feed them something they shouldn't have. Any number of things."

Charlie felt her brows lift. Wow. He said that with a lot of passion.

"But we could have a handwashing station and very closely monitor who is there and how they are interacting with the animals," Tori said, stepping forward. "Just like at the barnyard. We'll want people to wash their hands, and we'll, of course, provide any feed they give the animals."

"People are going to be feeding the barnyard animals?" Griffin asked, scowling.

"I think we could incorporate that," Tori said, her voice even and calm. "At designated times and with a limited number of people."

"Who would be supervising?" Griffin asked.

Charlie snorted. Then she shook her head. "Sorry."

"What's funny about that?" he asked.

"Well, obviously, *you* would be supervising," she said. "No one else would do it right, would they?"

He narrowed his eyes. "No. They probably wouldn't."

Charlie grinned at him. She knew his grumpy, bossy thing was supposed to put her in her place, but... it didn't. It made her want to poke at him. And make him smile.

"I don't really have time to supervise a bunch of tourists messing with my animals."

His animals? She knew the animals were actually, technically, Tori's. But he clearly felt protective. That was... sexy.

"We'll do the feedings at designated times, and I'll be sure, as your assistant, to keep those times free on your clinic schedule." She smiled at him sweetly.

He sighed.

She was going to take that as not-a-no, which was maybe as close as she was going to get to an agreement on this. At least for now.

Charlie turned to Sawyer and Maddie. "As it is now, people are only taking in the otters and petting zoo while they wait for boat tours, is that right?"

Sawyer nodded. "Yeah. When the otter family grew, and we wanted them to have a safe space, we decided to build an enclosure and figured we could locate it down by the docks. It really was, initially, intended just to be a place for the otters to live. But people love watching them, and it's right there so... Tori suggested bringing some of her other animals down there to a little barnyard as an added attraction and—" Sawyer shrugged. "Here we are."

So the petting zoo was kind of an accidental petting zoo. That was funny and pretty in character for her family, Charlie had to admit.

"Of course, that means sometimes they're over at the petting zoo instead of hanging out at Ellie's bar and enjoying a pre-tour cocktail," Maddie said with a grin. "Which annoys Ellie. She calls the otters 'varmints' who are stealing her business."

"We had to promise Ellie to really sell the bar on the tour, so the people stop over there afterward," Sawyer said. "We've started extending the time after the tour before the busses leave."

Charlie nodded. Her grandpa, Leo, and her cousin, Mitch, drove the busses that picked tourists up and returned them to their hotels in New Orleans. "Good idea. Does Ellie have kid-friendly options?" Charlie asked.

Maddie and Sawyer looked at one another. "She's got soda and lemonade," Sawyer said.

She was going to have to work on her grandmother too, Charlie realized. "Well, we need a kids' menu. Things that would make a family want to go in. Maybe coloring pages—"

They all laughed. Even Griffin. She really liked the sound of his laugh.

"Ellie's bar is a... bar," Maddie said. "She's got food, but it's gumbo and boudin balls and fried pickles. Stuff like that."

"Kids from other places should try local cuisine," Charlie said. "It's part of the travel experience. Especially when you can have it homemade in a family-owned, roadside spot."

But even as she said it, she knew Ellie's wasn't the kind of place most families would take their kids for lunch. For one, the building itself was pretty... ramshackle. It didn't leak when it rained, but it also wasn't anything anyone would call quaint or adorable. It was a big square building full of mismatched chairs and tables. The décor was a mix of photographs and sports team banners. It would need a makeover if they were going to make it into a tourist stop for anything other than a quick hurricane or beer before or after a boat tour.

"You know Ellie's not going to be into the idea of sprucing things up for a bunch of strangers," Maddie said. "She figures people can take her and her bar as is or leave them."

Maddie was right. Charlie could maybe talk Ellie into letting Mitch paint the outside, and maybe... no, that was probably about it. The bar had been exactly as it was for as long as Charlie could remember. It was often full of people she knew and loved—and the best etouffee and bread pudding in the entire world—but she could understand why it might look a little dingy to outsiders.

"Fine, then we put in a concession stand," she said.

Sawyer looked less enthusiastic about that, but it was Griffin who actually groaned.

"What now?" she asked.

"Trash, discarded containers, and wrappers that can get into pens. Goats will try to eat almost anything. People feeding the ducks popcorn..." He scowled. "No."

Charlie sighed. This guy definitely said that word a lot. It was her *least* favorite word in the English language. By far.

"Maybe Ellie would be open to serving some people at picnic tables outside the bar or something," Charlie said, also making that note. She'd talk to her grandma about it. Ellie was stubborn and truly liked things as they were with her business, but she was also the matriarch and, as such, wanted everyone to be happy and successful. Charlie could sell this to her. Probably.

She couldn't be any more difficult to win over than Griffin.

And Charlie thought Griffin was at least a little won over by her.

"We need to work on making this all one big package, one big experience," she went on. "We need to make sure people know what to expect when they come down here, so they can plan their time. We need to pick people up earlier for their swamp boat tours, so they have time to spend at the petting zoo. Or figure in lunch and drinks after the swamp boat tour. The longer people hang out, the more likely they are to head into the gift shop too."

Maddie winced. "The gift shop could also use some work."

Charlie already had plans for that too. They would, for instance, have to sell duplicates of the jungle hats the kids could wear while in the petting zoo. And the stuffed animals she was going to put up as prizes for their online interactions.

"We're going to figure out a way to encompass all of that for people coming down to the bayou and spending the whole day versus just a few hours the way they do now," she said.

Ellie and the family already had a crawfish boil every Friday night, and often, tourists would opt to stay for that after their tour. Boys of the Bayou also ran some special tours for bachelor and bachelorette parties, sunset tours, even night tours a couple of times a week. They needed to expand to jungle-cruise-themed kids' birthday parties, though. At least. She knew more ideas would be coming to her.

"So there will be more people milling around for longer periods of time?" Griffin asked

"Well, hopefully," Charlie said with a smile. "If I do my job, anyway.

Sawyer was clearly thinking this all through. "We'll have to hire more people to manage the extra traffic for longer periods of time. And add lots more supplies to the budget."

Charlie nodded. "We will definitely need to hire more staff." Someone was going to have to make the popcorn and snow cones and...

"How do we pay for that?"

Charlie reeled in her thoughts about what the concession stand could include. "With the profits. Like any business."

"The swamp boat company is going to have to support increased staffing and hats and stuff at the petting zoo?" Sawyer asked.

"Increased business at the petting zoo will be supported by the proceeds from the petting zoo."

"We don't have proceeds from the petting zoo."

Charlie stared at him. Then she looked at Maddie. Then she looked at Tori. "You don't charge for the petting zoo?"

"Do we charge people to stand at the fence and look at our alpacas and goats?" Sawyer asked. "No."

"All they do is look?" Charlie asked, looking at Maddie.

Maddie shrugged. "What else would they do?"

Charlie stared at her. "Have you ever *been* to a petting zoo? The word *petting* is kind of a giveaway."

"Of course," Maddie said. "But in order for people to go in and interact with the animals, we would have to have staff and, as Sawyer pointed out, to have staff, we would have to pay them, and to pay them, we would have to have money."

"Which is where charging the visitors comes in," Charlie said. "We charge them tickets for the petting zoo just like any other petting zoo. To do the 'tour' where they can wear the hat and get a keepsake booklet they pay a little more. Same with the otter encounter. They'll pay for the concessions. And that money helps to support the petting zoo and the otter encounter." She looked over at Tori. "How do you support the animals now?"

Tori hesitated for a moment. Then shrugged. "With our love."

Charlie laughed and shook her head. "Love is wonderful, but it doesn't really pay the bills."

"We would have to get decent staff to interact with the animals. Not just anyone can do that."

Oh good, more Griffin input. Honestly, she'd done easier presentations to billionaire CEOs. She was here to do a job that Griffin clearly didn't want her to do. That was just great.

Now she had reason to look at him again, though. Charlie gave him a smile. "Yes, Dr. Foster. We would have to get animal lovers and then train them to work in the petting zoo and the otter encounter. Which would be a great experience for any kids who'd like to go into veterinary medicine or other careers with animals. Just think of the amazing influence you could have."

Though billionaire CEOs probably didn't feel as passionately about their products as Griffin seemed to about the animals in his care.

"And how do you find these people?" Griffin asked, not commenting on the influence he could have on a whole new generation of animal enthusiasts.

"We'll be relying heavily on the animal expert already here in Autre to help us find the right people," Charlie said, literally batting her eyes at him.

He sighed. "Now I'll also be training people to work at the animal park?"

"Oh my God." Charlie made her eyes go round and gave him a huge smile. "*Thank you* for volunteering, Dr. Foster. No one could do a better job." Charlie turned to Sawyer. "Now we have a volunteer trainer, so that won't even cost us any money."

"Char—" Griffin started.

"Dr. Foster?"

Griffin's response, which was probably going to be a resounding *no*, was interrupted by Andre.

Griffin gave Charlie a this-isn't-over look but turned to speak with his patient's family. She was startled by the way his entire countenance changed. His shoulders relaxed as he looked down at the boy.

"Hey, Andre."

"Here you go. He's ready." Andre handed Brownie over to Griffin.

And again, Charlie's panties got a little damp as Griffin's big hands cradled the puppy, his biceps bunching under the edge of his t-shirt sleeve, and his smile. That I've-got-this-you-can-totally-trust-me smile he gave the little boy made *her* have to shift and swallow hard.

"We said our goodbyes for now, so I think we're ready to go," Michael said.

"Can I come to visit him later?" the little boy asked Griffin. Andre looked like he was trying very hard not to cry.

Griffin nodded. "Brownie will be out of surgery and feeling better after dinner. So when you're done, you can come to see him. And don't forget to bring Charlie the picture of him you're going to draw, okay?"

Charlie felt a flutter in her chest. He'd remembered about the drawing. And he'd called her Charlie.

He might be shooting down most of her ideas about the

petting zoo, but she still wanted to kiss him. And see how sturdy those exam tables in the back rooms were.

"He'll be okay for us to see him?" Michael asked.

Griffin nodded. "I think he will." He looked at Andre again. "I think he'll be ready for a visit, but I *might* ask your dad to wait until tomorrow if Brownie is still feeling a little sick. Part of being a good puppy dad is understanding that sometimes they need us to do things we don't want to do."

The little boy nodded. "I remember what you told me. Sometimes Brownie needs stuff that I can't do or don't want to do."

Griffin gave him a smile and put his hand on Andre's head. "You're doing such a good job, Andre."

Charlie actually sucked in a breath. She knew that it was an overreaction because Maddie gave her a funny look, meaning she'd heard the quick breath. What the hell was with this guy? Why did he affect her like this?

"And some of those things we don't want to do don't just include picking up poop in the yard, right?" Griffin asked.

"Right," Andre said. "Sometimes it means not letting him eat things he wants to eat or maybe not visiting him if he is sick."

Griffin nodded. "Very good."

"Can I bring him a new toy? When I was in the hospital getting my tonsils out, my grandma brought me balloons."

"Dogs and balloons don't go very well together," Griffin said, shaking his head. "But the great thing about dogs is that you don't have to bring them toys and balloons. He'll just be excited to see you when you get here. You're all he needs."

Andre smiled. "Yeah, you're right."

Griffin turned to look at Charlie.

Charlie knew she was looking at him like teenage girls looked at the movie stars they had crushes on. But damn. No wonder that she'd dropped her panties so easily for him in the barn. He was smart and kind and loved animals and was good with kids, and was going to fix Andre's puppy in time for his birthday. She'd be an idiot *not* to want him. Actually, that all made her feel a lot better. She did have good taste in men, after all.

"Do you mind?" he asked.

Charlie looked around and realized he was talking to her. "Do I mind what?"

"I need to get them an appointment tomorrow at three o'clock to pick Brownie up, and you're in the way," he said. "Although, that's one of those things that my assistant should probably be doing."

Oh, right. Yeah, probably.

Charlie turned to the front reception desk and saw that she had her marketing plans spread out across the desk in the way of any scheduling or appointment books. She leaned over, grabbed a sticky note off the top of the stack, grabbed a pen out of the pen holder, wrote down three o'clock p.m., added a smiley face, and handed it to Michael. "See you tomorrow."

He chuckled. "Thanks again, Griffin."

"No problem. I'll text you later."

"But I'll text you before that!" Charlie called. She'd promised photos and updates after all.

Griffin focused on her again after the door shut behind them.

"What if I'm busy tomorrow at three? You didn't look at the schedule."

"I promise to work it out," she told him. After she dug the schedule book out. Then she would get them set up to schedule online with a calendar that would connect to both of their phones, so they didn't have to dig the schedule book out every time. "I'm here to make your life easier."

He gave her a look that clearly said, *you're full of shit*. But there was maybe a, *but I'd still really like to kiss you again anyway* tacked onto the end of that thought. At least, she was going to tell herself there was.

"Anything else I can do for you, Dr. Foster?"

If that sounded like innuendo, she was absolutely unapologetic about that.

"As a matter of fact, there is."

Oh... good. Though that didn't sound enough like an innuendo for her taste.

"What's that?"

"Kennel three needs to be cleaned out."

"Okay then." A dirty kennel. That sounded as opposite from the work she'd been doing forty-eight hours ago as she could get. Charlie looked at everyone else with a smile. "I'm going to get to work, and you all think about what animals we should add to the petting zoo."

"We really are adding animals?" Sawyer asked

Maddie, Sawyer, and Charlie all looked at Tori. Her eyes were already twinkling.

Sawyer gave a little groan that Charlie interpreted as yes, they were adding animals to the petting zoo.

"Hedgehogs," Charlie said. "Hedgehogs are so cute and would be easy for kids to handle, wouldn't they?"

Tori's smile was wide and bright. "I love hedgehogs."

Sawyer shook his head. "They're animals. Four legs and fur, right? Of course you love them." But the way he smiled at Tori was resigned and affectionate.

"You've already looked into animals to add to the petting zoo?" Maddie asked.

"Of course. I never come to meetings unprepared."

"And who is going to take care of all of these new animals?"

She turned to face Griffin. He already knew the answer, of course, but she was glad he'd asked. The more chances for her to work with the grumpy hot veterinarian, the better.

"Well, probably not the pregnant veterinarian who's soon to be a mother and have all the time in the world," she said.

Griffin sighed. "No. Probably not."

Charlie shrugged, fighting a grin. He was so easy to poke. And it was so fun. "I'm sure we can find someone online. They can just use Google to figure out what to do with hedgehogs, right?"

Griffin didn't sigh, but he frowned this time. "I know you're kidding, but I still feel compelled to say that is completely unacceptable."

It might only be for animals, but he had some softness underneath the gruff exterior. And it wasn't so much that she would use it against him, as it was her finding it incredibly sexy.

"Well, we'll have to work something else out for the hedgehogs then," she told him. "And the rabbits."

"I *love* rabbits," Tori said.

Charlie grinned.

Griffin did not. "The cute girl who's going to be cleaning out the veterinary clinic kennels will have to help clean up after these new animals, you know."

Her eyebrows arched. Holy shit. Even though he was clearly annoyed with her coming in here and making changes, that was almost *flirting*.

"You have a cute new girl cleaning the kennels of the veterinary clinic?" she asked.

His eyes tracked over her from the top of her head to the toes of her tennis shoes. They came back to rest on hers. "I do. Apparently."

Charlie smiled at him. He didn't smile back, but his eyes were hot as they took her in.

After a few beats, he said, "Charlie?"

It was the first time he called her Charlie to her face instead of Charlotte. It did a funny swooping thing to her stomach.

"Yeah?" Was her voice a little husky? And did anyone else notice? Did she care?

"Kennels. They're down the hall. Numbers three and five.

"The cute new girl is going to clean kennels, *now*?"

"Yeah. It's one of the reasons I'm really glad to have an assistant actually. Kennel three had a St. Bernard in it."

Oh.

Oh.

St. Bernards were big dogs. That was about all she knew about them, but she could surmise that they also made big... messes.

"Is this payback for bringing hedgehogs into your life?" she asked.

"It's payback for bringing *tourists* into my life."

He said "tourists" the way some people would say "roadkill."

"So you like hedgehogs?"

"Who wouldn't like hedgehogs?" he asked.

It was clear Tori wasn't the only one who was a sucker for anything with four legs and fur. And because of that, Charlie would clean up after the St. Bernard.

But she was definitely going to pray the dog hadn't been here for gastrointestinal issues.

"I better get to work then," she said. "Because there *are* hedgehogs and tourists in your future, Dr. Foster." She turned back to the others. "You guys go ahead and head out. Talk everything over. Come up with any questions or ideas that you've got. I'll see y'all later at Ellie's."

"You sure you're okay here?" Maddie's gaze went from Charlie to Griffin and back again, the corner of her mouth twitching now.

All of this arguing and banter on top of the way they'd disappeared into the storeroom together earlier clearly made her curious about what was going on between them.

Charlie was curious about that as well. Griffin said no to picking up where they'd left off—after being the one to suggest picking up where they'd left off. But maybe they could just start new now.

Not that she'd be able to forget about the barn...

She looked over at Griffin. "Yeah, I'm just fine."

She was also highly amused to see the look of trepidation on Griffin's face when she said that.

8

If he didn't know better, Griffin would have thought Charlie brushed against him on purpose as she stepped around him on the way to the kennels.

Actually, he did know better. He knew she had done her best to rub up against him on her way past. He should probably be more irritated by that. His new assistant couldn't be brushing up against him at every opportunity. Especially when he was trying to be annoyed with her. And avoid that body at all costs.

But why was he annoyed with her? She was going to do what he just asked her to do. It was cleaning two big dog kennels, but she hadn't blinked an eye when he told her what the job was.

He faced Maddie, Sawyer, and Tori as Charlie headed down the hallway behind him. All three of them were wearing knowing grins.

He sighed.

There was no way they could really know what was going on between him and Charlie or, more specifically, what *had* gone on between him and Charlie, but they were clearly picking up on something.

"Charlie is our cousin," Sawyer said to Griffin. "We're just helping her out with a job. Temporarily. Probably."

That *probably* sent a shot of *dammit* through Griffin. He nodded. "I know who she is."

"They met at our wedding," Tori said.

Sawyer looked at Griffin with interest. "You already know her?"

Did he know Charlie? Well, he hadn't known her name was Charlie. But he supposed overall that was a small detail. Charlotte "Charlie" Landry being here, though, was a big deal.

"We met," Griffin said. "Talked outside the reception for a little while."

That wasn't untrue. They had talked. He wasn't about to tell Sawyer what other things he had done to Sawyer's younger cousin. He wasn't sure Sawyer really wanted to know.

He was also going to stop thinking about things he had done to Sawyer's younger cousin in the barn. Because that was over now.

Charlie was back, and she was his new assistant and, more than that, she was a Landry. He could not get involved with the Landrys. Especially one who walked into his clinic and turned everything upside down in the space of about fifteen minutes.

It wasn't his business, exactly, but he was the vet for Boys of the Bayou Gone Wild.

"Since when are you interested in expanding the petting zoo?" he asked Sawyer. He'd heard nothing about it.

Sawyer shrugged. "I guess as of now."

"All of this really is just Charlie's idea, and none of you had any input into it?" Griffin asked.

"Well, we did talk about bringing her on as a marketing consultant for us," Sawyer said. "And Charlie is... a dynamo."

He shrugged. "Charlie takes everything and makes it ten times bigger. We probably should have expected this."

"*You* should have expected it," Maddie said. "I haven't been around her as much since we were teens."

"I'm new to the Charlie Show too," Tori said. "This is on you, Sawyer."

The Charlie Show.

Griffin wasn't sure if that should make him feel better or worse. Better, because he wasn't the only one susceptible to her charms. Worse, because he didn't stand a chance, and it seemed no one else could slow her down either.

Within an hour of being here, she'd instituted a program to text updates and photos to puppy owners, implemented a jungle tour theme at the petting zoo, and brought hedgehogs into his life.

The jungle theme wasn't a reality at the moment, but he fully expected to see kids running around with plastic jungle hats, collecting stickers, and asking four million questions in the petting zoo within a couple of weeks.

He did like hedgehogs though.

"But you're the owners, and she's only here temporarily, right?" Griffin asked. "Surely you can pull this idea back."

"Why would we do that?" Tori asked. "She's expanding the business. Exactly what we need to do. And I think this sounds fun."

Sure, fun. Tori had never worked in a place where animals were used to entertain people and make money. Yes, he'd worked at zoos. He'd *wanted* to work at zoos. He'd still be at a zoo if he hadn't let his temper get the better of him, in fact.

But as a vet, he cared for the animals. He helped them stay healthy or get healthy when they weren't. He'd specifically worked to help increase the population of endangered tigers in the propagation program at the National Zoo. To work, propagation programs needed secure places where the animals could be protected. In the U.S., that meant zoos and preserves, so he hadn't had a lot of choices. Whether he liked it or not, the current state of the planet, saving many animals from extinction, meant keeping some in captivity.

But that was different than coming up with ways for people to ogle animals and, worse, invade enclosures and handle animals for their own entertainment.

Unfortunately, Maddie was nodding her agreement with Tori. Griffin sighed internally. Charlie had already won them over. Of course, this was her family, and it was possible that they would have been on board no matter what.

He had a feeling that they hadn't been actually looking for a marketing consultant or to expand the business. Charlie showing up here, unemployed, meant now they suddenly had a marketing consultant whether they—or he—liked it or not. And she was going all in.

But even if they hadn't been family, Griffin knew Charlie would have won them over easily. She had a way about her. Maybe with anyone else, her presentation would've taken twenty minutes to convince them versus the ten that she'd given Sawyer, Maddie, and Tori, but it was clear that these three were on board.

And Griffin couldn't really object. He was technically an employee of theirs. His partnership was in the vet clinic with Tori. Boys of the Bayou Gone Wild hired him and Tori to take care of their animals.

It was a little more complicated since Tori was married to one of the partners. It wasn't like they would've hired anyone else. And the petting zoo was made up mostly of her own animals.

Still, Griffin was a partner in the Autre Animal Hospital, and if one of their clients took on more animals, then Griffin would take on the care of those animals.

Charlotte Landry had been back in Autre for a few hours,

and already she was complicating his life. Not just by being gorgeous and completely kissable and now off-limits, which was a problem all on its own, but now she was going to make his job harder.

The goats loved attention, so it was not as difficult for him to imagine opening the little barnyard to a more interactive setup. The alpacas would be okay too. The otters performed for audiences, and he knew that they would be ecstatic to be fed fish by tourists all day long. But they would have to rotate which otters were on display so that he didn't end up with a bunch of fat, sassy otters who would only show off for fish all day.

However, there were plenty of animals that shouldn't have to be subjected to that. The potbellied pig, Hermione, would not like the visitors. She was shy and easily over-stimulated. They'd need to find her another place to be during petting zoo hours.

Griffin knew where his line was with all of this, and he wouldn't hesitate to hold it. Not even with big blue eyes blinking up at him, looking at him like he was amazing.

Yeah, the look on her face when he'd been interacting with Andre and Brownie had given him a hot kick to the gut.

Charlie looked at him like he was a rock star. Or a big piece of chocolate cake. Or both. Dammit.

And Tori, Sawyer, and Maddie clearly liked this idea.

That meant he couldn't shoot it down entirely.

Tori had given him a job when he was jobless and trusted him completely as she began relinquishing more and more of the practice to him. Besides that, he really liked her. He also liked and respected Sawyer, Maddie, Josh, and Owen, and everyone else who worked with Boys of the Bayou. The Landrys were an amazing family, and he was getting close to counting them as friends.

Of course, his loyalty would always be with the animals

first. Which meant speaking up if he thought things were getting out of hand.

"Who's going to consult with Charlie on which animals to add?" he asked. "We all know she's not going to stop at hedge-hogs." He sighed. She'd already added rabbits to the list. "And someone should set guidelines for how this will all go. How much and often the animals are fed. How to rotate the ones who are interacting with people and which ones are off display. I don't think any of them should be interacting with tourists all day, every day."

Tori nodded. He knew that Tori would want the best for the animals as well.

"I think Charlie will be fine with guidance on the animal care portion of the idea by someone with expertise," Tori said.

"Absolutely," Sawyer agreed. "She's gung-ho for sure, and she will have big ideas and move on them quickly, but she'll listen to you."

"Me?" Griffin asked.

"You're the one with concerns," Sawyer said.

Yes, he most definitely did have concerns where Charlie Landry was concerned. But he wasn't sure that his primary ones had anything to do with adding hedgehogs to their petting zoo.

"Will you give me full authority to approve or disapprove any animal additions?"

Tori gave him a contemplative look. "Of course, I trust you completely, Griffin. And I know that you will guide Charlie appropriately. But you can't shut down all of her ideas."

He really wanted to shut down her ideas.

He had a very bad feeling that Charlie was going to stir up a whole lot of things for him that he'd, so far, successfully kept under wraps since coming to Autre.

The job was straightforward. A little boring even. The otters were, by far, the most interesting animals he dealt with. And that was fine with him. He didn't need big, crazy ideas or anything "interesting" or challenging. Anymore. He needed basic, routine, unexciting. Like an addict needed to avoid their substance of choice, he needed to avoid situations that might get him worked up, passionate, and... fired.

"Right," Maddie agreed with Tori. "Obviously, Griffin and Charlie are the perfect people to work on this together."

Griffin felt a very strange mix of trepidation and excitement swirl through him. The excitement was obvious. Charlie Landry was someone that he would very much like to spend more time with. It would be torturous, of course, but she was like a bright light, and he was a moth.

The trepidation came from knowing that excitement always led to big disappointment. The universe had proven that to him over and over. Excitement was definitely cause for worry as well.

This girl was going to be big trouble for him. And he no longer had the great buffer of an ocean between them.

"For sure," Tori said. "With your experience working with animals on display, whatever you can bring to this project is far beyond anything I could do."

Tori was already moving toward the door of the clinic, and Griffin had the impression she was trying to escape before he could make a really good point about why he shouldn't be brought into this project. Or why the project was a bad idea.

"This is a Boys of the Bayou project," he said. "I shouldn't be involved in actually expanding the business. I'm not part of the Boys of the Bayou."

Maddie was also moving toward the door. She waved a hand as if his comment was unimportant. "Of course you're part of it. You're part of the family, Griffin. We know that you have our best interests at heart, and we're so glad to have you onboard."

Dammit. She had to pull out the *you're part of the family*, didn't she? Of course, anyone who spent more than about ten minutes with the Landry family was one of the family. He'd been living with Mitch for about six months. That had clinched it. But even though he now had a place of his own, he still ate most meals with the Landrys and, of course, worked with many of them. And whether they knew it or not, the idea of being accepted into a big, boisterous, loving family was hard to resist.

He'd tried. He had put up every wall that had worked in every other place to keep the Landrys out. But they'd gotten past all of his defenses.

He only had his brother in the world now, and Donovan was busy traveling the country as a wildlife rehabilitation expert. They'd had some rocky times for sure, but they were good now, and he'd even go so far as to say they were friends. They didn't, however, live near one another or have regular meals or tease and fight good-naturedly the way the Landrys did.

Griffin liked all of that. Too much.

"And," Sawyer said, also taking steps toward the door, "we trust you implicitly. We know that you're going to do whatever you can to make the business successful, even while watching out for all of our animals, as well as our visitors." Sawyer shrugged his big shoulder. "Really, there's no one else who could do this job. Charlie can come up with a plan, and you'll be sure it's implemented perfectly."

He should object. He should tell them he wasn't going to do it.

But he wanted to do it.

He'd prefer that Charlotte Landry's sweet ass was still planted in some swanky café in Paris. But if she was going to be here and doing this, he wanted in on it. He wanted to be sure it was done right.

And she *was* going to do this. He'd seen the sparkle in her eyes. She was excited about this. The chances of talking her out of it were zero. He already knew that.

"Do you have a long mop?"

He turned at the sound of Charlie's voice. When he saw her, all thoughts left his mind except, *Shit, I really like her.*

Charlotte Landry, the most beautiful woman he'd ever seen, the woman that he still had very dirty dreams about even two months later, the woman whose mouth he could still feel and taste if he closed his eyes, now stood in front of him in short shorts, wearing rubber boots that went up to her knees, rubber gloves that went up to her elbows, and a facemask that covered her nose and mouth.

He couldn't help but grin. Kennel three seriously had been a mess. But Charlotte had headed in there without an argument and was cleaning it up. From the looks of her boots, she had waded right in.

Griffin glanced behind him to get the reactions of her cousins but found they'd already left. Cowards. They'd taken the chance to escape when he'd been distracted. He turned back to Charlotte.

And boy, was he distracted.

"All the cleaning supplies are in the closet across the hall."

"Great. I hope you've got plenty." Her voice sounded nasally.

"Is that mask pinching your nose?"

She lifted a hand and pulled her mask down. Her nostrils were plugged. By two tampons.

He stared. Huh. He knew that they sometimes used tampons to stem the flow from bloody noses. He supposed the tampons would also keep smells out.

Creative. He would absolutely have to add creative to the list of adjectives he used to describe Charlie. He hadn't realized that he had a specific list, but looking at her now, he realized he absolutely did.

Funny, intelligent, sexy as hell, a little manipulative, willing to hold a goat in an eight-hundred-dollar cocktail dress—yes, he realized that was more than one-word—and now creative.

He watched as she turned on the heel of her rubber boots and headed back down the hall.

That view made him think that having her around the clinic might not be so bad.

Or *really* bad. Actually terrible.

Because she was untouchable.

He didn't actually think the Landrys would have a problem with him and Charlie having a fling. The family was passionate, slightly crazy, but all about pleasure and having fun. If they thought he and Charlotte were having a consensual let's-have-a-great-time affair while she was in town, none of them would have any issue with it.

He was the one who had an issue with it.

Charlie was more than just a gorgeous woman he wanted to do extremely dirty things to—even when she was wearing rubber boots. She was someone who made him laugh, could imagine himself talking to for long periods of time, and who, dammit, had him eager to work with some hedgehogs.

She was someone he could get attached to.

She was trouble.

He turned away from the hallway even though she'd already disappeared into the storage room.

Speaking of creative... His eyes landed on the papers that she had been showing Maddie and Sawyer and Tori. This was her big marketing plan for Boys of the Bayou.

Curious in spite of himself, Griffin stepped forward and flipped through a few pages.

It only took him five pages to realize that he *really* should shut this idea down.

Not because it was bad.

On the contrary, it was pretty great.

And if she pulled it off, he would have even more animals to care about, and he'd be even more attached to this business, and this town, and this family.

He didn't want the petting zoo to be great. He didn't want to be crazy about the otters. He was already attached to the animals that were here, and if they added more, it would make it even harder in the end.

It would be even more for him to be protective of and for him to worry about. And for him to potentially get fired over.

Charlotte Landry was such a bad idea for him.

But she was now his assistant. And he had a surgery to do.

Dammit.

Of course, Charlotte Landry was seemingly good at everything she did.

Herding goats, blowjobs, turning his professional life upside down, and assisting in surgery.

She took a selfie with Brownie—who licked her cheek as she snuggled her face in next to his—to text to Michael and Andre with the caption, "Best dog kisses ever."

Then she took every direction Griffin gave her to get the surgical area and the puppy prepped. She was calm and sweet with the dog, petting him and talking to him softly as Griffin administered the anesthesia. As they performed the procedure, she wasn't a bit squeamish. Her hands were steady and confident. She followed his instructions to a T.

She also somehow looked sexy in the scrubs he gave her to wear. She smelled amazing. He didn't mind at all having to stand close to her and press against her as she positioned the dog for him.

But she would not. Stop. Talking.

She listened to his instructions and did what he needed her

to do, but in between his directions, she talked. And talked. And talked.

"I had no idea otters could get to be *sixty* pounds," she said, turning Brownie ten degrees to the right. "There are even some up around Alaska that can get to be 100 pounds. And they have the densest fur in the entire animal kingdom. They have like a million hairs per square inch."

Her tone made it clear that she thought this was absolutely an amazing fact.

"I know," Griffin replied, feeling that she was waiting for a response. He didn't have much else to add to that, however.

"And I had no idea they almost never come on land. They spend most of their time in the water."

Griffin shook his head as he began stitching Brownie back up.

"The funniest thing I saw was some baby otters bobbing up and down in the water like little corks." Charlie laughed. "They were wrapped in kelp to keep them safe while the mom was off hunting. They were adorable."

"Charlie?" Griffin asked as he bent close and placed the stitches. "You spent time researching otters?"

"Of course."

"Why?"

"Because I always research my projects before I start them."

"And the otters are your new project?" Griffin asked.

"Well, they are part of my new project."

Griffin finished the stitches, and Charlie handed him gauze and a bandage.

"But you must find otters interesting," she said.

"Why do you say that?" He wrapped the gauze around the dog's leg, securing it with the bandage.

"You work with them every day."

"The otters belong to the business that has contracted me

for my veterinary services. I work with the otters because they're here."

"But you do like them, right?" Charlie asked. "And you know a lot about them."

Griffin braced his hands on the edge of the table next to the still-asleep dog. He did like the otters. But that didn't matter.

"What do you want?" he asked.

"What do you mean?"

"You're getting ready to ask me for something. What is it?"

She looked surprised. "How can you tell I'm getting ready to ask you for something?"

"You've been asking me for things since you got here."

There was a flicker in her eyes, and he couldn't tell if it was amusement or heat or a combination of the two. "Are we talking about since I got back this time? Or the last time I was here? Because yes, there were some things I wanted from you last time for sure."

This woman was dangerous. He needed to remember that she was quick and bright and was never going to let him get away with anything.

"The things you asked me for last time were a lot more fun than the ones you want now."

"What if I told you I want some of those things this time too?"

He shook his head. "Not possible."

"You're not really my boss, you know," she said. "I'm really working for Boys of the Bayou and helping you out on the side. No one's going to hold it against you if something happens between us."

"I'm going to hold it against me."

"Why?"

"Because I like things simple, Charlotte. And you are anything but."

She didn't seem offended by that. In fact, he almost suspected she took that as a compliment.

"So, the last time I was here, it happened because I was leaving, and there was no chance for it to get complicated?"

"Yes."

"Would it make a difference if I told you that I was leaving again this time too? I'll be here a little longer this time, but I'm not staying."

He studied her across the table. It should make a difference. It should make him happy to think she wasn't staying. Not only because he wouldn't have to spend years of his life resisting her, but because the havoc she was wreaking on his professional life would end, hopefully, at some point. But for some reason, the idea of her leaving made him even more convinced that nothing should happen between them.

Charlotte Landry was definitely the type of woman to break a guy's heart. She was blowing in like a hurricane, and everyone knew that even after a minor storm, there was cleanup to do.

He felt as if he'd been doing cleanup in the aftermath of storms in his life for years. He'd settled in Autre, in part, because he thought chaos couldn't find him here.

Then Charlotte Landry showed up.

"No, that wouldn't make a difference."

Charlie blew out a breath. "I grew up around Cajuns, but you are possibly the most stubborn man I've ever met."

"You grew up around people who never told you no," Griffin said. He shouldn't have been surprised to find that he was fighting a smile. This woman had that effect on him. It had been stronger last time before she was here messing with his job, but even now, he found himself amused, and he had to admit that watching her brainstorm earlier about turning the petting zoo into a jungle tour had been fascinating. A little over-the-top. But fascinating.

She nodded. "You're right about that."

"So, you just see me as a challenge," Griffin told her. "But having a man around who's not wrapped around your little finger could be good for you."

Her smile grew, and Griffin felt a definite *uh-oh* in response.

"You think you can be good for me, Griffin?"

With that tone of voice and the look in her eye, he had all kinds of ideas about how good he could be for her. But those were exactly the reasons that she was bad for him.

"I think that I could be good for you in a number of ways," he said. "For instance, I can teach you the difference between sea otters and river otters."

"Really? I don't have every one of those facts exactly right?"

He knew instantly that she already knew that she'd been sharing facts about sea otters rather than river otters, like the ones the Boys of the Bayou had on display.

"What do you want that has to do with otters, Charlie?"

"What do you mean?"

"While it's not impossible for me to believe that you were talking about sea otters while I operated simply because you cannot stand silence," Griffin told her, "I think there's a better chance that you were doing it for a purpose. You knew that I would know the difference."

"It's hot that you're figuring me out."

Desire hit him hard in the gut. The woman was not only bright and surprising and entertaining, she was also very blatant about her attraction to him.

He wasn't used to people being quite so straightforward. In fact, most of the people he'd dealt with prior to coming to Autre had been focused on being political and always saying things in just the right way. But the Landry family was different. You knew exactly where they all stood on nearly every topic, they always said what they meant, and most importantly, they meant what they said.

Charlie was absolutely a Landry in all those ways. And now,

he wanted her more than he wanted any woman in as long as he could remember. So having her constantly putting their attraction out there between them made it impossible to ignore.

"You're not really that hard to figure out," he said, refusing to comment on how hot it was.

"Yeah, ditto."

Strangely, he played the political game rather well when he wanted to. He'd bitten his tongue and smiled through frustration more times than he could count. But maybe some of the Landry ballsiness was rubbing off.

No, it wasn't the boldness he appreciated. It was the lack of filter he enjoyed about the Landrys. It seemed that his filter had been slowly dissolving over the past few months in Louisiana.

"Then you must have figured out that I'm not interested in a fling."

"Actually, I think it's that you're not interested in a fling with *me*," Charlie said, tipping her head. "It seems that maybe flings are exactly how you like to do things. They're much more superficial and—what was the word you used?—simple."

He recovered quickly, but she'd caught him off guard. She *had* figured him out. Maybe it wasn't hard to tell that he was more of a fling guy now, but they hadn't known each other long. How was she reading him this well?

Maybe she'd talked to her cousins. The guys here had made a note of the fact that Griffin wasn't looking for anything serious. Maddie and Juliet, Sawyer's wife, had tried to set him up a couple of times, but he'd rebuffed every one of their efforts, and they'd now given up.

However, he'd lived with Mitch for several months and hung out regularly with the younger, single Landry boys, including Fletcher, Zeke, and Zander. They were the ones who introduced him to women who wanted nothing more than a fun, physical encounter.

It didn't surprise him that they would have shared that fact with the rest of the family. The Landrys had no secrets as far as he could tell, and apparently, that extended to the people they adopted into the family.

Yes, he was one of those people. Once they brought you into their fold, it was impossible to truly want to escape. He told himself regularly that he wanted to escape, or at least avoid getting any closer to any of them. But in his less resolute moments, like when he'd had a couple of shots of Leo's moonshine, or when he was alone in the otter encounter and was spilling his guts to his—thankfully—nonverbal friends, he would admit that he loved the Landry family and enjoyed all the time he spent with them.

So, maybe someone had shared his determinedly single status with Charlie.

But no, he realized a moment later. That was impossible. She had been surprised to find out that he was the veterinarian here. If she'd talked to any of her family members about him and used his name, that would've come up. He had to assume that she hadn't asked anyone about him after the weddings.

Good. That was good. He didn't want her interested in him any more than he wanted to be interested in her. Because already today he'd seen what could happen when Charlie got interested in something.

She was going to turn their tiny barnyard into a full-scale petting zoo. She wanted to put in a concession stand, for fuck's sake. He could only imagine what would happen if she decided to pursue a man she was interested in.

"Yes, I am much more into simple and superficial," Griffin finally answered.

"I can be simple and superficial." Charlie gave him a little smile that he found, in spite of himself, adorable. Nothing about this woman was simple.

"I'm not interested, Charlie," Griffin said, telling the biggest lie of his life. "I hope that doesn't affect us being able to work together."

She studied him for a long moment, then nodded. "Actually, I think that makes it even more important that we work together."

More important? He wondered what she meant by that but quickly squelched the curiosity. He didn't need to pursue anything with Charlotte Landry, even a conversation, at the moment.

She ran her hand over Brownie's still form. "I think it's fascinating that baby otters can swim as soon as they're born."

"They can't, actually. They're born with fur that keeps them from sinking, and they can bob along in the water," Griffin said. "But they have to learn to swim. The mothers teach them. Just like human parents teach their kids."

Charlie gave him a bright smile that hit him right in the chest. "That is a great fact."

He narrowed his eyes. Damn. She'd pulled him right in. One seemingly off-hand comment—incorrect comment, by the way—about an animal, and he engaged.

She had figured him out all right.

"What do you want, Charlie?" he repeated.

"If we're talking about the otters specifically, there is one thing." She paused. "Okay, two things."

"We are talking about otters. Or at least we're talking about anything *except* you wanting to have a fling with me."

"For now."

"For good." He shook his head. "It's off the table, Charlie."

"So you're going to try to resist me?"

"With everything in me," he said with a nod. "I realize that that's a difficult concept for you."

"It really is," she agreed. "So much so that I'm not sure it's going to sink in."

He had to fight to keep from snorting. Her confidence and

audacity, while sure to be a huge headache for him, was amusing and, yes, attractive. "I'm sure if you give it enough time, you'll get used to it."

"Well, the thing about resisting something is that it means it's something that you want."

"I never said I didn't want you." And that was exactly the wrong thing to say.

She clearly really liked that answer. "True. You said you weren't interested in a fling."

"Correct."

"So you want to be my boyfriend?"

He most definitely did not want to be her boyfriend. "No."

"So what do you want to be?"

"Your boss."

"That's it?"

"Yes."

"Too bad. Just my boss isn't an option."

"No? And why is that?" And when was he going to learn to quit engaging in these conversations with this woman?

"Because we're already more than that," she said. She waited just a beat.

Which was enough time for him to recall all of the things they had done that bosses and employees *really* shouldn't do to one another.

"We're friends," she told him.

They were? But of all the labels they could put on this... thing... between them, he supposed that was the safest.

"Okay," he agreed. "We'll be friends."

"Great." She looked pleased. "And now that we're friends, I need a favor."

She wouldn't actually ask for sex as a favor between friends, would she?

And if she did, he would most certainly say no, wouldn't he?

"I'm not really into baking cookies, and I'm pretty bad at

painting fingernails, and I'm absolutely certain I would be a terrible wingman if you're going to pick someone else up."

She laughed. And the sound made heat streak through his gut.

"You think that women friends get together and bake cookies and paint each other's fingernails?"

"I haven't given it a lot of thought," he said. "I'm just telling you what I won't be good at."

"Those are the only things you're not good at?"

There were all kinds of innuendos dripping off those words. Which he resolutely ignored. Mostly.

"And making snow cones or whatever you have in mind for this concession stand," he added.

Her eyes widened. "How did you know I was thinking about snow cones?"

"Well, it's a concession stand. And it's summer. Why wouldn't you have snow cones?"

She was grinning as she nodded. "Exactly." She tipped her head. "But why would you be a bad wingman if we went out, and I was looking for someone who was into a short-term fling? Seems you could help me identify the assholes."

He snorted. He completely understood her it-takes-one-to-know-one insinuation. "Because I would never be able to tolerate another man touching you."

Right. Another thing he shouldn't have said out loud if her reaction was any indication.

Her brows arched nearly to her hairline, and her mouth dropped partially open. She stared at him for several seconds before saying, "Wow. That does not seem like you're not interested."

"I'm not interested in having a fling with you. I'm also not interested in making snow cones. And I'm not interested in watching other men hit on you. Simple."

She swallowed hard as she considered everything he just

said. "Then I guess that only leaves one other favor that I need you for."

Griffin told himself not to ask. Not to encourage her. Not to seem at all willing to help her with any of her crazy ideas.

But he didn't have to ask. This was Charlie. She clearly rarely had a thought that she didn't share out loud, just like a Landry.

"I need someone to help me put signs up at the otter enclosure."

Griffin shrugged. "Mitch does all of the construction and repairs to the enclosures and pens. I'm sure he can help you."

"Oh, I don't mean actually hanging the signs up. I mean deciding what to put on the signs."

"What kind of signs?"

"Otter facts. Trivia. Interesting things about the otters."

"Facts about *river* otters?" he asked.

She nodded. "Of course."

"Of course," he repeated dryly.

"Will you help me?"

"You think we need signs with otter facts on them at the enclosure?"

"I do."

"Fine. If you write out the facts, I will review them and add anything I think is important."

She nodded. "And..."

He sighed. He should've known there was more to it. He knew there was always going to be "more to it" with Charlotte.

"I need you to repeat these facts. And more. Out loud. On Friday."

"No."

"Oh, come on, Griffin. Doesn't that word ever get old? We have a group of kids visiting the enclosure on Friday to learn all about otters. It would be so amazing to have *the* veterinarian who works with them on a regular basis there to give the kids the information and answer any questions they have."

"I wasn't aware there was a group of kids coming to visit on Friday."

"That's because you're the first person I've told."

"So how did *you* find out there was a group of kids that wanted to learn about otters?"

"I would think *any* kid would want to learn about otters."

"Is there actually a group coming Friday?" Griffin asked.

"Sure there is. As soon as I invite them."

Griffin shook his head. "So there *might* be a group of kids coming to visit on Friday."

"Oh, there will be kids here," Charlie said. "I just haven't gotten the word out yet."

"And you're so sure it will work?"

"Griffin, there is something that you should know about me," Charlie said.

He braced himself.

"I always make things work."

Yeah, that didn't surprise him. That was a lot like if she'd said, "I always get my way." Not at all hard to believe.

She was tempting as hell. She wanted him. They already had a scorching hot encounter that had been fueling dirty dreams for him for weeks. And now she was here, to stay for a while, but not permanently.

That should all be pointing a huge flashing neon sign to *take her up on this*. Instead, he suddenly needed to get some space from her. Quickly.

"I need to go do some calls. Outside of the building. For the rest of the day."

She looked like she didn't believe a word of that. "Okay. Just tell me what to do with Brownie. And if I can text an update to Andre."

He checked the dog over, and they got him settled in one of the kennels where he would wake up slowly.

Charlie sent Michael an update with a little video using a filter that made her look like a dog. She sang the first line to Elvis's "Hound Dog" before she cut herself off laughing and telling Andre that she didn't know any other songs that had dogs in them but that she'd just realized this song wasn't really appropriate. Then she told him everything had gone well and that Brownie was resting, and they would text another update later.

As soon as he was sure that the dog and Charlie would be fine without him, Griffin got the hell out of the clinic. And away from the most intriguing woman he had maybe ever met. Before he backed her up to the examination table in room two.

But not before he wished he had a copy of that video to watch a few more times.

Dammit. She really was delightful.

9

"Yeah, yeah, she's everything I remember. And more."

The two otters took the chance to give their opinion. They chattered to him for a good two minutes. Unfortunately, when they were finished, Griffin still felt completely mixed up about Charlie.

"She's been here for one day. One. Day. And already I'm feeling pressured. And annoyed."

Gus, the adult male otter, and father to four of the other otters, climbed into Griffin's lap. He told Griffin he was being ridiculous and then pawed at the pocket on Griffin's shirt. Griffin gave him a couple of treats and then stroked his hand from the animal's head to tail.

He did love these guys. He hadn't intended to. He'd come to join Tori in the practice believing that he would see mostly cows, horses, cats, and dogs. But the otters had already been a part of the Landry family, and it had only taken them about a day to win him over.

The otters weren't the best listeners though. In fact, they hardly ever shut up long enough to hear someone else speak. But they followed him around, excitedly noisy whenever they saw him. He was like an otter celebrity. They thought he was great, even when he didn't bring them treats. They were easy to make happy.

And all of that reminded him of Charlie.

Griffin rolled his eyes and shoved a hand through his hair. "I'm never going to be able to *not* think about her, am I?" he asked Gus.

Gus wasn't sure, but he thought another treat might help him form an opinion.

Griffin handed it over.

"She comes off as this woman who is used to everyone just nodding and saying, "Yes, ma'am." Griffin actually gave a short chuckle. "She even admitted she always gets her way. But..." He thought about her in those knee-high rubber boots and then the scrubs, not only taking direction but doing a damn good job. The kennel had been clean, and the room even smelled good when she was done. "She doesn't hesitate to jump in and get things done. She's pushy as hell, but she does listen."

At least, kind of. When he'd expressed concern about how people would be interacting with the animals, she'd listened. That was really fucking nice.

He knew what he was talking about. He had more knowledge and experience in human-animal interactions than she did. He was overly protective sometimes, but it was with all the right intentions. She seemed to realize that. Even if the "no's" weren't what she wanted to hear, she respected his expertise.

That was *really* fucking nice. He'd butted heads so many times with so many people who didn't respect his experience and training. It had led to him getting fired twice.

Well, that was the underlying reason. The real reason he'd been fired and not just had a stern talking to was that he let his passion and protectiveness override the *you shouldn't call him a selfish bastard* thought at the back of his mind, and *don't grab the mega-donor's wife by the arm and march her out of the tiger exhibit in front of everyone* warning his brain had tried to give him.

It also seemed easy to make Charlie happy.

Yes, physically. He couldn't *not* think about that when he thought about giving her things she wanted. She'd been very upfront and vocal about what she liked when he'd been kissing and touching her. And yes, that was a huge turn-on.

But it seemed easy enough to make her happy otherwise as well.

And damn it, he wanted to.

She wanted him to talk about otters to little kids. How hard could that be? She also wanted his help coming up with otter facts to put up at the enclosure. He could do that.

He looked around. The enclosure was impressive. Mitch Landry had designed it and built it with the help of his cousins Fletcher and Zeke. It included rocks and logs and branches that gave the otters plenty of things to climb on and play with. There was also a long, winding river and two swimming pools for the otters to splash and swim in. The river even had a riverbank made with dirt, mud, and grasses taken from the actual river just a couple of miles away. The otters slipped and slid on it and had built a den in the bank just as they would have in the wild.

The enclosure had been designed to look and function very much like a real otter environment, but it was surrounded by a tall see-through wall that allowed human visitors to observe the otters while keeping the animals protected.

There was also a rise up behind the otter river with a flat grassy area where Mitch's girlfriend, Paige, did otter yoga with local women three times a week.

Charlie was going to love that. He wasn't sure if she already knew about it, but she would absolutely want to advertise that and push for more classes. Not that Paige would mind. She was a firecracker on her own and might just stand toe-to-toe with

Charlie if she didn't want to do it, but... why wouldn't she want to do it?

Charlie wasn't really asking for anything *that* crazy.

She wanted to do things that would make the place more fun and more appealing to more people. Which would, in turn, make it more profitable for her family.

A few hedgehogs, some snow cones, collectible stickers.

Those weren't big things overall.

He should probably cool it a little.

But it wasn't the snow cones he was worried about. It was how much more likable she was. Already. Watching her brainstorm and muck out a dog kennel had made him like her even more.

A couple of weeks with hedgehogs and kettle corn—because, of course, they'd have kettle corn too, right? What was a good concession stand without kettle corn? He might have to suggest that...

Yeah, he was totally screwed.

Griffin gave Gertie, the adult female otter, a stroke as she climbed over his lap. Gertie was Gus's girlfriend, and they were hoping that she would be having pups again soon to add to the brood they were already raising that was getting more independent.

"I'm thinking about kettle corn, Gert," Griffin said. "She's got me thinking about kettle corn."

Gertie squeaked her approval.

"Yeah, yeah," he said, petting her again. "This woman is going to have a merry-go-round and Ferris wheel in a month. I'd put money on it."

"There's the troublemaker."

"Zander!" Charlie exclaimed as she entered the front part of Ellie's bar, through the kitchen, five days after arriving in Autre.

She'd just pilfered some shrimp and grits from the stove for the third time since arriving in Autre and was heading in to join the family for dinner for the fifth time. There was rarely a time in Ellie's bar when there weren't at least three Landrys in attendance. Most nights saw a good portion of the family come together for dinner, though there were so many of them it was hard to get them *all* together at once.

"I can't believe I've been here for five days, and this is the first time I've seen you!" she told her cousin.

Zander caught her up in a big bear hug, squeezing her tightly. But when he set her back on her feet and looked down at her, he shook his head.

"Why is it that you Landry girls are almost more trouble than the boys?"

She laughed. "Considering you're one of the boys, you should know the answer to that."

"It's because you look and talk like a sweetheart, right? You fool everybody into thinking that you're a lot better behaved than you really are."

She leaned in and lowered her voice to a whisper. "Exactly."

"Sweetheart" was not a word most people used to describe any of the Landry boys. Well, maybe Mitch. Possibly Josh. But that was definitely it. The rest of the Landry boys were a lot of things—charming, intelligent, hard-workers, smart asses, good looking, and always up for a good time—but very few of them were *sweet*.

Zander laughed. "So you're profiling me based on my long hair and tattoos and liking motorcycles?"

"I'm profiling you based on your past bad behavior and the fact that you cuss like a sailor."

"All you girls cuss like sailors and have *plenty* of bad behavior."

She nodded. That was actually one of her favorite things about being in Autre and always had been. "But we're better at hiding it."

He wasn't buying that. "I never witnessed much hiding when it came to you staying out late, sneaking bottles of whiskey from behind Grandma's bar, and making out with guys down by the bayou."

"Well, I didn't hide it from *you*." She grinned at him. "Of course, now I probably should since you're a cop."

One of the family's favorite things was that Alexander, one of the wildest of the Landry bunch, had become a law enforcement officer. He'd worked in New Orleans, first as a cop right out of the academy, then moved up to detective three years later. But when the local sheriff, George, had retired, Zander was first in line to run for the position. He'd won easily.

"I wouldn't worry too much about *this* cop," Zeke, his twin brother, said as he came to join them. "He's way more into fishing and gossiping than breaking up parties or arresting anyone." Zeke's long hair was pulled back in a bun, while Zander's was loose, but it was easy to tell the two apart.

Zeke was the more mischievous one, who loved to joke and tease, and had a quick grin. Zander was more laid back. The older of the twins by three minutes, he was definitely a lot of fun, but he was quieter of the two. They both had long hair and tattoos, but Zeke had more ink and had piercings in both ears. And possibly other places Charlie didn't know about. They also both rode motorcycles, and loved to party. Zeke did construction around the area. And accounting. Which the family found hilarious. He was the least math-geek looking guy any of them had ever met. But he was a whiz with numbers and he loved it.

"I never got arrested," Charlie pointed out.

"Because George figured there was no way such a *sweetheart* would have been trespassing or drinking underage," Zander said.

Zander had a point.

"But gossiping?" Charlie asked with a grin. Gossiping was a favorite pastime of most people in Autre and especially her family, but Zeke's comment had her picturing Zander sitting around with the old men at the end of the bar trading fishing tales and talking about the latest couple to have a big fight at the grocery store.

"Hey, I've been in New Orleans for the past three days helping a cop buddy, if you must know," Zander said.

"See, that's a perfect story because we can't check it," Zeke said.

"You don't need to be checking my stories," Zander told him.

Charlie didn't believe for a second that Zander had any stories that Zeke didn't already know. She doubted he had many stories that didn't *involve* Zeke, in fact. They were identical twins and had been inseparable for as long as she'd known them.

"So you're saying that you didn't stop into Trahan's Tavern, and you didn't meet up with any hot brunettes?" Zeke asked with a knowing grin.

"Well, the stop at Trahan's might've been about the case. Undercover work requires a lot of different activities."

Zeke nodded. "Undercover work."

Zander shoved him. "Yeah, undercover work. Don't be an asshole."

"The ship has sailed on me not being an asshole," Zeke said.

Charlie laughed. They could go on like this all night. "And

why have I only seen *you* once since I've been back?" she told Zeke.

"I've been working over in Bad. Remodeling the coffee shop."

"Bad?" Charlie asked. "I didn't realize that you guys did anything *helpful* or *productive* over there."

Zeke nodded. "Sure. I'll do just about anything if the person is willing to pay enough."

"But it's *Bad*," Charlie said. The town about twenty miles up the bayou was Autre's biggest rival. And that extended to everything from high school football to actual business rivalries.

Charlie had always found Bad to be a fun town. The guys—known as the Bad Boys—certainly had been. Probably still were.

The name had come from a very short-lived settlement of Germans who had named the town something much longer and harder to pronounce. When they had been run out by the French settlers, they shortened the name to the first three letters only. B-A-D. Since then, the town had shown its sense of humor by leaning into the name.

All of the businesses in town had "bad" in their names. There was the Bad Egg, the town's café. Bad Hair Days, the salon. The medical clinic was even called Bad Medicine. Charlie found it quirky and funny.

The guys from Bad also leaned into the name, and their reputations showed it.

Charlie had spent some time in the truck beds of a few Bad boys down by the river. They were definitely not the type of boys she'd bring home to her mom and dad, but they were sure fun to spend time with when it involved bonfires, loud country music, and moonshine.

The fact that Zeke, Zander, Fletcher, and even Mitch, at times, hung out with the Bad boys said a lot about her cousins' reputations as well.

Zander's familiarity with the jail cell in Autre hadn't started when he started wearing a badge. Zeke and Fletcher had similarly had experiences that made people wonder just how far that city limit of Bad, Louisiana, actually extended.

"Well, you're at least charging them double, I hope," Charlie said.

"I think the sweet, bubbly coffee shop owner might be a perk that makes that drive up the bayou a little easier," Zander said.

Charlie looked at Zeke, waiting for a reaction. He just shrugged.

She laughed. "Actually, there were a couple of Bad girls..." She hesitated. The girls from Bad were known as Bad girls, but they didn't live up to the name quite the way the boys did. Still, she knew some of the girls who had come to the parties down by the water were just as much fun as the guys—"came over for otter yoga the other day, and I'm pretty sure a couple of the moms in the crowd for the otter talk were from Bad."

"Is this the otter talk that Fletcher did?" Zeke asked.

Charlie nodded. "He was great."

"'Course I was." Fletcher joined them. He was really at the bar for a refill on his beer, but he'd overheard his name.

"Oh yeah, really impressive to have a fan club full of five-year-olds and married women," Zander said.

Fletcher leaned an elbow on the bar and looked at his younger brothers. "It is a truth universally acknowledged that a man who is good with little kids and animals can have his pick of women. And those kids don't have to be that woman's."

Charlie wasn't surprised by Fletcher's adaptation of the first line of *Pride and Prejudice*. He was a teacher. He actually taught third grade at Autre Community School. And it was no secret that he was the most popular teacher at the school. Not only was he amazing with his third-graders, but the parents all loved him. It was true that many of the moms found him good-looking—he also wore his hair on the longer side and had a few tattoos—charming, and were attracted to how great he was with their kids, but the dads liked him just as much.

Fletcher becoming a teacher was as funny as Zander becoming a cop. But they were both very good at their jobs. And when Griffin had turned her down for doing the educational talk at the otter enclosure today, she immediately thought of Fletcher as a fill-in. It'd been a great call. There had been a bigger crowd than she expected, and several of the moms had been downright gushy about his presentation.

"So you're telling me that you being sweet to some other lady's kid makes you more attractive to everyone else?" Zeke asked.

Fletcher looked at Charlie, one eyebrow up. "Charlie?"

She nodded without hesitation. "Absolutely. There's just something about a man and little kids."

Even Griffin.

She took a moment to look around the room, wondering if he was here. He'd been avoiding her for five days. They worked together, of course. She saw him at the clinic. But he seemed to have a lot of calls outside of the clinic, and when he was in the office, they were busy with clients and animals. So they hadn't had more than a few minutes alone, and whenever she got too close, he immediately widened the distance between them.

She found it amusing, if not frustrating. She liked the idea that if he was going to try to resist her, it would take an actual conscious effort and physical distance for him to do so.

Her gaze landed on where he was sitting at the bar. He was a few stools down and was bent over his plate of food, clearly trying to ignore everything going on around him.

She'd missed him.

The thought surprised her. She'd seen him every day. They'd spoken several times over the past few days. But she missed actually *talking* to him. And definitely flirting with him. And absolutely kissing him.

She hadn't kissed him since she'd been back, and that felt like a travesty every time she thought about it.

He didn't want things to be complicated. She understood that. She agreed with it. But she liked him, she was attracted to him, and vice versa. Yes, she thought he even actually liked her. In spite of the fact, she was kind of a pain in his ass.

"Well, speaking of people doing crazy things," Zander said. "I need to hear the story about how you got fired, Charlie."

She focused on her cousins again. "Were we talking about people doing crazy things? I thought we were talking about Zeke remodeling a coffee shop and Fletcher being adorable with little kids. And having several not-so-secret secret admirers."

Zander nodded. "Those are both crazy. Zeke is making a 'quaint little coffee shop' out of some old rundown building in Bad. And Fletcher is being adorable with kids. Who would've thought?"

Charlie nodded and gave a little shrug. "You've got a point."

"Yeah, but Charlie fucking up some guy's Porsche and getting fired isn't really that crazy," Zeke said with a grin.

Fletcher nodded. "True. But I think we need to hear about *why* she did it. That might be the crazy part."

"I'll tell you the whole story," Charlie said. It was amusing that her cousins on this side of the family considered her a crazy, fun bayou girl. That was completely the opposite of who she was in Shreveport. Or really anywhere that didn't have swamp water running past it. She was sophisticated, classy, well mannered, and composed everywhere else. Autre brought out another side of her. But she loved the free feeling and being unfiltered, and that she had people who would love, respect, and back her up no matter what she did.

"Hang on now," Fletcher said. He turned to the bar. "Hey, Ellie," he called to their grandmother.

Ellie Landry had always been known to her grandkids as Ellie rather than Grandma or Maw-Maw or any other grandmotherly nicknames. Some people thought that was strange, but it was just how it had always been here.

"Charlie is about to tell us why she trashed that poor guy's Porsche," Fletcher said. "You need to come over and see if you win."

"Win? What's she win?" Charlie asked.

Fletcher laughed. "The family's got bets on what made you go after that guy. But we should all hear it at once to see who wins. Cash money, of course."

Charlie shook her head. She should have known that she had to share this story at some point, and it didn't shock her at all that her family was making a game of it. She was curious, though, about what reasons they'd all guessed for her outburst against Alan.

She looked at her grandmother as Ellie joined them at the end of the bar and passed over beers to all of them.

"You put money down on what you think I did too?"

Ellie nodded. "Absolutely. Winning twenty bucks off any of these yahoos always makes my day better."

Charlie wouldn't be surprised to find out that Ellie winning bets with her grandkids happened a lot.

"You don't know you're going to win," Zander told her. "We all know Charlie pretty well too."

Ellie looked at Charlie. "Maybe. Guess we'll see."

Charlie knew that Ellie would definitely have the closest guess. She may not have nailed all of the details of what would lead Charlie to deface an expensive sports car, but she would get pretty close.

That was partly because, despite not living in Autre full-time growing up, Charlie was a lot like her grandmother.

She'd been told so over and over again, but as she'd gotten to know Ellie as an adult, she understood what people meant by that.

Ellie was fiercely loyal and protective of the people and things that mattered to her. But she was also incredibly insightful and nearly magical when it came to reading people. She always had something to say and said it as bluntly and loudly as anyone else. But she was also an observer. She knew things about her family, especially her grandchildren, that they didn't even know.

That was how she and Charlie were alike. Passionate and insightful. Charlie considered it the highest compliment that she was like her grandmother.

"Well, come on then," Zeke said, grabbing Charlie's hand and pulling her toward the big, long tables that sat at the back of the bar where the family gathered.

"Hey, Leo!" Fletcher called to their grandfather, who was sitting at the opposite end of the bar talking, as always, to the group of men gathered there. "Charlie's going to tell us her story!"

Leo grinned and immediately got up off his stool. "I'm coming. Could use twenty bucks."

Charlie laughed. She loved her grandfather. He was outspoken, funny, and absolutely rough around the edges, but she'd never met a more loving soul in her life.

However, there was no way Leo was going to guess what had happened in Paris. Leo thought all of his granddaughters were perfect angels. She was pretty sure deep down he knew they got into plenty of trouble, and he'd heard all of them cuss, and he'd seen each of them drunk at least once, but he always blamed the boys for being bad influences.

Which wasn't entirely untrue.

Well, except with Kennedy. Kennedy, Josh and Sawyer's younger sister, and the girl who'd spent the most time on the bayou was a spitfire, and everyone knew she was an instigator. But she was Leo's very obvious favorite.

Leo was definitely one of the people Zander had been talking about when he said that the girls got away with more than the boys. Leo could be won over and wrapped around a little finger of one of his granddaughters faster than anyone.

"Wait for me," one of Leo's friends said, scrambling off his stool as well. "I've got money down too."

Charlie looked at him with surprise. "Elias, you think you know what I did to get fired?"

"I got caught up in the moment when everyone was guessin' and bettin'," he said with a grin. "Happens a lot around here."

He had a point.

She tugged her hand free from Zeke's hold. "Well, don't you guys move. I'll just sit here in the middle."

She headed for the stool in the middle of the long wooden bar. It just so happened to be right next to Griffin. Coincidentally.

Okay, not so coincidentally.

He might want to avoid her, but she didn't want to make it easy on him.

She slid up onto the barstool and looked over at him. He'd stopped eating but was stubbornly not looking in her direction.

"Hey, boss."

He sighed. She grinned. He had been the one to make a point of her being his assistant—especially when it came to cleaning up dog vomit and various types of animal bodily fluids —but when she called him "boss," he always sighed.

"Charlotte," he greeted simply.

It was different seeing him here than it was at the clinic.

He was dressed in jeans and a t-shirt. A dark blue shirt that stretched over his muscled shoulders and arms enticingly. He wore jeans and t-shirts a lot when he went out on calls outside of the clinic, but she didn't really get a chance to ogle him in them. When he had somewhere to go—i.e., a great reason to get away from her—he was out the door almost too fast for her to get a good look at his ass in blue jeans.

Almost. She always made a point of watching him leave.

But when he was in the clinic, he was in scrubs. Which was also stupidly hot. They made him look so capable and in charge.

She liked this look now though.

He'd showered since she'd last seen him. His hair was still a little damp along his collar. But he hadn't shaved. He had more than a five o'clock shadow. That was serious scruff, and she loved it.

"How's the cow?" she asked. He'd left that afternoon to go visit a pregnant cow.

"Not pregnant anymore."

She smiled. "Everything went okay?"

"Yep. But no need to send a video of you with a cow nose and ears or anything," he said. "Clive doesn't have a cell phone."

She'd been sending the little update videos to patients for the past few days after Andre had said the one she'd sent him was *so cool*. After Brownie had been home for a couple of days, Michael had sent *her* a video showing the dog cuddled up on the couch with Andre watching cartoons. That had been one of the highlights of her week. So yes, the videos were now a permanent part of the care at Autre Animal Hospital.

She used filters to turn her into whatever animal they'd been caring for. She'd been a cat three times, a dog again, a rabbit, and a guinea pig. Which had led to her putting guinea pigs on her list of petting zoo additions.

Griffin had not only rolled his eyes, but he'd adamantly declined her invitation to be in the videos too. Still, all of the clients had commented positively on the videos, and one of the cat owners had said her daughter had wanted to bring Sally, the tabby, into their clinic *because* of the video Andre had shown her. And Charlie *knew* Griffin had loved that video of Andre and Brownie at home and that they were doing well.

In fact, right now, Charlie could *swear* the corner of Griffin's mouth was trying to tip up thinking about her becoming a cow for a video.

Even that tiny bit of reaction made her want more. A lot more.

At the clinic, he was all business, purely professional, and focused on his tasks and patients as he should be. She just really wanted to be on his mind.

"Okay, but I should definitely take a congratulations gift out there. Is the appropriate baby gift for a cow a bouquet of flowers or a cake?" she asked.

"She'd eat the flowers." He paused. "And maybe the cake too, which would be bad for her."

"Well, it wouldn't be a human cake," Charlie said as if that was obvious.

Finally, he turned his head to look at her. "What would you make a cow a cake out of?"

"I would think we could somehow mix grains and... alfalfa?" she guessed.

"You really would make her a cake, wouldn't you?"

She would. If it made him look at her with that hint of wonder. Okay, a lot of the look in his eyes was *you're-kind-of-cuckoo-you-know-that*? But there was a *hint* of wonder, and she liked that.

"Oh my God, it's a girl? I'll have to figure out how to make the grains pink."

"Food coloring could be bad for her."

"Could be? Don't you know?"

"I've honestly never had an occasion to worry. I've never known anyone who might make a cow a pink cake to celebrate her new calf."

"Huh. That's weird," she said, trying hard not to laugh. "I mean, it's rude, really."

He shook his head.

She smiled. She'd been doing some homework on the animals the clinic served. "I guess we can leave the pink coloring out. Maybe there are some pink flowers we could put on top."

"And when you say 'we,' you mean you."

God, she'd love to get Griffin doing something like that. That would be funny. And sweet. "You can totally help."

"I'm not making cakes for cows."

"Cupcakes? Like a mouthful. We could just do three or four." She didn't really mean any of this, of course. Though if she thought it was something their clients would like... and would talk to other people about... she'd do it.

But Griffin looked like he couldn't tell if she was being serious or not. And she liked to keep him guessing.

"I'm not making cupcakes. Or cookies. Or pie."

"Just for the cows?" Charlie asked. "Or for any animals? Or for any reason whatsoever?"

"Let's say for any reason whatsoever," Griffin said. "God knows what you might get me to do."

"Well, if I'm going to get *you* to do things *I* want, I don't think I would start with cow cookies. Or any cookies. Or even baking, for that matter."

That flash of heat, and then exasperation, that was becoming awfully familiar, flickered in his eyes. "Stop it."

"Because we're in my family's bar surrounded by a ton of people?"

"That's one good reason."

"How many good reasons are there?"

"Several."

She didn't agree. She didn't even really believe him. But they were in public with a lot of other people, and she was about to be the center of attention. She could let this go for now.

"Maybe you should hang out here more often," she told him, "if you think being around all of these people will make me behave."

He snorted at that, and Charlie felt her smile grow.

"I'm not sure you're entirely capable of behaving. And this particular group of people is definitely not one I would expect to be a good influence."

That was an accurate statement. Okay, those were maybe both accurate statements.

"Okay, let's hear it!" Owen called from the back.

He was one of the partners in Boys of the Bayou and married to Maddie. He'd certainly had his days as a hellion, though he settled down a lot since Maddie had come back to town. Then again, a couple of the best family stories included crazy stuff Maddie had done as well.

Charlie looked at the group and grinned. They all had money out, and Fletcher had his phone out.

"I've got everyone's bets right here," he said, holding the device up.

She really loved these people, and she loved the laid-back, take-it-as-it-comes, live-life-out-loud attitude that permeated this place.

Zeke and Zander and Fletcher had rejoined the group at the back of the bar and were lounging at the table with almost every one of her other cousins. Owen and Maddie were there, as were Sawyer and Juliet. Josh was there too, but Tori was missing, and because she now had access to the clinic schedule, Charlie assumed it was because she was feeling either a little sick or just tired from the pregnancy, since she didn't have any appointments scheduled for tonight. Tori and Griffin both got called out at strange hours for various animal needs.

Mitch and Paige were also there, and Charlie gave Paige a

big grin. She liked the newest addition to the family. Mitch and Paige weren't married yet, but it was very clear every time they looked at one another that they were headed in that direction. Mitch was definitely one of the nicer of her cousins when it came to teasing and hell-raising, but it seemed that when he fell in love, he fell as hard and as passionately as the rest of them.

She'd already chatted with Paige a couple of times because of the expanded otter yoga sessions and was looking forward to getting to know her better.

"Before I tell the story," she said to the group. "I want to hear what y'all think happened in Paris."

This should be entertaining.

Fletcher held up a finger indicating this was number one on the list. "He cheated on you."

Charlie wrinkled her nose. "Ew, no. We weren't dating. I'd never date that dickhead."

Four people groaned and tossed their twenty dollars into the middle of the table. Charlie laughed.

"I wouldn't have risked getting in trouble and having to pay for that paint job for a guy who cheated on me," she said. "Just being without me would have been punishment enough."

They all laughed, and Leo said, "That's my girl."

"Well, if you weren't dating, that knocks out him just breaking things off," Fletcher said.

Only one person tossed money into the middle of the table for that one. Charlie smiled at Juliet, Sawyer's new wife. The other woman was also fairly new to the family and didn't know Charlie very well.

Fletcher held up a second finger. "He ruined one of your projects and cost you a client."

Charlie shook her head. "Nope. He's the CEO's son and is the Vice President of Development. He has nothing to do with marketing."

"What does the Vice President of Development do?" Zeke asked.

Charlie shrugged. "Just means he's the CEO's son, she paid for a very expensive college degree, but no one will hire him because he's an asshole."

Three people tossed money into the middle of the table now.

Charlie laughed. "You think I would key a guy's Porsche because he stole a project from me? In that case, I would have just gone around him to the client and proved that my new idea, which he wouldn't know anything about, and was way better, and I would've stolen the client back."

Ellie gave her a big grin. "Keying a man's sports car is an act of passion. Stealing an account from you would have simply stoked your competitiveness. He did something that made you beyond angry."

Charlie nodded. "Exactly."

"So something that would make you enraged, but that had nothing to do with a personal relationship," Zander said.

Charlie was aware that Griffin was listening intently. He was done eating and had pushed his plate away. But his arms were folded, and his elbows were resting on the bar. He didn't look like he was in any kind of hurry to get out of here. Either he was highly entertained by her family, or he was actually interested in knowing more about her and what happened to lead her back to Autre. She liked the idea that he might want to know more about her.

"I'll give you a hint," Charlie said. "He did something to someone else."

Zeke and Zander both nodded as if that made total sense. Charlie cast a glance toward Griffin. He had turned to look at her.

"Someone guessed that he cheated on one of your friends," Fletcher read from his phone.

Charlie looked at Ellie. "That was your guess?"

Ellie nodded. "You're passionate about things you care about. Of course, that includes your work and projects. But nothing as much as the people in your life. If you are going to risk jail time for something, it will be on behalf of someone else."

Charlie liked that her grandmother knew her so well. She also liked Ellie's observation. She was a passionate person, but it was true that it took a lot to push her to the point of property damage.

"Well, that's as close as anyone's gotten," she admitted.

Ellie gave a little whoop and held out her hand toward Fletcher, who had gathered all the money from the middle of the table into a stack.

"Let's hear her story first," Fletcher said. "She said it's just close."

Ellie scoffed. "But nobody else is going to win it this way."

Fletcher sighed. She had a point. He handed the money over, and Ellie sat back in her chair with a big grin and started to count it up.

"I still want to hear the story," Zeke said.

"For sure," Zander agreed. "Did he call the cops on you?"

Charlie shook her head. "He wouldn't dare. He wouldn't have wanted to explain to them *why* I'd done it."

Zander scowled. "I want to hear the story, Charlie."

"Me too."

She looked to her right to find Griffin watching her closely. He looked concerned.

That made her stomach flip. The rest of the people in the bar were protective of her and would be appalled by this story when she told them. But something about having Griffin's concern made her feel warm. It wasn't that she thought he wasn't the type of guy to care about a woman having issues with a man that might involve the cops. But when their eyes met, she could see that his concern was personal. That might have seemed like a strange thing to be able to read in someone's expression, but that was how it felt.

"Alan, that's the guy with the Porsche, had asked one of our interns out a couple of times before I got to Paris," Charlie started. "She was a lovely girl, young, a little naïve. But she absolutely did not like Alan, and she had turned him down both times. She shared that with me one day at lunch when he had left her a message on her phone saying that he wanted to speak with her after work."

Charlie shifted on the barstool. She was facing the room with the bar behind her. She now pivoted so that she could rest her right elbow on the top of the bar. That also caused her to lean closer to Griffin. He didn't move back an inch. In fact, he seemed to lean in a little closer.

"She was nervous that he was going to pressure her to go out with him again and possibly use his position over her as leverage."

Zander's scowl deepened, and Ellie sat forward in her chair now.

"I told her I would go with her, but she turned me down. I insisted that I wait for her after the meeting though." Remembering that day and how Isabelle had looked stepping off the elevator after her "meeting" with Alan made anger tighten Charlie's chest even now.

"Turns out that he got on the elevator with her, stopped it, and physically assaulted her."

"What?" Zander growled. "Tell me he was bleeding when you saw him."

Charlie shook her head. "He didn't get off the elevator with her. He'd gotten off on the floor earlier. Or he definitely would've been bleeding." Charlie would have definitely gone after him. It might be a blessing that he had been a chicken shit and gotten off the elevator early, but she still felt the helplessness and rage.

"He'd backed Isabelle into the corner, and put his hands up her shirt. She told him no repeatedly, and he wouldn't stop. Her blouse was ripped, and she was shaking so hard when I saw her she almost couldn't walk."

Zander's hand came down hard on the table in front of him. The people around him jumped, but he was frowning at Charlie. "There was a camera in the elevator, right?"

"He'd turned it off."

Zander shook his head. "So it was premeditated."

Charlie nodded.

There were frowns and gasps throughout the room, which she appreciated. Of course, these people would think that was horrible. It *was* horrible.

"I walked her out to her car and tried to get her to let me take her home. She refused, but I decided to follow her. But on my way to my car, I saw his."

Everyone nodded at that, obviously figuring out that was when she pulled her keys out.

"Please tell me that is not all you did to that asshole," Zeke said.

Charlie took a deep breath and made herself smile. She tipped her head. "Gosh, what do you mean? You think he deserved more than just 'I have a tiny dick' scratched into the side of his most prized possession?"

"He would have been walking with a permanent limp if I'd been there," Zeke said.

"And never would've fathered children," Fletcher added.

Charlie glanced at Griffin. His jaw was tight, and his gaze locked on hers.

"What did you do, Charlie?" he asked. His voice was low enough that no one else could hear it. It was low and rumbly as if he was ignoring the rest of the room.

"You think I did something?"

"I do." He paused. "And I'll bet it was something he won't forget soon."

"You're figuring me out."

"It doesn't take long to figure out that you can handle whatever is thrown at you, and you do it perfectly."

10

She stared at him. She hadn't been expecting a compliment. She definitely took what he just said as a compliment. She knew that Griffin liked a few things about her. He certainly seemed to like kissing her. He definitely liked her mouth wrapped around his cock. And while he didn't like all of her ideas for the petting zoo, she thought he did kind of like her little update videos she sent to their clients and that she'd gotten Fletcher to fill in on the otter talk rather than continuing to press Griffin for it.

"I wrote down everything she told me and everything I witnessed about her after the incident. Then, the next day I got on the elevator with him, stopped it just the way he had with her, backed him up into the corner, and told him if he ever went near her again, I would sneak into his house and cut his dick off with a rusty knife. He stammered and stuttered and said that he hadn't meant to scare her or hurt her. Basically, I got a full confession out of him. And I had a recorder in my pocket. Which I gave to Isabelle to take to the cops."

"Well done, Charlie," Zander said. "That's amazing. I don't

love that you were stuck on an elevator with the scumbag by yourself, but you handled it. I hope he was arrested."

Charlie realized she'd been looking at Griffin the entire time she'd told that portion of the story. The intense blue of his eyes and swirling emotion there wouldn't allow her to look away.

"He was taken in for questioning," Charlie said. "But I'm not sure what else happened at that point. I was fired later that day because of the car."

"His dad fired you even after hearing what he'd done to the intern?" Zeke asked.

Finally, Charlie glanced at her cousins. "The CEO is his mom. And yes, she did. She, of course, wanted to believe that what happened with him and the intern had been a misunderstanding. But even if not, she said that my lack of impulse control was concerning."

Ellie snorted at that. "She was clearly already intimidated by your fire. You don't need people like that in your life, girl. You need to be surrounded by people who love your passion and encourage it."

Charlie caught her breath. That was something she'd been dealing with a lot of her life. She'd learned to manage her impulses to an extent and realized that a lot of the time, it was inappropriate to do and say exactly what she thought and felt. However, she very much appreciated her grandmother's stance. It would be so nice to have a job where she could just be herself and do what she was moved to do.

Surprisingly, the petting zoo had already given her a taste of that. Everyone was going along with her ideas and plans—even if they were hesitant or didn't want to be directly involved themselves. She cast another quick glance at Griffin. He was no longer watching her. His jaw was tight, and he was gripping his glass of iced tea tightly in his hand.

The petting zoo was small, and there wasn't much room for

growth, literally for the business but also for her as head of marketing. It would always involve things like new items for the concession stand and event planning around the holidays, and made-up reasons to do special activities to bring business in. It wasn't world-changing work, but it had definitely given her a taste for what it was like to be completely in charge of a creative vision.

That was what she wanted ultimately. A job where she could grow a company beyond its core business and make an impact on the community as well as the world at large. Of course, changing the world could take many forms, but she was comfortable with the idea that she could grow a company to the point of being socially influential or at least have enough assets and resources to assist with charities and nonprofit work.

And she'd only been here five days. If she could grow Boys of the Bayou Gone Wild while she was here, it would look good on her resume for her next step. The experience would also stay with her, and she would continue to look for positions where she could be influential not only to the company's bottom line but to their overall vision.

"Thank you, Ellie," she finally said. "I wish I could have done more."

Ellie shook her head. "Not only did you alert the authorities and give this guy an important warning, but you also showed the woman that someone had her back. Sometimes that's the most valuable thing of all."

Charlie nodded. It would've been nice for someone to have had her back when she was being fired. But now, looking around this room, she realized she had a whole troop of people who would take her side and back her up.

Ellie slapped the stack of bills against her other open palm and got to her feet. "I definitely won this money," she said. "I was the closest, for sure."

Leo laughed. "I'm not sure why any of us doubted that for a second."

Ellie patted his cheek as she passed him. "You're a wise one, my love."

It only took a few minutes for everyone to settle back into their usual routine. People started laughing, talking, and eating again.

Charlie was happy that everyone's attention had shifted off of her. Maybe now she and Griffin could talk more privately.

That was a sure sign she liked the guy more than usual. She never shied away from the spotlight.

But as she turned to face him more fully, she found him getting to his feet.

"You're leaving?"

"I have some early patients tomorrow. My assistant apparently sent out letters from Brownie the dog telling his 'friends' that they should come to see me at the clinic."

She grinned in spite of the fact that he was leaving. "That was actually your marketing manager that said that, and yes, I got Brownie's owner's permission to use his name."

Griffin didn't smile but again, like so many times before, she had the *impression* of him smiling.

"And I rest my case," Griffin said, pulling his wallet out and tossing money onto the bar to cover his food tab.

Charlie was certain that Ellie never made him pay and that he insisted on doing it anyway. She suspected that her grandmother found ways of sneaking the money back into his possession. Or, at the very least, she made donations in his name to various groups. She refused to take money from family and friends, and after living in Autre and working with her family for this long, Griffin would absolutely be considered both.

"Your case?"

"You're not capable of behaving, and this group is a bad influence."

Yeah, he was right.

She frowned. Was he bothered by the fact that she'd keyed Alan's car now that he'd heard the story? Or was he bothered by the way she'd confronted Alan in the elevator?

If he was bothered by either of those things, he could fuck off. She wasn't sorry about any of it. And she would much rather be surrounded by people like Ellie and the rest of her family who were supportive of her actions than worry about the uptight, too serious, overprotective veterinarian.

And it was completely stupid that she wished his protective tendencies would maybe extend to her.

But as much as he'd seemed to like her curves the one night he'd let her close, she clearly didn't have the right kind of tail to get his lasting affection.

"I'll see you tomorrow, Charlie," Griffin said, tucking his wallet back in his pocket.

She stubbornly ignored how much she liked watching the way his t-shirt pulled tight across his chest with the motion. "You sure will." Whether he liked it or not.

She frowned, watching him leave, thinking about the fact that maybe he really didn't like it. She was increasing the business and helping his schedule run well and cleaning up all of the gross stuff in the clinic, and he still didn't like having her there? Yeah, fuck him, for sure.

She also stubbornly ignored the tiny voice in the back of her head saying *yes, you'd really like to, wouldn't you?*

She slid off the barstool and headed for the tables where her cousins were sitting. Now that Griffin was gone, she had no desire to sit at the bar away from the group. She should've just sat at the back tables from the beginning. These people, at least, liked her.

She took a seat next to Paige and crossed her legs. She also crossed her arms. It might look like she was pouting, but dammit, she really wasn't used to people not liking her. Especially men she'd given a blowjob.

Yeah, she'd given him a blowjob. A really good one, at least judging by his reaction to it. She'd made him *smile* that night. If she remembered correctly, he might have even laughed.

So it was only when she was helpful to him professionally that he got annoyed.

No, it was also when she was standing up for another woman who had been put in a terrible situation.

If he didn't like that about her, then she didn't like him as much.

"Hey, Fletcher," Josh said, pointing to the TV that hung over the bar. "It's Jason Young. Your favorite musician."

Fletcher looked over to the TV, and Charlie followed his gaze.

"Don't care," Fletcher replied flatly, turning away.

Jason Young was a new rising country music star. He also happened to be from Bad. He *also* happened to be dating Fletcher's best friend. In fact, he'd been dating Jordan for about ten years now.

Fletcher and Jordan had met in kindergarten and been instant friends. The little girl had taken care of Fletcher, doing everything from tying his shoes for recess to sharing her chips at lunch. As they'd grown up, they'd been nearly inseparable.

Charlie had hung out with Jordan several times during the summers she'd been in Autre. Jordan was fun, smart, and fearless. She'd always had a natural beauty versus being interested in makeup or doing her hair the way Charlie and her sisters had, but they'd still managed to find plenty in common. Of course, Fletcher had always been around. And where Fletcher was, typically Zeke and Zander were. And where the three younger Landry boys were, there was almost always a party.

Leo was absolutely correct in thinking that the boys had been behind most of Charlie's naughtiness growing up.

The boys had been behind most of the mischief that people their ages had gotten into.

"Oh my God, he looks so hot," Maddie said of Jason. "I mean, he's always been really good-looking, but they've clearly done a makeover or something. Or maybe it's just stardom that makes him look like that."

Charlie watched as Maddie shot Fletcher a sly grin.

Fletcher just raised his middle finger to her.

"I love his music," Charlie said.

There were several heads nodding around the table. "A lot of us do," Owen said. He pointed to the bar, and Charlie glanced over.

How had she never noticed the poster of Jason Young hanging by the register behind the bar? Of course, there was a lot of other stuff hanging on that wall too. Photos and flyers—many outdated, she was sure—and a few certificates declaring Ellie to have the best gumbo and the best bread pudding, and the best hurricanes in the area.

"Ellie's his biggest fan," Owen told her with a grin. "But we're not supposed to say nice things about him around Fletcher."

Charlie looked at Fletcher. "And why is that?"

Zeke patted his older brother on the shoulder. "Because Fletcher is a dumbass and didn't kiss Jordan when he had a chance, and now she's off touring the world with her big star boyfriend who can shower her with gifts and take her to Australia and shit."

Fletcher didn't react, but Charlie had to wonder how accurate Zeke's take on the situation was. Fletcher jealous of Jason Young because of Jordan? That wouldn't be crazy.

Charlie assumed that Fletcher had been given multiple opportunities to kiss Jordan over the years. They'd spent nearly all of their time together. She remembered several times in the summers when Jordan and other kids would crash overnight at Fletcher, Zeke, and Zander's house, sleeping on the couches and even the floor of the basement rec room.

Surely there had also been several sprigs of mistletoe and New Year's Eve parties over the years where he could have taken advantage if he wanted to.

"You wanted to kiss Jordan?" Charlie asked.

Fletcher frowned at her. "No. My brother is the dumbass."

Charlie thought he seemed more annoyed than he should by the question.

Zander laughed. "Okay, you want to *marry* Jordan and have babies with her and grow old with her in Autre. But kissing comes with that package, bro."

Owen nodded. "Damn right it does. And a hell of a lot of other fun things too."

Fletcher shifted on his chair. "How about you all shut the fuck up?"

Yeah, that was too annoyed for simple, typical Landry teasing if it didn't hit at least a little close to the truth.

Charlie leaned over to Paige. "Is there more to this story?"

"He's been progressively crabby this year about Jason's success. Apparently, Jason just got signed to tour with and open for Brett Eldredge, and Jordan is traveling with him full-time now. Which means she quit her job. He just found out when Jordan came home for the weddings in April."

"He's not happy she's touring with Jason?"

Paige shook her head. "No, and I think it really bugs him that she's not teaching anymore."

"Very interesting." But Charlie didn't know if that meant he wanted to kiss Jordan or if he was just concerned for a friend.

"Well, it's entertaining. At least for his brothers and cousins," Paige said. "Jason's been getting a lot of publicity and is regularly on the entertainment news, and they never fail to point it out to Fletcher. Ellie's fawning over him doesn't help either. Though last week there was a shot of Jordan with him at some country music festival, and everyone thought that was really cool. Except for Fletcher. He thought she looked tired and stressed."

Charlie looked at Fletcher again. He was still frowning and resolutely not looking at the television. "Well, honestly, if anyone could tell if Jordan was tired and stressed just by seeing her for a minute on television, it would be Fletcher. They've known each other forever and are really close."

Paige nodded. "That's what Mitch said. I can't help but wonder if part of his frustration is that they're not as close now. If all of her time and attention is focused on Jason and his new career, maybe Fletcher's feeling left out."

It was like a freaking soap opera around here, and Charlie loved it. Life in Autre was so much more fun than Shreveport had been, and now, even after only five days, it was more entertaining than even Paris, France. Sure, Paris had amazing food, and it was exciting to be in a foreign city and see new sights, but she'd been essentially alone. She was acquaintances with a few people in the office and had started making friends, but she'd only been there for a few weeks. Besides, she knew that she could live in a place for ten years and see the same people every day and never feel as close or comfortable with them as she did with this group.

"Hi, Paige."

Charlie and Paige both looked up at the woman who just approached the table.

"Hi, Lisa," Paige greeted. "How are you?"

"I'm great. I don't mean to interrupt, but I had to come over."

"You're not interrupting anything," Charlie assured her. Besides, if anyone wanted to speak to any of the Landrys inside of Ellie's bar, they'd have to interrupt. The family talked nonstop and very often over one another. And anyone else.

"Well, I just wanted to come over and tell you how much my daughter enjoyed the yoga class yesterday."

Charlie recognized the woman from the class and, now that she mentioned it, Charlie remembered that she'd had a teenager with her.

"I'm so glad to hear that," Paige said with a smile. "She's going to come back then?"

The woman nodded. "Oh, definitely. I know this sounds strange, but the class was like a breakthrough."

Paige shifted to sit up straighter on her chair. "How do you mean?"

"We lost my dad two months ago," Lisa said. "Morgan has been deeply depressed ever since. She barely talks to us and spends most of her time in her room. I got her to come to the yoga class only because of the otters. Afterward, she talked the entire way home in the car, during dinner, and then sat on the couch watching television with me that evening." Lisa's eyes got a little shiny. "I know she misses my dad terribly. They were very close. But it's been breaking my heart that I can't do anything to cut through the depression to make her happy. The yoga class, and of course the otters, did something I've been unable to do."

Paige looked incredibly touched, and Charlie had to admit that she felt a little sting in her eyes as well.

"I am so happy to hear that," Paige said sincerely. "Yoga has always been an important stress reliever for me, but when I started doing classes with cats back in my hometown, I noticed that not only did my happiness level increase, but my class participants seemed even lighter and happier after class as well. I'm so happy the otters are doing the same thing here."

Lisa nodded. "I think the yoga is really good for her, and she did enjoy that, but I would never have gotten her to the class if the otters had not been a part of it. So, thank you for that too."

Paige nodded. "I'm going to be doing a lot more classes, and I would love to see you and Morgan back again."

"You can count on that," Lisa said. She gave them both a big smile and then turned to leave.

Charlie looked at Paige. "That was amazing."

Paige nodded happily. "I'm always pleased when people enjoy my classes, of course, but it's stuff like that that really makes it matter. I've had people get over back pain and lose weight and meet new friends all because of my classes. And of course, I used to get cats adopted because participants would do yoga with them and then want to take them home." She grinned. "This makes me so happy."

Paige had shared with Charlie that she'd run a combination yoga studio and cat café back in her hometown of Appleby, Iowa. She'd been in Autre since January, having come for Josh and Tori's wedding—which had been postponed to April—but she now readily admitted that Mitch had been the main attraction. They'd met in Appleby, and Mitch had invited her to come spend a few months in Louisiana, and Paige had happily taken him up on it. Now it seemed clear that she wasn't going to be leaving. At least not permanently.

Charlie glanced toward the door where Lisa and her husband were just leaving. The otters had been the attraction for Morgan, but the entire experience had opened her up. That really was amazing. And it made her imagination start to turn. Was there more they could do? Was there a way to make other portions of the petting zoo more meaningful than they seemed on the surface?

And even if she did come up with some ideas along those lines, would Griffin go for them?

She frowned. The clear answer to that was probably not.

Which got her thinking about Griffin again. Which got her

thinking about how Griffin had left right after hearing her story about getting fired. Which got her thinking about how he'd essentially complimented her, then acted like he couldn't wait to get away from her.

What was with that guy?

He'd liked her just fine back in April. Sure, that had been very physical. But it hadn't been only physical. He might try to say that it was, but she knew better. They'd had a connection.

Why was he fighting this? Getting involved with her would be "complicated,". Or so he said. But maybe getting involved with her would be for him what otter yoga had been for Morgan. Maybe it would be... therapeutic.

Clearly, the guy had some issues. He was grumpy, gruff, and unyielding. And yet, he was sweet with animals and even seemed amused at times with her ideas.

Charlie suddenly got to her feet.

Paige looked startled. "Are you okay?"

Was she okay? No, not really. She needed to talk to Griffin. She wanted to be okay. Part of the whole reason she was here in Autre was to get okay. And that guy was holding her back from that.

"I'll be okay," she told Paige. "But I need to go right now."

"Will I see you at otter yoga tomorrow?"

"Oh, yeah, I think I might need some help finding my Zen by tomorrow."

Griffin Foster was definitely messing with her chill.

———

Charlie stepped out of the bar and started to turn east to head to Griffin's house. It was a little farther than most of the Landry houses, but it was still within walking distance.

Of course, just then, she heard thunder overhead. It was a

low deep rumble which meant she hopefully still had a few minutes before the rain would start.

But before she had gone more than a few steps, she stopped. She heard a low voice and immediately smiled.

"Sugar, we gotta get you home. It's going to start raining, and I need to get some sleep. We can't have a date tonight."

Griffin was still here. Perfect.

Thank you, Sugar, you little stalker.

Charlie pivoted in the direction of his voice, and when she stepped around Zeke's big truck, she saw Griffin with his hands on his hips looking down at his biggest fan.

Of course, Sugar wasn't alone. Stan was there too, as was Mike, the duck, and Hermione, the pig.

Thunder sounded overhead again, and the pig shrieked.

"See?" Griffin asked Sugar. "You got Hermione out here, and it's going to storm. You know how she feels about thunder."

Charlie found herself curious about how Hermione felt about thunder. She assumed she wasn't a fan.

"Need some help?"

Griffin turned. He didn't seem surprised to see her. "I made the mistake of stopping to chat with someone. Sugar heard my voice."

Charlie nodded as she approached. "Your voice has that effect on me too."

He stepped back as she drew near. "You gotta stop that."

"Telling you that I'm attracted to you? It's not exactly a secret, is it?"

"Putting it out there all the time."

"Why?"

"Because it..."

She smiled. He wanted to tell her how it affected him. Which probably meant that it affected him in a good way. At least in a way that she would consider good.

Then she frowned. Clearly, he didn't think it was good.

"What is your deal?" she asked.

"Excuse me?"

"You've been avoiding me for the past few days. And tonight, after I told you how I got fired, you couldn't wait to get away from me. I have to tell you, Dr. Foster, if you have an issue with what I did to Alan's car, we are going to have a problem."

He looked at her for a long moment. Then he said, "If we have a problem, will you stop being so..."

Charlie planted her hands on her hips when he trailed off. "Oh, you better finish that sentence."

He hesitated for a moment, then shook his head. "I was going to say tempting. But I don't think you can stop being tempting."

She dropped her hands. Again, he'd surprised her with a compliment. Or at least saying something she considered a compliment. "What does that have to do with the way you hightailed it out of the bar a little bit ago?"

"It has everything to do with why I left the bar."

"After I told you about how I got fired? How was that tempting?"

"Because the more I learn about you, the more I—"

The next clap of thunder was much louder and sharper. It made Charlie jump and Hermione squeal. It also made the pig take off toward the road.

"Dammit!" Griffin immediately started after her.

Charlie watched them, then looked around, feeling discombobulated. That was unusual. Discombobulated was definitely not a usual state for her.

But she snapped out of it as Sugar took off after Griffin, and then Mike took off after Sugar. The other goat seemed unconcerned with anything but the patch of grass he was munching on. Charlie cast him a glance, decided he was probably staying put, and that Griffin needed her help more. She took off after the pig, the man, the goat, and the duck.

Griffin caught up with Hermione after just a few steps. Fortunately, his legs were much longer than hers. He scooped her up, no easy feat considering she weighed well over a hundred pounds and was wiggling and clearly terrified.

Sugar stopped beside him, looking up and bleating her displeasure over another animal getting the attention she wanted.

Knowing that the duck would follow Sugar, Charlie bent and scooped the goat up.

Griffin glanced at her, took in the situation, and started for the barn without a word.

But they'd only gone a few feet when the skies opened up.

The rain poured down as if someone had dumped a bucket from the clouds, and Charlie was completely soaked by the time they reached the barn door.

With his arms full of a wriggling pig, Griffin was unable to slide the door open, so Charlie set Sugar down and slipped in around him to shove the heavy wooden door to the side. She stumbled inside with Griffin right behind her.

She turned and, sure enough, found the goat and duck right behind them.

"Stan!" Griffin called. He added a whistle.

The goat across the road looked up, seemed to realize he was getting wet, and started ambling toward the barn.

It was a really good thing that the road wasn't very busy this time of night.

As Stan strolled into the barn, Griffin slid the door shut behind him. The rest of the animals were already inside for the night. He turned and headed for the back of the barn. Sugar, of course, stayed right next to him, and the duck waddled along beside her. When he reached the final stall, he stepped inside with the pig. The next thing Charlie knew, he disappeared behind the wooden slats.

Unable to help herself, Charlie headed in that direction to see what he was doing.

She found him sitting on the floor with Hermione half on the hay beside him and half in his lap. He was gathering more hay around the animal into a little nest and talking to her soothingly.

"It's okay. It's okay. You're fine. I'm here. I've got you."

Heat bloomed in Charlie's stomach. She wasn't scared of storms, but she very much wanted to be held in Griffin Foster's lap and told that everything was going to be okay. About anything. Or just held in his lap and petted the way he was stroking Hermione's head and back.

Sugar knelt next to him on the side opposite Hermione, and the duck settled in next to her.

"You can come in too."

Charlie looked at Griffin.

He was sitting on the floor of a barn stall with a pig in his lap. His hair was wet, his T-shirt was plastered to his body, and his skin was shiny with the rain. And he looked delicious, competent, calming, and yes, tempting.

"Are you sure?" she asked. "You think Sugar and Hermione will share?"

Griffin looked down at the pig, then the goat. "If you don't want to be in my lap."

"Oh, I very much want to be in your lap, Dr. Foster."

Heat flared in his eyes. He shook his head and seemed to decide not to comment on that directly. "I can't move Hermione until Sylvester gets here."

Charlie thought she knew everyone who worked for Boys of the Bayou. "Sylvester?"

"Her cat."

That was Griffin's full answer. Charlie tipped her head. "What do you mean, *her* cat? The pig has a cat?"

"Well, I suppose Sylvester is maybe more of a friend than a pet. But he's her comfort animal."

Griffin chuckled at what had to be the you've-got-to-be-kidding-me look Charlie was giving him.

"Sylvester wandered into the barn one night as a kitten. The next morning we found him curled up next to Hermione. He was pretty sick, and we weren't sure he was going to make it, but Hermione got very upset when we tried to take him out of her pen. So I did an exam and gave him some medicine and food and water right here in her stall. He bounced back and is perfectly healthy now, and they still are best friends. He sleeps in here with her every night, and we've noticed that when he is here with her on stormy nights, she's much calmer than she was before."

Charlie looked at the pig, who was being petted like a lapdog by the handsome vet. She was jealous of having that big hand running up and down the pig's body. "Why is she scared of storms?"

"We're not really sure why, but storms and particularly thunder make her anxious. Tori brought her here from Iowa. I guess she's always been this way."

Wow. Charlie shook her head. She was good at a lot of things. She knew a lot of things. There were very few situations that really threw her for a loop. But all of this animal stuff was definitely new territory.

She'd always considered herself an animal lover, but they hadn't had pets growing up. She and her sisters had wanted a dog, but their parents had said it wouldn't be fair to the animal since they were all so busy and gone a lot.

Her dose of dogs and cats had come—as had all really special things in her life—from her trips to the bayou. And now that animals, and definitely nothing as normal as cats and dogs, were part of her daily life here in Autre, she found herself fascinated.

The story about Hermione and Sylvester also reminded her of what Lisa had just told her and Paige about Morgan.

"Just now, a mom came over to tell Paige that being at otter yoga had helped her daughter open up for the first time since her grandfather died."

Griffin simply nodded.

"I mean, of course, I know about comfort animals. I've heard stories about dogs that can tell when their owner is going to have a diabetic episode or seizure. I know there are cats in nursing homes that comfort patients as they pass away. But I've never really *thought* about it beyond, 'wow, that's really nice,' But it's a real thing, huh?"

"It's definitely a real thing." Griffin looked down at Hermione and patted her side. "Animals won't judge you. Animals are loving, and loyal, and trusting. Even when the human they're loving and trusting doesn't deserve it. There's nothing quite as humbling as having another living being depend on you and fully trust you to take care of them." Griffin lifted his head to look at Charlie. "I find people who understand and love animals to be more understanding and loving of humans as well."

That made sense, of course. Being able to be empathetic toward any other living thing could clearly extend to all living things.

"You seem much more loving toward animals than toward humans," Charlie couldn't help but point out.

"Animals deserve it more," he said without hesitation. "They're easier. They don't have agendas, they're not selfish, and they don't say one thing and do another. Animals have simple needs that are easy to understand and meet."

Charlie studied him. "You know, if you want me to quit talking about being attracted to you and putting it 'out there,' you need to stop *being* so attractive."

He gave a soft chuckle, and Charlie felt her body warm. It

wasn't exactly desire. At least not in the sexual sense. But it was pleasure at having made him laugh and a desire to make it happen again.

"I just been drenched by rain, and I'm sitting on the floor of a barn with a pig in my lap," Griffin said. "How's this attractive?"

"I don't totally understand it either."

11

That wasn't true. Charlie completely understood what was attractive about Griffin Foster.

"Okay, I lied. It's how upfront you are about how you feel about things. It's how passionate and caring you are. And it's how you know who you are and what you want."

He didn't answer for several seconds.

Charlie took the opportunity to join him in the stall. She really wanted to know more about this guy. This seemed like as good as a time as any to dig a little. He clearly wasn't going anywhere for a while—at least until Sylvester showed up.

She pulled the door open to the stall and stepped inside. She looked around for a moment, wondering where she should actually sit. She chose a spot across from him so she could look at him.

Charlie leaned back against the side of the stall the way Griffin was and stretched her legs out, crossed her ankles, and folded her hands in her lap. Her feet didn't quite reach his boots.

They weren't touching at all, but inside the barn, alone, with the rain pounding on the roof, it felt intimate.

"We have that in common," he finally said after she was settled.

"We do?"

"You know who you are and what you want."

She nodded.

Well, she was pretty sure she knew what she wanted. She knew her ultimate goals. She was just having trouble formulating a plan to get to them. "We both also say what we mean when we mean it."

"I guess that means I'm supposed to appreciate it when you comment on being attracted to me?"

"Exactly." She grinned at him.

He didn't respond to that.

After a few quiet seconds, she asked, "Have you always wanted to be a vet?"

He shook his head. "No. That's not how I started out, anyway. I grew up in love with animals. My parents were huge animal lovers. We had all kinds of pets."

Griffin rested his head against the wall behind him, and his hand stroked rhythmically over Hermione's back again. The pig seemed completely relaxed now, and Charlie couldn't blame her.

"I went to college, studied biology, figured I'd become a park ranger or a game warden. But in my second biology class, I met Kamali. He was from Zimbabwe and was heading to Zambia for the summer to work on a wildlife preserve."

"You went along?"

"I did and ended up staying for a year."

"Wow."

He nodded. "The elephants were the first to win me over, but I also just fell in love with the whole idea of wildlife conservation and keeping the animals protected in their own environment. I had planned to stay there indefinitely."

"What happened?"

"My parents were killed in a car accident, and my little brother needed someone at home."

Charlie gave a little gasp. Okay, she hadn't expected an answer like that. "Oh, Griffin."

Griffin was looking down at the animals now. "He was only sixteen, and I was twenty-one, so I was able to become his legal guardian. He could have gone to live with our grandparents, but I couldn't just stay that far away, knowing that his whole world had been turned upside down."

Charlie stared at him. She had been fascinated by his rough exterior from the beginning, but she never guessed what was behind it. He'd given up his dream to take care of his brother. That was... okay, sexy. But it was also so in character. Which struck her as an odd realization. Did she know him well enough to think that?

But yeah, it definitely fit.

She swallowed hard and resisted the urge to crawl over and hug him. And maybe push Hermione out of the way so she could curl up in his lap. "I'm really sorry about your parents."

He gave a short nod. "Thanks. It's been nine years, so it's a little better now."

"You have just one brother?"

"Yeah, Donovan is actually a wildlife rehabilitation expert." He said it with a noticeable touch of pride.

"What does that mean?"

"He helps rehabilitate sick or injured wildlife and return them to their natural environment whenever possible. His expertise is big cats, cougars, and bobcats, for instance. But he works with wolves and bears and eagles and just about anything. Right now, he's in North Carolina, but he travels extensively."

She smiled. It was clear that Griffin loved his brother. "That's pretty great that you share that passion for animals."

He lifted a shoulder. "It's nice to have anything in common.

Things were pretty rocky when I first came back after Mom and Dad died." He looked up and met her eyes. "I tried my best to be there for him, but he got into partying heavily. A lot of drinking. He's a recovered alcoholic."

Charlie could tell Donovan's hard times had hurt Griffin too. He was loving and sweet under all of that gruff exterior. And she'd never wanted another man the way she wanted Griffin.

"So you ended up in vet school when you came back?"

He nodded. "Eventually. I finished my bio degree while Donovan finished high school. Then after he graduated from high school and was doing well in counseling, I decided I could take the time. I went to vet school while he went to college. He double-majored in biology and ecology."

"And then you went to a zoo so you could work with elephants and lions and zebras like in Zambia?"

"I worked in a regular old veterinary clinic for about a year. A friend from school called me about a job at the zoo in Omaha, but I initially turned it down. I didn't like the idea of animals in captivity. They should be wild. But she kept after me. She convinced me that I would be in a position to help protect them from any mistreatment and could help ensure that being in captivity was safe and healthy for them. And, of course, that I could be a part of protecting vulnerable animal species. Sometimes captivity is the best place to keep them and certainly the best place to try growing populations that are in danger."

Charlie nodded. "And there's something to be said for having a place where people can learn about animals and observe them and even interact at times, isn't there? That's the best way to get people interested in protecting species and doing what they can for conservation, isn't it?"

"Sounds like a pretty good marketing brochure."

Charlie frowned. "That doesn't sound like a compliment."

He shrugged. "My brother says similar things. That you have to educate people before they'll care, and they have to care before they'll put their time and effort and money into things."

"He's right."

Griffin just shrugged.

"You can't tell me that having people come and see, personally, how gorgeous and majestic wild animals are doesn't make them more engaged in trying to help them."

Griffin nodded. "Yes, it does happen."

"So zoos can be good."

"Wildlife preserves are better."

She sighed. The guy just wouldn't give an inch. "Why not go back to Africa now then?" she asked.

"Donovan," he said simply. "Even though we don't live in the same place, we see each other a lot and stay in contact. We're the only family we have, so we need to stay at least on the same continent."

Charlie understood that. Being back in Autre had made her realize that she wouldn't have lasted for too long in France. She would have worked and built her resume there for maybe a year or two, but it hadn't been a long-term situation.

"So how did you get into marketing? I'm guessing you could have done anything."

She tipped her head. "Now, see, *that* sounds like a compliment."

"I think that probably is."

Charlie gave a short laugh. "Okay, well, I got into marketing because I saw what it did for my dad. And because I believe that if a business can grow and be as successful as possible, they can then turn around and be a positive influence on their communities and sometimes even on a bigger scale."

He frowned. "What do you mean?"

"My dad first went to Shreveport to work for a big company after he graduated from college. But he figured out that as their profits grew, they were only increasing the salaries of their executives and paying out more to their shareholders. They weren't reinvesting in the company itself, never in the employees, and never in the community around them. So, he quit and opened his own business with the opposite model. It's a cleaning business for homes and businesses. His salary didn't increase until all of his employees had paychecks well above the average, great benefits packages, and other perks like help with tuition if they went back to school and childcare. He also donated huge amounts to the community. Only then did he ever take any more money himself. And now it's a huge multi-state company with some of the best employee satisfaction scores in the business."

Griffin was listening with interest, so she went on.

"About five years ago, Dad used his brand to start a line of cleaning products. They are all-natural, so better for the environment, and the manufacturing of the products created more jobs. Dad insisted on hiring locally first, so our community benefitted from that as well."

She took a breath. "And *now*, after all that hard work and making all of those decisions that were sometimes hard, but always according to his mission, he now has a lot of community and state-wide influence. He has the ear of politicians who can influence legislation that protects workers' rights and the environment. And he is able to pass on his experience and advice to other business owners, encouraging them to treat their employees and communities right."

Griffin didn't say anything for several seconds. He just stared at her.

"What?"

"You helped him to do all of that?"

"A little bit. Over the last couple of years, I worked with him a little bit more. But he did a lot of it while I was growing up, so he's actually been more of my inspiration."

"And that's why you chose to go into marketing? You're going to help other companies do what your dad did?"

"I hope so. I'm willing to start at square one. I want to find a company that has the potential for growth and help them build. And along the way, as a trusted part of their team, I can be influential in how they use their increased profits and brand recognition."

"I never thought of marketing like that," Griffin said. "I figured it was always just convincing people to buy things."

"It is that. But there's a bigger picture, a long-term plan, with what to do when that works, and people *do* buy things." She took a breath. "I want to be involved in helping smaller businesses grow. There were a lot of different ways I could have done that, but my whole life, my dad has told me that I can talk anyone into anything. That meant that I could probably be a very good political lobbyist, or I could sell a ton of cars or something. But marketing is bigger, I think. It's about creating a whole brand and then really thinking about what you can *do* with that brand."

"So what's your dream job?"

"Well, working for a makeup company that just launched a skincare product line and wanted me to work in their Paris office," she said. "Just, for instance."

Griffin looked at her seriously. "You're heartbroken over the job?"

She thought about his question then lifted a shoulder. "I don't know about that. I mean, I don't regret what I did, and if they were to fire me for that, they weren't the company I wanted to work for. I guess it's possible that I could have helped them get bigger and more successful and more profitable, and they *wouldn't* have done good things with it."

Griffin studied her. He shook his head. "No chance."

"No chance of what?"

"You definitely would have talked them into doing good things."

Now that was definitely a compliment.

"Do you have brothers and sisters?" he asked.

She nodded. "Two younger sisters. Amelia and Abigail. Abi is in college. She wants to go into healthcare. Ami is... trying to find herself."

Griffin lifted a brow. "Oh?"

"She was Miss Louisiana two years ago," Charlie said.

"As in, went to the Miss America pageant?"

"Yep."

"Well, that's something you don't hear every day."

She laughed. "I guess that's a way to say it. Anyway, I think she thought that was her ticket to whatever she wanted. Turns out, it wasn't that easy."

"What's she want to do?"

"Travel the world. Have lots of money. Get paid to be pretty." Charlie sighed. "Sorry. That makes her sound very superficial and awful. She's very sweet. She's just... used to getting her way, and when it doesn't happen, she isn't sure how to work for it. She's the middle daughter and, I guess, feels a little ignored?" She shrugged. "I'm not sure. I love her, but we don't have a lot in common."

He snorted.

"What?" Charlie asked.

"If she's very used to getting her way and holy-shit gorgeous, I'd say you have a lot in common."

She gave him a smile and shook her head. "There's one of those is-that-a-compliment-or-not comments."

"It's... mostly... a compliment."

He gave her a little grin that made her panties definitely feel warmer.

"You'd better watch yourself, Dr. Foster. Throwing out so

many compliments in such a short timeframe might make me think you're starting to like me."

"Well, I definitely wouldn't want that."

They sat for several seconds without speaking, smiling at each other stupidly. Until a loud *meow* came from the stall door, pulling Charlie's attention away from Griffin.

A large black cat with a white chest, white paws, and a streak of white on his nose walked past. He entered the stall as if he belonged there. She assumed he did.

"This is Sylvester?"

Griffin reached his hand out toward the cat, which approached him without hesitation and rubbed its cheek along Griffin's fingers. "Yep. Sylvester, this is Charlie. Charlie, this is Sylvester."

Sylvester sniffed Hermione, and they touched noses.

Griffin ran a hand down the back of the cat and then shifted Hermione off his lap and onto the pile of hay next to him. He got to his feet, and the cat immediately took his spot. Some might have guessed it was because the spot was warm from Griffin's body, and the cat had just come in from the rain, but as soon as he lay down, and Hermione moved to rest her forehead against his stomach, it seemed clear he was here for his friend. The warm spot in the straw was just a bonus.

Griffin brushed the seat of his jeans off and came toward Charlie. He reached out a hand.

She took it, letting him pull her to her feet.

He didn't let go of her once they were both standing. Nor did he step back.

"They'll be fine now," he said, his voice low.

She looked up at him and was struck with the urge to lean in, wrap her arms around him, and hug him.

It was a very different urge than she normally had around him. Those urges tended to oscillate between wanting to take her clothes off and wanting to tease him. This was a much softer feeling, and as it curled through her, she realized it came with an undeniable feeling of *I just really like him.*

That shouldn't be a revelation. Of course she liked him. It seemed most of the people who knew him liked him.

She loved watching him with patients and their owners. She'd loved hearing his chuckle from his office yesterday when he'd seen the new *This Probably Has Dog Hair In It* mug on his desk. She'd loved *imagining* his grin when she'd sent *him* one of her video messages to tell him about a change to his schedule. She'd made herself look like she had otter ears and a nose and whiskers. She was ninety percent sure he'd at least smiled. Even ninety-five percent sure.

She'd also like to think that she liked most of the men she was attracted to. But this was different. This was a feeling that made her think that she'd like to see him every single day, that if she didn't, she would miss him, and that even if it wasn't physical or romantic between them, she wanted to be his friend.

He was a good man. He was grumpy, said no way more often than she liked, and was stubborn as hell. But she really liked him.

"Why did you leave Washington, D.C.?" she asked.

She had been wondering about it since Tori had first mentioned it, but she hadn't had the chance to ask Griffin yet. Suddenly, she needed to know. She wasn't just curious now. She felt like she truly *needed* to know. She wanted to know everything about him.

When the thought hit her, she looked up into his eyes. What was his favorite sports team? What was his favorite breakfast food? What was his favorite color? What was his mom's name? Did he have a favorite animal?

All of these questions were swirling through her mind all at once, and Charlie was as shocked by them as anyone.

"I got fired."

His answer to her question stopped those spinning thoughts.

She frowned, studying his face. But as his words sunk in, she realized that maybe she wasn't shocked.

They seemed like opposites. Where she was outgoing and creative and a little pushy, he seemed serious, introverted, and perpetually annoyed.

But he was very good with his patients' families and when they had a common concern, he was honest but compassionate. He also had to be creative in a way as well. Just yesterday, he had needed to sweet talk an older woman into fixing her cat after it had delivered its fourth litter of kittens.

He wanted the cat to be healthy while cutting down on the population of unwanted kittens and reducing the number of cats the woman was currently living with. He'd had to find a way to communicate those concerns to the woman in a way she would understand and agree with. He'd finally told her he was looking for someone to foster the kittens people turn over to him. He felt that the mother cat would be excellent at nurturing and teaching other kittens, and he knew the woman would be a fabulous foster mother.

Then, he'd pulled out the big guns. He'd introduced her to a litter of kittens that had been dropped off just two days before. The woman hadn't stood a chance. Not only had she agreed to the spaying of her adult cats, but she and the kittens had happily gone home together.

Of course, when Charlie had complimented him on the arrangement, he'd said simply, "Now I don't have to bottle feed a bunch of kittens."

Charlie had rolled her eyes. Griffin had maybe bottle-fed those kittens at one point or another, but Paige had been coming in on a regular basis to do it. It was how Charlie had first met Paige and found out that she was the otter yoga instructor.

And, along with all the other things they had in common, he could definitely be pushy.

Charlie knew her family thought she had been getting her way on almost every idea. What they didn't know was that Griffin had shot down her suggestion for selling organic, homemade cat and dog treats in the clinic. He'd also said, "hell no" to the petting zoo acquiring a sloth. He had not just said no to doing the educational talk at the otter enclosure but had declined her idea about selling a calendar with photos of him and various animals featured. He hadn't even liked the idea that fifty percent of the proceeds could go to the animal charity of his choice.

Of course, the calendar idea had been her teasing him rather than anything serious. Not that she thought it wouldn't sell like crazy, but she wasn't so sure she could get twelve smiles out of the guy.

Though he was pretty damn sexy when he *didn't* smile too.

And she was still working on the homemade cat and dog treats.

She was also pretty sure he knew that.

"Did it have something to do with the animals?" she asked about him getting fired.

"Yes."

"And humans doing something that bothered the animals or exploited them somehow?"

"More or less."

She smiled at him. They had plenty in common. She'd been fired because of a passionate reaction to a horrible behavior. Griffin's situation was similar.

"Tell me the story," she said.

"It doesn't matter."

She took a step forward, bringing them mere inches apart. She put her hand on his chest. His shirt was still damp, but the skin underneath was hot, and she was immediately warmed by the touch. Though, a lot of that heat was coming from her as well.

"It matters to me," she said softly.

Emotion flared in his eyes. He lifted a hand to cover hers where it rested over his heart. She felt the drumming under her palm and knew hers matched. He didn't move her hand. He simply rested his on top of hers.

"This is what I'm talking about." His voice was rough.

"What do you mean?"

"You can't help being tempting."

Charlie felt like she just downed a shot of her grandpa's moonshine—warm all the way through her body, tingly to her toes, and a little dizzy.

"Yeah, well, ditto." She curled her fingers into the damp cotton stretched over hard muscles. "You know my story. I want to know yours."

"Aren't you cold? You got drenched."

She shook her head and wet her lips. "Definitely not cold." She paused. "How about you?"

His thumb stroked across the back of her knuckles, where her hand was still resting on his chest. "No. Not cold."

"Tell me."

He took a breath and then slowly blew it out. "Let's sit."

Charlie liked that idea. It indicated that his story might be more than just a sentence. She looked around and spotted a hay bale and a big, plastic bucket they used for feed. Reluctantly, she pulled her hand from his and went to the bucket. She turned it over and dropped onto it like a stool. She gestured toward the hay bale.

"Have a seat."

To her mild surprise and definite pleasure, he did. He sat on the hay bale facing her, elbows on his thighs, his big hands dangling between his knees. It took a few seconds for him to speak. "I was in charge of the tiger propagation program," he started. "We very much wanted to have a Sumatran tiger cub but were having very little luck. The female tiger didn't want to mate with any of the males, and none of the males were, for whatever reason, strong enough to convince her otherwise."

Charlie smiled. "Discerning tastes. I can respect that."

"Yes, well, when you're an endangered species, you shouldn't be quite so picky."

"Maybe she just didn't want to be a wife and mom."

"Maybe. We actually were talking about acquiring a new female. But she had very strong genetics, and we knew that any cub of hers would do well. So, we finally artificially inseminated her. Four times. Never took."

Charlie frowned. "That's too bad. Must've been really frustrating."

"It was. Of course. It was the entire reason I'd gone to D.C. from Omaha. Well, other than getting fired in Omaha."

Charlie's eyebrows shot up. "Wait, you got fired from the zoo in Omaha too?"

He nodded. "I get... riled up about animals."

She snorted. "No kidding."

He shrugged. "That's not how I would characterize it, but the zoo director put it that way. I'll admit I get protective. And short-tempered. And..."

"Easily irritated with other human beings?"

He blew out a breath and actually gave her a faint smile. "Yeah, something like that."

"Okay, so now we have to start in Omaha," she told him. "What happened there?"

"Well, it had to do with some animals." Now he gave her a half smile.

Which was at least a quarter smile more than she'd gotten from him in a couple of days.

It made her smile even bigger, and the warmth in her stomach notched up a few degrees. "I'm shocked, Dr. Foster."

"I know. But yeah, they wanted to bring in some new penguins but weren't willing to add onto the enclosure. I got into a huge yelling match with the zoo director and our primary donor."

"They fired you for giving them advice that you were essentially hired to give them?"

"It wasn't the advice I was giving so much as it was calling our donor a pompous ass and the zoo director a selfish bastard. Loudly. In front of most of the staff. And some of the public."

Charlie felt her eyes widen. But her smile spread too.

"Oh, and to fuck off," Griffin said, almost thoughtfully. "That definitely didn't help."

Charlie laughed out loud. "Just so you know, I love everything about this story."

And now she got a full-on grin.

And she wanted to climb right into his lap and kiss the hell out of him because of it.

Well, also because he'd told off the guys in Omaha. She had no doubt that they'd deserved it.

"That's because you're a troublemaker," Griffin told her. "Most people know that I shouldn't have reacted like that."

"Sometimes, when you're dealing with selfish bastards, the only thing to do is call them out."

He looked at her for several beats before asking, "You think I was right?"

"Of course."

"You don't know how the whole conversation went or any of the details of the situation."

"No, but I've been around you for five days now."

"Exactly. You've only been around me for five days."

She leaned in, rested her elbows on her thighs, mimicking his posture. She met his eyes directly. "Griffin, it only takes a few hours with you around animals to see what kind of guy you are and what matters to you."

Again, several ticks passed with him simply watching her before he said, "And there you go, being irresistible again."

She laughed lightly. "I'm not sure you're using the word irresistible correctly. You seem to be doing a fine job of resisting me."

"I don't think that's going to last."

Her stomach swooped, and heat shot through her belly straight between her legs. "You probably shouldn't have admitted that."

He nodded. "Probably not."

"Tell me what happened in D.C." She swallowed hard as tingles raced through her bloodstream. "Quickly, though."

"There's a timeline?"

She nodded. "There is. I'm about three minutes away from kissing you. And once I start, I'm really not going to want to stop. Even to talk about tigers." She leaned in a little closer, her voice dropping a bit as she said, "And I don't think you'll want to either."

His eyes were hot on hers as he said, "We finally got the tiger pregnant. She had a cub that was perfectly healthy. We decided to have an event to celebrate and invited all of our mega-donors to the propagation program to come see the cub before we introduced him to the public. A donor's wife climbed into the nursery pen and picked him up for a photo."

For a moment, Charlie was distracted from her delight over how quickly he was talking, clearly to get the story over with so the kissing could commence. "She got *into* a *tiger pen*?"

"The mother wasn't in there. It was only the cub. But yes, even after being told that no one could touch the cub. Her husband was our biggest donor, and she obviously thought the rules didn't apply to her. And I lost my shit."

"Was she okay?"

"Yes. But honestly, that was not my first concern. If baby tigers are handled too much by humans, it's possible that their mother will reject them. We had just successfully had a tiger cub born after multiple tries, and to think that the mother might not take care of him made me see red."

"My God, I can totally understand that." Charlie felt herself frowning and her heart pounding, but now her heart rate had nothing to do with Griffin. Well, that wasn't entirely true. Her heart rate was always a little elevated when Griffin was around, and when he was growly and protective of animals, it especially made her hormones rush. But now, she was sharing his frustration and anger. At a woman she had never met.

"What did you do?" Charlie asked. For some reason, she knew this went beyond raising his voice and calling people names.

Griffin blew out a breath. "I grabbed the cub away from her, put it down, then took her arm and started to escort her out of the building. When she resisted and started yelling, I wrapped an arm around her waist, picked her up, and carried her out."

Charlie felt her mouth drop open. Okay, that was a relationship-with-a-donor nightmare as well as a horrible publicity situation. She still wanted to kiss him. "And you were fired right on the spot," she guessed.

Griffin nodded. "You got it. But, I would've quit the next day if the director had tried to side with the donor."

Charlie nodded. That was totally in character. "And then you came here?"

"A mutual friend called Tori, and she called me."

Charlie stood from the bucket and took a step forward. Griffin didn't change his posture at all except to tip his head slightly to look up at her.

"Is Autre going to be enough for you?"

"My goal now is simplicity. I want things uncomplicated and straightforward. I don't have to deal with politics here, or mega-donors thinking they have rights that they don't, and—"

He sighed. "I don't have exotic, endangered animals here. That should keep me from losing my shit."

She took another step, and now he spread his knees and straightened slightly. She stepped between his knees and put a hand on his face.

"I don't think anything can actually take away a passion like yours." She took a breath. "At least I hope not."

With a resigned groan, Griffin's hands went to her hips, and he pulled her forward and into his lap.

She straddled his thighs, thrilled that they were on the same page here.

She slid her hand up the back of his neck and into his hair, cradling his head and looking into his eyes.

He ran his hands from her hips up her back, pressing her close as he took a big, deep breath.

"You are a really good man, Griffin Foster."

He shook his head. "And you are absolutely irresistible."

"I'm very happy to hear you say that."

12

Griffin felt an intense mix of desire and relief as Charlie's body melted into his.

He'd been trying to stay away from her for days. The five days that she'd been in Autre felt like five weeks. And like five minutes.

He'd enjoyed all of it, except for the part where he'd tried to keep his hands to himself. That had been getting progressively more difficult the more they worked together at the clinic and the more delightful ideas she implemented. It was everything —her voice, her smile, her ideas, her enthusiasm, her warmth —that had come together to make him realize that his life had become very small. And dim. And a little boring.

Of course, that had all been his intention. Clearly, his plan to lay low in a small town and take care of cats and dogs had worked.

But dammit, now that Charlie was here, his heart was beating again. His own mind was spinning with ideas. He was getting excited about things.

And all it had taken was kettle corn and hedgehogs—actually, just the *idea* of kettle corn and hedgehogs—to break through his nothing-works-out-so-I'm-destined-to-just-be-miserable thoughts and his sullen attitude.

Well, and a gorgeous, happy, optimistic, won't-take-no-for-an-answer blonde who thought "why not?" and had the best mouth—for talking, teasing, and tasting—he'd ever encountered.

He couldn't imagine what it would be like around here without her now.

And it had been five days. *Five.*

He'd had a strong inkling from the start—and a pretty big shot of trepidation—that she was going to become even more irresistible, but tonight had cinched it.

Seeing her with her family had caused a huge crack in the wall that he'd tried to erect. Just as he'd known it would. He had especially tried to avoid seeing her with the rest of the Landrys.

As of tonight, he was done resisting *all* of the Landrys.

Dammit.

He liked them and enjoyed being around them, and respected them. However, he hadn't realized just how strong his affection for them was until he'd seen Charlie with them.

But he'd been expecting that to be the final nail in the you-can't-keep-fighting-your-feelings-for-her coffin. He'd told himself that he should eat quickly and try to get out before she showed up, but for some reason, his spoon had not moved any faster. For the past few days, he'd been coming into Ellie's earlier than usual and had eaten at home twice, just to avoid the big family reunion.

And sure enough, when Charlie came through the swinging doors from the kitchen, his heart had beat especially hard in his chest.

And, as expected, the Landrys were as fucking charming as always, and adding Charlie to the mix made his gut tighten with want.

Her story about how she been fired and the way they all backed her up and assured her she'd done the right thing had made him realize that he wanted to be a part of this group.

And then, hearing that she'd been fired because of a passionate, emotional reaction to something unjust had made his blood pound, and everything in him crave her.

He hadn't seen that coming. Now that he knew she had taken a man by the balls, literally, when he was being an asshole and was someone who would defend another person even at risk to herself, he could admit he was gone for her.

Charlie Landry was amazing.

And now, she was in his lap, kissing him, clearly wanting him as well. Even after he'd tried to keep his distance and had shot down a number of her ideas and had told her about his failures as an employee and as a brother.

He hadn't expected being accepted and supported for who and how he was to be such a turn-on. Though he probably should have. Those were two things he wanted more than anything.

The third thing he wanted desperately was to touch every inch of her.

He wanted to hear every sound and feel every bit of her. And judging by the way she was already working his shirt up his torso, her hot hands sliding over his ribs, it seemed she felt the same.

He pulled his mouth away from hers, staring into her eyes. The look he gave her was intense enough to stop her hands for several seconds. She paused with her hands on his sides, where his jagged breathing moved them in and out. Then she gave him a soft smile and continued moving the still-damp cotton up his body. He lifted his arms, letting her peel it off.

That was an amazing idea. His hands slid under the hem of her purple t-shirt and quickly stripped it up and off, tossing it on top of his on the floor beside them. Griffin immediately unhooked her bra and tossed it in the same direction.

He filled his hands with her breasts, rubbing his thumbs over the hard tips and relishing her moan. He bent forward as she lifted herself off his thighs to get closer to his mouth. He swirled his tongue around the tip and then sucked hard. Her fingers curled into his scalp.

"Oh, *yes*, Griffin." She urged him on, arching closer.

He sucked and licked and nipped at that breast before moving to the other.

Charlie shifted on his lap, clearly growing restless. Her fingers went to the button and zipper of his fly, opening them and running her hand down along his length. But in their position, it was hard for her to get as much skin on skin contact as they both wanted.

He nudged her back, and she got to her feet. She was breathing hard, her jaw had slight whisker burn, and her lips and nipples were both darker pink from his mouth on them.

"Strip," he ordered, his own hands going to his jeans.

She toed off her tennis shoes, and her fingers worked on the button and zipper of her own jeans. The whole time, her eyes were locked on what he was doing.

He bent to untie and remove his boots, then stretched to his feet, shucking out of his jeans and boxers.

As he watched her shimmy out of her thong, he fisted his cock, needing the pressure.

Her eyes were hot as she watched, her thong dangling from her fingers.

"Please tell me you have a condom this time."

Without a word, Griffin reached for his jeans and pulled a foil packet out of his back pocket.

Both of her brows rose. "And please tell me you've been carrying that around for me."

He should say something funny and flirty. Maybe he should make her guess a little bit.

Instead, all he could say was, "Since the day you got back."

She sucked in a little breath and dropped her thong, then reached for the condom in his fingers.

"You keep doing what you were doing. I got this."

He wrapped his fingers around his cock again, stroking up and down. She licked her lips as she tore open the foil packet. She liked watching him do this? Hell, she should've been with him in the shower every morning for the past four days. Of course, if she had been in his shower with him, he wouldn't have needed his hand.

She pulled the condom from the wrapper and stepped forward, nudging his hand out of the way and rolling the condom down his length.

Her touch was enough to send a shudder of need through him, and Griffin gritted his teeth. He wanted to make this last more than two minutes, but that was about where he was already.

She stroked again and then again.

Griffin caught her by the wrists and pulled her hands away. "As much as I appreciate that, I'm pretty on edge here, and I have a much better idea about what could be milking me right now."

Her eyes jumped from his cock to his face.

"Absolutely," she said breathlessly.

Griffin grabbed his shirt and spread it over the hay bale, then sat back down—bare ass on hay was not particularly pleasant—then he pulled her back into his lap.

"While I would love to take a few hours with you, or even all night, for now, I can't wait, and we'll have to be quick. Never know when someone might come out to check on things."

Her eyes flew to the barn door. "Maybe not in a downpour," she said.

She clearly wasn't bothered by the idea that someone might come out and catch them. There were a couple of open stall doors and two wooden barrels between them and the door that would block enough for them to grab clothes or at least duck into Hermione's stall again to avoid being completely exposed.

Griffin didn't really care at the moment, however, about what anyone else was doing, including plans for coming to the barn. All he cared about was Charlie. He ran a hand down her side to her hip and then slipped between her legs to cup her.

She was hot and wet, and he wanted every inch of her. He stroked over her clit, causing her to shiver.

"God, Griffin, that feels so much better when you do it than when I do."

"Have you been touching yourself while you've been back? Thinking of me?"

She nodded. "I was touching myself before I got back here thinking about you."

He circled her clit again and then slipped his finger into her tight heat. He leaned in and kissed her, long and deep, and he felt her pussy clench around his finger. He stroked her gently, making sure she was wet and ready, then added a second finger. He curled his fingers, finding her G-spot—validated by her, "Oh my God, Griffin, *yes*, there," as she gripped his shoulders. He rubbed lazily over the sweet spot, gradually increasing the pressure and rhythm until her fingers digging into his shoulders became nearly painful, and she threw her head back, moving against his fingers, seeking release.

"Griffin, Griffin, Griffin," she chanted breathlessly. Her eyes were closed, her hair was swinging, her breasts bouncing.

His name on her lips was so fucking sweet.

"*Charlie*," he groaned in response.

He was never going to recover from this.

And then she was there, clamping down and calling his name.

"Charlie, you are—"

She leaned in and covered his mouth in a hot kiss before he could finish the thought. He slipped his hand from her body and gripped her hips, bringing her against his aching cock. She held his face and kissed him deep and hot. Then she sat back, breathing hard. And grinning.

"You ready for me?" she asked.

No. No way. "I've been ready for you for two months," he told her.

That was true if they were talking about sex.

Not if they were talking about falling in love with her.

But he'd deal with that later.

Especially after she wrapped her hand around his cock and lifted her ass, moved forward, and then lowered herself onto him.

He slid in easily. They both moaned. She took his face in her hands again and kissed him, their bodies fully joined. He cupped the back of her head, holding her still as he stroked her tongue, tasting her, drinking her in.

Finally, they broke apart. She rested her forehead on his. They both just breathed. Hard.

"This is... this feels... better than... anything."

She was having trouble finding her words. Damn. He felt downright *proud* about that.

And that was all it took for him to fall face-first the rest of the way into infatuation.

He'd made Charlotte Landry stumble over expressing herself. That was a trophy-worthy accomplishment right there.

"It sure fucking does," he agreed, squeezing her hip.

"Is it... the hay?" She lifted her head and gave him a mischievous smile. "Because I might just replace all my furniture with hay bales."

And he was grinning. Like a dumbass. While balls deep inside of her.

What the hell did this woman do to him?

"It's the hay," he said. "But only *this* hay bale. You want to feel like this"—He lifted her and then lowered her on his cock, slowly, relishing every inch as he sank deep— "you have to keep coming here."

Dang, he was flirting. And telling her that he'd really like her to stick around. Or at least come back after she left.

But all of those thoughts were obliterated when she rewarded him with another lift and lower, taking him fully. She was tight, but it was like a glove around him. A hot, wet glove.

"Well, Dr. Foster, you have *very* nice hay."

He was saved from having to flirt any further, thank God, by her picking up the pace.

He was right there with her. This he understood. This he could handle.

He gripped her hips, she gripped his shoulders, and they moved together.

Until... a loud *bleat* interrupted them.

They both froze.

No. *No.* Damn goats. He looked over to find Sugar watching them.

She bleated at them again.

This was not okay. How the fuck had he forgotten about the animals?

Of course, that needed no actual thought. Charlie. Charlie was how he'd forgotten about the animals. And forgotten not to get attached and to protect his heart.

"She's going to take a bite out of my ass, isn't she?" Charlie asked.

He moved his hands to cover her cheeks. "No." But he wasn't entirely sure that was true. It might be her leg if it wasn't her butt.

Charlie frowned at the goat. "Knock it off. You're not his type."

Sugar bleated in answer and took a step forward.

"Swear to God, little girl, you even take a *nip* at me, and I'll keep Griffin out of this barn and away from you for two weeks," Charlie told her.

Sugar gave her a loud, "*Blaaaaa!*" But she didn't come closer.

"That's right. He's mine. You can flirt with him when he comes to feed you and give you medicine or whatever he does, but keep your hooves to yourself. Got it?"

Griffin was shocked to feel laughter rippling up from his gut through his chest.

He was fucking Charlie Landry. On a hay bale in an animal barn. With a goat looking on.

And not only was she completely into it and not upset about the hay and the smell, but she was engaging his goat stalker in conversation.

Sugar lifted her chin and gave her another blast of annoyed goat language.

"Fine. I'll get you a boy goat," Charlie said. "But you need to go to your stall now. Stalker *and* voyeur is not cool."

Griffin stared as Sugar turned and headed for Hermione's stall. It wasn't hers, but he wasn't going to argue.

Charlie turned back to him. "Now, where were we?"

She started to lift herself, but he gripped her hips, stopping her.

She looked startled, but he quickly shook his head. "That was..."

Her expression softened.

God, she was so...

He lifted her and then lowered her. "So." He did it again. "Fucking." And again. "Delightful."

"Well, I now need to talk to you about boy goats."

God, they were bantering even while having the hottest sex of his life.

But Griffin quickly realized that the sex was so amazing because of the banter. Because of this woman.

"I'll talk to you about anything you want if you keep working my cock with this sweet pussy," he told her.

The graphic talk did its job. She moaned and started moving on him faster.

She did, however, manage to say, "Even sloths?"

Because of course, she did. There was nothing that could keep Charlie from talking when she had something to say.

"You'll do anything for a sloth?" he teased, even though his voice was rough, and he was trying very hard not to just slam up into her.

She tightened her inner muscles around his shaft, and he groaned.

"I am definitely open to negotiation about how we can both get what we want, Griffin."

Fuck, the way sex with Charlie was going so far, he was going to end up with a hippo or something.

And, at the moment, anyway, he didn't care. All he cared about was Charlie and how damn happy she made him.

He moved her faster and harder. She tipped her hips so his cock would hit that magical G-spot, and his thumb found her clit.

And in mere minutes, they were climbing toward the summit and then plunging over the edge. Together.

Griffin felt his orgasm roar through him, from deep in his gut, maybe even his bones. Everything in him strained to be a part of her, and he came hard as she clamped down on him like a vise.

"Griffin!"

"Charlie!"

Shudders of pleasure continued to wash through them both for several long moments, even after Charlie finally slumped against him, wrapping her arms around his neck and hugging him close.

Griffin found his hands stroking up and down her back.

He felt completely contented and also protective and like he'd really like to lift her up, turn her around, and start all over again against the stall door behind them.

But then Charlie turned her head and whispered in his ear, "It wasn't the hay."

C harlie thought maybe she was the first one to stir, but she'd climbed out of Griffin's lap very reluctantly, and his hands lingered on her hips as she stood and started to look around for her clothes.

She smiled, thinking about it even as they walked across the road toward Ellie's.

She'd hung around while he checked the animals one last time. She'd leaned over the edge of the stall and given Sugar the gesture that meant, *I'm watching you.*

Griffin had chuckled, and the sound, as always, made heat and a deep sense of contentment roll through her. She'd been teasing, of course, but she did intend to get Sugar a boyfriend.

Then Griffin put his hand on her lower back as they stepped out into the steamy night. It was a small gesture, but it had made her heart trip.

They stopped by his truck, and Charlie turned to face him. "Well, that was fun."

He didn't laugh. He didn't even grin. He nodded seriously. "It *really* was."

She opened her mouth to tease him about the fact that maybe he didn't understand the word *fun* meant he could actually smile, but before she could, he reached up and tucked a strand of hair that was trying to frizz and curl in the humid air, behind her ear.

It was a sweet gesture. Nothing earthshaking or all that unusual, except that it was Griffin who did it. To her. It was almost affectionate, and she realized that she wanted that. Not just for him to find her attractive. Not just to enjoy her time around him. She wanted him to feel more for her as well.

Dammit. Maybe Griffin had been right to try to avoid complications. Because this was starting to feel like a lot more than a hot summer fling, and she had no intention of staying permanently.

Or did she?

Things definitely felt good in Autre. Her family, at least a huge portion of it, was here. She could definitely be herself here. It'd only been five days, but she felt happier and lighter than she had in a while.

And Griffin was here.

That shouldn't matter. Especially after only five days. But it strangely felt like it did.

But she didn't have a job here.

Well, she was being paid for her work in the vet clinic as well as the marketing plans. She felt there was a lot of promise for future income based on the increased revenue of the petting zoo. But it certainly wasn't on level with what she'd done in the past or even a huge nonprofit organization or healthcare system.

Could she actually make a career here in Autre? Working for a tiny petting zoo?

Maybe.

She was startled to realize that word went through her mind when she asked herself that question. But yes, maybe.

Maybe not at the level the petting zoo was now. Maybe not even with the changes she had proposed to date. But was there potential for growth? Could she make the petting zoo even bigger? Could the business expand further? Could the petting zoo become an influential part of conservation efforts in this area of Louisiana? Just as she'd proposed teaching kids who visited about the wildlife and ecosystem around them, were there things their business could get involved with right here? Bennett Baxter, Kennedy's husband and a partner in Boys of the Bayou, was an environmental activist along with his political endeavors. His foundation was dedicated to helping preserve the Louisiana coastline. Certainly, they could expand that mission and include, more directly, the animals in the area.

Her mind was already spinning, especially after the conversation with Griffin about the work he had been drawn to in Africa. Selling snow cones and letting kids pet goats might not seem like anything big or influential, but even just hearing about how doing yoga with otters had touched a depressed teenage girl, Charlie couldn't help but think that there could be more here, under the surface of the petting zoo, if they tried.

But would they want to try? And if they did, was she willing to stay and help with that growth?

The answer to all of that was... maybe.

Okay, it was bordering on yes.

Wow, Griffin Foster was making her really think about her career plans. It took a lot for anyone to mess with any of her plans. She had always known what she wanted, for the most part, and it had never involved goats, pigs, or even otters.

Then again, there'd never been a man like Griffin Foster in her life.

"I have to be at the clinic early tomorrow," he finally said.

She nodded. "Susan is really worried about Petunia," she said of the woman and her cat that were meeting Griffin at 6:30 AM.

"I guess I'll see you sometime tomorrow then," Griffin said.

"Yes, and if I am staring at your mouth at any point during

the day, rest assured that I am definitely remembering every-thing about us having sex in the barn."

She waited for all of that to sink in with the growing grin. She really did love teasing this man.

"And if my hand ends up on your ass at any point during the day," he said, crowding close and backing her up against the truck door. "Rest assured that you can just tell me to back off rather than grabbing my balls or threatening to key my truck."

She took his face in her hands and said seriously, "If my hand ends up on your balls at any point tomorrow, rest assured you will be *very* happy to have it there."

And then the best thing happened. He laughed, then lowered his head and kissed her long and hot and deep.

"I'll see you tomorrow, Charlie," he said as he lifted his head.

"For sure, Griffin."

They just stood looking at one another.

Finally, Griffin said, "I'm gonna watch you until you get to the front door."

She was staying with her grandmother, whose house sat across from her bar. It was about a hundred feet from where they stood right now. She glanced at the house and back to Griffin with a smile. "Really?"

"Really."

"Why?"

"Well, for one, I really like watching you walk away."

She laughed. "I'm going to assume that means you like the *view* from behind rather than because you're always happy to see me go."

"That's definitely it," he said. "Though, if I'm honest, some-times I'm glad to see you go."

She laughed louder. "That's fair."

"But tonight," he said, his voice dropping. "It's more because I just want to be sure you're okay."

"I'm never more okay than I am when I'm here in Autre," she said honestly. The truth of that fact hit her harder than she would've expected.

There was even a flicker of what could have been surprise but also looked like satisfaction in Griffin's eyes.

"Then, it's really because I feel like I should be walking you to the front door, but if I do that, I'm afraid something might happen that would scandalize Ellie."

Charlie grinned up at him. "I can't even imagine what it would take to scandalize Ellie."

"You really have no idea all the things I want to do to you, then."

Her smile dropped as heat streaked through her. She started to reach for him, out of instinct, she supposed, but he caught her wrist. He turned her hand and lifted it to his mouth, pressing a hot kiss to the center that sent tingles dancing up her arm. But then he dropped his hold and said, "No more touching right now, Charlie. I don't have the self-control."

She took a deep breath and let the sense of satisfaction seep into her. She was testing Griffin Foster's self-control, and it had nothing to do with him protecting an animal. That was definitely worth being proud of. She nodded and stepped back. "Fine. But don't think that I'm always going to let you off the hook so easily. I would love to see you lose some of that self-control."

"Just keep being you, then," he said. "And stop scheduling me such early patients so I can stay up all night."

Flirting with Griffin was an entirely new experience for her. She never knew when he was going to say something hot or sweet or funny. And she loved it.

She lifted up on tiptoe to press a kiss to his cheek. Then turned on her heel and walked toward her grandmother's front door, very aware of his eyes on her the entire way.

When she was on the porch with the front door open, she

turned back and gave him a smile. He was indeed watching her, and a warm flurry of butterflies fluttered through her stomach.

She lifted a hand and blew him a kiss and then stepped into her grandmother's house with, she was sure, a very obvious I'm-falling-in-love smile on her face.

And on her way up to her bedroom, she wondered what exactly went into getting a license to own an elephant.

13

"So what do you know about elephants?"

Tori looked over at Charlie with her muffuletta halfway to her mouth. "Um, can you be more specific?"

Yes, she could. But they were all going to think she was nuts. Oh, well.

"Specifically in regards to having them in zoos. Or animal parks."

Tori set her sandwich down. "I know that there is *a lot* of licensing involved. Who can own what animals varies state by state."

Yeah, Charlie had figured there was a lot of paperwork involved. At least. She'd tried looking some things up online, but it was stupidly hard to get a direct answer. Still, she hadn't stopped thinking about growing the business with more animals in the past two days since she and Griffin had heated up the barn.

"Right. For individuals. But what if an established animal park or zoo wanted one?"

"Zoos have connections to get animals," Tori said simply.

"What about animal parks?" Charlie pressed.

"Are you getting us an elephant?" Zeke asked with a chuckle. He was leaning back in his chair, nursing a glass of tea, with half his attention on the TV over the bar.

"I was thinking about it," Charlie admitted.

That caught Zeke's full attention. "No shit?"

Tori leaned in. "You were wondering about getting an *elephant* for the petting zoo?"

"Well..." Charlie realized that everyone at the table—Tori, Maddie, Zeke, Fletcher, and Owen—were all listening now. "I was just *wondering* about the potential for expanding beyond the petting zoo."

Maddie's eyebrows rose. "You want us to have a *zoo* zoo?"

"An animal park."

"What's the difference?"

She wasn't sure. Animal park sounded smaller and less formal than a *zoo*. "I was just... talking... to Griffin the other night, and he mentioned that he'd fallen in love with elephants while he was in Africa."

"You want to get *Griffin* an elephant," Tori summarized with a grin.

Charlie really should have tried to have this conversation with Tori privately. It was just so damn hard to do anything privately with this family.

"It just got me thinking that if we want to really grow the business, maybe one way is to expand with more animals," Charlie said.

"What do elephants have to do with the swamp?" Owen asked.

"What do you mean?"

"Maddie and Sawyer said you were working on a way to tie the llamas—"

"Alpacas," Charlie and Tori corrected at the same time.

"And goats and shit to the bayou," Owen went on as if they

hadn't spoken. "So how does adding another definitely-not-from-the-bayou animal help?"

Charlie nodded. He had a point, of course, but her mind was already working. "Our 'safari' can span continents," she said simply. "The kids and families will start their adventure in North America, starting on the farms of the Midwest and traveling down to Louisiana to the swamp. Then they'll travel to Africa to learn about other animals."

Owen just stared at her.

"Well, then why not keep going and get some penguins and take them to Antarctica too?" Zeke said. He tossed a fry into the air and caught it in his mouth.

Charlie frowned at him. "Maybe I will. Maybe I'll get a panda too and have them tour Asia."

"You *have* to get kangaroos then and have them 'visit' Australia," Zeke said, putting air quotes around *visit*.

He was teasing her, she knew, but dammit, now Charlie couldn't stop thinking about all of this. Kangaroos would be awesome.

"Would it be easier to take care of a kangaroo than an elephant?" she asked Tori, assuming the answer was yes.

"Um..." Tori looked at her as if she couldn't believe Charlie had actually asked that. "Definitely."

"But Griffin likes elephants," Maddie pointed out. "So, why would you get him a kangaroo?"

More importantly, *how* would she get him a kangaroo?

"He likes it all," Tori said to Maddie. But she was watching Charlie. "He's very fond of tigers. He loves zebras. He loves lemurs too. He *really* loves lemurs. They're endangered, you know."

Lemurs. Those were much smaller than elephants. And they were endangered. That meant Griffin could care for something that really needed him.

"Could lemurs be a part of a petting zoo?" Maddie asked. "Can people interact with them?"

"Maybe," Tori said after a moment. "I know there are a few places that allow people to feed and interact with them for short periods. But, like with any wild animal, we'd have to be careful and supervise it."

Charlie nodded, still thinking. "But even just having them —and Griffin being able to take care of them—would make *him* happy."

Tori's smile was wide. "Yes. It would."

Yes, it would.

"You wouldn't have any idea about how to get lemurs for a park like ours, would you?" Charlie asked.

"Now it's a park?" Zeke asked. "I thought it was a petting zoo."

"Well, it *could be* a park," Charlie said.

"Sawyer is going to roll his eyes so hard it will hurt," Owen said.

"Oh, Sawyer will be fine," Maddie said. "We'll just have Charlie explain it to him. No one can say no to her."

Charlie appreciated the vote of confidence and couldn't help the little flip of excitement she felt in her chest. Getting Griffin a lemur sounded like the perfect idea. She wanted him to be excited about the petting zoo. But after their talk, she thought that she was possibly already at the limit of how excited he could be. He was a wonderful vet and obviously cared a lot about the animals, be it pigs or goats or otters. But that was because he was a great guy. He was doing his job, and he would feel the same way even if those animals were simply someone's farm animals and not in a tourist attraction. In fact, making this a tourist attraction was what was making him less than enthusiastic.

Maybe lemurs could change that. She would really love to get him something he could be truly enthusiastic about. Sure, tourists would want to look at the lemurs and possibly feed and interact with them, but they would be for Griffin first and foremost.

"And yes, to answer your question," Tori said to Charlie. "I do know someone who would know about how we could get a couple of lemurs."

"Mitch is going to have to build an enclosure for that, right?" Zeke asked. "That would be cool."

Charlie grinned at him. "Yes, it will be all hands on deck. As always."

Zeke nodded, tossing another fry in his mouth and chewing. Then said, "Awesome."

It was hard to do anything privately here, but that was awesome. Even the craziest ideas actually got considered, and when something was going to happen, everyone was willing to play a part.

"Let me make a phone call," Tori said. "I'll let you know later today."

Charlie was excited. "Great. And no one says anything to Griffin."

Owen chuckled. "Don't worry. I'm not gonna be the one who tells him about this."

Three days later, when the front door to the clinic opened, Charlie looked up, admittedly hoping it was Griffin. She was always hoping it was him. She had it bad.

It wasn't him, though.

The woman was tiny, with lightly tanned skin, dark curly hair, and an instantly contagious grin. She was around Charlie's age and walked in as if she was in exactly the right place.

"Hi," Charlie greeted, getting to her feet. "Can I help you?"

"You're Charlie, right?" the woman asked.

"I am."

"Awesome!" The woman's smile got even brighter as she approached the counter. She was dressed in blue jeans with a bright red tank top and red Converse on her feet. When she walked, she nearly bounced.

Energy seemed to radiate from her, and Charlie found herself grinning without even knowing why. "Have we met?"

The woman shook her head. "Tori called me. I'm Fiona."

"Oh, if you're meeting Tori, she isn't here yet."

"I'm sure she's on her way. But I'm here for *you*," Fiona told her and propped her elbows on the front counter.

The counter was high enough for her that she had to stretch slightly. She couldn't have been more than five foot one, and Charlie noticed that everything about her seemed small. She had a cute turned-up nose, and her blue eyes practically twinkled. For just a moment, Charlie had the thought that Fiona reminded her of an elf. Or a sprite. Or something else with positive energy and maybe a magical touch.

"You're here for me?" Charlie repeated. "What about?"

"I hear you're in need of a lemur."

Charlie's eyes widened. "Yes, I'm interested in talking with someone who can tell me what it would take to care for a lemur at a place like ours and give more information about purchasing and licensing and all that."

Fiona laughed, and the sound was light and happy, and Charlie found that contagious as well. She laughed too, without being really sure why.

"We'll go over all of that when I introduce you to Larry."

Charlie shook her head. "Who's Larry?" Maybe Larry was the lemur expert who could help her decide if she should do this or not.

"Larry is one of the lemurs I brought you."

Charlie stared at Fiona. "You brought me a lemur."

"Three of them, actually. Larry, Curly, and Moe are outside just waiting to move into their new digs."

Charlie let that sink in for a moment, then asked again, "You *brought me* a *lemur*?"

"Tori said you wanted to get some lemurs for Griffin. I am one thousand percent on board with that idea. So I brought you some." Fiona said it as if it was the most obvious thing. Almost as if she had just brought Charlie a new pair of shoes to try on. Something simple and not at all crazy.

"You just brought them? I don't know anything about lemurs."

"But Griffin does," Fiona said.

"Griffin doesn't know that we're getting lemurs," Charlie said, feeling a tiny bubble of panic rising in her chest. She had intended to do a lot more homework. She never went into a presentation without being fully prepared. And presenting the idea of lemurs to Griffin seemed like something she needed to be very prepared for.

"Griffin Foster needs to be shaken up out of his boring, trying-to-be-a-normal-guy routine, and I think a hot blonde and lemurs are exactly what he needs," Fiona told her.

"Wait, do you know Griffin?"

Fiona nodded. "Oh, sure. Griffin and I were in Zambia together."

This woman had been in Africa with Griffin? The place he loved so much? The place that had shown him what he wanted to do with his life?

Suddenly Charlie was completely jealous of the woman standing in front of her, and it had nothing to do with Fiona's seemingly perfect hair or the fact that she clearly knew a lot about lemurs.

The stab of jealousy was strangely intense as well as completely surprising.

Charlie didn't get jealous, and she really shouldn't be jealous about Griffin.

But a cute brunette in possession of lemurs seemed much more like the type of woman Griffin should be with.

"You know that Griffin likes lemurs and knows a lot about them, so you think he'll be okay with this?" Charlie asked, focusing on the situation at hand. She could deal with who Fiona was to Griffin later. Or never.

Griffin and Fiona's relationship and history had nothing to do with her. Just because Charlie had been flirting with him, and even stealing kisses, and exchanging lots of innuendos over the past five days since their hot barn encounter, didn't mean that Griffin was hers to be jealous over.

And even if he did have a relationship with this woman, Charlie still wanted him to have lemurs.

"Oh, lemurs are the perfect thing for Griffin," Fiona said.

Good. That was good. Charlie frowned. "You said that he's got this boring thing where he's trying to be a normal guy?"

Fiona nodded. "Yeah, after what happened in D.C., he decided he was going to just be a regular vet. Which, of course, he's great at, but he's got a passion for bigger things. More meaningful things. Not that being a small-town veterinarian can't be meaningful," she said quickly. "It's very meaningful. Especially to the animals and families of those animals that he's taking care of. Tori is completely content doing that kind of work. And God bless her for it. It's just that Griffin has a... wilder streak." She grinned. "Of course, that sounds funny, considering Griffin is one of the most solid and steadfast people I know. He's just got a heart for wild animals."

Solid and steadfast. Charlie thought about that. That did seem to be Griffin. He definitely had things he felt strongly about, and he wasn't shy about expressing his opinions and feelings, but he was very consistent. It was easy to know where Griffin stood on most topics. And she really liked that.

Autre and the Landry family had given her the chance to express her wild side and be herself, but anyone who wanted to spread their wings and push boundaries needed a steady foundation under them. Griffin was that type of man. He was someone who could be counted on. If she were going to take a chance on staying in Autre and trying to build an animal park —something very outside her bubble of experience—she would need the Landrys telling her she could do whatever she wanted and get on board with her crazy ideas. But she also needed someone like Griffin, who would pull her back when it got too crazy and would give her the blunt, honest truth about what could and could not be done.

She felt excitement bubbling up from her stomach into her chest, like bubbles fizzing up out of a glass of soda. This could happen. She had everything she needed to make this happen. No, it wasn't a big international company with an office in Paris, but this was starting to feel like exactly where she should be and what she should be doing.

"So the lemurs will help him feel a little more excited about this plan, right?" Charlie asked Fiona. Fiona was a stranger. They'd literally met minutes ago. But the fact that they both knew—and clearly cared about—Griffin made Charlie ask.

Fiona nodded. "What Griffin needs is to do amazing work with a variety of animals and feel like he's making an impact, while not answering to bosses who know less than he does and without being beholden to donors. If he can be his own boss and in charge of the care of the animals, Griffin will be very happy and will be able to make a big difference."

"A big difference?" Charlie asked.

"When he was in Africa, he wanted to do all kinds of teaching. About the animals and what was going on with their populations and their ecosystems. He wanted to help people understand how they could get involved and why they *should* get involved. He was very passionate about conservation efforts and anti-poaching laws, and environmental issues that threatened various groups of animals. He was ready to be a huge fundraiser and to go to D.C. to lobby Congress and all kinds of other things. And even after he got back to the states, he really tried to make the best of it by going to vet school and hoped to move up the ranks at zoos where he could have even more influence over his zoo as well as networking with others."

Charlie stared at her. Griffin Foster had wanted to do public presentations and lobby Congress and grow his influence over zoos so that he could positively impact how animals were treated in captivity?

If that were true, all of her reasons for going into marketing would have resonated deeply with him.

It seemed they were even more alike.

"So, what kind of things can he do if he is in charge of a tiny animal park in a small town in Louisiana?"

"Education, possible propagation programs, public awareness, fundraising, helping other animal parks, and petting zoos with their care standards," Fiona shrugged. "Whatever he wants to do. He certainly has the credentials and the passion. He just needs a place to apply those. Something to get excited about."

"I want to help make that place," Charlie said.

Had she just committed to staying in Autre and building the park—for Griffin no less—to a near stranger?

"I like you," Fiona said. "I mean, I like anyone who's interested in lemurs. But someone who's willing to work at pulling Griffin back to where he needs to be in this world? Oh yeah, you're going to be one of my favorite people."

Yes, it seemed she had just made such a commitment.

Charlie felt her heart flutter in her chest. "Well, I'm creating a job for myself as well."

Fiona gave her a knowing smile. "Sure," Fiona said. "But I

think you could make a lot more money somewhere else. A lot more *guaranteed* money."

Charlie shrugged. "I like a challenge."

"Well, Griffin is definitely a challenge."

Charlie just gave a little nod with a smile.

"And you like Griffin."

The flutter in her chest got more intense. "Yes," she admitted. "I really like Griffin."

"That shows impeccable taste," Fiona told her.

"How much do *you* like Griffin?" Charlie couldn't help but ask. Fiona struck her as a straightforward type of woman.

"A lot," Fiona said. "He's like a brother to me. Except that he's a lot smarter and more responsible than my brothers."

Like a brother. Charlie took a deep breath and blew it out. She could deal with Griffin and Fiona being close friends. Definitely. She was starting to like Fiona quite a lot as well.

"Just so you know, I would want Griffin to have this even if I hadn't decided to stay."

Fiona nodded. "Yeah, that's how love works. You want the other person happy no matter what's going on with you."

Love.

Was that what she was feeling for Griffin? She was definitely in lust with him. She also liked him a lot. And she would even go so far as to say it was infatuation. But love?

It had only been a couple of weeks. That shouldn't be enough time to fall in love. But she could almost hear her grandma Ellie's voice in her head asking, *well, how long should it take then?*

In the Landry family, there were very few rules when it came to love. They just did it. They just loved. Big and loud and fiercely. And they didn't get hung up on things like it not making sense or it being too fast or two people seemingly not fitting together. Love was love. If you felt it, you felt it. And if you were a Landry, you embraced it, and you celebrated it, and you fought for it.

The Landry family tree had many amazing, crazy love stories. There wasn't one person currently residing in Autre, Louisiana, who would tell her that it was bonkers to think she was in love with Griffin Foster after only two weeks.

Except maybe Griffin Foster.

But she had no intention of telling him that she thought she was in love with him.

"Fiona!"

Charlie swung around at the sound of Griffin's voice. He'd evidently come in through the back of the clinic.

"Hey, Griff!"

A moment later, Griffin had his arms wrapped around Fiona and her feet dangling several inches off the floor.

"Saw that huge purple truck in front of the clinic," Griffin told her, setting her back on her feet. "You can't really surprise anyone with that thing, you know."

"It does make me a bit conspicuous," Fiona agreed. "But it also makes me feel like a badass, so I'm going to keep driving it."

"Not to mention that you need a huge old truck to pull those animal trailers you're always hauling all over."

Oh great, her surprise was ruined. He knew Fiona was here with animals?

He glanced at Charlie, and she felt her stomach flip at the warmth in his gaze when their eyes met. "You didn't ruin my surprise, did you?" he asked Fiona.

"Nope, we were just having some girl talk."

Wait, surprise? *He* had a surprise?

"Girl talk?" Griffin looked back and forth between them.

"Yeah, heard all about this hot guy Charlie is falling for," Fiona said.

Charlie's eyes went wide as Griffin's gaze clashed with hers.

"Is that right?" he asked, his voice almost nearing drawl-level. Hot and slow and full of *isn't-that-interesting*.

She didn't know which of them he was talking to exactly, so she simply swallowed hard and stayed quiet.

Fiona was happy to jump in. "Yeah, apparently he's super smart and really dedicated and passionate about his work and good looking and has a huge..."

Charlie's mouth dropped open, and she made a little squeaking sound.

Fiona gave her a sly smile as Griffin's brows shot up.

"...heart," Fiona finished.

Charlie snorted, and Griffin even grinned.

"Well, maybe I should leave since you haven't had a chance to talk about all of my other huge parts."

He was staring right at her when he said it, and Charlie felt her mouth drop open even wider. He always caught her off guard when he flirted, but he'd never done it in front of someone else and never so blatantly.

She looked at Fiona, who was grinning broadly.

Yeah, she liked Fiona too. Griffin was clearly very comfortable with the other woman, and seeing her made him happy. Anyone who could make Griffin smile like that was someone Charlie could like.

Especially if they were more like brother and sister.

"Yeah, I haven't had a chance to tell her about your huge ego or your huge negative attitude toward sloths," Charlie said.

Fiona gasped. "Don't tell me he turned you down about getting a sloth."

Charlie nodded, propping a hand on her hip. "Yep. Shot it right down."

Griffin groaned. "The last thing I need in my life is the two of you conspiring against me."

"Too late," Fiona said. "We've met, we've fallen in love, we're going to be BFFs. And just remember, Foster," she added. "You invited me here first."

"He did?" Charlie asked.

"First?" Griffin asked on top of Charlie's question.

Fiona just gave them both a sly smile.

They looked at one another.

"You invited her here?" Charlie asked.

"Yeah. So, did you?"

Charlie shook her head and looked at Fiona again. "No, actually I didn't know she was coming but... She brought something I need." She said those last five words slowly.

Griffin turned narrowed eyes to Fiona. "Who called you besides me?"

"Tori," Fiona answered.

"To bring something Charlie needs?" Griffin asked.

"Yes."

"Something for Charlie besides what I asked you to bring?" Griffin pressed.

Charlie looked at him quickly. "You had her bring something for me?"

Fiona shook her head. "Wouldn't this be easier if we just went outside and looked at everything?"

Charlie figured that hiding a bunch of lemurs would probably be difficult, so she might as well show them to Griffin now.

Griffin nodded. "Oh, I definitely need to see this."

Charlie snuck a glance at Griffin as they followed Fiona out to the parking lot.

He met her gaze and gave her a half smile. "I would've warned you about Fiona, but I wanted this to be a surprise."

"Fiona needs a warning?"

He chuckled. "Um... Yes. She can be a lot." They stopped at the doorway together and turned to face one another. "Fiona is one of my favorite people in the world. One of my best friends."

Charlie nodded. "She told me you were in Africa together."

"And we stayed in touch and see each other periodically since she's been back in the states. And it hit me the other day when I was talking to her that you two have a lot in common."

"Fiona and I?" Charlie didn't see that. Fiona was an exotic animal expert of some kind. She'd traveled to and lived in Africa. She'd worked on a wildlife game preserve. And she somehow was able to procure three lemurs with only a couple of days' notice. Charlie didn't know much more about her than that, but all of those things set the two women apart drastically.

"Fiona doesn't really believe in asking for permission. She follows her gut and is perpetually certain that all situations can be better. And doesn't take no for an answer."

"So she's pushy and bossy?"

Griffin grinned. "Definitely. But she is also an optimist and wants to change the world. And believes she can."

Charlie felt a warmth spread through her chest. "And that reminds you of me?"

"Yep. And, I know that the two of you together will cause me some major headaches at times, but I also think that the world better watch out once you two get together."

Charlie stepped closer and took his hand, giving it a squeeze. "I consider that a huge compliment."

"I seem to be getting a little better at those."

"You are. And, in the spirit of putting everything out there, it also makes me want to kiss you even more than usual. Which, by the way, is a lot."

Then Griffin completely shocked her by cupping the back of her head, tipping her head back, and covering her lips with his.

Right in the doorway of the veterinary clinic with Fiona just on the other side, and the potential for anyone to drive up and see them.

It was one of the sweetest kisses yet, and Charlie immediately grabbed the front of his shirt in her fists to hold him close for a little longer.

But they only truly got a few seconds before Fiona let out a shrill whistle. "Get your asses over here. Your new friends want to meet you."

They pulled apart, their gazes lingering. Griffin captured Charlie's hand and tugged her toward the huge purple pickup parked in front of the clinic.

It was one of the biggest trucks Charlie had ever seen. The wheels were enormous and lifted the truck at least a couple extra feet into the air. It was an extended cab and, though Charlie was no expert, even the front of the truck looked extra-large as if encasing a larger than usual engine.

It was also purple. Really purple. Like, grape soda purple.

Charlie hadn't known Fiona long, but already she felt like that truck fit the woman's personality. It was big, bright, colorful, and impossible to ignore.

Added to the whole picture was the huge trailer she had hooked to the back of the truck.

Again, Charlie knew very little about animal trailers or even transporting animals at all. But she was suddenly worried that lemurs were possibly bigger than she thought they were if they required that size of a trailer.

The sounds from the trailer would've been startling if Charlie didn't know what Fiona had brought with her. However, it sounded as if Griffin had asked her to bring something too, and Charlie assumed that the various squeaks, chirps, growls, and barks were not all from the lemurs.

Griffin was already frowning as they stopped next to the trailer. "You brought lemurs?"

Charlie grinned. Of course, he would know the sound of a lemur.

Fiona went to the back of the trailer and pulled the main door open. "When I heard that Charlie needed some lemurs for her new animal park, I knew that Larry, Curly, and Moe would be perfect."

Griffin moved to the back of the trailer to look inside. He looked like a kid on Christmas morning. His expression was a combination of happiness and excitement and wonder.

And Charlie wanted him to look like that every day.

"You asked her for lemurs?" He turned back to Charlie.

"With some input from Tori," Charlie said. "I was looking into what it would take to get you an elephant."

He just blinked at her for a few seconds, then shook his head. "You're serious, aren't you?"

She shrugged. "You told me you loved elephants."

He took the four steps that separated them, cupped her face, pulled her up onto her tiptoes, and kissed her again. She leaned into him, ecstatic that he loved the surprise and wasn't already saying no to keeping the lemurs and expanding the park.

He lifted his head a few seconds later and stared at her. "This is... One of the best things..."

"Hey, how about a little love for the woman who drove these guys from Florida?"

Griffin gave her a grin. "I appreciate it, Fi, but I'll show my gratitude to you in some other way."

"You better. Like with etouffee with shrimp and pecan pie."

"Ellie will be happy to see you," Griffin said with a laugh.

So this wasn't Fiona's first trip to Autre. She knew Charlie's grandmother, and Charlie could only assume, the rest of the family as well.

"Are you going to show Charlie what you asked me to bring for her?"

Charlie's eyes widened. "You *did* ask her to bring me something?"

"Come see." Griffin again looked excited.

Charlie really liked that look on him.

He pulled her to the back of the trailer, and they looked inside together.

Charlie gasped as she first caught sight of the lemurs. They were, in fact, bigger than she'd expected. Of course, she knew from her reading that they were part of the primate family. They did remind her a little bit of monkeys as they climbed up the side of the cage and swung from bars overhead. They were also very vocal. They were going to give the otters some competition for the loudest exhibit.

"Wow, they're really beautiful," she said.

Griffin grinned down at her. "This is the best surprise."

Yeah, now she wanted to get him an elephant too.

"And those are for you." He pointed.

"Hedgehogs!" She grinned up at him. "I wondered if we were going ahead with that."

"Hedgehogs will be great," he said. "And then there's him."

Charlie lifted her gaze and looked past the lemurs into the back, darker part of the trailer. And gasped.

"No," she said softly. "Really?"

"Really."

He'd gotten her a sloth.

A *sloth*.

"I've decided that saying yes to you maybe isn't the worst idea I've ever had."

"Oh, Dr. Foster, you really shouldn't have admitted that."

14

Fiona cleared her throat, and Charlie realized she and Griffin had been grinning at each other stupidly for several seconds.

"So, should we take them over to their new pens?" Fiona asked.

Oh, crap. They needed a place to put these animals. Charlie hadn't expected to have three lemurs today. She hadn't talked to Mitch or Zeke about building new enclosures. Hell, she didn't even know what kind of enclosures these animals actually needed.

"Oh..." She started.

"Yeah," Griffin told Fiona. "I'll ride with you and show you where to go."

Charlie looked up at him in surprise. "We have a place to put them?"

He nodded. "Mitch and Zeke have been working on it for the past few days." He shrugged. "I'm assuming they added a lemur enclosure to their plans as well."

Charlie supposed that Tori would have let them know

about the new plan. But she shook her head. "I haven't seen any new pens down by the petting zoo."

"They are over behind Mitch's place."

Charlie's eyes widened. The land behind Mitch's house was several acres of unused grassland that extended from the back-yards of three family homes to the bayou. Mitch, Zander, and Fletcher lived in those houses, and Zeke had built his own house at the end of the dead-end road everyone now referred to as Bachelor Row—even now that Paige had made Mitch not-a-bachelor-at-all.

The land had been in the family ever since the Landrys had settled here back before Autre was even officially a town. They'd turned down at least a dozen offers over the years for the purchase of the land, dedicated to the idea of keeping the land in the family.

It was exactly where Charlie had envisioned putting Griffin's elephant.

Obviously, elephants need a lot of space, and while the land became marshy the closer they got to the bayou, there was plenty of space on nice, firm ground that could keep several animals with the proper fencing.

Over the past couple of days, her vision for the area had become more specific, including buildings like barns and concession stands, paved pathways for people to walk, and various structures to keep a variety of animals safely.

Okay, she had envisioned an entire animal park behind her cousins' houses.

She hadn't told anyone that yet though.

The Landrys had done a lot of crazy things over the years, but she wasn't sure any of them were quite this crazy.

But Griffin was telling her there were already new enclosures built for the sloth.

"The poor sloth is going to be housed out there all by

himself?" Charlie asked, her heart thrumming with anticipation and excitement.

"Well, it looks like he's going to have some lemur friends," Griffin said.

Charlie nodded. "But you didn't know that." She tipped her head. "What were you thinking, Dr. Foster?"

"Just that it might be nice to have room for some expansion. The alpacas could use a little more room. And Fiona and I were talking, and she has a baby ostrich that might need a new home."

Charlie swung to face the other woman. "What do you *do*?" she asked. Who had access to sloths, lemurs, and ostriches at the snap of her fingers?

"I run an animal park outside of Orlando with my boyfriend," Fiona said with a smile. "We specialize in giraffes, but we have lots of other animals."

Charlie knew her expression was one of shock and amazement. "You have *giraffes*?"

Fiona nodded. "A bunch. They are my favorite. That's who *I* fell in love with in Africa."

Wow, Fiona was fascinating.

"You can get us more animals?"

"Oh, definitely—"

"Hang on," Griffin interrupted. "Let's not go crazy. How about we get the sloth and lemurs settled and see how things go."

"But you're willing to talk about more?" Charlie asked. Her heart was definitely pumping hard now. She was asking about more than the animals. She wondered if he realized that.

"I am." His gaze was intense and steady. "But in regards to the animals, I'll need a team."

So, yes, he did know she was talking about more than the animals.

Charlie took a deep breath herself. Just a few minutes ago,

she admitted to Fiona that she was committed to this idea. In large part, because of Griffin. But now, she was about to admit the same to him. That would make it even more official. And... complicated. Exactly what he'd wanted to avoid.

It would also mean she could quit sending out her resume to marketing firms and companies.

She took one more deep breath. Then said, "I'm in."

"Okay."

It wasn't just the word, it was the look in his eyes and the tone in his voice that made that one simple word into a much bigger promise.

Charlie opened her mouth to respond with more, but just then, a car came screeching into the parking lot. They all whirled around.

A man jumped out of the passenger side the second the car came to a stop. "Dr. Foster!" He had a dog in his arms.

Griffin immediately shifted into professional mode and bee-lined for the man.

"What happened?" Griffin took the dog and turned toward the clinic as the man fell in step beside him.

"We just found it by the side of the road. Hit by a car, I'm sure. We were driving by and thought it was dead, but it lifted its head, and we knew we had to stop."

The dog whined in Griffin's arms and was clearly in distress. Charlie stood frozen to the spot in the parking lot watching them as the man pulled the door open for Griffin, and they disappeared inside.

"You need to go in?" Fiona asked.

Charlie shook herself. Yes, of course, she should go in. She was Griffin's assistant, and obviously, he was now at work. But she didn't really want to. This seemed next level and far beyond her ability to help.

But she swallowed. Griffin needed someone to assist him.

She finally nodded. "Yeah, I should go in." She glanced around. "I don't know what to do about the lemurs."

Fiona waved that away. "No worries, I'll call Tori or Fletcher or Mitch. We'll get them taken care of."

Right, Fiona knew everyone here, and obviously, knew more about lemurs than Charlie did. Still, Charlie wanted to go with the lemurs a lot more than she wanted to go into the clinic.

"Okay." But she was still just standing looking at the clinic door.

"It's not exactly any of my business," Fiona said. "But you're not a veterinary tech, are you?"

Charlie shook her head. "No. I am just the receptionist and another pair of hands here. I'm in... marketing." That sounded so weak and stupid suddenly.

"But you want to help Griffin expand the animal park."

"I do."

"Well, working with animals is amazing and can be very rewarding," Fiona said. "But it can also break your heart. Animals, like people, get hurt and sick, and sometimes they don't recover. Exotic animals can be especially a lot of work and can be difficult to treat."

"What are you saying?" Charlie asked though she knew.

"If you're going to have a collection of animals, and if you're going to support Griffin in this, you have to be prepared for the bad things that happen too."

Charlie took a moment to really focus on the other woman. Fiona was clearly very friendly and, as Griffin had described her, an optimist. But right now, she was being completely serious and, if Charlie wasn't mistaken, protective of Griffin.

"I just want Griffin to be happy," Charlie said.

Fiona nodded. "I believe that. But taking this on, expanding with new animals, is going to be a big deal for him. It's a risk.

The fact that you've got him thinking about it in the first place is huge. But there will be times when it's hard on him. He hates seeing animals suffer, and he hates losing them. And that will happen, of course. He knows it will be painful at times. So if he's willing to do this, it must be because he trusts in your support."

Charlie sucked in a little breath. Basically, Fiona was telling her that Griffin was willing to do this because of her and that if she wasn't up to the task, now was the time to realize it. And get out.

But she was in too deep.

Not only did they already have hedgehogs, lemurs, and a sloth, and not only had Mitch and Zeke put time and resources into the new enclosures, and clearly, the Boys of the Bayou would've had to put money into that, but... she was also in too deep emotionally.

With Griffin.

She wanted to make him happy. She wanted to give him something that he would find rewarding and that would make him smile and feel like he had a purpose. Yes, as cliché as it sounded, she wanted to save him. She wanted him to use his passion and potential, and it seemed she had found a way.

She couldn't bail now.

"I understand what you're saying," she told Fiona. "And I'm going to go inside and help Griffin right now."

Fiona looked at her for a long moment but finally gave a little nod. "Okay. I'll see you later."

Charlie turned on her heel and faced the front door of the clinic again. She took a deep breath, blew it out, and headed inside to be Griffin's assistant.

"I am so fucked, you guys."

Griffin was seated on one of the large boulders in the otter enclosure. It was dinner time, and he knew everyone would be gathered at Ellie's, including Fiona. He knew he should go up there. They'd probably make him feel better.

But Charlie would probably be there. And she'd had a really bad day.

The dog that had been hit by a car along the highway hadn't made it. It wasn't his first, of course. Sometimes, no matter what he did, animals didn't survive. It always tore him up a little, of course, but it was a part of being a veterinarian.

Today had been made worse because Charlie had been there.

He'd felt like a damn failure.

In every other way, Charlie made everything better. His days since she'd come to Autre had been some of the most exasperating yet fun days he'd had in a very long time. She'd brightened everything up. And not just with the new bright paint colors around the petting zoo or the colored caramel corn she'd ordered for them to sell in their pseudo-concession stand that would eventually be replaced by a much bigger, better-stocked snack shack. Not just in the various colored t-shirts she'd convinced Maddie to add to the green and white tees Boys of the Bayou had been selling. The brightness she had added was deeper than all that. She made him happy. She made him smile, laugh, and look forward to his day in a way he hadn't in a long time.

But today, having her there as the dog slipped away had been heart-wrenching.

She hadn't handled it well at all. Tears had been streaming down her cheeks, and the moment he said, "I've got this, Charlie, you can go," she'd spun and run from the room.

There was no way he was going to make her stay and clean

up. Or help him track down the owners. Or anything else involved in dealing with an animal that had died.

He'd wanted to go after her, but there was nothing he could say that would make it better. The dog had been hit by a car and died. Yes, it had been in some pain. And yes, there was a family out there who was going to be heartbroken tonight when they found out their dog had been killed.

There was nothing he could say or do to make that better.

His line of work came with a lot of joy and fun. Animals amazed him on a regular basis. But it also came with sadness. Veterinarians had one of the highest suicide rates of any of the professions, not only because it was always hard to lose a patient but because of the human beings who were devastated by those losses. Veterinarians were often blamed for not doing more or working harder and faster, and having that piled on top of already feeling like they hadn't done enough led to a lot of stress and depression.

But veterinarians knew death was part of life. Just like human physicians did. And when they went into practice, they knew there were going to be times when patients didn't pull through or when euthanasia was the humane thing to do.

But knowing it didn't always make it easier.

He was used to working with other animal experts. When an animal had died on the preserve or in one of the zoos, it had been hard, but he hadn't felt it was his obligation to comfort his co-workers. They got it. They'd dealt with the same things he had.

Seeing the woman he was eighty percent sure he was falling in love with heartbroken, had made his heart ache in a whole new way.

"What was I supposed to say?" he asked Gertie, who was perched on his lap, lecturing him.

He handed her treats, and she quieted for a moment.

"Do you really think that going after her and telling her that if she was going to be involved with animals, she'd have to get used to this was really the right thing to do?" he asked the otter.

She did *not* think that was the right thing to do, but she kept insisting that he should have said or done *something*.

"If I thought just hugging her would've been enough, I would have done that."

Gertie gave up on him, slipping off his lap and sliding into her man-made river.

He turned to Gus with a sigh. "So, I'm not great at the boyfriend thing. Big shock."

Gus told him he was being dramatic.

"Easy for you to say," Griffin said. "Human females are a lot more complicated than otter females, Gus."

Gus told him to fuck off if he thought he had it so bad. Gus was living and raising kids with his girlfriend.

Griffin stroked the otter's back. "Okay, so you might know a little bit about relationships. But I can't tell her that we'll never lose another animal. I can't tell her that I can save them all." God, he really couldn't tell her that. "I can't promise there's never going to be heartbreaking moments. She'll get used to it. It was harder on me in the beginning too."

Gus informed him that that was not the right approach with Charlie.

"Well, I'm not going to *tell* her that she has to just get used to it, but it *will* get easier with time."

It didn't actually get easier. It just became less of a shock when things didn't turn out as expected.

The otter in his lap chattered at him again, and Griffin shrugged. "Yeah, okay, I was wallowing a little bit about things not turning out in D.C., but I've been getting better."

For a guy who claimed to know that life didn't always go according to plan, Griffin had definitely let the situation at the National Zoo throw him for a loop.

He'd come to Louisiana with a plan to approach his life and

work with animals completely differently than he had in the past. Rather than looking for ways to make it all work and pushing for bigger and better, he had been determined to simply be content with what he had and to take one day at a time.

It had taken the bubbly, pushy, addictive blond Landry to shake him up and make him wonder what the hell he was doing.

"But I never would've come up with the idea of having an animal park here," Griffin told Gus. "It's not like I was missing some obvious answer."

Gus didn't agree with that either, even after being given a treat. He sat in Griffin's lap, chattering about what a dumbass Griffin had been.

Griffin shook his head. "Yes, I know the Landrys are hugely supportive and always willing to think outside the box. And yes, I feel a definite kinship with Tori and her willingness to take on any and all animals. But I wouldn't have thought about having an elephant in Louisiana."

Gus asked him why the hell not.

"Because having an elephant here is definitely over the top," Griffin explained to the otter. "But," he said over the otter's protest. "Lemurs, and a sloth, and an ostrich, and... Maybe some other stuff could work."

Remembering Charlie's face after he told her the dog had died made his entire chest hurt, but he also thought about how she'd lit up when she noticed the sloth in the trailer. And, he knew it wasn't because she was particularly fond of sloths. In fact, he doubted very much that she'd spent much time in her life thinking about sloths.

He'd put that look on her face. Because he'd surprised her and done something that clearly said he was listening to her and wanted to make her happy. The only other look that was even more poignant had been the look on *her* face when he'd first seen the lemurs. It had been clear that it meant a lot to her to give him those.

Charlie cared about him. It was obvious, and it made his heart swell and ache at the same time.

He'd had relationships in the past. He'd been serious with a couple of women. He'd known women who cared about him and possibly even loved him. But the idea that Charlie Landry would want to give him an elephant and had succeeded in giving him lemurs did more to him than any other woman had ever done.

Charlie was special. She knew almost nothing about animals, particularly exotic ones. She had come to tiny Autre from Paris, France. And yet she looked around the little town and the dinky petting zoo that hadn't even had proper signage and saw nothing but possibility.

And that was how she looked at him. She saw possibilities for him. In him. She wasn't going to let him hide out in Louisiana or wallow in the things that had gone wrong in the past. She was going to push him to do more, and be better, and go after his dreams.

"Okay," Griffin told Gus. "I'm probably more like ninety percent in love with her."

The otter told him it was about time he realized that.

"So, what do I do about it?"

Gus turned and scampered off Griffin's lap, slipping into the river with Gertie.

Griffin sighed.

It was possible that he needed to start getting relationship advice from creatures with two legs instead of four.

C harlie was depressed.

That was something that so rarely happened, she didn't really have good coping mechanisms for it.

She got upset. Angry. Frustrated. Sad. But depressed was very unusual.

Of course, it was also unusual for her to see a dog die.

That had really sucked. She wasn't a Pollyanna. She knew the animals died. She'd just never seen it happen herself.

And she never wanted to see it happen again.

But worse, she never wanted to see Griffin giving his all to save an animal, only to have it not work.

He'd clearly been devastated.

Again, she was an adult, and she knew what veterinarians did. She didn't think that this was the first time it happened to Griffin, nor would it be the last. Still, seeing the man she cared so much about and who she was trying so hard to help heal knocked down like that had been really hard.

Now, she sat in her own personal therapy session—i.e., at Ellie's bar with a plate of homemade beignets in front of her and her crazy, loving family surrounding her.

And she was still depressed.

The beignets were delicious, the chicory coffee was strong, and her family was, well, her family.

All of that was perfect.

But Griffin wasn't here, and she didn't know where he was, and she had no idea what to say to him even if she found him.

Still... she wanted to find him.

She wanted to hug him. She wanted to tell him that he was amazing even if he hadn't been able to save the dog. She wanted to tell him that no matter what happened, she would always consider him a hero.

She wanted to tell him that watching him work on the dog had actually been sexy.

But that was very inappropriate, she realized.

She was sad the dog had died. She was sad thinking about how they needed to find the family. She hurt for Griffin.

But watching him today had been sexy. She wasn't going to admit that to anyone else because it sounded very strange, but this was the first time she'd seen him truly worked up. He'd been intensely focused, working quickly, barking orders, and clearly pouring his all into saving the dog.

There had been blood, and a sense of desperation, and definite sadness. But seeing Griffin determined and confident, yet still clearly working with emotion, had been, yes, sexy, dammit. She didn't care how that sounded. Well, she cared enough not to say it out loud, but she wouldn't apologize for being attracted to Griffin in those moments.

"You need a shot of something in that coffee?"

Charlie looked up at Ellie. She smiled. "Promise it will help?"

Ellie shook her head. "Nope."

Charlie sighed. "No magic potion, huh?"

Ellie put her hand on Charlie's head, an affectionate gesture she used with all of her grandchildren. "Some hurts just have to hurt."

Well, that wasn't what she wanted to hear. "You know what happened?"

"Sure. Pete Cochran and Billy Melancon were the ones who found the dog. They came in here for lunch."

"Griffin tried so hard," Charlie said. She looked down at her coffee cup. "I didn't know what to say to him."

"You couldn't just say you were sorry it went sideways?" Ellie asked. "Or say that you knew he did his best?"

Charlie lifted a shoulder. "That wouldn't have changed anything."

Ellie stroked her hand over Charlie's hair. It was such a

familiar, comforting gesture, Charlie felt her throat tighten. "You don't have to change things all the time, Charlie."

Her grandmother's words hit her and made her heart skip. "But..." She really felt like she did. "Isn't that what we should try to do? Change things? Make them better?"

"Well, maybe you're not looking at changing the *right* things," Ellie told her.

"What do you mean?"

"You can't change the fact that dogs die. But you being there to give Griffin a big hug when it happens can change how it feels for him afterward."

Charlie studied her grandmother's face. "I like changing things."

"I know. Even more, you like being the savior," Ellie said with an affectionate smile. "You like making your mark. But maybe you need to start realizing that you make your mark in lots of ways. Maybe you didn't send Isabelle's attacker to jail, but you made her feel supported. Maybe Boys of the Bayou isn't going to be worth ten million dollars, but they're all excited, and everyone is pitching in on the new projects and having fun. And you can't keep Griffin from never facing tough times, but you can definitely be there for him when those times come."

Charlie let all of that sink in. Yes, she did love being the one who swooped in with her big ideas and plans, took everything to the next level, and then stepped back and saw that everyone was happier and more successful when she was done.

Yes, she'd envisioned doing that here.

But maybe Ellie was right. Maybe she was making people happier and more successful in smaller, quieter ways.

And maybe she couldn't make *everything* better, but she could do her best with the things in her control.

Who was she kidding? Of course, Ellie was right.

"Thanks," she told her grandmother. "*That* helps."

And now she needed to hug Griffin. Of course, first, she

needed to *find* Griffin. He wasn't answering his phone, wasn't at his house, and wasn't down at the petting zoo barn. She'd left the clinic after the dog passed away but had gone back to see if Griffin needed her after she'd cried for about ten minutes. She'd just been overwhelmed, but she realized running out was the wrong reaction.

Griffin had been gone when she got back though. And she hadn't seen him since. She'd been hoping he'd come to Ellie's, possibly needing the camaraderie of the group the way she did, but she hadn't seen him yet.

Ellie grinned at her and leaned over to kiss the top of her head before stepping away. "Good to know I'm still better than a shot of whiskey."

"An ostrich? Really?" Tori asked Fiona.

The question pulled Charlie's attention back to the conversation around the table.

"Yes," Fiona said. "And I won't tell you that this ostrich is possibly the dumbest bird I've ever met."

Tori chuckled. "Ostriches aren't really known for being all that smart."

"But you love them anyway," Josh said. He had his arm over the back of Tori's chair and was playing with a strand of her hair. He tugged on it playfully. "Or you probably love them *because* the poor things are dumb."

Zeke laughed. "Ah, she loves dumb things. That finally explains why she's with *you*."

Josh flipped him off.

Mitch and Paige were also there at the far end of the table, and Maddie, Owen, Sawyer, and Juliet were also present. Zeke, Zander, and Fletcher were lounging at the next table.

The seating arrangement made Charlie smile. The big tables at the back of Ellie's had always been where the family gathered. It was a big enough space for them all but also kept them out of the way of paying customers. They helped themselves to the kitchen and behind the bar for their food and drink.

It seemed that the single guys hung out at the smaller table to the side while the couples gathered at the bigger, longer table. It was very similar to having a kid's table at Thanksgiving, and Charlie found that amusing.

Of course, Charlie joined her three bachelor cousins rather than sitting at the couples' table.

Fiona was at this table too, and Charlie was certain Zeke and Zander had been flirting with the bubbly, brunette animal expert before she arrived.

Charlie looked across the table at Fletcher. He was sitting back with one ankle crossed over his opposite knee. He was watching the group, smiling but seemingly not as engaged.

Fletcher wasn't the outright flirt that Zeke and Zander were, so he probably hadn't been hitting on Fiona. Now that Charlie thought about it, she really never saw Fletcher flirt. He was very good-looking and very friendly and had plenty of women's attention. The mothers of the kids in his class—and kids in several other classes—found him charming, and he got lots of cookies and brownies and gushy, "Oh, Mr. Landry, you're *such* a good teacher." Maybe that was enough for him.

Or maybe he was trying to be a good role model. As a male third-grade teacher, he was in the gender minority in his profession, and she was sure he got plenty of attention for that too. It was very possible that he felt increased pressure, as a single guy teaching young kids, to be an especially upstanding citizen. Flirting with the moms probably wasn't the best example for the kids. Or the best way to endear himself to his bosses. Or the dads.

Especially the dads who had grown up with him and knew his past.

Especially the dads who had been right beside him as he'd partied and drag raced and fought and swiped his grandpa's homemade moonshine and played strip poker—and strip anything else they could think of.

He was a great guy. But he was a Landry, and he came from the wilder branch of the family tree for sure.

"You okay?" Charlie asked him softly.

He looked at her and gave her a wink. "Better than okay."

She didn't quite believe him, but he either didn't want to talk about it or figured this was the last place he should.

"So, we're really going to get in a bunch more animals?" Zeke asked.

Charlie realized he directed the question to her. She glanced at Tori, but Tori was watching her as well.

Charlie looked at Sawyer, then Maddie. They, too, were watching her as if waiting for her answer. So the other veterinarian in town and two of the major partners in Boys of the Bayou weren't making this decision?

But yeah, Charlie had kind of plowed ahead with many of the plans, and over the past few weeks, had mostly just informed everyone after the wheels were already turning.

Still, talking to Mitch about building a snack shack and getting in touch with a few food vendors, and adding to their t-shirt and stuffed animal inventory were relatively minor.

At least compared to bringing in sloths and lemurs.

And especially compared to bringing in anything more.

"If you all are interested," Charlie started, using her marketing presentation voice. "I think there is a lot of potential for growth, and I think it could result in not only increased revenue but also increased business for other parts of the family—the swamp boats and here at Ellie's—as well as increased awareness of animal care and the ecosystem and conservation efforts and..."

Suddenly, she ran out of steam.

Just like that.

That never happened. She always knew what she was going to say and how to say it, and she was always prepared.

But now, sitting here with her family and wanting more for them, but also for herself and, of course, for Griffin, she found that she couldn't spin it.

They were all watching her expectantly. A couple of them seemed surprised because none of them had ever known her to run out of words.

She sighed. "I really want to do more here. I want to turn this into a bigger animal park. I want to bring in all kinds of animals. I want this to be a place people want to come and interact with animals and learn to love them and... make memories. Smile and laugh and have a good time." She took a breath and blew it out. "But I'm not really sure I know what I'm doing. And it's probably crazy, and I don't know if we have the resources to do it. But yeah, I want to make Griffin an animal park. Somehow. If I can."

There was a long beat of silence.

Charlie realized what she'd said immediately. She wanted to do this for Griffin. And she'd just confessed that out loud. To her entire family.

Tori was the first one to speak. "We're in."

Charlie blinked at her. "In? For what? Which part? It's just one crazy, mixed-up, probably-too-big idea."

Tori nodded. "Yeah, that part." She grinned. "We'll make it work. We've got everything we need. We have people to help us build and maintain the animal enclosures." She looked at Mitch and Zeke. "We've got our favorite accountant." She grinned at Zeke again. "We've got enough hands to get started, and we can hire as we go. It would be great to become a bigger employer in Autre. And we've got animal experts. Griffin and I can handle a lot of it. We've got Fiona to call on if we need her. But Griffin and I have contacts that we can tap as needed." Tori looked around at the group, seemingly choked up suddenly.

"We'll do it together. As long as this group takes it on together, we can make it happen."

Charlie took all of that in. Her throat tightened. Yes, she liked being the savior. But it was really nice to have people who could, and *would*, step in and save *her* sometimes too. Like when she got way in over her head with building an animal park out of a petting zoo.

She looked around the group. Tori was right. These people could do this. This could actually happen.

"Okay," she took another deep breath. "I guess we're getting an ostrich," she said to Fiona. They already had an emu. It couldn't be that different. Probably. Could it? See, she really didn't know what she was doing.

"What the hell is that big ugly purple thing in the parking lot?"

Charlie turned on her seat toward the deep, low voice coming from behind her.

The man was huge. He was tall, at least six foot four inches, broad, and muscular. He also had an air of confidence, and annoyance, that made him seem even bigger. His brown hair touched his shoulders, and he ran a big hand through it now, sweeping it back from his face.

"Hey, Knox," Zander greeted with a grin. He pointed at Fiona. "It's hers."

"You drive that thing?" Knox took stock of Fiona.

Fiona was also clearly taking stock of Knox. "Yeah, and if you're nice, I'll take you for a ride later," Fiona told him.

Charlie covered her laugh with a cough. Zeke, Zander, and Fletcher did not. They laughed out loud.

"I'm gonna warn you right now," Zeke told Knox. "You take her up on that invitation, and you'll come back a changed man."

Knox looked from Zeke to Fiona and back again. "You've been for a ride with her?" he asked Zeke.

Zeke shook his head. "No way, man. I tend to piss women off, and this one could literally feed me to the lions if I made her mad."

Knox looked at Fiona again. "Literally?"

"I only have two lions, and they're well-fed, so there's not much risk. But for the right guy, I'd let them get hungry," she said with a nod.

Knox clearly had no idea what to think of Fiona. "Your truck is taking up several parking spots."

"Yeah. I like big things," she agreed.

"It's kind of in the way," Knox told her. "You gonna move it?"

"It's gonna be big no matter where I put it."

Charlie didn't know about anyone else, but she thought that sounded very dirty. She glanced at Knox. He was watching Fiona with a look that was part confusion and part interest.

But Fiona had a boyfriend, so she probably hadn't meant it *like that*.

Though, looking at Fiona looking at Knox, Charlie wasn't *entirely* sure about that.

Finally, Knox looked at Zander. "Can't you do something?"

Zander shrugged and rolled his head to look at Fiona. "Hey, can you move your truck, so it doesn't take up so many parking spots?"

She gave him a sweet smile. "No."

Zander looked up at Knox. "I tried."

"You're a terrible town cop."

"Or am I just a gentleman and good friend? What do you expect a chick with a trailer full of lemurs and sloths to drive, and where is she supposed to put it when she needs gumbo and bread pudding?"

Knox's frown deepened. "A trailer full of *what*?"

"Fiona brought a sloth and some lemurs to add to the Boys of the Bayou Gone Wild," Zeke informed him. Seemingly with glee.

"And hedgehogs," Fiona added.

"A *sloth*?" Knox said. He looked at Tori, then Sawyer. "A sloth?" he repeated.

"His name is Slothcrates. He's *really* cute," Juliet chimed in.

Sawyer shrugged. "I don't know what to tell you," he said to Knox. "Sloths are really cute."

Knox muttered something under his breath that sounded a little like *pussy whipped*.

Charlie grinned but ducked her head so he wouldn't see it.

He focused on Zander. "If ya'll keep adding animals, the traffic and parking are going to get even worse."

"You really think so?" Charlie asked, perking up. "You think it will bring more people in?"

Knox looked at her with one brow up. "Is that not your goal?"

"Well, of course, but... you really think it will happen?"

He sighed. "Yeah. I do. And I think it's going to be a pain in the ass."

"Who are *you*?" Fiona asked. "You with the USDA or something?"

Charlie did know from her reading that the USDA oversaw the animal care in petting zoos and animal parks and zoos. At some point, she supposed they'd get a visit. But she was going to depend on Tori and Griffin, and now Fiona, to know what they needed to do.

"He's our city planner," Zander said with a grin. "And he gets his panties in a wad whenever something might muck up the traffic patterns in our great metropolis."

Knox—and was that his first name or last?—didn't *look* like a city planner. Or the type to get his panties in a wad about things like traffic patterns. That seemed a little... nerdy... for a big guy who looked like he could be on the line for the Saints or right at home knocking out drywall with Zeke or pouring cement with Mitch or even slinging hay bales for the goats and alpacas. He was brawny. He looked like a big, hot, blue-collar Cajun. Not a guy who sat behind a desk with perfectly sharpened pencils and schematics hanging on the wall behind him.

"I'm going to enjoy watching you have to actually get up and write a ticket or two when people start having fender benders all over our 'great metropolis' because our traffic lights and parking areas and roads aren't up to an increase in traffic," Knox returned. "Mayor Landry's gonna love her first city council meeting after all of this."

Okay, but he *sounded* like a nerdy city planner.

And right, Mayor Landry. Kennedy. Was this really going to be a mess for her now?

Charlie sighed. She tended to get ahead of herself in her mind and her overall plans, but she always had set parameters to work with. Here, it seemed that "sure, whatever" was going to be the motto. That *sounded* great, of course, but maybe it was dangerous.

She glanced at Fiona. Griffin had said they were going to probably cause him headaches together. It looked like others in Autre were going to need more ibuprofen too.

But Fiona just gave her a wink and then leaned in, resting her elbow on the table and her chin on her hand. "Are you going to be here making a fuss every time I show up with new animals?" she asked Knox. Her voice was sweet, but her expression was mischievous.

Knox didn't seem overly impressed with her batting eyes or her sweet tone. "You're going to be showing up with new animals again?" he asked.

"Well, they can't just go pick up an ostrich at Target, you know," Fiona told him.

He looked at Zander. "An ostrich?"

Zander held up both hands. "Animal procurement is above my pay grade."

"Is exerting some control over the crazy around here above your pay grade too?" Knox asked.

Zander nodded. "*Waaaaay* above."

Knox sighed and looked at Fiona again. "Do I need to call the USDA?"

"Are you not-so-politely asking if these animals are legally obtained and well cared for and will be properly licensed?" Fiona asked, sitting back, apparently realizing that her flirting wasn't getting her anywhere.

"I am," Knox said simply.

"The answer to all of those are 'of course,'" Fiona replied.

"You have a license for them all?"

"I do."

"In Louisiana?"

That made her pause. And that pause was just a little too long.

"Get it taken care of." Knox looked around at the group, including them all in the directive.

"Why does the *city planner* care about all of that so much?" Fiona asked. *City planner* could have been *stinky pile of garbage* with the way she said it.

"He *really* likes paperwork," Zander said.

"He really likes *not* having to do extra paperwork," Knox corrected. "Like the paperwork required to put in new stop signs and to fix potholes and to increase garbage pickup. And he *really* doesn't like having city council meetings where he has to explain to the people of this town that we can't do those things because the budget doesn't allow for it."

"Does he like having the area businesses thrilled with the uptick in customers stopping for gas and food and souvenirs?" Fiona asked.

"He does," Knox said, still speaking of himself in the third person.

Charlie watched Fiona and Knox square off, hiding her smile by pressing her lips together.

Knox was a big guy, and when he planted his hands on his hips and glowered, he seemed even bigger.

Petite Fiona wasn't the least bit daunted, however. She continued to sit. In fact, she was now leaning back, her legs crossed, looking at Knox as if he was boring her. But her cheeks were pink, which spoke to either anger... or excitement.

"Well, then, he should be thanking this group for providing an increase in traffic and business to the town," she informed him.

"Except that, a lot of the businesses in town won't see an increase in revenue from this," Knox said, clearly exasperated. "The clothing shop, the hardware store, the mechanic. But they'll have to deal with the increased motor and pedestrian traffic, littering, not to mention animal noises and smells."

Fiona shook her head. "Don't be ridiculous. Families will decide to stick around for the crawfish boil and will head downtown and look around the shops and buy stuff. And inevitably, someone will have car trouble while they're here and will need the mechanic. And you can't tell me that Mitch doesn't buy a lot of his supplies from the hardware store when he's building new pens for the animals, especially when the woman bringing the animals doesn't give them a whole lot of time to order things in."

Knox just stood looking at her. Then he sighed. "Is your last name Landry?"

"Why do you ask?"

"Because you sure act like a Landry."

Fiona gave him a smile. "Well, thank you very much. But no. It's Grady. Do you want my number too?"

"I have a feeling I'm going to be seeing a lot of you without needing to call."

Her smile widened. "Lucky you."

"Yeah," he said dryly. "Exactly what I was thinking." He looked at Zander again and pointed a finger at the town cop. "You realize this means less fishing and more actual police work?"

"Oh, I'll be in the front row at the next city council meeting," Zander said. "We really are going to need more traffic lights to cut down on fender benders."

"You mean cut down on the paperwork you have to do," Knox said.

"Potato potahto," Zander said with a shrug.

Knox sighed, seemingly at them collectively. "Make sure you get the licensing taken care of. The last thing we want is the USDA making a big deal about all this."

He headed for the door, and they all watched him go.

Fiona was the first one to speak. "Wow." She looked at Fletcher. Then to Zeke. "You all even grow the nerds big and hot down here."

Zeke, the contractor-slash-accountant, stretched his arms straight out in front of him, fingers interlaced, and cracked his knuckles. Then he sat back in his chair, arms spread wide, and said, "Thank you very much."

They went back to talking, laughing, and eating.

Charlie thought about everything Knox had mentioned. He had actually made some good points. Again, she hadn't fully thought out her plan and how it would impact people beyond the Landrys. But yes, an increase in traffic would affect Zander, the local businesses, and simple things like the roads and parking lots.

She sighed. She was used to making plans that involved a lot of other people who handled details like this, but here, it was all a lot more up close and personal. And frankly, she didn't really know what she was doing when it came to things like stoplights and paperwork for the USDA.

She needed some air.

She pushed her chair back and stood. The whole group looked at her.

"I'm going to head out."

Several nodded, and a couple wished her a good night.

But Mitch said, "He's probably with the otters."

Charlie paused and looked back at her cousin. "What do you mean?" She knew who "he" was, and she wasn't going to deny she wanted to go looking for him.

"Griffin hangs out with the otters when he's had a bad day," Mitch said. "And if you are real quiet going over there, you might overhear their conversation."

"Whose conversation?" Charlie asked.

Mitch chuckled. "Griffin's conversation with Gus and Gert."

"Gus and Gert, the otters?"

"Yep."

"He talks to the otters?" Charlie felt the familiar warmth in her chest that always occurred when it came to Griffin interacting with animals.

"Yeah, and it's pretty funny," Mitch said with a grin.

She smiled. Of course he talked to the otters.

Charlie knew Mitch and Griffin were good friends and that Mitch wasn't making fun of Griffin. But he was wrong.

Griffin talking to the otters wasn't funny.

It was downright delightful.

15

Griffin heard the footsteps approaching the otter enclosure. He handed out the rest of the treats to Gus and Gertie and stretched to his feet.

His heart thunked hard when Charlie came around the bend in the path.

She spotted him immediately and lifted her hand.

The high glass walls around the enclosure weren't sound-proof, but he didn't want to have to raise his voice to talk to her. He gestured toward the door to the side of the enclosure. She nodded.

They met at the door, and he pulled it open.

"Are you okay?" he asked.

"I'm sorry," she said at the same time.

They stopped and smiled at each other.

"What are you sorry for?"

"For not handling losing the dog well. For leaving without making sure you were all right."

That made his chest tight. "It's part of the job, Charlie," he said. "It's not that it's easy or no big deal, but it happens. It's not your job to make sure that I'm all right."

She stepped closer and tipped her head to look up at him. "But... it kind of feels like my job."

That made it hard to take his next breath. He had friends. His brother Donovan and he were a lot closer now, and since coming to Autre and meeting the Landrys, he'd felt more cared for than he had in a very long time. But it had been years, even before his parents had died, that anyone had felt like they needed to take care of him.

He didn't think that Charlie actually believed that he couldn't handle this without her. But she wanted to make it better. And dammit, her being here, with concern in her eyes, did make it better.

And he wanted to make it better for her too.

He realized that should have sent a wave of panic through him. Instead, it felt right. Like this was part of what he was supposed to be doing.

He took her hand and lifted it to his chest. He pressed it over his heart, the spot where she often touched him. "I'm okay. Are *you* all right?"

She wet her lips and then shook her head slowly. "That was really hard. Not just the dog dying but watching you work so hard and having it not turn out. I wanted to help *you*, and I couldn't, and that also felt bad."

"Honestly," he told her, realizing he was about to confess something that was going to change things between them and realizing that he wanted to say it anyway. "You just being here now helps me a lot."

Her eyes widened slightly. "Really? I don't know what to say or do."

"You came looking for me."

She pulled her bottom lip between her teeth and nodded.

"I guess that's all I needed. I feel a lot better already."

She looked at him for a few seconds, then said simply, "Me too."

That made the tightness in his chest loosen slightly. Not only had it been a long time since someone had wanted to take care of him, it had also been a very long time since he'd wanted to take care of another person. Not since he'd failed with and then finally gotten Donovan on the right track. Caring about animals, and dealing with feeling inadequate when things went wrong for them, was hard enough. Caring about and being unable to help human beings was just not something he wanted to take on again.

Or so he'd thought.

Then Autre, Louisiana, had happened to him.

And then he'd met the Landrys.

And then Charlotte Landry had walked out of Ellie's bar and into his life.

And now, like it or not, he had even more things to care about, worry about, and potentially be disappointed by.

Which didn't explain at all why his next action was to gather Charlotte close, wrap his arms around her, and hug her.

She was wearing tennis shoes rather than her heels, and her head fit perfectly against his shoulder. She seemed to melt into him, wrapping her arms around his waist and snuggling in. He felt her back rise and fall as she took a big breath and let it out.

She felt amazing. This was the perfect fit. Physically, for sure, but seemingly in every other way as well.

They just held each other for a few minutes. They didn't talk, they didn't move, they just breathed together. And Griffin felt the tension and the disappointment of the day fading.

Charlie was the first to speak. Of course. But he grinned as she said, "So..."

He didn't respond, knowing she would go on anyway.

"You don't seem like much of a hugger. But you're really good at it, for the record."

"I'm not much of a hugger, no," he agreed.

She tightened her arms around him. "Thanks for making the exception for me. I really needed this."

"You have a lot of people in this town who would happily hug you, Charlie."

She nodded, her cheek moving up and down against his chest. But she didn't let go. "I do. And they always make me feel better. But this"—she squeezed him slightly—"is officially my favorite hug."

It was a stupid thing to feel proud of, but the Landry clan was a very touchy-feely bunch. There had been lots of hugs in Charlie's life. If he could out-hug Ellie Landry, that was something.

"Well, you have a way of making me willing to make a lot of exceptions."

He realized giving that knowledge to a woman like Charlie —someone who epitomized the saying "give her an inch, and she'll take a mile"—was dangerous. But it was true. And if she didn't know it already, she was surely starting to figure it out.

"You mean like owning a sloth?"

He smiled against her hair, but said, "Like not getting attached."

That made her lift her head from his chest and look up at him. Her lips, right there, were tempting, but he knew she was going to use them to ask him a bunch more questions, and even if he kissed her now, those questions would come up. It was maybe better to have this conversation first.

"You try not to get attached?" she asked. But it didn't really sound like a question. It sounded more like a clarification.

He nodded. "I do. I try not to get attached to people or animals. Anymore."

"Because of what happened in the past? At the zoos?"

"Yes. It felt like getting invested and pouring a lot of emotion into things ended up making me overreact and eventually lose everything."

"But you know the things you did were the right things to do," Charlie said.

"I don't regret doing them," he said. "Just like you don't regret what you did to get fired. But that doesn't necessarily make it easier to have lost those things that mattered."

"The animals?"

"Yes. I was very attached to some of them. But I also lost all the work I put in, the potential for the programs, and my respect and trust in the people that I worked with. I thought I was on the same page with my colleagues and bosses, and they put other priorities ahead of my expertise and beliefs."

"So you came here, to what you thought would be a simpler job, to work with Tori—who you knew you could trust—and figured there wouldn't be as many animals and people to get attached to and be disappointed by," she summarized.

"Exactly."

"But now you are getting attached?"

"You know Autre. It's pretty hard not to get attached," he said.

She nodded. "Of course, I've never tried *not* to get attached."

"Trust me when I say it's impossible. Especially with your family."

"And with otters and goats who fall in love with you and pigs who are scared of thunder?" She smiled up at him.

"Yeah, all of that too." His voice was rougher now as he looked into her eyes.

"And Ellie's gumbo?"

He nodded. "Yep."

"And now you have lemurs."

"Yep."

She wet her lips again. "Anything else?"

"Definitely. In spite of my best efforts and better judgment."

"You don't want to be attached?"

"I didn't."

"But you're changing your mind?"

"I'm starting to understand that falling for things in Autre, Louisiana, is different than getting attached to things other places. For one, here, it's deeper. I also realize that things here last. People do what they say and say what they mean here. And people do the right things for the right reasons. Or if they screw up, they say they're sorry and do better next time. And everyone still has their back. That's the kind of place I want to be."

He could tell by the look in her eyes that that touched her and that she was very pleased that was his answer.

"So, you're attached to my family, the otters, Ellie's gumbo, the way everyone is fully accepting of everyone else—even when they screw up—and now you've got lemurs," she said. "Is that the full list?"

He needed to tell her that he was falling for her. It would be dangerous. Charlie already knew that she had him pretty well wrapped around her little finger when it came to this new animal park idea. Knowing that she was working her way into his heart as well would make her even more brazen about the big, crazy ideas she brought into his life.

But he suddenly wanted big and crazy.

Actually, he'd always wanted big and crazy. The big and crazy ideas had once been his. But he'd let circumstances rob him of that creativity and joy.

It was back now. Because of this woman. Of course, he was falling for her, and he was willing to take the risk of admitting that to her. No matter how much that was going to turn his life upside down.

"If I was another guy, here is where I would say something sexy and flirtatious," he told her, dropping his hands from her lower back to her ass and pulling her closer to him. "But I'm not. I'm pretty straightforward. So, I'll tell you that the number one thing on the list of things I'm getting very attached to is a sassy, sweet, larger-than-life hot blonde who has no idea what the word 'no' means and is, for some reason, insisting that I need to be happy."

Her eyes widened slightly and then, much to his chagrin, filled with tears.

"Jesus, Charlie," he said, loosening his hold on her. "I'm sorry if that's too much."

She immediately tightened her arms around him, holding him close. "No, no, it's not too much. Or, maybe it is, but I feel the same way."

He paused, searching her eyes. "You're getting attached too?"

She smiled. "You really can't tell?"

"It's been a while. I'm pretty good at keeping people at arm's length."

"Except my family. And me," she said with a grin.

"You people have no respect for emotional boundaries," he said. "Thank God," he added with a smile.

"Yeah, I don't think I'm going to apologize for that."

"Good." He lowered his head and took her mouth in a kiss that started soft and sweet.

But she unlinked her fingers from behind his back and slipped her hands under the bottom edge of his shirt. Her hands on his bare skin made heat arrow through him. Just that simple touch, and he wanted to devour her.

The kiss turned hot and dirty quickly, and before he knew it, he had her backed up against the otter enclosure door. Her hands came around the front, running up over his abs to his chest. He slipped his hands under her shirt as well. Her skin was hot and silky, and he stroked it greedily, loving the way her stomach muscles tensed under his touch, and goosebumps broke out as he stroked his fingertips up her sides to cup her breasts.

They made out against the door for several delicious minutes but were soon noticed by the otters.

The furry family came scampering over to meet the new girl and ask Griffin if this was the one he'd been pining for over the past couple of months whenever he came to the enclosure to talk.

They really needed to stop making out where there were animals around.

He pulled back from Charlie, chuckling as the otters surrounded them, slipping between their feet and going up on hindlegs on Charlie's calf, welcoming her to their home.

She looked down, her eyes wide. "Well, hello there."

"Charlie, this is Gus and Gertie and their kids. Snickers, Skittles, Rolo, Hershey, and Baby Ruth." He named them off, pointing to each in turn. He didn't even feel like an idiot telling her they were named after candy. "Everyone, this is Charlie."

"Nice to meet ya'll," Charlie said, grinning widely at their names and playing along with the introduction.

"They've heard all about you," Griffin told her.

"Yeah, Mitch said that you and the otters have regular conversations," she teased, running her hands up and down his sides again.

Even with a family of otters looking on, his desire for her hadn't cooled a bit.

"You can't believe everything Mitch tells you."

"Actually, I think I can. Mitch is one of my nicer cousins. And, frankly, you talking to otters is really not that hard to believe. I'm sorry if that ruins your tough-guy image."

Griffin's hands were resting on her hips now, and he slid a hand to her ass and gave her a little pinch. "Good thing me being an animal nut is such a turn-on for you."

"It really is," she said sincerely.

"And you think that you can still be into me if we go back to my house instead of having sex in a barn?"

She laughed. "I think it's worth a try."

Griffin wanted nothing more than to spread this woman out on his bed, lick her from head to toe, make her come at least three times in a row, and then keep her there all night.

That would seal his fate, he knew. Having Charlie in his bed would make it so that he would never want another woman there.

And still, he knew that was exactly how this night was going to go.

"Let's get out of here," he said.

"But—" she said, actually looking disappointed.

"But?"

She looked at the otters. "I've done yoga with them, but I haven't really had a chance to pet them and feed them... Or have a deep, meaningful conversation with them."

"You want to stay and hang out with the otters for a little while?"

She shrugged. "I mean, we're already here. It would be rude for me to leave after just meeting them officially for the first time."

Griffin looked down at the otters and back to her. He narrowed his eyes. "Okay, fine. We'll stay for a little while. But if you think you're going to make them like you more than they like me..." He blew out a breath. "It's very possible that could happen."

She gave him a bright grin. "You really think so?"

He pushed back from her, catching her hand and linking their fingers. He shook his head. "I really think so. You are, after all, quite delightful."

B aby goats in pajamas were probably the cutest thing Charlie had ever seen.

She'd hung out with the sloth and lemurs for the past five days, learning about them and how to handle and feed them from Griffin. And they were awesome for sure. But the cute award definitely went to the tiny goats that were now prancing around the barnyard. In pajamas.

She'd stumbled across a video of goats in pajamas when she'd been researching the animals. She'd immediately come up with the idea for the party and had thrown it together in just two days. But it was going very well. Ticket sales had been higher than they'd expected, and everyone involved seemed to be having a good time.

Well, the visitors seem to be having a good time. The staff looked a little harried, and the animals looked a little confused.

That was fair. Charlie was feeling a little harried and confused herself.

Why wasn't she enjoying this more?

The pajama party was going off exactly as she'd envisioned it.

Families had been invited to come to the petting zoo, also in pajamas, to watch a kids' movie and enjoy some snacks with the goats.

The kids were thrilled, the parents were all grinning, and the money from the event was going to be at least double what Charlie had spent on supplies.

The movie was being projected on the side of the goat barn, and the guests were sitting around the pen on hay bales or blankets spread out on the ground. The kids were eating raisins, strawberries, carrots, and celery, all of which they were able to share with the goats. All, of course, were Griffin-approved.

Charlie found him across the goat yard. He was roaming,

keeping a close eye on the activities within the pen. For the most part, things had gone smoothly, but she could tell he was on edge.

Maybe that was why *she* was on edge.

Maybe spending the last five nights having the best sex of her life with him—in an actual bed—had made her even more in tune with him.

"Hey." Fletcher moved in next to her, leaning onto the fence, mimicking her stance.

"Hey."

"You okay?" he asked.

She shrugged. "Yeah. Why?"

"Because you're scowling at a bunch of little kids watching a cartoon movie and a herd of goats in pajamas. Which are probably some of the cutest things ever. If *that* is making you frown, something is up."

She definitely shouldn't be scowling. Because she should *like* this. But also because it would look bad to any of the parents who noticed.

"This is... not feeling the way I expected," she told her cousin.

"How so? This looks pretty fun. My kids were really excited about it."

She looked at him. "Your kids? You have some students here?" She didn't know why it hadn't occurred to her that he would know some of the kids. Of course, he would.

He nodded. "A bunch of them. About ten of these kids were in my class this past year. And I've taught probably half of the older kids here tonight."

Charlie turned toward him, resting one elbow on the fence. "You've taught here for what? Three years?"

"Just finished my fourth."

"And you love it."

"I do."

"And you reached out and talked kids into coming tonight," she said. It wasn't a question. She'd just realized it, but she wasn't surprised.

"I might have sent an email."

She reached out and squeezed his arm. "Thank you. You didn't have to do that."

He chuckled. "It wasn't a have-to. This is a fun event, and I knew they'd enjoy it. Besides, you know we all do our part for family stuff."

They did. They were all a part of everything everyone else did. That, she was sure, could seem meddlesome, but it was nice.

Yes, working here with the Landrys and very few boundaries or guidelines was definitely different from her past jobs. But she was quickly getting used to knowing that there was a whole group of people who would have her back and believe in her no matter what she wanted to try.

"So, you think it's going well?" she asked Fletcher.

"I do. Why don't you?"

"This is the first major event we've hosted with multiple children."

Over the past two weeks, they'd seen an increase in visitors, but all the children had been with parents, and there had been no formal activity.

They had definitely been enthusiastic about the jungle tour hats and the sticker books, but there hadn't been one big coordinated activity for kids until now.

The other activities she'd tried, including an extra session of otter yoga and a knitting class held in the alpaca yard on picnic tables and using yarn made from alpaca wool—not wool from *their* alpacas yet, but that was on the research-this list as well—had been a huge hit. But those had been attended by adults. This was different.

This was a much bigger group and included kids from ages

four to about ten. The kids were enthusiastic about hanging out with the goats. Maybe a little too enthusiastic. She doubted that anyone could really hear the movie over the excited kid chatter and laughter, and she tried to take that as a good sign. Of course she wanted people participating in their activities to be excited and laughing.

But she was a little bored.

Well, maybe not *bored*, exactly, but she was feeling restless. While the event had definitely brought more visitors in, it also seemed... gimmicky. The kids were interacting with the animals, but it felt chaotic, and she wondered if the younger kids in the group would somehow be misled into thinking the goats actually wore pajamas to bed.

And that was a sure sign that Griffin Foster was rubbing off on her. He'd spent the past week and a half insisting that no, she couldn't have an event called Lunch with the Llamas because they didn't have llamas, they were alpacas.

He'd made changes to nearly every one of the informational signs she'd wanted to put up around the otter enclosure. He'd tried to get her to offer bundles of hay to the guests tonight in place of the fruits and vegetables for the goats and hadn't seemed at all concerned about the fact that hay bundles were not edible for the human guests.

She knew she was driving him crazy. And, apparently, he'd gotten under her skin as well because she didn't want kids leaving tonight thinking that goats wore pajamas on a regular basis. She was now more worried about accurate animal facts than she was about their guests having fun and bringing in more business.

But people were having fun, and there was nothing wrong with that, she reminded herself. In fact, if people had fun, they'd be more likely to come back. So, in the future, she could do something more meaningful—whatever that would be— for the same crowd. Tonight was a great kickoff to more community and family activities at Boys of the Bayou Gone Wild.

She'd just started to believe her pep talk when she heard, "That's enough!"

Charlie straightened immediately. That was Griffin's voice. That was Griffin's angry voice. Not that she had experienced a lot of Griffin's angry voice. She was much more used to his obstinate voice. And his know-it-all voice. And his exasperated voice. But she didn't have to have direct experience to know that that was most definitely an angry voice.

She located him immediately. He was standing near a family of five who was seated on two hay bales toward the middle of the group.

The father was on his feet facing off with Griffin, and one of the little boys was standing just behind his father's leg, looking sheepish.

Charlie was through the gates and beside Griffin in seconds.

"Hey, back off, man. He's just a little kid," the man said.

"But he's old enough to listen to directions from adults. He's also old enough to be taught how to handle animals. In fact, the sooner, the better," Griffin said.

"The goat's fine," the other man said, taking a half step closer to Griffin. "I've been around goats. You can't really hurt them."

Griffin took a step closer to the man. "No wonder your kid doesn't know how to treat animals and doesn't know the word no."

"Hey, guys," Charlie said, in her best calming and friendly voice. She stepped between the two men. "What's going on?"

"This gentleman and his family were just leaving," Griffin said, his eyes still on the man.

"Hey, we paid to be here. We're not going anywhere." The man glared at Griffin.

Charlie would've put serious money on the fact that Griffin was right. However, the man and his family were customers. Paying customers. And the confrontation was happening in the middle of the rest of their paying customers.

"Maybe we can take this discussion into the barn," Charlie suggested.

"No further discussion is necessary," Griffin said. "They're on their way out, and they're not welcome back."

Charlie's eyes widened, and she took in the other man's tight jaw, as well as the clenched fist at his side. She didn't have any brothers, but she'd seen more than one disagreement between her male cousins turn into a physical altercation. Every one of her cousins that she could think of at the moment had suffered a black eye and or a bloody nose at some point in his life inflicted by a family member.

"They're goats, man," the father said. "They're not made of glass."

"Yes, they're goats. They're animals. Living, breathing beings. And if your kid keeps yanking on Happy's tail, he's going to turn around and take a bite out of your kid. And I'm guessing you're going to be pretty upset then."

"He's only six," the man said. "He's still learning."

"And if you don't *teach* him how to interact with animals, he's never going to learn. Or he'll learn by getting hurt," Griffin said.

"I don't want to get hurt!"

They all looked down at the little boy. He was staring at the arguing grown-ups with wide eyes and a trembling lower lip.

"Then you need to be nice to the goat," Griffin told him bluntly.

"I love the goat!" the boy insisted.

"You're not acting like you love him," Griffin said. He put his hands on his hips and looked down at the kid.

He looked intimidating, even to Charlie, and she knew the soft, caring, sweet, passionate side of him.

She grabbed Griffin's forearm and squeezed, willing him to look at her. "Griffin."

Suddenly Fletcher was there. He dropped to one knee next to the little boy and put his hand on his back. "Hey, Hunter."

"Hi, Mr. Landry," the little boy said, seemingly shy now.

"Let's talk about goats for a second, okay?" Fletcher asked.

"Who the hell are you?" the father demanded.

"That's Fletcher Landry," his wife told him. She was smiling at Fletcher. "He's one of the third-grade teachers. Colt and Jonah both had him. You should come to more parent-teacher conferences," she added with a frown at her husband.

Even in the midst of this chaos, Charlie rolled her eyes. Fletcher had a fan club, and they were definitely not all elementary-aged kids.

Fletcher was mostly ignoring the adults. He was talking to Hunter in a low voice.

Charlie felt Griffin's arm tense under her hand. She glanced at him. His jaw was tight, but he was watching Fletcher and the little boy rather than staring down the father.

"Do your brothers and sisters ever pinch you or hit you or pull your hair, Hunter?" Fletcher asked.

The boy nodded.

"And that doesn't feel good, does it? And it makes you not like them for a little bit, right?" Fletcher asked.

Hunter's bottom lip stuck out slightly, but he nodded. "Right."

"That's how it feels to Happy when you pull his tail," Fletcher said. "It hurts him, but it also makes him not want to play with you for a little bit. If you can be nice to him, then he'll want to come over and be friends."

The little boy sniffled but nodded. "Okay."

"But he'll forgive you," Fletcher added. "Happy knows that

sometimes kids don't know how to play with goats. Don't worry. He'll be your friend again."

The boy managed a little smile.

"See, everything's fine," the father said, directing the comment to Griffin.

Griffin tensed again. "No thanks to you. *You* should be teaching your kid how to treat animals. They need to learn it from people they respect and trust, and it needs to be reinforced all the time."

"Look, man. I work two jobs. And we don't have any goats," Hunter's dad said.

"Kids can learn to be gentle and kind and patient and to care about animals in a lot of ways," Griffin said. "You can read to him. You can watch programs about animals."

"And you're some kind of animal expert?" the man said.

Charlie tensed at that. The man was questioning Griffin's expertise? And even if the man didn't know who Griffin was, Griffin was clearly right. Every adult here should recognize that.

"This is Dr. Foster," she said, her tone indignant. "He's the veterinarian here. These goats are all in his care. If he tells you something about how to treat them, you need to listen."

The man looked slightly chagrined. "Okay, fine. But I grew up on a farm, and I know that farm animals aren't exactly delicate."

"All animals, farm or otherwise, deserve to be treated with kindness and respect," Charlie said. "One of our goals here at this petting zoo is to teach people more about the animals and to give them a chance to interact and understand them better. However, first and foremost, we are concerned with the treatment of our animals. And if you cannot be responsible enough to ensure that our animals are safe with your family, then yes, you will be asked to leave and not allowed to come back."

The man stared at her. "You're overreacting."

"Am I?" She took a step forward. "Or am I calling you out on bad behavior? I'm sorry that it has to be in public and in front of your children, but that's on you."

She felt a finger hook into the back waistband of her jeans and tug slightly. She took a step back, realizing as Griffin tucked her under his arm that she'd been only inches from the other man.

"Thank you," Griffin whispered, softly enough that only she could hear. Then he released her and went down on his knee by the little boy the way Fletcher had.

He didn't reach for the kid, and he was several inches back, not invading the boy's personal space, but he said, "I'll tell you what, Hunter, let's set up a time for you to come to my clinic. We'll play with a couple of kittens together. Maybe a dog. Then, if that goes well, you can come back, and we'll play with some rabbits and hedgehogs. We'll talk about how to handle them properly and how to know if they like what you're doing or not. And once I think that you're doing a good job, I will give you a special animal handling certificate. Then you bring it with you to the petting zoo for our next big event."

Hunter's eyes were wide.

"What's the next event?" one of Hunter's brothers asked.

Griffin glanced up at Charlie. "You'll have to ask Ms. Landry. She's in charge of all the good times around here."

Charlie couldn't tell if he meant "good times" sarcastically or not, but she did realize that he had just put her on the spot to announce another event. One that, no doubt, he had major reservations about before even hearing it. He hadn't wanted to do the pajama party, and she'd had to assure him that everything would be fine. Of course, now it wasn't, and she was feeling like an idiot.

But everyone in the barnyard was now listening. Someone had paused the movie, and all eyes were on her.

Well, this was Griffin's fault, she supposed.

"Yeah," she said brightly as if she'd been fully prepared for this announcement. "We're going to do Lunch with the Lemurs." She looked at Griffin as she said it and noticed his small grimace. Well, he was the one who'd said no to Lunch with the Llamas. And Lunch with the Alpacas didn't have the same ring to it.

But as the words came out of her mouth, she realized she could have called it Alpaca Lunch. Wow, that would have been perfect. The alpacas would have been a better choice too. The lemurs weren't as used to visitors. And they were endangered animals. Maybe they shouldn't be around humans much. She honestly didn't know. But now she blurted out Lunch with the Lemurs, so she had to keep going.

She was definitely going to do an Alpaca Lunch though.

Her mind worked to catch up with her tongue. "Everyone will come and get a brown bag lunch which will also include some fun treats for the lemurs. We'll go out to the lemur enclosure, and spread out picnic blankets, and..." She glanced at Fletcher, who was also watching her attentively with a very amused grin. "Mr. Landry will teach you all about lemurs and what they like to eat and how they like to play, where they're from, and what we can do to help protect them as endangered animals."

Fletcher looked surprised for a moment, but then he gave her a small nod that said he would be there for her. Of course he would. She smiled with gratitude.

"So be watching for more information on our website and in the paper," she encouraged everyone. We'd love to see you all." She glanced at Hunter again and felt compelled to add. "But if you would like to interact with the lemurs and actually feed them, you will have to also attend a special handling seminar with Dr. Foster at the Autre Animal Hospital and get your special certificates. There will be more information about those on the website as well. And, of course, those are free to attend."

There was a long moment of silence, then Hunter said, "Cool!" He turned to his brother. "You can get a special certificate too, and we can both be special animal experts!"

Charlie kept her smile firmly in place, but she wanted to sigh with relief. At least Hunter seemed happy about this turn of events. And looking at his parents, they seem to have calmed down as well.

The rest of the guests started chatting about what had just unfolded, and Fletcher said something to Hunter and then stretched to his feet. He grinned at her. "Nice save." He looked at Griffin, who had also gotten back to his feet. "You too."

Charlie, on the other hand, was stoically avoiding looking at Griffin.

She had, as usual, taken a tiny kernel of an idea and blown it up into something much bigger. Something that would involve Griffin, without his input or permission.

This was becoming a habit.

When she'd first come to Autre and started talking about things like plastic jungle adventure hats, stickers, and kettle corn, she found it fun to poke at him. But now, she truly cared about him, and she realized it was unfair of her to keep signing him up for things that were very likely annoying or even uncomfortable for him.

Griffin stuck his hand out toward Hunter's father and said, "I look forward to seeing you at the clinic. You can call tomorrow morning, and Charlie will help you set up time."

The other man hesitated for only a second before taking Griffin's hand and nodding. "I think that sounds like a great idea."

The men shook and then stepped apart. Charlie breathed out.

But that relief was short-lived.

She felt Griffin's big hand wrap around her upper arm, and he said near her ear, "A word, Ms. Landry?"

Oh, she was certain it was going to be more than one word.

She let him escort her across the barnyard to the barn and then around to the back of the building. They entered through the back door, which allowed Griffin to pull her into the first stall to the left. It was across from Hermione's stall and was used for general storage rather than any animals.

"Okay," Charlie said, turning to face him with her hands up before he could say anything. "I'm sorry."

He looked mildly amused. "What are you sorry for?"

That was a trick question. Because there were a few things she should be sorry for. She wondered where she should start. The beginning, probably.

"Becoming the marketing consultant for Boys of the Bayou."

He blinked at her. She seemed to have surprised him. "Why are you sorry about that?"

"Because that's what led me to being the marketing consultant for Boys of the Bayou Gone Wild. Which led me to opening up the petting zoo to being an *actual* petting zoo. Which led to ideas like a pajama party with goats. Which led to kids interacting with the goats. Which led to us getting lemurs. Which led to the debacle of Lunch with the Lemurs."

He seemed to take a moment to process that. Then he asked, "Lunch with the Lemurs is going to be a debacle?"

She shrugged. "It's very likely, isn't it?" Hell, she'd already missed using a really great name for it and picked the wrong animals.

Griffin crossed his arms, his stance wide as if he was settling in. "The only thing I have to say about Lunch with the Lemurs is that I'm going to be doing the presentation, not Fletcher."

Now Charlie blinked at him. "You want to do the presentation?"

"I do."

"That would be... wonderful. You're not upset about the idea?"

"I think it's great, actually."

She took a step toward him. Had he hit his head at some point? Was he drunk? "You think it's a great idea for a bunch of people to come and look at and interact with the lemurs? And for you to give a presentation in front of all of those people?"

He nodded. "I do."

"Who are you, and what have you done with Griffin Foster?"

"I realized that if I want people to learn, especially kids, how to treat and interact with animals, then maybe I should be a part of teaching that. That little boy didn't know any better. Instead of yelling at him, I should take this chance to turn him into an animal lover. Instead of making that interaction scary and embarrassing."

Charlie loved that. That was actually huge. Not only was that going to be great for the kids and the animals, but it was also great for Griffin. Instead of caring for the animals alone and feeling like their only protector, he could help teach others to protect them as well.

From what Fiona had told her, that was in line with some of the original plans he'd had for his career. Maybe a petting zoo in Autre, Louisiana, was small-time next to the National Zoo in Washington, D.C., but anywhere there were animals, there was a need for human beings to treat them well and protect them. And who knew? Maybe Griffin would help inspire a bunch of new veterinarians or humans to travel to Africa to work on the game reserves.

"Seeing Fletcher interacting with Hunter inspired you?" she asked. "Because I've seen you with little kids. Like Andre. You're very good."

He shook his head. "I wasn't inspired by Fletcher and Hunter. I was inspired by you and Hunter's dad."

Charlie frowned. "What do you mean? His dad wasn't exactly won over by me."

Griffin nodded. "Exactly."

Charlie felt offended. Even though she wasn't sure why. "I don't know what you mean."

Griffin snorted. "You being protective of the goats was hot. But I realized as you were getting into that guy's face that that was possibly not the best way to get our message of kindness across."

She gasped. "Are you telling me that you decided to have this handling clinic and teach everyone about lemurs because *I* acted inappropriately?"

He shrugged but reached out for her arm, tugging her close. "You also heard the part about where I found you protecting the goats hot?"

She sniffed. "Sometimes people need to be yelled at."

Griffin nodded with a grin. "I agree a thousand percent. But I realized at that moment that I've already turned you into an animal advocate, and I haven't even been trying. Maybe if I'm just a little patient and realize that people sometimes act inappropriately simply because they don't know any better, I can help them learn."

She narrowed her eyes even though she didn't fight stepping closer to him. "I knew exactly what I was doing."

"I know. I was talking about Hunter." He chuckled. "I know very well that if Hunter's dad had a Porsche, there's a very good chance that he would end up with 'Goat Hater' scratched into the side of it."

"No, I think I might stick with 'I Have a Tiny Dick' as my go-to Porsche graffiti. I feel like men who drive Porsches may have that same general problem no matter what their specific asshole actions are."

Griffin pulled her even closer. "Probably a good thing he doesn't have a Porsche."

"For the record, I'm not sorry I got in his face."

"I wouldn't expect you to be."

She swallowed. Griffin understood her. He was very much like her family in his general acceptance of her quirks. Whether it was her, okay, overreaction to certain situations or her over-the-top brainstorming ideas, he was generally resigned and amused. And accepting. She really liked that about him.

"Also, for the record," she said. "I think your ideas for the special handling clinics with the kids are brilliant."

"Yes, I noticed that it's for the kids—plural—now," he said dryly.

"I'm not really sorry about that either," she said. "Except that, I do recognize that I could probably slow down a little bit and ask your input and opinion on things before I just throw them out there."

"Charlie," Griffin said, his voice low and a little husky. "I don't want you to change a single thing. I want you exactly as you are. You are pushing me outside of my comfort zone, yes. But that's a good thing. You're amazing. I'm very happy that you got fired and ended up here as the marketing consultant to Boys of the Bayou."

She swallowed hard. "Me too," she admitted.

She could tell from his expression that he understood what that meant. Not only was she happy with how things turned out, but she wanted to stay and keep doing this.

"I think I'm even glad that I got fired from the National Zoo."

And she understood that that meant a lot. He was now glad to be here. And from the look on his face, she thought that might have more than a little to do with her.

She wasn't sure what to say exactly, so instead, she went on tiptoe, wrapped her arms around his neck, and pulled him down for a long, sweet kiss.

When she finally let him go, she said, "And later tonight, at your place, you can practice your lemur lecture on me."

"Unless that's a very strange innuendo, that was not at all what I was thinking about us doing at my place later tonight," Griffin said.

"Oh?" Charlie asked. "Because I was thinking that every time you tell me a fact about lemurs that I don't already know, I'll take a piece of clothing off."

His brows went up. "How much do you know about lemurs?"

"I have been reading up about them," she said. "But I was also thinking that every time you tell me something about lemurs that I *do* already know, *you'll* take a piece of clothing off."

"Strip lemur lecturing," Griffin said thoughtfully. "I could get into this."

"You'll maybe even want to start doing more lectures," she said innocently. She started to step around him. "I'm sure there are some things that I don't know about sloths, and otters, and alpacas, and ostriches, and porcupines."

Griffin turned to follow her to the barn door. "We don't have any porcupines."

"No, but Fiona does. And I don't know much about them."

She reached for the door, but Griffin caught her around the waist, his big hand splayed across her belly as he pressed her back into him. He put his mouth against her neck, sliding his stubbled jaw up and down the sensitive skin, before saying gruffly in her ear, "And of course, you found a way to make me even want to do public lectures now."

She gave a happy sigh and leaned into him. "Is that a yes about the porcupine?"

"Maybe. But I think I'll have to come up with a different

game that you'll have to play whenever you want to add a new animal to our collection," Griffin said.

That sounded like a *fabulous* idea. "Oh, yes, please tell me more, Dr. Foster."

Griffin groaned and let her go. But he was grinning widely as he pulled the door open and ushered her out of the barn.

"You know I can't resist you. We're going to have a freaking elephant, eventually aren't we?"

She *loved* his use of the word 'we' and the idea of an ongoing, sexy game between them. She stepped through the door. "Oh, I don't know. That's a lot. But... maybe a camel? Or two?"

He groaned again but then said, "You better keep up with that otter yoga then. I've got elephant-sized plans for you."

Charlie stumbled slightly at that, and Griffin caught her with a hand under her elbow.

He gave her a knowing look.

"I'm just always surprised when you tease," she said. "It's so unlike you."

He lifted a brow. "I wasn't teasing."

Charlie felt a shiver of pleasure dance through her. It was a combination of desire and pure contentment. She was willing to do anything that made Griffin happy. But playful too?

Oh yeah, one of these days, she was going to have to let him in on all the things she'd be willing to do to get a kangaroo.

16

"Did you know that lemurs will lay around in the morning and bask in the sun? It's even a group activity."

Fiona laughed. "Yes, I did know that. In fact, I've witnessed it many times."

Charlie grinned at her computer screen, where she had Fiona on a video call. They'd started making this a more regular thing over the past two weeks. Charlie had lots of questions about lemurs and sloths, for one thing. She had to study up for the strip lecture series that Griffin had going at his house twice a week.

Fiona was also very interested in all of the new community activities they had going.

"And did you know that the word lemur means 'shadow tail' in Greek?" Charlie asked.

Fiona was amused by the facts she was picking up, and so Charlie always shared a couple with her when they started their calls.

"Actually, that's not true," Fiona said with a tiny frown. "I think that's squirrels. Lemur is Latin for 'spirits of the night.'"

Charlie frowned. "You sure?"

"Completely sure," Fiona said. "Where did you learn that?"

"Griffin told me." After which, she'd had to remove her final piece of clothing—her panties.

"Griffin told you that?"

"Yeah, when we were... working on his presentation."

Fiona knew that Griffin was doing a weekly presentation during the Lunch with the Lemurs but didn't, of course, know exactly how Charlie helped him prepare.

Charlie's eyes narrowed. Every time Griffin told her a fact about lemurs she didn't know, she had to remove clothing. Would he have lied to get her panties off?

But she knew instantly the answer to that was yes, definitely.

They'd both been down to their underwear in their game of strip lecture preparation, and as soon she'd been completely naked, he'd put her up on the dining room table and made her very happy to be completely naked.

The game truly was a win-win, but she couldn't believe that he'd cheated.

Oh, tonight she was getting him back. And it would be just as fun being the winner as it was when she was the loser.

"So the Lunch with Lemurs is going well?" Fiona asked.

Charlie focused on her new friend again. "Yes, and so is Sloth Storytime." She grinned. "I'm not sure the kids heard every word of the story because they were pretty fascinated by the sloth, who was also listening, but we had a really good turnout, and all the moms seemed thrilled." Charlie laughed. "Of course, that might've been in part because Fletcher was the one reading the story. He has an interesting fan club. Everyone from four-year-olds to about forty-four-year-olds." She shook her head. "Scratch that. I'm pretty sure the one grandma who brought her grandkids is at least seventy-four, and she was pretty enamored with him too."

Fiona laughed. "I cannot imagine a person not being enamored with Fletcher."

Charlie nodded. "Yeah, he's pretty cute with those kids. Growing up, I never would have believed that he would become a teacher, but he is really awesome."

"And very hot," Fiona said.

Charlie rolled her eyes. She had been hearing how "hot" her cousins were since she'd been about thirteen. She, of course, didn't see them that way, and it was often strange to hear her friends talking about them.

"I thought it was Zeke you thought was hot," Charlie said.

"Oh, Zeke is very hot. He clearly likes to push buttons. And Zander," Fiona added. "He's very sexy. Of course, part of that is the uniform, but I really love his don't-get-all-worked-up attitude too."

Charlie shook her head. "That would get old, trust me. For someone like you who is such a go-getter, I can't imagine that you and Zander would have much in common."

"He's a cop. He was a detective for a few years. I think he's got more underneath than shows," Fiona said. "I think he enjoys Autre just being sweeter and more slow-paced than what he used to do."

Charlie leaned in and rested her forearms on the desk. "Are you defending my cousin to me?"

"I am. The guys are great."

"I don't disagree. I love them very much."

"And next time, you should completely record Fletcher reading the story with the sloth and put it up on YouTube."

"Won't it defeat the purpose of having people come if it's up online?" Charlie asked.

"Oh, just put a couple of them up there. Mostly for me so I can watch Fletcher be sweet with little kids."

Charlie laughed. "I can just send you the video straight to your phone."

"Oh, trust me, if moms see that online, you'll definitely get more business out of it."

"You go for the bad boy turned good guy?" Charlie asked Fiona.

"Actually, I think I go for the big, grumpy nerd type."

"Aha, you did feel a little spark with Knox, didn't you?"

"I cannot get the picture of that guy in a necktie out of my head," she admitted. "And if he wears glasses, even better."

Charlie knew for a fact that Knox did wear glasses sometimes. And she could definitely see that attraction. She wasn't related to Knox. The guy was big and muscular, and she wouldn't at all be surprised if there were some tattoos underneath his linen shirt sleeves. She loved that he wore his hair long in spite of being a serious city employee. Knox hadn't grown up in Autre. He'd moved here in high school, just in time to run around, party, and get into trouble with Fletcher, Zeke, and Zander.

"I thought you had a boyfriend," Charlie said to Fiona. Of course, she also had a boyfriend and still noticed how sexy Knox was.

At least she assumed that's what she should call Griffin. They saw each other every day and every night, and spent a lot of time talking, laughing, planning, and being naked. They'd even played with some silk ties and a blindfold. Griffin definitely got into bossing her around and in the bedroom she was completely fine with it.

The animal park was growing, and her family was excited about the increased revenue. She was equally excited about the lemurs and the sloth and the idea of adding additional animals. She loved hanging out with her family and being at Ellie's every night for dinner, and becoming friends with her cousins' new wives and girlfriends.

But, if she was completely honest, she was still in Autre because of Griffin. Without Dr. Foster here, she wouldn't have stopped sending out resumes to marketing firms and companies three weeks ago.

"Yeah, I do have a boyfriend," Fiona said. "But I've also got two eyes. And I'm not going to not appreciate hot bayou boys when given the chance."

"Tell me about your boyfriend," Charlie said.

"Oh, he's —"

She was cut off by the front door of the clinic banging open. Startled, Charlie shot up out of her chair. Griffin was stomping across the tiles of the waiting area. He had something brown and furry cradled in his arms.

"Oh my God, Griffin! What happened?" Charlie asked.

"It's Snickers."

Charlie felt her stomach knot. It was one of Gus and Gertie's pups. Now was definitely not the time to reflect on how cute it was that they were all named after candy bars. "What happened?"

"I'm not sure yet. He's really sick." Griffin continued down the hall toward one of the examination rooms without even pausing.

"Charlie, go with him."

Charlie looked at the computer screen, having forgotten Fiona was there. "Yeah, okay."

She really didn't want to go with him. This was just like the day with the dog who had been hit. Only worse. This was one of the otters. An animal she knew. An animal Griffin knew well and loved.

She was fine when they were doing procedures that she knew were going to turn out well. Giving shots, even spaying and neutering. Even the first day with Brownie, she'd trusted Griffin's confidence that everything was going to be all right.

Griffin's face when he came in the front door just now did not look like he thought things were going to be all right.

"Charlie!" Fiona repeated. "Go. Call me later."

Charlie nodded. "Okay." She reached out and disconnected the call.

Then she headed for the examination room. She had to be stronger than she'd been with the dog. This was going to happen sometimes, even with the animals they personally loved. Snickers needed her. Griffin needed her. She could do this. Whether she liked it or not.

But she really didn't like it.

She took a deep breath and stepped into the room. Griffin had already covered his clothes with one of the paper gowns he used when the work might get messy.

Charlie swallowed hard and looked at the animal on the exam table.

It looked dead. Her heart squeezed hard, and she had to force another deep breath.

"What can I do?" she asked.

"We need to figure out what's going on," Griffin said shortly. "He hasn't been eating for about a day and has been lethargic. We need to run some tests. Figure out if it's a virus or what actually is going on."

Charlie nodded. "Okay, just tell me what to do."

They worked for the next couple of hours. Charlie could hear the phone ringing but ignored it. At one point, she'd run to lock the clinic door and turn the closed sign out.

They'd run blood tests. They'd done a scan. Now Griffin was doing an exploratory procedure.

"Dammit," he muttered. He was frowning.

Charlie was assisting by handing him tools and helping position the otter. She'd like to think that she was also helping him just by being there, but she doubted that was true. She had no idea what was going on and couldn't get past her intense fear that this wasn't going to turn out well.

But she reined her thoughts in every time they started to go down the path of, what will we do if the otter dies?

It would devastate the Landrys, Tori and Kennedy in particular. On a more superficial note, it would not be good publicity for the park. Of course, in the back of her mind, she knew that they would have to deal with sick animals and animals that passed away, but having it front and center made her realize that not only was it emotionally hard on the family, but they would have to deal with a public message around it as well.

Where she would not allow her thoughts to go, even for a moment, was to Griffin.

He was the primary caregiver to these animals and closer to them than anyone. Tori might've been closer to some of the barnyard animals, but Griffin had a special place in his heart for the otters.

She couldn't even allow herself to think about how this would affect him.

"Fuck," Griffin held up a pair of tweezers.

From the end protruded a bloody object that looked like a tiny stick.

"What is that?" Charlie asked

"A fucking toothpick." Griffin's tone was angry. "He swallowed it."

"Why would he eat a toothpick?"

"He wouldn't unless it was stuck in something he did want to eat."

Charlie frowned. "How would a toothpick get into the otter food?"

"Someone tossed it or dropped it in his pen. It might've had food on it or have been attached to something else he ate. It looks like it's just about half of one. I need to make sure the other half isn't inside somewhere."

He tossed the bloodied toothpick into the basin next to him and bent over the otter again.

Charlie felt a little lightheaded. A *human* had obviously

tossed the toothpick—intentionally or accidentally—into the otter enclosure.

"Is the toothpick poison to him or something?" she asked.

"No. There's a chance it would just pass through. But this one punctured his intestine and is causing leakage into the rest of his body. That's a serious infectious condition situation. I need to see if there's more toothpick in here, repair the perforation, and then we'll have to treat him for the infection."

He said all of this while carefully exploring and not sparing Charlie even a glance.

"Will he be okay?" she asked softly.

"I've no idea.

The otter might not be okay. The otter might die from a toothpick.

It might have just been a careless act, but negligence was just as dangerous to the animals. Maybe more so in some ways. If people didn't realize what could happen, they could do it again. There could be other toothpicks in the otter enclosure or in other animal pens.

Charlie felt her throat tighten. With fear.

Next time it could be a lemur. Which was not only special to Griffin but was an endangered animal.

Charlie felt her heart pounding hard in her chest.

People had been feeding the otters and the lemurs and the sloth and all of the barnyard animals over the past few weeks. Because of her. As part of the stupid activities she'd come up with to drum up business and increase their bottom line. She'd pushed for all of this. She was the one who had pressed Griffin into agreeing to more human interaction with the animals. Even before she'd known his past encounters with human beings who hadn't properly respected the animals they were interacting with, she'd known that he was against the idea in general. Now that she knew what he had been through before, she realized that he was not only right, but she'd been very wrong.

"I'm not seeing any other pieces of the toothpick," Griffin said after a few minutes of tense silence. "I'm going to repair the perforation."

Charlie worked on breathing and not crying as she assisted. The only conversation was him giving terse instructions. Which was fine. She had no idea what to say to him. She needed to apologize, of course, but she didn't think this was the time. And she wasn't sure she could get the words out without breaking into tears.

Griffin finished the procedure and gave the animal a huge dose of antibiotics. Then they settled Snickers in one of the cages.

Finally, after what seemed like a day, Griffin was cleaned up, and he took the first big breath Charlie seen him take.

He turned to her. "Are you okay?"

That was all it took to make the tears start running. He was asking if *she* was okay?

"We had fruit kebabs," she blurted out.

He frowned. "What?"

She nodded, tears tracking down her cheeks. "We had fruit kebabs during Sloth Storytime. We also had them for Lunch with the Lemurs. They were two or three pieces of fruit on a toothpick for the kids. They were told to pull the fruit off to hand it to the animals. But they easily could have dropped one."

She was certain at this point that's what had happened. Toothpicks didn't randomly show up. People didn't routinely carry toothpicks with them. Did they?

"If they dropped them around the sloth or lemurs, Snickers wouldn't have gotten a hold of it," Griffin said as if processing what she was saying as he spoke.

"Maybe a couple of the kids saved their kebabs and thought

they would feed them to the otters later. Then they couldn't get in to hand the food to the otters like they did with the lemurs, so they tossed it over the enclosure wall," she said.

Griffin nodded slowly. Of course, he did. It made sense. That *had* to have been what had happened. Which meant that not only was it her fault that there was more human interaction with the animals, but the toothpick was *directly* her fault. The fruit kebabs had been her idea. With each animal interaction, they had food that the animals could also eat. Not just so the kids could have the fun of feeding the animals, but to also show that humans and animals had some things in common. For instance, the love of fruit kebabs.

"Charlie—"

"Do you need me to stay?" she interrupted.

He studied her face. "No," he finally said. "You can go."

Yeah, she needed to go. She needed to give him some space. She also needed to deal with what she'd done.

If the otter died, it was her fault. She would've killed one of the animals that was most special to Griffin. She would've come into his life, turned it upside down, thought that she knew more than he did about how to make the animal park success-ful, and in the process, endangered the animals and put him through more pain and frustration that came from a human being interacting with an innocent animal.

On her way past the front desk, Charlie glanced at the laptop computer where she'd been talking to Fiona. She grabbed it quickly, tucking it under her arm, then practically ran to her car.

She headed to her grandmother's house. She needed to be alone. She hadn't spent more than a couple of nights there in the last couple of weeks because she'd been at Griffin's every night.

The whole family had known, or at least assumed, and it seemed they thought it was natural that's where she would be.

But she needed to be alone right now. And being alone in Autre was extremely hard to do.

Which was why, when she pulled up in front of Ellie's, she only paused for three seconds before she put her car back into drive and pointed toward the bayou.

There were a few nooks and crannies along the bank where the ground was solid enough to park a car and walk on without sinking into the marshy ground. It wasn't that no one would be able to find her, but it would take them a while to look for her there.

She needed to think about what happened and what she was going to do to fix it.

"Where is she?" Griffin strode into Ellie's bar five hours later.

He hadn't seen Charlie since she'd left the clinic. He'd been unable to go after her until he was certain Snickers was stable. He tried calling her cell, but she wasn't answering. He'd called Mitch and Fletcher and Maddie, but none of them had seen her in the last two hours.

He'd been hoping she'd come back to the clinic after she had a few minutes to breathe and think. But she hadn't. She wasn't at his house, she wasn't at the petting zoo, and she wasn't at Ellie's.

"We were hoping you could tell us," Sawyer said. "What the hell's going on?"

Griffin stopped by the family table at the back of the bar and planted his hands on his hips. "We had a problem with one of the otters. She was pretty shaken up and left to get some air. Five hours ago. I haven't seen her since."

"Oh my God, do you think she's all right?" Tori asked.

"Well, she's been around," Sawyer said, seeming exasperated. "There are signs all over the petting zoo and the otter enclosure that say we're closed until further notice."

"*What?*" Tori asked. She looked up at Griffin. "What kind of issue was it with the otter?"

"Snickers got a hold of a toothpick, had an intestinal perforation. He's still in serious condition, but I think he'll be okay."

Tori looked a little pale. "A toothpick? Oh crap."

Griffin nodded. "Obviously, he got a hold of it because a human tossed it in there. And I'm sure Charlie is blaming herself."

He knew that was exactly what was going on in his girlfriend's mind. He'd seen the distraught look on her face and recognized the guilt immediately. She'd pushed to have more human interaction with the animals, and the interactive feeding activities, in particular, had been a pet project.

He was angry too. And worried. And he wanted to lash out at the humans who had been reckless. But the last couple of weeks had shown him something very important. Humans didn't know how to act around animals unless they were taught.

Working with the little kids in the handling techniques clinic he'd started doing twice a week in the afternoons had shown him that they needed to be taught but also that they were eager to learn.

It wasn't just the kids who had been attentive students. The adults who brought them to the clinic had all hung around and listened as well. Hunter's father had brought him to the second session, and the man had been clearly excited to get to handle the hedgehogs as well when Griffin offered.

There were horrible human beings in the world. That was just a fact. They hurt people and animals and the environment around them without any thought and without any remorse. Sometimes on purpose.

But that was not the majority of people. The majority could

be taught and wanted to learn. And Griffin had found incredible reward in being the person to instruct them and to answer their questions, and be a resource they felt they could come back to.

No one had hurt Snickers on purpose. He knew that. Did they need to do a better job of instructing people during the feeding times? Yes. Did they need to be more careful with using things like toothpicks? Yes, absolutely. But that could be done.

Yes, this was Charlie's fault. But he wasn't angry with her. He hadn't supervised the feedings as well as he should have, and he knew that her intentions had been nothing but good.

"What the hell is going on?" Maddie came marching across the bar just then. She was holding onto a piece of paper that she waved at them all as she stopped by the table. "Where's Charlie?"

"Question of the hour," Sawyer said. "She shut down the petting zoo and the rest of the animal encounters."

"Where's Charlie?" Paige came through the kitchen door, stopping at the table. "I've been getting phone calls for the past two hours telling me that otter yoga and the kids' otter exercise classes have all been canceled indefinitely. What's going on?"

Griffin sighed. "She canceled otter yoga?"

"And she sent out an email to everyone who went to Sloth Storytime and Lunch with the Lemurs telling them that someone had been careless and dropped a toothpick and might've killed an otter and there were to be no more activities because the people of this town can't handle the responsibility."

Maddie waved the paper she held again.

"You've got to be fucking kidding me," Sawyer said. "She *said* that?"

"Practically," Maddie said. "She basically said that because people can't be more responsible around the animals that we are no longer going to be offering encounters."

Griffin shoved a hand through his hair. Yeah, clearly, she was feeling responsible. And clearly, she was taking this very seriously.

But, in typical Charlie fashion, she was doing this big and passionately as well.

"That's it," Sawyer said, shoving back from the table and standing. "We need to find her. This is ridiculous."

"Well, one of the otters being harmed by a feeding encounter is kind of a big deal," Tori said, frowning at Sawyer.

"Fine. Then we'll have people look at the otters and hear presentations about them without feeding them," Maddie said. "But we can't shut it all down. It's going so well."

"You weren't even that excited about expanding the petting zoo in the beginning," Tori said.

Maddie frowned at her. "I was fine with the idea. Charlie talked me into it easily."

"Okay, okay," Griffin said. Now Tori and Maddie were going to argue? This wasn't good.

Tori pushed back from the table and stood as well. "The animals and their safety have to be our first priority. I'm glad it's going well and that the business is making more money, but that can't be our only focus."

Maddie gasped and squared off, facing Tori directly. "I can't believe you said that to me. I'm not only worried about the money."

"The increased revenue is really great though," Sawyer inserted firmly. "Charlie came and talked us into this idea. We went along with it, trusting her to lead the way, and every-thing's been great. She can't just pull the plug like this all of a sudden."

"If people can't be trusted around animals, then pulling the plug all at once is maybe the best way to go," Tori said. "I realize this is an extension of Boys of the Bayou, but these are *my* animals."

"The otters aren't yours," Maddie said. "The otters adopted us. And we *all* love them and want them to be safe."

"Well, to keep them safe, we need to keep them away from people, obviously," Tori said.

Maddie drew herself straighter. "I don't think—"

"That's enough!" Griffin roared.

Everyone stopped and turned to face him. Most eyes were wide with surprise. Yeah, he didn't say much when he was around the Landrys in the first place, and he certainly never yelled when he was with them.

But dammit, sometimes with this group, yelling was the only way to be heard. Ellie Landry herself had told him that and it was certainly proving true. These people were all passionate and had no trouble standing up for what they believed in.

But *he* believed in Charlie. And he was definitely going to stand up for her.

"The animal and human interaction encounters are *fine*," he said.

He saw Tori's shocked expression. Yes, initially, he had been the one pushing back on the idea. But he'd seen it in action over the past few weeks. Not only had the animals thrived with the additional stimulation, but the people in Autre were more engaged and invested in the business than ever before, and the kids and their families had been learning more and coming to care more about animals every day. And, of course, the increased tourist traffic had been great for the business as well as the town.

"All of this is a great idea," Griffin said. "We need to keep Boys of the Bayou Gone Wild going."

That he was now the advocate for the business that Charlie had brought into his life uninvited and initially unwelcome, was ironic he knew.

"We need to protect the animals," he said to Tori. "But we

can do that. We can keep them safe and still have people interact with them. This was a fluke. Do we need to get rid of toothpicks? Yes. And we need to review the materials that are being used at the events more carefully. But this was an unintentional consequence. And one that we can fix. Snickers is going to be okay. But even if he wasn't, we all need to understand that this is never going to be perfect, and all we can do is our best."

Griffin almost couldn't believe that those words were coming out of his mouth as he said them. That was not how he had felt when he worked for either zoo. But now he realized it was all true.

This small town with everyday regular people, and adorable, unique animals had taught him that. Watching their interactions, teaching them how to interact had shown him that while it was messy sometimes, it was important.

"Fine," Tori finally said. "I trust you."

"Well, you don't have to convince *us*," Maddie said, gesturing at herself and Sawyer. She wiggled the paper in her hand again. "You need to convince Charlie. She's clearly freaking out."

"Where *is* Charlie?" Paige asked.

"I don't know for sure. But yes, she's freaking out a little," Griffin agreed.

"A little?" Sawyer repeated.

"Okay, fair enough," Griffin said. "Landrys don't do things 'a little' and certainly not when protecting things that matter to them." He looked at the whole group gathered. "This means everything to her, and she feels like she's losing it. Shutting it down is easier than the idea of losing it because the animals are in danger or because people stop coming. She's willing to sacrifice what makes her happy to do the right thing."

"Shutting it down isn't the right thing," Paige said. "People all over town are talking about the animal park. They're excited to see new events. They can't wait to see what other animals we have coming, they're hoping for baby animals." She sighed. "We really need Charlie to stay and help us grow."

They really did. *He* really did. Griffin knew that he would not be the person he was at this moment if it wasn't for Charlie. She had pushed him, it was true, but for all the right reasons. And it had turned out to be the best thing that could have happened to him.

"You have to promise to figure out a way to keep these animals *completely* safe," Tori said. "No more emergency surgeries."

Griffin regarded his friend and partner. Tori Landry was possibly the second-most passionate animal lover she knew. Fiona Grady was the first. But Tori's first priority would always be the animals.

And until Charlotte Landry walked into his life, they would've been his as well.

"Tori, you know there's no way to promise that nothing will ever happen to any of the animals."

She pressed her lips together. Of course, she knew that. She worked with large farm animals as much as she worked with pets. She knew the animals didn't live forever and, just like in humans, sometimes illness and injury happened, as unfair as it sometimes seemed.

"But you know I'll do my best." Griffin took a breath and blew it out. "Six weeks ago, if this had happened to one of the otters, *I* would've been the one putting those closed signs up all over the petting zoo and emailing everyone. But yeah, now I want to keep the animal encounters going. I want to keep the petting zoo open. I'm going to do whatever I can to talk Charlie into that." He looked around the group. "But, at the end of the day, she's doing a hell of a lot more here than just making us more money. If I have to choose between keeping this animal park going and keeping Charlie here and happy, I will pick Charlie every time."

"Really?"

Griffin spun at the sound of her voice behind him.

And his heart turned over in his chest, looking at her. It was relief, combined with concern, with a healthy measure of what could only be love.

Her hair had been pulled up and piled on top of her head under a Boys of the Bayou Gone Wild cap. She wore a pale yellow t-shirt that was streaked with dirt, cut off denim shorts, and the rubber boots she wore in the clinic when mucking out the dog kennels. Her mascara was smudged under her eyes as if she'd been crying, and she had no lipstick on.

In other words, she looked as different from the first night he'd met her as she possibly could.

And he had never seen anyone more beautiful in his life.

He quickly crossed the floor to where she stood just inside the swinging door from Ellie's kitchen.

"Really," he said simply.

"You want to keep the animal park? And all the animal encounters?"

"Yes."

"You fought me on those. You didn't want them."

"You changed my mind." He reached out and took her hand, tugging her close. "You changed my mind about a lot of things." He noticed she had a couple of broken nails, and there was dirt around her cuticles. "What have you been doing besides hanging up crazy signs?"

"Trying to be sure there aren't any more toothpicks in the otter enclosure."

His eyes flew to hers. "You've been digging around in the enclosure with your bare hands?"

"It seemed like the only way to be sure."

God, he loved her so much. "Thank you," he said simply. "But we would have all helped you."

Her lower lip trembled, and her eyes filled with tears. "I had to do it right away. I took away the thing that matters most to you. I killed one of your otters, Griffin!"

There were gasps from the few tables occupied around them. Griffin quickly turned to the room and held up his hands. "No, no, it's all okay. The otter is going to be fine."

"He is? Are you sure?" Charlie asked, her voice scratchy.

Griffin turned back. "He is. It was serious, but we got to him in time."

"*You* got to him in time," Charlie corrected. "You're the one who saved him. I'm the one who almost killed him."

"It's going to be okay. You didn't mean for this to happen."

"No, but I was careless. I didn't think it all through. I got in way over my head. Like I always do," she said. Her eyes slid shut, and she shook her head. "I was one of those people who hurt you in the past. I thought I knew better, thought I knew what I was doing, didn't give it enough thought, and just went ahead. And it ended up threatening another living thing. A living thing that you love."

She opened her eyes and looked at him with an expression that nearly tore his heart in half. She was hurting. For him.

"You told me you didn't want to get attached. You had so many good reasons. And I ruined it all! I made you get attached. I pushed you. You didn't want any of this, and it all happened because of me."

He ran a hand down her arm and linked their fingers. She tipped her head to look up at him. "Yes, you did all of that. You pushed me. You made me do things I didn't want to do. And you made me get attached."

She swallowed hard and nodded. "I'm so sorry, Griffin."

He shook his head. "Don't you dare be sorry for making me fall in love."

Her eyes widened. "What?"

He nodded. "I fell in love. Because of you, Charlie. With your family, with the animals, with all of these big ideas and plans, with teaching, with interacting with people and watching them learn and fall in love with the animals themselves." He reached up and cupped her cheek. "Okay, I was already falling in love with the place and your family when you got here. But you pushed me the rest of the way. And," he added, running his thumb over her bottom lip, "you made me fall in love with you. I was an idiot to think that I could possibly resist that."

She sucked in a quick breath, and her eyes filled with tears again. "I fell in love with you too, Griffin."

His heart expanded almost painfully. He took a deep breath, realizing that he needed to hear that more than anything. "Charlie—"

"And that's why I don't know if I can do this." She took a deep breath. "I don't know if I can watch you get hurt. And you will. Things will go wrong with this park. I didn't think about that before. It was just a big project for me. It was all just on paper and in sketches. But now, it's real. They are real living things. And they're dependent on us to keep them safe. And keeping them all safe and healthy is a lot. And sometimes they will get sick and hurt, and even if it's not because of humans, it will still hurt *you*. And I don't know if I can help build this up knowing that it could hurt you someday."

He shook his head. "I know how this works, Charlie. I've been a vet for a long time. It's part of the job. And yes, I've been hurt in the past. And yes, I'll be hurt in the future. But what I've realized since being here, is that the fun, and discovery, and adventure, and teaching, all of the wonderful moments, are worth it. And," he said, moving his hand to cup the back of her head, "doing it all with you and your family is the only way I want to do it."

A tear slid down her cheek. But this time, Griffin was sure that it was a happy tear instead of the ones she'd been shedding previously.

"Please stay. Please open the animal park back up. Please do this with me."

She swallowed. "I might have done something stupid. I emailed a bunch of people."

"Yeah, I'm about to fire your ass for it as a matter of fact," Sawyer said.

Charlie's eyes widened, and she turned her cousin. "You can't..."

But clearly, she realized that he could, in fact, fire her.

"That is a fair reaction," she said instead. "I'm so sorry. I... overreacted. But I can fix it. I'll send another email. We'll have a big event. Beer and..." She looked at Tori. "How quickly could I get a beaver?" Then she looked up at Griffin. "Maybe just Oreos and otters? Use it as a teaching experience about the tooth-picks. Can they eat Oreos? Or maybe..."

"The email will be enough," Griffin interjected.

"You're sure?"

"Maybe not for a normal human being, but for you? The most charming woman on the planet? Yeah, I'm sure." He was also sure his smile was full of love and wonder and God-I-fuck-ing-want-you-so-much.

She blew out a breath and nodded. "Okay." She looked at Sawyer. "Let me fix it."

"You sure you *want to* fix it?" Sawyer asked.

Charlie looked up at Griffin.

She could leave. This would be a good reason. She could cut and run. Go back to Shreveport. Find another marketing job. One with less mud and blood and lots of other messy stuff.

But she smiled for the first time and nodded. "Yeah, turns out this little job, in this little town, with this little petting zoo,

ERIN NICHOLAS

is the biggest, most important thing I've ever done. Next to falling in love, of course."

That hit Griffin hard. She meant it, and it filled him with a strange sense of happiness, contentment, and possessiveness. Not just because she wanted this job, in this place, with him. But because he was going to be able to make her dream of growing a business into something truly influential and meaningful while also fulfilling his dreams of working on wildlife conservation and education initiatives right in his own backyard.

He could give the woman he loved her dream. That meant more to him than anything he'd done before.

"Bigger than Paris?" Griffin asked gruffly, teasing.

"The only thing I fell in love with in Paris was a chocolate croissant. I'll take a bunch of otters, a trio of lemurs, a sloth, and some goats any day."

He noticed he wasn't on that list, and he leaned in, nearly touching her nose with his.

"And we're going to have kettle corn here. That beats chocolate croissants, right?"

She lifted her hand to his chest, placing it over his heart. He covered it with his own.

"Oh yeah, I'm totally here for the otters and kettle corn."

"Well, and a kangaroo, right?" His voice dropped a little lower.

"I did do some pretty... *hard*... work for that the other night, didn't I?" she asked, her smile mischievous.

"You really did."

"But I'd definitely be willing to work toward two or three."

"Hmm. Kangaroos are somewhat solitary animals. I don't know if we need more than one."

Her smile was so sweet that Griffin felt his heart squeeze. She loved when he teased because he didn't do it that often.

But she might have to get used to more of it.

"Oh, well, then I guess I won't need to do the thing I was planning on doing..." She said, trailing off.

"Okay, fine. Five kangaroos," he said.

She laughed.

"And don't forget... you're still trying to talk me into an elephant."

Two months later...

"This kettle corn is terrible," Sawyer declared. "Again."

"Shh!" Charlie told him sharply. They couldn't let Ellie or Cora, her best friend and head cook at the bar, overhear.

They were standing outside of the new snack shack that Zeke had just finished building two days before. This was the grand opening, and Ellie and Cora had insisted on making much of the food themselves. The mini beignets, meat pies, and fried alligator balls had all turned out great. It was nice to have some authentic Louisiana food alongside the typical snow cones, ice cream sandwiches, nachos, and pizza slices. They'd even been discussing how to do gumbo in easy-to-handle containers.

Unfortunately, the one snafu was the kettle corn. For some reason.

"But how can it keep getting *worse*?" Mitch asked in a loud whisper.

"Seriously, how is it possible that the two best cooks I know *can't* make kettle corn?" Fletcher asked.

"Yeah, someone needs to tell her that we're going to start buying the kettle corn from somewhere else," Owen said.

"Not it!" Zeke was quick to exclaim.

"Definitely not fucking it," Zander agreed.

"No fucking way," Fletcher said. Then he looked around quickly. Spending more time at the animal park with his family had come with the added pressure of constantly running into kids from school. He was struggling to keep up his good-influence vibe when he was with his cousins and brothers. That wasn't anything new, of course, but being surrounded by little kids all the time was.

"Fine," Charlie finally said with a sigh. "I'll handle it with Ellie."

"You sure you want to do that?" Sawyer asked.

What, was she stupid? Of course, she didn't want to do that. But she was in charge of making sure everything at the animal park was as good as it could be.

She'd given up on the idea of perfection. Well, she was *working on* giving up on the idea of perfection. She was also trying to give up the idea that her ideas were always the best ones. But, when it came right down to it, she took responsibility for making the park everything that she and Griffin had dreamed of.

With a lot of help from her family.

And Fiona, of course.

"Wow," Fiona said, joining them from where she'd just picked up her own kettle corn. "This really sucks," she said around the first few kernels.

"What really sucks?"

Charlie grimaced as she heard her grandmother's voice.

Zeke suddenly said, "Gotta go," and headed in the opposite direction.

"Yeah, just got a call," Zander said, holding up his phone and backing away.

"I've got to—" Fletcher started.

"Don't even think about it," Charlie said, catching the sleeve of his shirt.

She turned with a bright smile for her grandmother. Which instantly morphed into a very real grin when Charlie saw Griffin was with Ellie.

"What really sucks?" Ellie repeated as they stopped near Charlie, Fiona, Fletcher, and Sawyer.

Except, when she looked again, Sawyer was gone too. He just hadn't announced his departure. Smart guy.

"This kettle corn," Fiona said, holding up her bag. "You all need a new vendor."

Ellie's eyes rounded as Griffin and Charlie both groaned.

"You don't like the kettle corn?" Ellie asked.

"No. It tastes burnt. Even though it doesn't look it." Fiona held her bag out. "Here, try it."

Ellie reached out and took three kernels. She tasted them, frowned, and said, "It really does suck."

Fiona nodded. "Told you."

Charlie looked at her grandmother. "You agree it's not good?"

"Of course, that's not good," Ellie said. "No one would think that was good."

"So, we were thinking that with everything else you and Cora are doing, maybe we should look to someone else for the kettle corn."

Ellie waved that away. "We'll try again. We'll try a new recipe. It will be fine."

Charlie sighed and looked at Griffin. He lifted a shoulder.

She didn't want her grandmother's feelings hurt, for sure, but looking at Griffin reminded her of all their plans and dreams, as it always did. Plans and dreams she was willing to do anything for.

Even insult her grandmother.

She took a breath. "Ellie, I love you, and I so appreciate everything that you're doing for the snack shack. Most of it is amazing. And I know it's a lot of extra work. But, we're going to find a new vendor for the kettle corn. You've tried a few times now, and it's just not working. Everything here has to be as good as it can possibly be."

Ellie regarded her with one eye narrowed. She crossed her arms. Then, after nearly thirty full seconds, during which Charlie shifted her weight from one foot to the other, twice, Ellie said, "It's about time."

Charlie frowned. "About time? What do you mean?"

"I've been waiting for you to say something. I wanted to know that even the kettle corn was important to you. Figured if it were, you'd say something eventually."

Charlie stared at her grandmother. "You've been ruining the kettle corn on purpose, waiting for me to say something? You were testing me?"

Ellie chuckled. "I wasn't ruining it on purpose. But I knew it sucked. Still, no one was saying anything. Hell yes, it was a test. If you can confront me about my cooking, then you can handle anything that comes up in the park."

Charlie let her eyes slide shut, and she took a deep breath. A deep breath full of hot, humid air that smelled like goats. And burnt kettle corn.

She could be working in a sleek, modern, *air-conditioned* office with other marketing experts and beautiful online slideshow presentations talking about the latest makeup trends and how they were going to support programs that got single moms successfully into the workforce.

But when she opened her eyes, Griffin was watching her with a combination of amusement and affection that told her she was never not going to be by his side taking care of goats. Of course, now she had three beavers to also help take care of.

"Okay then," she told her grandmother. "You are officially fired as the kettle corn maker for Boys of the Bayou Gone Wild."

Ellie laughed. "See, that wasn't so hard."

"The idea of it sent three grown men running," Charlie told her with a grin.

"Good," Ellie said. "I want to keep my grandsons scared of me."

"Speaking of grandsons who are scared of you and if the questionable mental health in our family is genetic, I'm going to go find somewhere else to be," Fletcher said.

"Oh," Ellie said, "you're the reason I came over here."

Fletcher sighed. "Why is that?"

"Jason Young is performing live tonight, and there is a rumor that he's going to do something big and exciting on stage," Ellie said.

Fletcher just blinked at her for a few seconds. Finally, he said, "I don't give a fuck what Jason Young is doing tonight, on live TV or not."

Ellie gave him an eye roll. "Well, it just so happens that Jordan's mother was at the grocery store the same time I was in buying more sugar for the kettle corn. And she thinks he's going to propose tonight. On stage."

Charlie snapped her head around to look at Fletcher. She could feel the sudden tension emanating off of him.

His jaw was tight, and he pulled in a long breath through his nose. Then he let it out and said, "I suppose it's about time for him to do that."

Ellie nodded. "That's what I was thinking. She's been there beside him through all of his trying to be a star. Quit her job to go travel with him. It's about time that boy put a ring on her finger."

Fletcher simply nodded.

"So, we're watching it at the bar. I think it'll be nice to see these two hometown kids doing something so great," Ellie said. "Starts in twenty minutes. You should be there."

"I have no desire to be there, Ellie," Fletcher told her.

"Fletcher Landry, Jordan is your best friend. You need to

witness her big moment. What will happen when she calls and asked if you saw it?"

"She knows I don't like Jason's music and don't watch him."

"And she knows I'm a huge fan and would definitely have it on in the bar. You have no excuse to miss this. You need to be supportive."

Fletcher sighed. "I'll think about it."

"Yeah, you think about it," Ellie told him. "If you're not there, no gumbo for two weeks."

Since her grandkids had become adults, or really since they become too big to sit in timeout behind the bar and read William Shakespeare out loud to Ellie while she worked, her favorite punishment was to withhold their favorite foods. Of course, for seven out of eleven of them, it was her gumbo. But she knew every one of their favorites and would not hesitate to cut them off if it meant making a point.

"Missing Jason Young singing might be worth two weeks of no gumbo," Fletcher muttered.

Ellie nodded. "Fine. Be that way. But if Jordan ever asks me if you watched her engagement live with the rest of the country, I'm not lying for you." Ellie spun on her heel and stomped back toward her bar.

Charlie looked at Fletcher. "You're not really willing to give up two weeks of gumbo, are you? He's actually pretty good."

Fletcher met her eyes. "You know very well that I don't hate him because of his music."

"But you hate him?" Charlie asked.

"He's not my favorite person."

"I understand," Charlie said. "But Ellie has a point. Jordan's going to want her best friend to have seen her engagement and to be excited about it."

Fletcher rubbed a hand over his face. "Bad enough that I have to think about them being engaged, isn't it? I have to watch it happen in person?"

"Jason's the hot rising star right now," Charlie said with a shrug. "But he still needs as much attention as he can get. This is a huge way to get all over the entertainment news and Internet."

"So he's using her," Fletcher said. "I'm supposed to support that?"

"If they'd just met, I'd be on your side," Charlie said. "They've been together ten years, Fletcher. They were going to get engaged eventually. Why not do it this way? Lots of women have fantasies about a big public declaration of love. And what better way to tell the world that he is off the market? Jordan might be eating this up."

Fletcher shook his head. "I promise you, she's not."

"We still need to be there for her."

He nodded. "Yeah, I suppose."

"We'll go with you," Charlie said, grabbing Griffin's hand as she volunteered him. "If that'll help."

"A couple shots of Leo's moonshine, and maybe you won't mind as much," Griffin said.

Fletcher nodded again. "That's about the only way to do this."

"Let's head over and get started. I actually wouldn't mind a shot of moonshine before listening to country music myself," Griffin said.

Charlie gasped. "Wait just a second there, Dr. Foster. Are you telling me you don't like country music? Because this could be a problem."

He put an arm around her waist, tucking her up against him as they started toward Ellie's. "I'll get you a kangaroo and be right back on your good side."

"And to think you are the guy who even protested the idea of hedgehogs."

"Actually, I thought the hedgehogs were great," Griffin corrected. "And no one ever said that hedgehogs would lead to me getting laid. You should have led with that."

She hugged him as she laughed. "You got laid long before the hedgehogs."

He nodded. "Actually, it was the goats, wasn't it?"

Actually, yeah, it had been—sort of.

They settled in for dinner with the family. The food had already been served in big bowls and platters when they arrived, and they slid into empty chairs just in time for the dishes to be passed to them.

They all dug in and chatted and ate for about ten minutes before Ellie yelled, "Shut up! It's starting."

She pointed the remote at each of the three televisions in the bar, turning the volume up on each.

No one in the place could avoid watching Jason Young take the stage and launch into his new number one hit.

Charlie looked at Fletcher. He had his eyes down, focused on his food, and was eating without a word.

Jason did three numbers before taking a break and speaking into the microphone to the huge live crowd in the MGM Grand in Las Vegas.

"Vegas, wow, that's fun," Tori said. "Bet Jordan's having a good time."

"Shhh!" Ellie told her.

Everyone's eyes widened. Tori never got snapped at, and since she'd been pregnant, she'd been treated like a queen, especially by Ellie, who was beside herself over the idea of her first great-grandchild.

"Hey, everybody, thanks for coming out tonight," Jason said into the microphone. The crowd in Vegas roared.

Jason grinned and waited for the noise to die down a little. "This last year and a half or so has been pretty crazy for me. All my dreams seem to be coming true, and there are some really important people who've been a part of that."

He went on to thank his manager, his parents, and a couple

of other people. Then he said, "But there is one very special person who's been here with me from the beginning, and who I have a very special question for tonight."

The crowd went crazy. The noise was incredible, and Leo reached for one of the remotes to turn the volume down a bit. Ellie slapped his hand, but he did succeed in lowering it a few notches.

"Yeah, I hope she feels the same way about it," Jason said, grinning into the camera. "Now I just need her to come out here with me."

Suddenly the camera panned to a blond woman who stepped out from backstage. Again, the crowd went wild.

It was Jordan. Though it didn't look much like the Jordan Charlie remembered. She was in a sparkly black dress and high heels with a denim jacket with lots of rhinestones. Her hair was in a twist, and she had full makeup on. Charlie honestly couldn't remember ever seeing Jordan in anything more than lip gloss.

She also looked terrified.

She lifted her hand tentatively and waved to the crowd, but she seemed focused on walking across the stage.

Charlie could understand. Probably every woman in the world could understand. If you're not used to high heels, walking in them, especially on a slick surface, not to mention with millions of eyeballs on you, was not a piece of cake.

"Daaay-um," Zeke said with a slow, appreciative drawl. "Jordan's got great legs. And other stuff."

Jason met Jordan partway across the stage and took her hand. He was smiling like someone had just given him a million dollars.

"Oh my gosh," Maddie said. "This is pretty exciting."

"I would die," Paige said. "I hate public proposals."

The group laughed. Yes, Paige said proposals, plural, and she knew what she spoke of. The girl had been proposed to five times before she'd come to Autre to be with Mitch. Mitch was letting her be in charge of her next proposal. She was going to ask him to marry her when she was ready. But the proposal was just a formality. The two of them were absolutely going to end up together.

"You already promised me you would ask Mitch to marry you here at the bar in front of all of us," Ellie told her.

Paige nodded. "I guess I don't consider you all public." She smiled at the group. "You're family."

"Aww," Juliet and Tori said together.

"Shhh!" Ellie told them again, waving her hand to shut them up as Jason pulled Jordan to the microphone at the front of the stage.

The crowd had been cheering the entire time, but now as he swung his guitar to his back and went down on one knee, they quieted.

"We've known each other forever," Jason said with Jordan's hand in his.

Charlie found herself holding her breath. But not so much for the words that were about to come from Jason's mouth but because Jordan still looked petrified and like she was about to wobble off of her heels at any moment.

"And we've been through a lot together," Jason went on.

Ellie was watching the TV, practically without blinking. Fletcher, on the other hand, had yet to look at the screen as far as Charlie could tell, and he looked like he was about to throw up.

"It just seems right," Jason said, "at this point in my journey, that I ask this question."

A couple of loud whistles came from the audience, but for the most part, everyone was quiet.

"I love you, Viv. Will you marry me?"

There was a long beat of silence.

Fletcher's head came up quickly. His eyes now focused on the TV.

Then Zeke asked, "Who the hell is Viv?"

Ellie swung to look at Fletcher. "Does he call Jordan 'Viv'?"

"What? Is that like her middle name?" Zeke asked.

But Fletcher wasn't looking away from the television. Charlie looked too. Jordan looked white as a ghost, and she visibly wobbled on her heels now.

No one in the live audience seemed to know what to do.

Jason quickly got to his feet, grabbing both of Jordan's hands. "Oh fuck," he said into the microphone.

That was going to be a problem with the television producers.

"No, I'm sorry, Jordan. Jordan. Of course. I want *you.* "

Suddenly there was a crash, and the camera panned to the drum set that was now partially lying on its side, the cymbals having crashed against the floor as the drummer bolted off of her seat and ran for the side of the stage.

"Uh, that's Viv."

They all looked at Zander.

"*What*?" Ellie demanded.

Zander nodded. "Vivian Holbrook. Jason's drummer."

Ellie turned to face him, her hands on her hips. "What are you saying?"

"I'm saying that Jason Young basically just proposed to Vivian."

"Why would he do that?" Ellie asked.

"Maybe because he's actually in love with her, but his management team told him that breaking up with a sweetheart like Jordan would look bad for him right now," Zander said.

"How do you know this?"

"I might have... read it... somewhere," Zander said.

"Do you follow country music celebrity gossip?" Ellie asked him, her eyes narrowed, daring him to lie to her.

Zander shrugged. "Maybe."

"I can't believe you've been holding out on me!" Ellie exclaimed. "We could have been talking about Kelly and Brandon and Brett?"

"Well, apparently, you wouldn't have been that great to gossip with," Zander told her. "People have been talking about Jason and Viv for a while, and you seem shocked."

"Don't you tell me Jason Young has been cheating on Jordan," Ellie said.

"Okay, I won't tell you. But *he* basically just told you," Zander said, pointing at the television.

Ellie shook her head, clearly not wanting to believe such a thing about her favorite musician. "Maybe he was just nervous in front of all those people. This is kind of a big deal. Maybe he just said the wrong name. Obviously, he knows Vivian really well too," Ellie said.

Zander snorted. "Asking a woman to marry you *is* kind of a big deal. But not exactly something where you get the wrong name. Especially when you've been with the woman you're asking for ten years."

"But—" Ellie started.

Suddenly Fletcher shoved back from the table and stood. He tossed his wadded napkin onto his plate, then turned and headed for the back door.

"Where are you going?" Ellie called after him.

He yanked the back door open and looked back. His eyes flickered to the screen in the back of his grandmother's bar. "Vegas."

Charlie pivoted in her seat to look at the television. Jordan was running off the stage, tears streaming down her face, and Jason was going after her. The camera showed a bodyguard stopping him as they let her pass. Then his manager joined him, and they had a brief, heated discussion.

"I can't believe they're not cutting to commercial," Maddie said, leaning in attentively.

"They better not cut to a commercial," Ellie said. "I'll call my cable company and complain so loudly they won't know what hit them."

"Won't matter," Zeke said. "That whole thing is going to be *all* over the internet in five minutes if it's not already. Everyone there has a cell phone."

God, he was right.

Charlie stared at the screen. She felt so terrible for Jordan.

But damn… the way Fletcher had gone storming out of here headed for Vegas? That was a whole new level of exciting.

She felt Griffin lean in.

"Just telling you now, when I propose, it might involve an otter or two. Or maybe a lemur. But it will be nothing like *that*."

When he proposed. That was like a proposal for a proposal, wasn't it? She gave him a huge smile and leaned in and kissed him. Then said, "As long as it's not the goats."

"No? But everything started with the goats and the barn," he said with a grin.

"Yeah, but Sugar isn't going to take my 'yes' well. Or," she said, leaning in and putting her lips to his ear, "the way we celebrate after. She might leave a scar this time."

Even though Sugar had a new goat boyfriend, Pepper, she still loved Griffin most, and if he and Charlie got too frisky in the barn, Sugar would come and bite Charlie's pant leg. So far, she'd only nicked the skin, but Charlie didn't trust her. And she refused to get completely naked in the barn anymore.

"Good point." Griffin's hand dropped to the upper curve of the butt cheek Sugar had tried to take a chunk from about three weeks ago.

"Is someone going to Vegas with Fletcher?" Paige asked.

"Nah, he's okay," Zeke told her.

"He didn't look okay."

ERIN NICHOLAS

"He better not beat Jason Young up," Ellie declared. "I like that pretty face, and I don't want his tour postponed."

"Wow, you're team Jason?" Maddie asked. "I'm *totally* team Jordan."

"Well, of course, I'm team Jordan," Ellie said. "I just don't want Fletcher all over the country music gossip pages as the guy who messed up that nice face."

"It's kind of fucked up that you care more about how Jason Young looks than how your own grandson feels," Zeke told her.

"Oh, shut up, you." Ellie threw a cornbread muffin at Zeke, hitting him right in the forehead. "That's not what I said."

Zeke picked up the muffin and took a big bite.

"What about how *Jordan* feels?" Paige asked. "My God, how humiliating."

"I'm team *Fletcher*," Zander declared. "I hope he does beat Jason's ass, and I hope he finally gets Jordan in his bed where she belongs."

"Well, that would make you team Jordan too, then," Paige said with a grin.

Mitch looked at his girlfriend. "Is that right?"

"Oh, for sure. Jason Young and Fletcher Landry fighting over her?" Paige fanned her face. "Go, Jordan."

Maddie and Tori both nodded.

"Well, I'm definitely team Fletcher," Owen agreed. "Fuck Jason Young."

"Well, no shit. I'm team Fletcher too," Ellie told them all. "I didn't know we had to pick sides."

"Oh, after *that*?" Maddie asked, pointing at the TV. "We *definitely* have to pick sides."

Griffin just shook his head. "This family..."

Charlie grinned up at him. "Crazy. I know."

"Yep. I'd even say... it's *otterly chaotic* around here."

She gasped. God, she loved when he teased and got playful. "And *that* is *otterly delightful*, Dr. Foster."

"I can't seem to resist," he admitted.
Charlie laughed and snuggled happily into his side.
He found them all irresistible.
Thank God. Because it was very, very mutual.

———

Thank you so much for reading *Otterly Irresistible*! I hope you loved Griffin and Charlie's story!

There is so much more to come from Boys of the Bayou Gone Wild and the Landry family!

Up next is Fletcher and Jordan in Heavy Petting!

**Find out more at
ErinNicholas.com**

———

And join in on all the FAN FUN!

Join my **email list!**
http://bit.ly/ErinNicholasEmails

And be the first to hear about my news, sales, freebies, behind-the-scenes, and more!

Or for even more fun, join my **Super Fan page** on Facebook and chat with me and other super fans every day! Just search Facebook for Erin Nicholas Super Fans!

IF YOU LOVE AUTRE AND THE LANDRYS...

If you love the Boys of the Bayou Gone Wild, you can't miss the Boys of the Bayou series! *All available now!*

My Best Friend's Mardi Gras Wedding (Josh & Tori)

Sweet Home Louisiana (Owen & Maddie)

Beauty and the Bayou (Sawyer & Juliet)

Crazy Rich Cajuns (Bennett & Kennedy)

Must Love Alligators (Chase & Bailey)

Four Weddings and a Swamp Boat Tour (Mitch & Paige)

And be sure to check out the connected series, Boys of the Big Easy!

Easy Going (prequel novella)-Gabe & Addison

Going Down Easy- Gabe & Addison

Taking It Easy - Logan & Dana

Eggnog Makes Her Easy - Matt & Lindsey

Nice and Easy - Caleb & Lexi

Getting Off Easy - James & Harper

If you're looking for more sexy, small town rom com fun, check out the

The Hot Cakes Series

One small Iowa town.

Two rival baking companies.

A three-generation old family feud.

And six guys who are going to be heating up a lot more than the kitchen.

Sugar Rush (prequel)

Sugarcoated

Forking Around

Making Whoopie

Semi-Sweet On You

Oh, Fudge

Gimme S'more

And much more—

including my printable booklist— at

ErinNicholas.com

ABOUT THE AUTHOR

Erin Nicholas is the New York Times and USA Today bestselling author of over forty sexy contemporary romances. Her stories have been described as toe-curling, enchanting, steamy and fun. She loves to write about reluctant heroes, imperfect heroines and happily ever afters. She lives in the Midwest with her husband who only wants to read the sex scenes in her books, her kids who will never read the sex scenes in her books, and family and friends who say they're shocked by the sex scenes in her books (yeah, right!).

Find her and all her books at
www.ErinNicholas.com

And find her on Facebook, Goodreads, BookBub, and Instagram!